IMPRISONED

A DEMMONICA HURT-COMFORT PARANORMAL ROMANCE

EMMA JAYE

purindoors publications

Copyright © 2022 by Emma Jaye

All rights reserved.

No portion of this book may be reproduced in any form without written permission from the publisher or author, except as permitted by U.S. copyright law.

IMPRISONED

Irritating people to death isn't easy.

End the line to earn your freedom, the demon lord promised. Four centuries later, Alastor ran out of Walpole heirs to kill, but the curse remained.

Angry, exhausted, lonely, and in constant pain, he craves to be seen and heard again.

But when a long-lost heir enters Walpole Hall to auction it, hope sparks, and so do emotions. Darien brings hope, warmth, understanding, and doesn't hate his pranks.

Time is running out to choose: kill the first heir who doesn't view him as a problem to eliminate, and walk free with a broken heart, or let Darien go and become a ghost until the sun explodes.

Possible Spoilers:

Themes: Demonic curses. Demons. Ghosts. Witches. Enemies to lovers. Opposites attract. Historical violence. Murder. Extreme brattish behavior. Historical class war. Culture clash, multicultural romance, Cameo appearances of other DeMMonica characters.

DeMMonica is a dark mm paranormal series set in the same world as INCUBUS and is intended for mature readers.

If fluffy, low angst is your thing, RUN AWAY!

CONTENTS

PROLOGUE	1
CHAPTER ONE	5
CHAPTER TWO	17
CHAPTER THREE	27
CHAPTER FOUR	46
CHAPTER FIVE	54
CHAPTER SIX	62
CHAPTER SEVEN	75
CHAPTER EIGHT	87
CHAPTER NINE	102
CHAPTER TEN	118
CHAPTER ELEVEN	131
CHAPTER TWELVE	143
CHAPTER THIRTEEN	150
CHAPTER FOURTEEN	162
CHAPTER FIFTEEN	168
CHAPTER SIXTEEN	177
CHAPTER SEVENTEEN	186
CHAPTER EIGHTEEN	209
CHAPTER NINETEEN	219

CHAPTER TWENTY	231
CHAPTER TWENTY-ONE	245
CHAPTER TWENTY-TWO	254
CHAPTER TWENTY-THREE	262
CHAPTER TWENTY-FOUR	275
CHAPTER TWENTY-FIVE	281
CHAPTER TWENTY-SIX	290
CHAPTER TWENTY-SEVEN	296
CHAPTER TWENTY-EIGHT	303
CHAPTER TWENTY-NINE	316
CHAPTER THIRTY	333
CHAPTER THIRTY-ONE	346
CHAPTER THIRTY-TWO	360
Afterword	367
Next In Series	368
About Emma	369

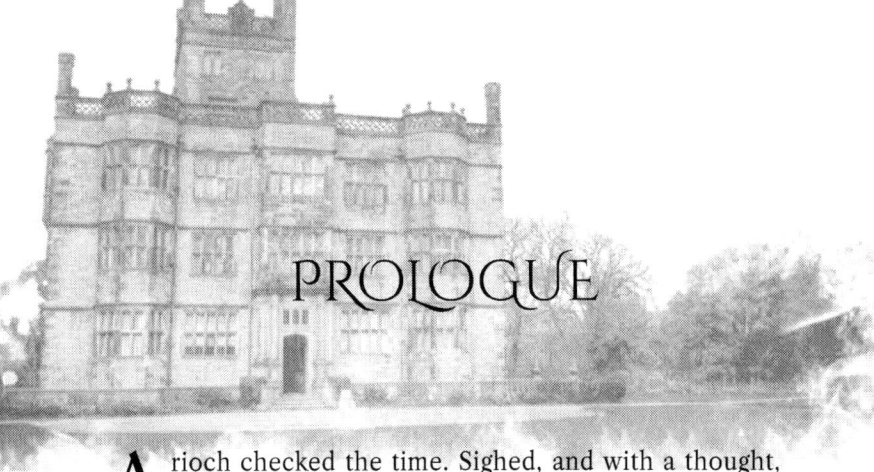

PROLOGUE

Arioch checked the time. Sighed, and with a thought, changed the office from their preferred bright, modern, work environment to something far more demonic. Appearances were everything in this game.

The rock walls glowed with a reddish hue, and screams and groans rent the overheated sulfur-scented air. Arioch changed form to a dark-haired, honey-skinned, red-suited woman but didn't put out the cigar. The sweet smoke counteracted the sulfur a little. It would also give their fingers something to do rather than strangling their next appointment to shut him up. Still, ten minutes once a decade was almost tolerable.

Checking the time, the Demon Lord counted down the seconds on the smartwatch wrapped around their slim, delicate wrist. As the dial clicked to 00:00, a second person appeared out of thin air in the doorless room. Arioch's peace shattered.

Frustration rolled off the young imp in almost visible waves. "I hate, I hate so damn much, and there's not a fucking thing I can do about it. And talking about fucking, I haven't got any in—"

"Revenge is a dish best served cold," Arioch murmured as they puffed on the cigar.

Alastor had probably been working on this rant for the last nine years, eleven months, three weeks, and six days, planning and refining every nuance, movement, and phrase to elicit Arioch's intervention. But even with all that forethought, his words were hardly original. It was all incredibly tedious. Pursing their lips, they blew a smoke ring while waiting for the imp to calm down enough to be able to listen.

Administration sucked, but as the leader of the vengeance demons, it was part of Arioch's responsibilities. A little darkness had to fall into everyone's lives, and Alastor was undoubtedly theirs. Arioch blew another smoke ring, pondering the possibility that Alastor was some convoluted punishment they'd earned back in the mists of time.

The red-haired, pale-skinned youngster, wearing only a mid-thigh length raw linen shirt, paced in front of the craggy granite desk, throwing his arms in the air with enviable energy. Arioch couldn't sense an ounce of contrition. The imp didn't even provide the vengeance demon with the equivalent of a human's canapé.

At least the black eye and finger marks on his neck provided some entertaining decoration, as it had the last seven times they'd met. Judging by the way the imp winced when he'd attempted to sit during previous meetings, his backside boasted a few marks too. Arioch didn't care. Alastor was paying the price of failure, but it irritated that they had to suffer alongside the imp.

"I get the idea of revenge being cold, but four hundred years is frozen, not chilly. No one even remembers that damn witch now." He picked at his dull beige undyed shirt. "Do you know how long I've been wearing nothing but underwear?"

Arioch sighed. The imp hadn't even gotten to the rank of being able to change his skin color, let alone clothes, size, or an appropriate gender for different circumstances—a mere baby in the scheme of things. Young demons were almost as impatient as humans and often far more volatile. If the imp didn't break the curse that bound him, he'd never free himself.

Nevertheless, even with his highly constraining circumstances, Alastor was a damn good imp. His work was intricate, full of finesse, and quite beautiful to behold when he had a subject to work on. Arioch found it hard to remember the imp's good points when faced with the excitable, child-like venting occurring in front of their desk.

"I'm going almost as mad with boredom as I send the damn humans. I haven't even had a sniff of a Walpole male in eighty years, and you know what that means." He ticked his restrictions off on his fingers. "No sex. No touching. No drinking. No eating. No healing. I'll tell you one thing for free, these bruises are getting fucking old. No—"

"Sit, now."

Alastor flopped into the purposefully small hard wooden chair in front of the desk. He gritted his teeth, glaring at the senior demon as if the pain in his ass was Arioch's fault rather than his own.

Still, this was the situation they found themselves in, and getting a little entertainment out of the meeting wouldn't hurt. Well, it wouldn't hurt Arioch. Most things that entertained a vengeance demon meant pain for someone.

How long has it been since I made someone spontaneously combust?

Arioch waved the smoking cigar as they lounged back in the incredibly comfortable demon-skin chair. "Boredom and pain provide motivation. Do your job, end the Walpole line, and then you can come home."

Angry steam rose from the imp's flushed skin as his jaw clenched. It showed progress but not nearly enough for Arioch's liking.

"And how—all fucking knowing one—can I do that when I can't damn well LEAVE THE ESTATE?"

Ranting was one thing. Rudeness was quite another. Arioch stood, expanding and transforming into their full male demonic form, including scarlet skin, huge curling ram's horns, forked tail, and cloven hooves.

The imp shrank back in his chair. His fearful respect was gratifying. Maybe he wasn't entirely stupid.

"My chair cover is wearing thin, so I'll be looking for some more material soon, something soft—" they looked Alastor over. "—maybe pale this time. If you want to keep your skin, do your job and end the Walpole line. I shouldn't have to remind you that you can use other humans to fulfill your goals. Now, our time is up, and I've got an appointment with the head of the vampire council. Don't make me suffer through another 'No progress' meeting in a decade because you might end up as a permanent office fixture."

With a wave of a hand, Arioch sent the imp back to his prison and set about the far more entertaining task of plotting how to reveal to Fabian that his heir wasn't all he seemed.

CHAPTER ONE

Darien FitzHenry checked the particulars of the auction listing agreement as he sat in the taxi and tried to contain his excitement about the building he'd see today.

His client was currently a resident of HMP Wormwood Scrubs, where he'd been incarcerated on remand pending his trial. Carl Anderson insisted on meeting with a representative of their family-run auction house before signing the auction contract for Walpole Hall in Darien's briefcase.

Buildings, artifacts—the past in general—fascinated him but meeting a client before an auction happened once in a blue moon. The CEO of FitzHenry auctions, his older sister, Juliana, usually conducted these contract meetings. Juliana was a shrewd face-to-face negotiator, but a male-only prison wouldn't be a comfortable environment for her. Hell, he didn't like the prison aspect either, but he still volunteered to go. Juliana's lack of argument spoke volumes.

The Victorian Grade II listed building held far more interest than his violent client, but it was too modern to stir real fascination. The style might be post-medieval, but it wasn't even two hundred years old. Like the gothic Tower Bridge that most of his fellow Americans cooed over, it was a fake, a Victorian copy of a previous style. At least it didn't make him shudder like the 1970s Tudor-revival housing estates.

"The Scrubs is coming up on our left," the driver said over his shoulder.

The towering stone entrance looked like a medieval castle. White stone embellished the corners of the towers flanking the giant studded wooden gate. The
depressing, dull brown brick urban setting of run-down shops and blocks of government-owned housing did nothing to lighten the mood of Hammersmith. Nobody in their right mind wanted to be here, but those who had no choice made the best of it.

Darien pulled out his wallet. "Can you wait? I shouldn't be more than half an hour."

"I'll wait for a ton."

Darien frowned. "Excuse me?"

The driver sighed at the ignorance of foreigners. "A hundred quid. I'll wait for a hundred pounds."

As usual, the locals were trying to get one over on a tourist. He opened the door. "I'll call another cab when I'm done."

"You try getting anyone decent to do a pick up at the Scrubs. You'll end up with a smoky old banger with sick on the back seat."

Darien held the man's gaze for a moment, assessing his honesty.

"It's no skin off my nose, mate. I'll just go back to Heathrow and pick up another fare; I just thought you'd prefer riding in comfort for the rest of your journey."

"Two hundred and fifty for the rest of the day." Darien didn't miss the gleam in the man's eyes at the amount.

"Three and you've got a deal, as long as I'm back near Heathrow for seven. The missus will have my guts for garters if I miss dinner again."

Darien wasn't entirely sure what the man had said, but it sounded positive. "Done," he said. "A hundred now, and the rest at my final destination."

"Which is?"

"Tandridge, Kent."

The man pursed his lips, squinted, and wobbled his head from side to side, probably assessing distance and time. "Done." He held out his hand. Darien shook it before depositing five purplish plastic twenty-pound notes into it.

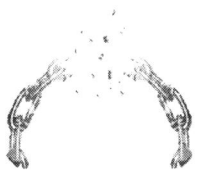

The clang of the gates behind Darien as he followed the navy-blue uniformed white guard down the corridor had him trying not to stare too much. In his world, handcuffs and being locked up usually had erotic associations.

Architecture. Concentrate on the architecture.

Men, women, and children, all the visitors had one thing in common, they looked as though they'd given up on life. His tailored suit set him apart, although his skin color didn't. BAME people made up around forty percent of prisoners and visitors, which stank considering Black, Asian, and Minority Ethnic people only made up around fifteen percent of the UK population.

Like every other visitor, he'd endured being searched and having his valuables locked away in the visitor center before entering the main prison. Even though he was a visitor, not an inmate, he got an inkling about what it would be like to be locked up here. Being watched was nothing new, but here he felt judged and found wanting rather than admired.

Instead of being dull and colorless like the other parts of the prison, the large visiting room was filled with bright blue and orange molded chairs and round white tables. A single orange chair sat on one side of each table while a trio of blue ones were opposite it. The rest of the visitors spread out, but they only sat on blue chairs.

After being scrutinized, the guards let Darien bring in the contract, but they disallowed the pen. He'd have to borrow one from a guard if—no, when—he got Anderson to sign the auction contract.

Darien found a seat on the edge of the room, nearest the entrance and the guards. Understandably, most visitors chose seats in the center, as far away from the watching staff as possible.

The contrast between the man who shuffled over to him and the one in the glossy publicity shot was shocking. How did a man go from the top of the heap—a billionaire movie producer with the world at his feet—to this?

Anderson looked broken, his shoulders rounded and drooping under the weight of his experiences, until he sat down.

He looked right at Darien, blue eyes bright, maybe even feverish. Darien had seen the same look many times in BDSM clubs. He never interacted with subs or doms with that look and always warned the staff of his suspicions that a potentially unsafe situation could develop. Subs with that attitude never safeworded, and doms with that look never heard. But he wasn't at a club now. This was business, nothing more.

"Thank you for meeting me, Mr. Anderson. I'm sorry it has to be under these circumstances."

Without a word, Anderson held out his hand for the contract. Darien passed it over. The hubbub in the room grew as other inmates entered and were greeted by their loved ones.

The charges against Anderson might still be upgraded to double murder. His wife hadn't survived being strangled. Although still alive, the pool boy had suffered permanent brain damage and might never leave the hospital.

Anderson looked up at him, eyes narrowing. "You're American, right?"

"Born and raised in Missouri, went to college in California."

"Do you believe in ghosts?"

Not rolling his eyes took a decade of perfecting his dom face. "I believe there's a lot of things that can't currently be explained. Although I fail to see how my personal beliefs impinge on my company's ability to conduct a fair auction for your property."

Anderson sat back in his plastic seat. Darien resisted the urge to attempt to move his seat. He'd tried when he sat down. The things were damn heavy, probably to stop the inmates from throwing them at the staff or each other.

"I want to specify the nationality of the buyer."

Darien blinked at the change in direction, but Carl Anderson probably wasn't playing with a full deck of cards.

"I'm afraid that's not possible." Anderson scowled, and Darien continued. "I also cannot favor or discriminate against a particular bidder because of gender, race, sexuality, age, or disability status. The only way you can legally ensure that the next owner of Walpole Hall belongs to a particular demographic is to gift it rather than sell it."

"There's no one I hate enough to land with that cursed place," Anderson muttered.

An argument broke out behind them, and it took determination not to turn and stare like most people around him. The guards moved in and dragged the irate inmate away. By the insults being thrown, the prisoner had just been dumped for another man.

"Does me being a fellow American have anything to do with you choosing my company to conduct the auction?"

Anderson snorted in amusement. "You betcha. At least with you as the auction house, a little more of the money from that cursed place will go home." He paused and fixed Darien with an intense stare. "I didn't mean to hurt either of them.

Something just came over me—" Anderson tensed, his hands forming fists "—the jealousy, that fury... it came from outside, not me."

Darien remained relaxed and quiet. He was here to auction the man's property, not give absolution or provide evidence for a diminished responsibilities defense.

Carl Anderson rasped out, "At least, for the love of God, make sure no one ever lives there permanently again. That place screws with your mind." He poked a thick finger in Darien's direction. "If you sell it to an individual, you'll condemn them. That'll be on you, not me."

If there was one thing he'd learned about human behavior, it was that people tended to mirror the energy level of a more dominant individual. "Mr. Anderson, I'm bound by the auctioneer code of ethics to bring all known possible negative aspects to the attention of bidders."

Anderson held his gaze for a moment longer. "They won't believe you."

"That's probably true," Darien replied without inflection, "but that won't stop me telling them."

"If I could, I'd bulldoze the entire place."

The last residue of sympathy he'd had for the man evaporated. The mere thought of destroying something that magnificent, that historic, turned his stomach.

"As that's not possible, would you care to sign the contract so we can take the property off your hands as soon as possible? Would you mind if we used the venue for a special auction of period pieces too?"

Anderson looked over at the nearest guard. "Do what you like, just get rid of it. Can I have a pen, please?"

A biro was produced, and under the watchful gaze of the guard, Anderson scrawled his signature and handed the pen back.

Just to be safe, Darien asked the guard to notarize the signature before putting the contract back in his inside pocket. His briefcase was back in a locker at the visitor center.

He turned back to Anderson. "I'll do my best to get a good price for you, but the Hall's recent history might make it a difficult sell."

Carl barked with manic laughter. "Recent? I looked into the history of the place after I bought it. Suicides, murders, fatal accidents, the place is drowning in unnatural death. The only people who survive owning Walpole Hall get out early and never look back." Carl grabbed his arm. "Don't ever sleep there. That's where he gets you, in your sleep. It'll start with—"

The guard came back over. "Now, now Anderson, let the nice man go." Anderson turned to the guard, tense, frantic.

"He doesn't understand; it's dangerous. I have to warn him. I have to—"

Another guard approached, and Darien made a swift exit as Anderson continued to shout dire warnings about ghosts. If he hadn't already had a signed sales contract from Melody Anderson's estate lawyer in America, he might have worried about the validity of the paperwork in his pocket. Although Carl Anderson hadn't been certified insane yet, such a diagnosis could add years of legal wrangling to the disposal of the estate.

To his relief, the taxi still waited outside on the busy London street as promised. Darien got in, and the driver turned on his blinker.

"Kent?" he confirmed.

Darien managed a 'yep,' before opening his briefcase and retrieving the glossy brochure Juliana had already produced from photos taken for the previous sale several years ago. It already included photographs of some of the pieces they hoped to sell, including furniture, tableware, art, and weaponry. The pieces came from all over the world, but all dated between 1550—just before the beginning of the

Elizabethan era—and the end of the English civil war in 1651. The Hall dated from 1600, three years before the death of Elizabeth I.

This was the most unusual and personally exciting sale the FitzHenry Auction House had ever handled. He and Juliana had stepped off their transatlantic flight four hours ago, but she had gone straight to the hotel in Kent with their luggage.

The auction would take place in ten days, but they would have viewings by appointment rather than an open house. They wanted genuine buyers, not a horde of tourists or ghoulish fans of murder scenes.

The Hall had been unoccupied since the last police officer had rolled up the crime scene tape over fifteen months ago. Darien had no idea what he'd be walking into. It could be pristine except for a little dust or a complete nightmare of trash. Just because a property had listed status, it didn't mean an owner wouldn't change or destroy things. The thought of all that priceless, unique history being destroyed by the deranged man he'd just left turned his stomach.

The brochure in his hand trembled. After laying it on the seat beside him, he flexed his fist then picked it up again. This was just another auction, just another job. Except, it wasn't. This was history, possibly his own.

Darien had planned to get here three weeks before the auction to seal the deal and supervise the clean-up of the property. Because of the lack of time, he'd ordered the carpeting the Andersons had apparently installed removed; covering the original stone and wooden flooring had been an almost unforgivable sin. He just hoped what remained had enhanced the property rather than scarred it. Who knew what a man capable of killing his wife could do?

Work, and the long-winded prison procedures to request and then grant a visit, had gotten in the way of arriving any sooner. Darien only had ten days to immerse himself in the atmosphere. Excitement, and a bone-deep dread that this would be a huge disappointment, meant going to the hotel first had never been an option. He needed to see, to experience, the history because he'd probably never see the property again after this brief visit.

Even with the high guide price, there were plenty of interested parties. The National Trust hoped to save this stunning example of an Elizabethan building for the nation, but there were also hoteliers, a theme park owner, construction firms who wanted to build on the parkland, and a scattering of private buyers.

Thanks to its Grade I listed status, the house itself was safe from development, but the rolling parkland could become an amusement park or a housing estate in the next few years. Anderson would probably approve of an amusement park.

Darien shivered at the thought, but as the auctioneer, he couldn't favor one bidder over another. Auctioneers suspected of giving particular bidders preferential treatment never worked in the industry again.

Personally, he hoped the National Trust bought and restored the Hall to its former glory. The building and land would be sold in one lot, but the new owner had the right to sell any artifacts and land as long as they kept the structure intact.

Darien and Juliana grew up among valuable colonial artifacts on an eighteenth-century plantation estate in southern Missouri. They had soaked up history and a love for antiques like other kids absorbed TV and games. His obsession with sixteenth and seventeenth England started at eight years old, when he discovered that their family name, FitzHenry, referred to the illegitimate offspring of an aristocratic 'Henry' possibly one of the Tudor kings.

Having inherited the small local auction house from the previous generation of FitzHenrys, Darien's parents had encouraged their son's obsession with history. Although, he'd resisted their push toward majoring in American history in favor of studying the Tudors. Juliana had majored in marketing, finding the business side far more interesting. They'd grown the business into a national organization, but this was one of their first international ventures.

This wasn't Darien's first visit to the UK; he'd come here many times to visit historic sites and absorb the culture. His homeland seemed pale, new, even raw in comparison, but his research proved the real reason that he felt so comfortable here. Part of his roots lay in this softly rolling, verdant green maze of lanes and hedges.

His introduction to the Tudors had come from studying the era's art. Paintings from the period both fascinated and frustrated. The faces were so stylized that getting a feel for the person behind the almost universally bug-eyed, moon-like faces was impossible. Instead, he'd poured over their homes, objects they'd touched, trying to get to know the people and the lives they'd led.

His personal genealogy became his passion, and his degree thesis had made a case for his aristocratic lineage. He'd traced his family back to an entry in the manifest of a colony ship that had sailed for Virginia from Southampton, England, in 1627.

One negroe, known as Tom Henry.

The entry came as part of the cargo owned by one Henry Walpole, the fourth son of the first Earl of Tandridge, the builder of Walpole Hall. Any disappointment that he wasn't related to Tudor royalty vanished as Darien discovered more intrigue and drama in the Walpole line than he could possibly imagine.

Most younger sons of sixteenth/seventeenth English aristocrats either went into the military, the clergy, or were married off to secure political alliances. Not Henry Walpole.

The man had been a colorful, wayward rogue, a gambler, a risk-taker, and an unrepentant hedonist. He left the family home under a cloud and had been struck from the majority of family records.

Darien suspected—hoped—that Tom Henry had been Henry Walpole's biological son. No information existed about the boy's mother.

Back in those days, it was common for enslaved people to be given their owner's name. The prefix 'Fitz' had been added sometime in the 1740s as the family became tobacco plantation owners and strove to hide their African roots from their white colonial neighbors and business associates.

Of course, Henry Walpole might have purchased Tom Henry. Still, Darien enjoyed the romantic fantasy of his family emerging from a love match between a couple from two such varied circumstances.

The races had come together again with Darien's generation as his blond, blue-eyed father married his Black college sweetheart. Being a mixed-race couple in the wealthy circles they frequented didn't cause many waves, but Darien had been stopped when driving his Lexus many times, unlike his pale-skinned paternal cousins.

Darien smiled as the gravel of the mile-long driveway, between stately, orange-leaved elm trees, crunched under the taxi's wheels.

What would Henry Walpole think about a black descendant returning to his family home after all these years?

The mixed race of his descendant might please Henry, but he wondered what he'd think of Darien's preference for young, pale-skinned male partners. Homosexuality had been officially outlawed in Elizabethan times, but Elizabeth's successor, James 1st, had several male lovers. Yet again, it was one rule for the poor and another for the rich.

His mind stuttered and then blanked as the Hall rose before him. He would describe the building as having first, second, and third stories; the British said ground floor, first and second floors. Built of red brick, with square turrets at either end of the hundred-and-fifty-foot-long roof, it owned the open, rolling surrounding parkland. The first Earl certainly liked to impress his visitors.

The car crunched to a halt, and almost in a daze, Darien paid the driver and got out. The feeling of kinship with a building he'd never seen outside of a page or screen was probably merely a flight of fancy, the product of a fertile imagination.

History oozed from the brick, hanging in the air like sweat. The shades of the many people who had called this place home over the last four hundred years seemed to hover at the edges of his vision. The births, the deaths, the loves, triumphs, and failures, the very details of lives lived.

Taking a deep breath, he told himself that this was just another job. It wasn't. The taxi departing made him realize he was still staring up like a moonstruck tourist. Shaking his head, he made his way up the twenty-foot-wide stone stairs that had been worn into shallow, central dips by centuries of feet.

CHAPTER TWO

A shiver went down Darien's spine as, unable to resist, he touched the propped open studded wooden front door that dated to the original construction.

What had Henry Walpole thought as he exited this door for the last time? Or did he sneak out of another door in the middle of the night? Did he think he'd return, or had he known he was leaving everything behind forever?

So many of his possible relatives had met with tragic, often bloody ends within these walls. In contrast, Henry had outlived all three of his brothers and many of his nephews and grandnephews. From birth and death statistics, Walpole daughters had fared far better in life than their fathers, brothers, and mothers. History showed that being the Earl of Tandridge, or his direct male descendent, did not lead to a long life or a happy one.

Suicide, accidents, and murders; misfortune plagued the male Walpole line. Looking at the records, you'd suspect a genetic mental health issue that Henry Walpole and his descendants had somehow avoided, but the so-called curse had passed to subsequent unrelated residents of the Hall.

The Walpole line had ended when the last Earl was killed in a riding accident a week before he'd been due to join the war effort in 1939. The estate had been bequeathed to his bereaved fiancée, who sold it within a month.

Since then, no one had remained in residence for more than five years, which added another complication to the sale. As with vehicles, house buyers preferred the number of previous owners to be as low as possible. The illusion of being a previously happy residence for an extended period—particularly when handed down through several generations—added a significant percentage to most sale prices.

Stepping inside, Darien let the atmosphere of the Low Great Hall permeate him. The stunning oak paneling seemed to have survived being covered in wallpapered plywood as it stretched twenty feet above his head. The room was dominated by a huge, gray stone fireplace with the Walpole family crest of a phoenix standing with spread wings above it.

For a second, Darien could almost see the hurrying servants, the long tables laden with food, could almost smell the smoky atmosphere, and hear the raucous laughter.

"At last. I thought you'd got lost." The click-clack of heels on the flagstones pulled him out of his daydream. "I take it he signed?"

Juliana snapped her fingers as he failed to tear his gaze away from the phoenix. He wondered if the first Earl had known how appropriate the symbol would prove for his family as they rose from the ashes of tragedy again and again.

"Earth to Darien, come in Darien?"

"Hmm?" he replied, wondering if the sculptor had left a telltale mark to advertise his expertise. If he could match it to others of the period, he—

Pain flared. His gaze shot to his sister as he rubbed his pinched arm. "Hey, cut it out, or I'll tell mom you're picking on me again."

Juliana snorted. "She'll agree with me when I tell her you were daydreaming again. Did you get the signature on the contract?" As usual, his sister got straight to the point when there was business to discuss. No way would anyone guess the perfectly made up, lavender-suited woman had been on a plane for nearly eight and half hours last night, had lost five hours, and was short on sleep.

Darien shook himself, trying to get his mind back on work.

She touched the back of her hand to his forehead. "You ok? You're not coming down with something, are you? Because a sick auctioneer snotting all over his gavel does not leave a good impression."

Darien let out a snort. "The same caring sister, no matter which side of the Atlantic we're on. But don't worry, I have your precious paperwork. I was just taking in the atmosphere." He opened his briefcase and handed her the signed agreement.

Eyes alight, she almost snatched it from him and scanned to the dated signature in case Darien had somehow forgotten something. She turned, going to walk away from him without saying anything further.

"Thank you, Darien, do take some time to look around," he parroted.

She waved a hand in the air as she made her way out of the room, heels clicking on the worn centuries-old flagstones. "Knock yourself out. But there are some potential bidders wandering about. Make sure you don't get too friendly; we don't want any bias accusations."

Darien sighed. Juliana hadn't even glanced at the carved wooden friezes on the paneling above her head or the fireplace. For her, history was a commodity, part of their business, not a passion. Sometimes he wondered if he should have become a museum curator or a professional historian rather than being dragged into the family business as an assessor and auctioneer.

However, right now, his job had provided the opportunity of a lifetime. He was actually here in Henry Walpole's birthplace, and maybe, just maybe, he might find something to connect himself to this magnificent building.

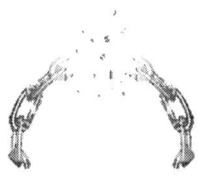

Unlike most later buildings, the stairs didn't lead off the main hall. Two staircases existed, one at either end of the house. After making his way up the larger staircase, with long shallow curving steps that boasted several landings, he found himself on the viewing gallery. The view of the double-height Low Great Hall below captured Darien again.

How often had the young Henry Walpole stood right here? Two parties of viewers crossed the flagstones below, one being guided by Juliana, another by an older, weather-beaten man.

The man, who looked as if he belonged here, had to be Harry Grimshaw, gardener and handyman who lived in the gatehouse at the edge of the property. The Estate had been home to the Grimshaw family for generations without them suffering from the supposed curse, but it appeared that streak had ended when the Andersons bought the place.

The clacking of high heels on the flagstones and the occasional phone ringing felt utterly alien in this ancient place, but they pulled Darien back to his job. He should be checking the particulars of the sale, doing his best for the client, but he couldn't help sucking up the atmosphere for a little longer.

He bet the hall smelled a hell of a lot sweeter now than when it'd been built. With no running water, toilets, fifty-plus unwashed bodies, and numerous hounds, the place must have hummed to high heaven. Now, only the scent of beeswax and old dust hung in the air.

"So, this is what fifteen million gets you," Darien murmured as he leaned on the carved wooden balustrade. Considering the price of some London and New York apartments, it didn't seem expensive.

A bird, probably the family crest phoenix, had been carved on the two newel posts at either end of the banister. Over the centuries, they'd become so worn with the touches of generations of hands that he could barely see what they had been originally. Had Henry Walpole stood here like this, plotting his escape?

"Death, pain, madness, heartache, and a shite load of woodworm and dust. Not much considering," a heavily accented English voice said.

Darien glanced sideways. A young man—with a striking purple bruise around his left eye and dark finger marks on his neck—leaned on the balustrade ten feet away. His fingers caressed the worn carving as he gazed at the scene below.

The barefoot, red-haired lad wore a raw linen shirt that reached his mid-thighs and nothing else. The overly large collarless shirt revealed a sharp collarbone and white skin smudged with dirt.

Why had an 'Elizabethan peasant' actor been engaged to provide ambiance, especially one who looked half-starved, beaten, and missing half his costume? Even though it was the end of October, this was business, not a Halloween tourist event. Glancing around, Darien confirmed that he hadn't missed anyone else in costume; it certainly hadn't been part of the marketing plan.

Maybe he'd slipped in with one of the prospective buyers and was an exhibitionist who had a role play kink. If so, both the redhead and his partner had balls, but Darien needed to have a word. The focus had to be on the auction, not a new scandal heaped on top of all the other controversy surrounding the property.

"I appreciate role play, but this is hardly the time even if the place has the right ambiance," he said, then frowned as the youngster ignored him. "What are you supposed to be? Scullery boy kicked out of bed too early? Stable lad? An overgrown chimney sweep on his day off?"

Darien wondered if the guy knew he wore the equivalent of modern underwear. An actual Elizabethan would never have walked around like this. They believed that exposing the skin allowed diseases to attack, so they covered up as much as possible. The belief was also the reason why bathing seldom happened. Exposing your entire body to air or water was certain to make you sick.

The guy was small and slim enough to play the part of a malnourished Elizabethan or Jacobean peasant. Darien's gaze was caught by a slight tear in the shirt; it teased on the curve of his buttock. White skin showed through; there was no sign of modern underwear.

He bet the guy's backside would glow like a beacon if the role play he enjoyed included corporal punishment. Darien's cock stirred at the thought of turning that white ass red with a well-deserved spanking.

A slight shift in the young man's stance revealed a different inch of skin and a thin black bruise. Someone had already beaten this guy with a cane hard enough to leave deep bruises. You could hit a lot harder without causing more than superficial damage on an ass, but the guy's movements were stiff. Darien changed his mind about the black eye and neck bruising being makeup. What other bruises and injuries lay under the youngster's clothes?

BDSM and getting into a role was one thing, but whoever was this guy's dominant, they weren't looking after their sub's health. That much pressure on a throat must have made him pass out. He also looked as if he hadn't eaten a decent meal in weeks. Slim could be attractive, but this stepped over the line into skinny. The man's poor condition pinged every caregiver dom nerve Darien possessed.

Straightening up, Darien rolled his shoulders. Abusing someone who gave you their full trust pissed him off. It gave the lifestyle a bad name. This guy couldn't be any older than twenty.

"Hey, red, I'm talking to you."

The man's startling blue-green eyes shot to his. Stepping back from the balustrade, his gaze didn't leave Darien. He rocked back and forth as if debating whether to run or throw himself at Darien. The second option held far more appeal if there hadn't been a dozen people within shouting distance. At least he'd get to see to the sub's injuries.

"I'm not going to hurt you, but someone has, haven't they?"

The youngster swallowed, his Adam's apple bobbing in his bruised throat. "You, you can see me?"

Darien frowned. "Should I not be able to?"

"But you... you're black." The guy seemed genuinely amazed. Darien hadn't experienced overt racism other than being stopped by traffic cops for a long time, but this amused him more than it pissed him off.

"And you're ginger. Guess it sucks to be you. Now, about those bruises?"

The costumed man licked his lips, almost vibrating with tension. "Why are you here? Who are you working for?"

"Strange as it may seem, I'm here for the auction, and I work for my family business."

The man's head tilted. "As what?"

Darien folded his arms, enjoying the interaction. "Are you usually this nosy?"

A grin that tugged directly on Darien's cock appeared. This guy wasn't the on the floor submissive he'd assumed.

"Oh, yes. I want to know everything about you. Including the noise you make when you spill."

A quick glance around them showed a group of four suited men making their way up the wide stone staircase to their left. Darien moved closer to the source of his irritation, his arousal.

"Cut it out, or I'll have you removed, no matter who your Dom is."

A line appeared between his eyebrows as if something briefly confused or upset him, then he was back to the questions.

"Are you buying for yourself or a company? I know what I'd prefer."

Darien's patience drained away. This guy clearly didn't need his immediate help. He could certainly imagine him goading his partner into going too far. Darien needed to shut this irritating, cocky, incredibly sexy man up before he embarrassed him in front of potential customers.

There were many influential people here, and if the auction went well, FitzHenry's might get more prestigious clients in the UK. Unfortunately, his preferred method of shutting up this bold flirter, by spanking him, was out of the question right now.

Closing the gap between them, Darien caged the man against the balustrade with his body.

"I'm the auctioneer; I run this show. Who the hell are you?"

The man's shoulders deflated as he looked up at Darien through his drooping, curly auburn hair. "Not a buyer?"

He looked so sad, so disappointed, that Darien's anger drained.

"No, I'm not a buyer."

"You'll be leaving after the sale next week?"

"Here you are, Darien. I was wondering where you'd got to." Juliana's voice had him glancing in her direction.

"I'll be with you in a moment," he said and turned back to his more immediate problem.

A problem that was no longer there. Darien turned, one way then the other; the guy must have ducked under his arm while he'd been distracted. There was no sign of him.

Jogging the few steps to the other side of the landing, he peered around the corner. Nothing.

"What is it? Did you see the ghost?"

Darien snorted. "Don't be stupid. You saw him as well as I did."

"Who?"

"Really? You didn't see a skinny redhead in a long shirt and nothing else? Black eye, bruises on his neck? He was standing a couple of inches from me."

A crease appeared between Juliana's dark eyes. His sister's skin was lighter than Darien's, but her eyes were dark brown compared to Darien's amber.

"I didn't see anyone. You sure you're not jet-lagged?"

Darien gave her a hard look. "I'm fine. There was a guy here. I doubt ghosts ask what sex noises you make."

Julie bit her lip but couldn't hide her grin. "Only you could meet a sexy gay ghost. Unfortunately, rather than doing an impression of the Scooby gang, you need to go schmooze. The local realtor has been showing prospective bidders around for the last week. He was heading up to the long gallery, probably to ogle the art."

"What's he look like?"

Julie rolled her eyes. "Done your research as usual, I see? I'll take you."

Darien grinned. "You do the people. I do the things. It's what makes us such a good team."

A loud 'whoo-hoo' rent the air from somewhere above him. Darien stopped in his tracks. Juliana bumped into him from behind.

"What the... Warn a girl, Darien," Juliana said as she staggered back a step.

Darien gritted his teeth. "This is a quality sale. We can't have people hollering like that; it lowers the tone."

"Hollering? No one's hollering. You sure you're ok?"

"You didn't hear a woohoo?"

Those perfectly shaped eyebrows drew together again. "Nope. No woohoo, yeehaw, or praise the Lord. I think you need to go get your head down sooner rather than later. Go meet the realtor—he's guiding a group on the upper floor up as far as I know—then head back to the hotel. I'll finish up here, ok?"

"I'm fine. Someone shouted. If you didn't hear it, you need to get your ears syringed again."

That no one down in the Low Great Hall appeared to be looking around for the source of the shout merely proved that all the activity down there had masked the noise.

Darien followed his sister up the smaller eastern stairs, wondering where the nameless battered costumed man had gone. There was no doubt that the shout had come from the elusive 'peasant' or that his mischievous grin promised all sorts of wicked pleasure.

However, stepping on another dom's toes was a huge black mark in the BDSM world. He needed to find out if the boy was being purposefully abused or if this was a case of over-enthusiasm, ignorance, and one hell of a bratty sub. Maybe then he could step in and provide some much-needed advice and education. But for that, he had to catch the intriguing little shit.

The 'if's' were snowballing, but all the best things in life took effort.

CHAPTER THREE

Alastor punched the air and let out a yell after relocating to the roof. Up here, he could see beyond the estate's borders to the village that had grown into a small town over the centuries. Knowing people were going about their lives, that things changed, helped dispel a little of his loneliness, but he didn't have to be lonely anymore.

An heir, a living heir after all this time. Waiting eighty years suddenly didn't seem too long if he got to play with a young, sexy, forceful man who clearly found him attractive.

Alastor needed to find out everything about him and his family. Could he be the last Walpole? The idea sent a tingle through him. After over four hundred years, was his sentence finally nearing its end? His first priority was getting more time to work on him.

But the man wasn't here to buy, not yet anyway. Alastor had exceptional persuasive skills, but getting this heir to spend millions in a week was a big ask, even if the man had that much money.

After standing still for so long in his quest to break the curse, it felt as if he'd been shot from a bow and was still accelerating. Every second counted. There had to be another way to keep the heir here longer than a week. He needed information, but more than that, he craved the ability to touch things again, to maybe, finally, quench his dry throat.

With a thought, Alastor located the heir and appeared behind him in the Long Gallery. He wasn't alone.

Driving Walpoles to insanity usually began as soon as they stepped within the grounds, but he needed this one alive, at least until he discovered how many more heirs

were out there. Cursing himself for forgetting this man could see him, Alastor slipped behind one of the many tapestry screens.

For centuries, the family and staff had complained about the cold, arctic-like drafts; Alastor simply wished he could feel what they hated.

The Long Gallery stretched the length of the rear of the second floor, a hundred and fifty feet long, thirty feet wide, and twenty-five feet high. The space had been used for exercise in inclement weather and to show off the family's standing to guests. Most Elizabethan country houses had long galleries, but they weren't on the top floor. The first Earl had wanted to show off the view along with his wealth. Multi-paned windows covered the entire wall, an extravagance that had boggled the minds of visitors. Glass had been hand-blown back then and incredibly expensive.

On the opposite wall hung portraits of previous owners and visitors, from modern times back to the first Earl. They varied in size from barely two hands wide to vast, six-foot square canvases.

The heir stood, tall, straight, and lickable, with an older suited man, who pointed up at the portrait of the man whose male progeny had been cursed. The painting bore little resemblance to the man Alastor remembered. The high forehead, heavy-lidded eyes, and prominent nose of the slim, middle-aged man had more to do with Elizabethan fashion than accuracy. The overly large lace ruff was correct, but the one in the painting wouldn't have fit around the neck of the corpulent man Alastor had known.

Thomas Walpole, the builder of the Hall, had been obsessive about making sure everyone he met knew his status. The bigger the ruff you wore, the richer the colors of your clothes, the more importance you exuded, and the more you trod on those beneath you.

The Grimshaws were more worthy people than any Walpole. Guilt wasn't an emotion a demon should experience, but he still regretted what had happened to Liam. The youngster wouldn't be a living corpse if he'd kept out of it.

He still didn't know if he'd do the same thing again, even if he'd known that the Grimshaws' suffering would bring him an heir. *Perhaps the final heir?*

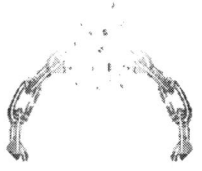

A year ago

"See the way she fucks him with her eyes? No one looks at someone like that if they haven't already done it."

The fifty-seven-year-old balding American watched his blonde twenty-five-year-old trophy wife rather than concentrating on the phone in his hand. For the fifth time in the last few minutes, she peered over her dark glasses, but it wasn't her husband she eyed with a slight smile on her scarlet lips.

The pair lounged on wooden beds beside the pool, sipping ridiculous cocktails in the late August evening. The atrocious new addition had been dug right in the center of the formal gardens.

The focus of Melody Anderson's attention, a brown haired, tanned youth—wearing nothing but a green sleeveless shirt and frayed cut-off blue jeans—dipped a large net into the shimmering water of the swimming pool.

Alastor couldn't blame her. Nineteen-year-old Liam Grimshaw would make everyone who found the male form attractive take notice. He yearned to have that much life touch him again. The visceral need to be touched, seen, or heard by another person ate at him with every passing day. It almost eclipsed the pain in his ass and his unending thirst.

Ugly modern music throbbed from what had been the hub of the house, the Low Great Hall. Now, it was a stark open space, devoid of life. In 1602, it had been the living, eating, and sleeping place of the lower servants and hounds. He'd give almost anything to have a dog snarl at him again. Tormenting beasts wasn't nearly as entertaining as driving people to distraction, but it beat being ignored.

At least the Americans couldn't destroy any of the Hall itself. Out of all the alterations they'd made, Alastor couldn't decide whether the pool, carpeting, the damn air fresheners, or the boarded over paneling on the lower two floors were more offensive. He'd thought encouraging them to buy the Hall two years ago was a fantastic idea at first.

As an imp, being irritating came naturally. Making the entitled pair suffer minor mishaps and annoyances had been his pleasure and delight, but Arioch's deadline meant he didn't have time to play any longer. Time to amp up the jealousy, greed, lust, and suspicion he'd been introducing into their minds, mostly while they slept. What he said didn't really matter—humans couldn't consciously hear him—but over the years, he'd found he could influence emotions if he tried hard enough.

He spoke into Carl Anderson's ear. *"New sheets on the bed again this morning. Efficiency, or is she hiding the stink, the stains, of what they did while you worked? Slick, sliding, hot, and wet. Moaning for him, sucking him, swallowing his cum, and loving it, giving him what's yours, what you worked hard to pay for. They're using you, laughing at you."*

Carl stiffened and stroked a hand down his t-shirt-covered paunch.

"Can you blame her for going for that? Look at you; look at him. She married you for your money, and when you divorce, she'll keep this place and him."

Alastor knee walked the few feet to Melody. His target didn't even get a subliminal message unless his mouth was within inches of their ear.

"Look at him. Fifty-seven, he could last another thirty years, maybe even forty, with money-eating medical care. You'll be stuck with a stinking, dribbling, pissing, and shitting old man while your looks fade. By the time he dies, you'll be just like him, unable to enjoy any of this. Divorce him. Take him for everything, then you can have whoever you like, whenever you like."

Whispering to Liam was a little trickier as the man moved around the pool, but Alastor managed.

"Why does he have all the luck? He can't even keep his wife satisfied. Draw her in, make her love you, then you can have a taste of this pie and be the one sitting in that chair. You and your family deserve it more than he does, more than that living blow-up doll. Your family has slaved in this place for generations; it's time you got to enjoy it. Don't your mum and dad deserve it? Take her; she wants it."

The young man cast an unsubtle glance at Melody's artificial breasts that almost hung out of her blue bikini top. Jealousy bubbled. These ephemeral humans could experience pleasure every hour of every day if they wished.

"Is there anything else you need before I go?" Liam asked, his gaze on Melody Anderson, not her husband.

"A good hard fuck is what she needs. First your cock down her throat, then deep in her pussy. Knock her up. She'll have to divorce him. Think of it; a Grimshaw will finally own Walpole Hall."

Melody sat up. "No, that's it for today. I'll drop you home if you like? I wanted to pick up something special for dinner at the store."

Carl's frown deepened. "Don't be silly, honey. He can walk; it's only a mile. You'd have to get dressed. I'm sure we've got something in the—"

Melody was already getting up, making the fabric of the bikini strain to retain her tanned, rounded flesh.

Melody smiled, jiggled a little. "Aw, you're so sweet, sugar. No, I'll go. I want to celebrate you finishing that movie." After a peck on her husband's cheek, she bounced back into the house. Both men watched until she disappeared.

"What are you, a man or a mouse? That's your wife, your property. She can't even remember the name of the movie you've been working on for a year. That's a real kick in the balls. Are you going to let a boy ruin everything? Do something, show him who the man is around here."

Carl put his drink down, sweat shining through his dark belly hair. Alastor held his breath. A nice messy divorce would be just perfect.

"Boy, are you up to anything with my wife?"

Yes! Alastor did a fist pump.

"I'm just doing my job, Mr. Anderson, taking care of your assets while you're away."

Alastor's jaw dropped open at the youngster's audacity. *Go, Liam.*

Carl heaved himself off the lounger, red-faced. "Why, you little shit!"

Alastor expected Liam to run or apologize like any servant confronted with an angry master; he didn't. Confident in his physical superiority, Liam simply stood and waited for Anderson to lumber around the pool.

The American's eyes bulged, but he halted a few feet from the gardener. He pointed a trembling finger at the younger man.

"You're fired, and I'm evicting your family."

White teeth flashed as Liam laughed. "Fired? That's all you got? As for evicting my parents, good luck with that. The law is on our side—we've had an assured tenancy for over three hundred years—so I'll still be living there even if I'm not working here.

"Who do you think will be warming her bed when you're off on location? Did you know that she really loves gagging on big dicks?"

Alastor rubbed his hands together. This was bloody priceless. Carl looked on the verge of having a heart attack.

The American's fist shot out and caught Liam on the chin. The youngster slipped on the wet paving stones, fell back. Alastor winced at the dull thud of the back of Liam's head hitting the flagstone. Blood mixed with the film of water.

Liam lay still, blinking up at the sky as if he couldn't quite work out what had happened. Carl put his foot under his rival, and with a heave, flipped him into the water.

Liam flailed, went under. Fear and panic screamed in the boy's eyes as he briefly surfaced. Spluttering, Liam stretched out an arm; his fingers brushed the side. Carl bent, picked up the pool net. Cool as ice, he pushed Liam away from the side, then put it over his head and shoved him down.

"No!" Alastor shouted, but Carl couldn't hear him. Forgetting for a moment, he tried to shove Carl, attempting to unbalance him to give Liam a chance. His hands passed straight through the man's body with a sickening sinking sensation. Alastor drew back, shocked into immobility.

The older man watched until his rival stopped moving and floated face down. Then, as if he didn't have a care in the world, Carl dropped the net in the now still water and walked indoors.

"Honey? Can you come here for a minute?"

Although he'd seen death many times, Alastor gaped at the body for a few seconds before he saw fingers twitch.

"Help, I need to get help."

With a thought, Alastor relocated to the gatehouse that always made him itch and found Mr. Grimshaw in his greenhouse, potting out cuttings.

Blowing out a breath to calm himself, Alastor concentrated and moved one of the little sticks the man reached for.

"Finally come to play, have you? My dad told me about you, how his dad saw you once, but I woulda thought it was more interesting up at the Hall. Getting on your nerves, are they?"

Alastor's jaw clenched in frustration. *Shit, this is too slow.*

A scattering of compost on the bench in front of Harry gave Alastor an idea. Wincing, the imp stepped into the space Mr. Grimshaw occupied and reached out a finger to draw, so damn slowly, in the dirt.

L

Die

Pool

Exhausted, Alastor watched Liam's father pound out of the greenhouse, knowing in his heart that it would be too late.

Heaviness pressed down on his shoulders, and he felt a little sick, despite not eating anything for almost eighty years.

Huh, so this is guilt.

Alastor decided he didn't like it and let the curse pull him back to the main house.

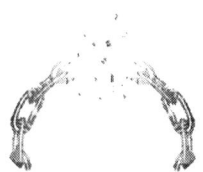

What happened to Liam hadn't been fair, hadn't been what he'd planned. But life and death weren't fair; Arioch and the curse had taught him that. The sooner he broke the spell, the sooner he could get out of the Grimshaw's lives. He needed to look to the future, not dwell on the past. And the future was the Walpole heir standing in the Long Gallery where his distant family had preened, played, and in more than one case, died.

The heir stood perhaps six feet tall, not particularly tall for modern times, but a near giant compared to many of his ancestors and far bigger than Alastor. The pale gray suit set off his dark skin perfectly. Broad nose, lush lips, close-cropped hair, and a strong, fit body. It would be such a shame to ruin him, but before he could even think about that, Alastor had to catch him.

The imp stopped contemplating his target as the man fell silent. Alastor followed his gaze to a particular painting. Crude in comparison to the others, it had only been kept because of the artist.

The widowed first Lady Walpole sat in the walled garden with two maids, one a young black girl. Behind them, Alastor leaned over the garden wall, wearing the same undershirt he had on today. Unusually for the time, the painted Alastor smirked. The artist had been Charles, the second son of the first Earl, before Alastor drove him to his death.

A week after the painting had been hung, Charles Walpole became the third Earl of Tandridge when his older brother Richard died in a riding accident the week before he'd been due to marry. Spooking horses had removed quite a few heirs. Unlike people, animals could see him.

Back then, Alastor had cut through the male heirs like a hot knife through butter. He'd even managed to set family members against one another a few times, causing them to do the hard work for him. But families back then had often been large. As soon as he crossed one Walpole male off the list, three others seemed to slither out of the snatches of various women.

It took having the five-year-old son of a servant saying 'Good morrow' to him a score years into the curse to realize that the spell didn't discriminate on legitimacy. Many English aristocrats were constant philanders, having mistresses in various towns and fucking maids without a care. That day reached Alastor's top three depressing days; the second on the list was the day he'd been ripped from a life he couldn't remember and dumped here.

The worst had been the day the last Earl of Tandridge, a childless man who had been the only child of an only child, died. As soon as the fucker who had just beaten him black and blue stopped breathing, Alastor ran for the edge of the estate a few hundred yards away, every fiber of his body alive with the anticipation of finally being free. He ended up on his bruised backside, staring at the grass a few feet away that he still couldn't touch. His throat still ached with the scream of frustration he'd let out over eighty years ago.

Finally, when he'd almost given up hope—had considered begging Arioch to end his existence the next time they met—Alastor found himself in the presence of another living heir.

The heir peered upward at the canvas, and his mouth dropped open. Alastor smiled. He'd seen the moment an heir recognized their tormentor in the painting many times.

"Ah, you've spotted the resident poltergeist," the agent said. "He's why Carl Anderson is trying for a diminished responsibilities defense. He claimed the ghost sent him temporarily mad. Personally, I'm sticking with the rumor that Melody Anderson seduced poor young Grimshaw, and Anderson caught them at it."

The heir indicated the painting. "How widely is it known that this is meant to be the ghost?"

The portly, balding man shrugged. "I have no idea. The groundskeeper, Harry Grimshaw, told me about it earlier this week. It's a cute story that will pull tourists here if it gets sold as a commercial property."

The heir pursed his lips. "Maybe. Why do you think the property has changed hands so often? No one has retained it for more than five years since the last Earl died."

The agent smiled as he also looked up at the painting. "You do your research, Mr. FitzHenry. As for the frequent sales, I don't know or particularly care. It just means more commission for people like us. I've sold this place three times in the last decade."

FitzHenry. Bastard of Henry. There had been many Henrys in the Walpole line, including the fourth son of the First Earl, who had run off with the black maid in the painting soon after Alastor started his sentence.

Shit, fuck, and hairy hanging bollocks. If that first Henry Walpole produced issue, and in the Americas judging by this man's accent... Alastor's mind boggled at the number of descendants he could have produced in four hundred years.

I could be here until the sun explodes.

The prospect of being stuck here, century upon century, causing death after pointless death while the world passed him by felt like a dray horse had kicked him in the balls. His despair lasted for mere seconds before anger burned it to ash.

I did my job; the legitimate Walpole line is ended. It's not my fault Walpoles breed faster than rabbits.

An image of the bare behind of this heir thrusting hard and fast into him, holding him down, using him as his ancestors had done, blanketed Alastor's swirling thoughts. Alastor thought he deserved a reward like that, even if he was stuck here for eternity.

"So, who do you think are our best bets?" FitzHenry asked. "You've shown the property to the majority of the bidders, correct?"

The middle-aged realtor became animated. "The hoteliers, the Majesty Group in particular. This is right up their street. They've tried to buy it before, but the price was never right."

"Severe woman in a grey suit, right?" FitzHenry asked.

"Yes, Mrs. Carmichael. She owns the Majesty chain. At least she'll keep the place essentially intact. The Foresters, the large Asian man in the black suit, will turn it into an amusement park." He indicated the painting again. "And I bet your little spook will get pride of place."

"Not my spook," FitzHenry said, a little too quickly.

Alastor smiled. *Not yet, anyway.*

"Do you know if—" FitzHenry started, then shook his head. "Never mind."

The estate agent checked his Rolex. "Well, I'll be going. Got a little more sucking up to do. I'll see you tomorrow. Feel free to soak up the atmosphere for as long as you like; you might never get another chance. The housekeeper and her husband hold the keys; just let them know when you leave. Personally, I'll be out of here as soon as I can. The place gives me the creeps. It always feels like I'm being watched."

The man walked away. FitzHenry moved slowly sideways, examining the plaques under the paintings that stated the subject, year, and artist, if known.

FitzHenry proved he knew about his ancestry when he stopped at the family portrait of the first Earl and focused on the smallest boy, Henry Walpole as a four-year-old.

On silent feet, Alastor moved up behind him. "Henry Walpole, born 1584, fifteen years before the Hall was built." FitzHenry jerked, eyes round, as he twisted to look at Alastor.

Alastor kept his focus on the painting, even though he itched to witness someone finally seeing him again. "He disappeared at the same time as Yaingo in December 1602. They called her Ruby; she's the slave in the portrait you looked at earlier. The second Earl wanted his younger brother prosecuted for stealing valuable property, but his mother persuaded him a manhunt would be another embarrassing scandal. It was a busy time for the Walpoles."

"You're a historian," FitzHenry stated, almost as if reassuring himself.

Alastor stuck out his hand. "Name's Alastor. Pleased to meet you."

"Darien FitzHenry."

The solid flesh closing around his hand after so long felt damn good. Alastor closed his eyes, swaying on his feet, savoring the experience.

"You gave me quite a— are you ok? Here, sit down. I'll call someone. I'm all for method acting, but starving yourself and getting beaten for a part is going too far."

Alastor found himself on one of the tapestry-covered window seats, with Darien squatted in front of him. A dark hand resting on his naked thigh. Blissful heat radiated through the longed-for touch.

The cane marks on his backside smarted at the contact with the seat. Alastor reveled in the new pain; feeling anything new outside of Arioch's office was heavenly.

"No, no, I'm fine. Just need to sit for a bit."

Darien frowned. "When was the last time you ate or drank anything?"

Alastor gave a wry snort. "You wouldn't believe me if I told you."

"Wait here. I'm going to get you something to drink."

Putting his hand over Darien's, Alastor looked into kind, concerned, amber eyes. Eyes that he would one day have to see filled with pain and anguish. But not yet. Unfortunately, he did have to start beguiling the poor clueless man right away. He needed information about his family before he left in a few days.

Widening his eyes, he pleaded, "Please, don't tell anyone I'm here. They'll throw me out."

"You're a squatter?"

Alastor knew the term from the Andersons' television. Living with the American couple had been difficult, but he'd learned so damn much about the modern world. Not having the device for the last two years—the crippling silence in the Hall—had been yet another thing to regret.

Pressing his lips together, he looked down at the hand he could feel touching him, then up at the heir's concerned face. "Sort of. I thought I'd get in early before they sold the place to some amusement park. The building is protected, but we both know the new owners might sell off everything that can be moved. I can't let that happen."

Darien's mouth twitched, then he indicated Alastor's clothes. "What were you hoping to do, convince them that the place is haunted by wearing your grandma's nightgown?"

Alastor licked his lips, saw Darien focus on them. Desire curled in his belly. Usually, he had to work far harder to attract an heir as most preferred women.

"Worked on you, didn't it? You didn't tell the estate agent about me."

"How did you disappear when my sister came over?"

Alastor grinned. "Ah, ah, that would be telling you the secrets of Walpole Hall, and those are on a need-to-know basis."

"Those bruises aren't more than a day or two old. Is the person who beat you hiding with you? Or are you hiding from him too?"

Reaching up, Alastor pressed on his bruised cheek and took a sharp breath.

Darien grabbed his wrist, pulled it away from his face. "You're a masochist," he stated.

"There you go with those odd words again, masochist, dom."

Darien snorted. "Now I know you're lying."

"Believe me, don't believe me, it doesn't make a difference. I'll still be here. But the man who made these bruises is no longer an issue. He died a few minutes after he made them. Fell off his horse, broke his neck. Dead. As. A. Doornail."

Darien frowned. "I suppose you're going to tell me he was the last Earl of Tandridge."

Alastor gave him a cheeky smile. "Now you're getting it."

"There's a flaw in your logic, Mr. Ghost. Bruises require living flesh, yours are only a day or so old, and the last Earl died over eighty years ago. Quit with the Halloween stories, although bruising yourself for the part shows a lot of dedication. How long have you been here?"

"Long enough to know my way around better than anyone else. The maps in the brochure left out an awful lot."

Darien pulled a folded catalog out of his jacket pocket. "Show me."

Alastor fixed his gaze on Darien's groin, then slowly dragged it up to his face.

"Only if you show me something equally naughty first."

Darien's eyes widened. "You want to trade sex for plans?"

"Not necessarily, but I find a good hard fuck oils the wheels of negotiation, don't you?"

For a second, Alastor thought he'd read this man wrong, then Darien leaned in until his breath tickled Alastor's ear. He could feel the damp heat of it, could smell his minty breath and sandalwood cologne. If there was one thing Alastor didn't miss about the seventeenth century, it was how much people's breath stank.

"I find brats need a damn good spanking when they're trying to blackmail their betters, but someone already tried to teach you that, didn't they?"

Alastor kept his voice equally low and throaty, loving this little cocoon of space they'd made. "More than one has tried. They all failed. I'm a challenge, but I'll give you a hint. I find choking on a fat cock far more effective than being beaten."

Darien pulled back, his lips curving into a smile. "As much as I'd like to continue this conversation, I am responsible for keeping this property secure. You are trespassing, half-starved, probably dehydrated, and you need those bruises treated.

"If you tell me where you're keeping your stuff, we can fetch it and get you off the premises without involving the police. I doubt a night in the cells would do you any good. You can come back to my hotel if you have nowhere else to go, but you'll be sleeping on the floor."

That Darien was a stickler for protocol and enforced his privileged position didn't come as a surprise. Involving the damn mutton shunters[1] was typical of an heir, not that they'd find him. Even though hundreds of years, an ocean, and the color of his skin separated him from the first Earl of Tandridge, Darien FitzHenry was a privileged bigot, just like all his line.

Any sympathy or regret Alastor might have had vanished. He needed to keep this man close and find out about the rest of his family, then lure another heir here before disposing of this one.

While Darien maintained physical contact with him, Alastor remained corporeal; he could be seen and heard by any passing human and couldn't relocate. As soon as Darien let go, Alastor would vanish for everyone except a direct male descendant of the first Earl.

However, the threat of involving the police sparked an idea to delay the auction and gain more time to pump this heir for information. Hell, who was he kidding? Alastor needed the heir for another kind of pumping too. Hopefully, sex with Darien would hurt as much as it had with every other Walpole, so he'd feel no guilt when he caused yet another life to end early.

Alastor blew out a breath, letting his shoulders slump in a parody of defeat. "My stuff is up on the roof, in the west turret. You can only access it from across the roof. Just don't call the police; my folks would have a fit."

Darien stood up, his hand leaving Alastor's thigh. The urge to reach out, to touch again as his body became insubstantial, proved almost impossible to resist. He could have relocated immediately but maintaining the appearance of humanity for as long as possible would mess with the heir's mind when he eventually revealed himself. He stood up too.

Darien rested his hand on Alastor's shoulder, and the weight felt fantastic. Alastor set off at a slow walk, feigning exhaustion and defeat. He headed toward the eastern staircase as it was the only one that led up to the roof. He didn't have to pretend that much. Yes, when he was incorporeal, he didn't require food, couldn't eat if he tried, but now he was solid, his belly rumbled, and his throat parched.

"Seriously, when was the last time you ate?"

They'd reached the painting depicting Alastor, and Darien's many times great grandmother. Alastor stopped, looking up at it. Time to mess with the heir's mind a little more.

"You know, you really should let someone know you've got a claim to this pile."

"Excuse me?"

"I always wondered what happened to Henry Walpole and Yaingo. She came from East Africa. Her belly was starting to swell when they disappeared."

"Don't be ridiculous," Darien said, but his gaze rested on the painting again.

Darien's words confirmed what Alastor suspected about the FitzHenry line.

"About her name being Yaingo, or about you being a long-lost Walpole bastard?" As he spoke, Alastor moved back, getting out of grabbing distance. With a thought, he relocated to the entrance of a room around thirty feet from Darien.

"Hey, FitzHenry," he called.

Darien's eyes went wide as he tried to work out how Alastor had moved so far in the blink of an eye.

"I wasn't kidding about knowing this place, and it needs to be preserved, all of it, just as it is. I won't allow it to be sold off in parcels to someone who will turn it into a housing estate. I intend to make it as difficult for you as I can, because as a spirit restricted to the boundaries of the estate, having it shrink will suck donkey balls." He grinned at the dumbfounded heir.

"You're crazy," Darien said.

"Maybe, but you'll never find out unless you're better at catching me than your relatives were." Alastor ducked inside the room behind the Long Gallery that had been a library since the early nineteenth century.

Pounding feet alerted Alastor to Darien getting closer. He let the heir catch a glimpse of him before he ducked out of the room. FitzHenry wasn't any better at playing tag than a legitimate Walpole, and Alastor had four hundred years of experience to draw on.

A second later, Alastor crouched beside one of the shiny automobiles sitting on the gravel outside the main entrance. Hopefully, FitzHenry would continue galloping around the house hunting for him like a dog chasing its own tail.

Gritting his teeth, using the spark of energy being corporeal again had given him, Alastor concentrated, reached out, and depressed the valve on the tire.

On a demon scale of one to a hundred, this small act of vandalism probably wouldn't even rate a one, but Alastor had to work with what he had. Moving or touching anything modern when not in contact with an heir took tremendous amounts of energy. Besides, as an imp, minor irritations gave him as much satisfaction as spectacular acts of vengeance did for demons like Arioch.

When the tire was almost flat, he moved to the next vehicle in the growing gloom, even though his head swam. But if he passed out, he'd wake up in the same place he always did when he wasn't touching an heir.

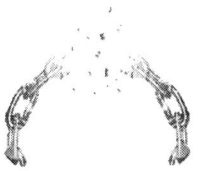

---

1. Mutton shunter: Offensive Victorian term for a police officer.
A large part of their work was moving on prostitutes—shunt is slang for move. Mutton is the meat of an adult sheep, but there's an English phrase, "mutton dressed as lamb" which means an older woman dressed up as a much younger one–often in an inappropriate, revealing way. For that reason, "mutton" was sometimes used as slang for low-class prostitutes.

Chapter Four

Darien swore to himself as he entered the room and couldn't see Alastor. There were multiple exits from the library leading to former withdrawing rooms and the High Great Chamber. In turn, those rooms linked to the Long Gallery and both staircases. Alastor clearly knew this house; it wouldn't be difficult for him to avoid one person.

He pulled his phone out. "Sis, we've got a security issue. That guy I told you about, he's still in the building, and he might not be alone. He's some sort of heritage warrior. He wants to disrupt the sale to anyone who's not going to keep the estate intact."

"What do you want to do?" Despite her earlier teasing, Juliana was a professional, from her straight bob weave to her designer high heels.

"Clear the place out, seal it, and do a thorough search. Who knows what he—"

"Mrs. Carmichael," Julia said, her tone professional, placating. "I'll be with you in a moment, I—"

"Whatever that call is about, it can wait," said a strident female voice. "My car and several others have been vandalized." Darien's heart sank. That little shit had fulfilled his threat.

"Darien, did you hear that?" Juliana said.

"On my way."

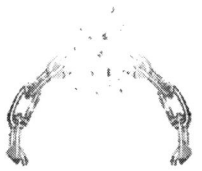

It took five hours to mollify the nine bidders with deflated tires and conduct an utterly fruitless search of the property. The local police lent three officers to the effort, bolstering the number of searchers to seven, including the two Grimshaws.

The police left after taking statements about a man no one but Darien had seen. The Hall had so many nooks and crannies, maybe even secret passageways, that not finding the little shit didn't mean he wasn't still here.

The remaining search party of five gathered in the kitchen for much-needed coffee at two a.m.

Darien took a scorching sip. Even though it was only eight in the evening at home, exhaustion dragged at him. Sometimes he could sleep on a plane, but it hadn't happened last night. He couldn't even muster the brainpower to work out how long he'd been awake.

"There's no point in looking again. None of us, except you, will find him anyway," the weather-beaten gardener told him.

Juliana put her cup down. "And why's that Mr. Grimshaw? Don't tell me you believe all this ghost nonsense?"

The older man pursed his lips. "I 'aven't got anything to say on that, but there is folks that see 'im, and folks that don't, so my grandad said."

Juliana rolled her eyes, so Darien stepped in. "He's not a ghost, Mr. Grimshaw. I spoke to him, touched him."

"That you did, but nobody else did, did they? My grandad thought the curse had been lifted when the last Earl died, but things kept 'appening, even though no one saw 'im. Like my boy getting half-killed."

Juliana blew a breath out of her nose, a sure sign of exasperation. "I'm sorry about your son, I really am, but just listen to yourself. This is the twenty-first century, not the Middle Ages."

Harry Grimshaw drained his mug, put it down, and looked at Darien. "Think what you like, but I'd watch out if I were you. People who see that boy don't live to a ripe old age. I'd also check your family history. Only those with a direct father to son link to the first earl sees 'im. Doesn't matter what side of the bed you come from, just that you come from an unbroken male line." He pointed his finger at Juliana, then at Darien.

"You, missy, are safe. As for you, I'd high-tail it back to where you came from and check your will is up to date, tonight." The man started for the door, silence echoing around him.

Darien concluded that the guy in the period costume wasn't the only one who enjoyed a dramatic exit.

"So, who is he, a relative of yours? Are you worried you'll lose the gardening contract?" Juliana called out. "And I'd appreciate you not threatening my family."

The man chuckled, turning back to them. "Aye, he might have been a relative in the same way you're a relative of the first earl. My family has lived in the village for as long as this house has been here. My ancestors probably knew yours. And I'm not threatening either of you, just offering to tell you the story, as much as I know."

Jules blew out a breath. "Oh goody, a middle-of-the-night ghost story. Shall we go somewhere more comfortable, like a drafty attic?"

"Mock not, young lady. Here is fine; you can't get away from him on this estate anyway."

Mrs. Grimshaw, who worked as a housekeeper for the estate, shared a glance with her husband. "I'll be going. I've heard the story. I'll see you at home, dear. Don't forget we're visiting Liam tomorrow morning."

She gave her husband's arm a rub as she passed him on her way out of the door.

It left Juliana and Darien with Mr. Grimshaw. "I'm sorry if I came across as rude," Juliana said. "I really am sorry about your son. How is he?" His sister could be spiky at times, but she had a heart of gold.

"He's awake, can't talk or move, though."

Darien thought this was probably when religious people would say they would pray for the person, but as Darien wasn't a believer, he just said, "You have our sympathy, such a horrible thing to have happened."

Silence stretched as they all took another mouthful of coffee as if someone had given them a cue.

"So, let's hear it, we've all got beds to go to, except for the ghost, of course," Juliana said.

Mr. Grimshaw's lips pressed together. "Oh, he'll 'ave a bed he wants to get in, just like he's done before, but it won't be mine or yours, Miss."

Mr. Grimshaw moved over to the vast kitchen table and sat down as if settling in for a significant time. Juliana didn't bother to hide her eyeroll, but Darien was intrigued.

Harry cleared his throat. "The troubles started with the first earl. He was given this land for services to Queen Elizabeth the first, but there were already some cottages on it. He paid them to leave, and all did apart from a widow woman and her son. A good-looking red-haired boy from the tales."

"Don't tell me; he tried to throw them out, the boy was killed, and she cursed the earl and all his male descendants?" Juliana said.

Darien frowned at his sister. "Even if it's only a story, this is real word of mouth history. I want to hear it. Go on." He nodded to the man.

Grimshaw leaned both elbows on the table, eyes alight. "That's where you're wrong. Walpole let them stay. It seems he took a fancy to the young boy. The kid tried to kick him when Walpole came to throw them out. He liked his spirit, see?

"As the boy grew, rumor has it that the Earl came to see the lad quite a lot, even preferred him to his own sons, treated him a bit like a jester. Well, time passed, the house was finished, and the Lord was away in London. One of the fireplaces had been smoking, so the first son called for the lad and shoved 'im up the chimney."

Grimshaw's violent arm movement made Darien startle. Juliana hid her smirk at his reaction with a sip of her probably cold coffee.

"But the lad got stuck. They say you could 'ear that poor boy crying for days, but the son refused to dismantle the walls to get 'im out. They even set a fire in the hearth to see if it would smoke him out. The mother, she wailed and pleaded for them to save him, but eventually, the boy went quiet." Grimshaw cast a baleful glance between the siblings.

"The next night, the distraught mother set her cottage alight. She screamed for the Earl to beg for her forgiveness before she died. As she stood in the burning doorway, she cursed every man of Walpole blood forevermore. Said they would die in anguish until her innocent boy was given a decent burial beside his father."

Grimshaw dropped his sinister act, sniffed, and scratched his chin. "The earl's eldest son turned up in time to hear the curse, called her a witch, and they pushed her back inside with pitchforks to burn. Rumor has it that it all happened because they wanted the land. Might be true. My cottage is rumored to have been built in the garden of that building, and I've found burned timbers and broken pottery."

The thought of there being a skeleton behind one of the walls sent a shiver up Darien's spine. No wonder the locals avoided this place.

Grimshaw leaned back in his chair. "Quite the tragic tale, ain't it?"

Juliana looked a little green. "What that poor mother went through, and the boy..." She shook her head.

"I take it that they never found his remains?" Darien asked. Even if the man he'd met was only playing the part of the poor unfortunate boy, he still imagined him trapped in a chimney shaft, choking to death.

Grimshaw shrugged. "There are a lot of chimneys in this place. But if they did ever find him, they probably fed the body to the pigs. Now, I'm not saying the boy's ghost had anything to do with the first earl's death, which happened only a couple of weeks later, but that was the first of many untimely deaths in the Walpole line.

"Family lore says that young Henry Walpole and a maid called Ruby disappeared about the same time. I bet the second earl killed his brother too, and the poor girl saw something she shouldn't 'ave.'

"And with no Christian burial for the boy, the curse will go on all the time there's a male of the Walpole line left in the world," Grimshaw finished.

He pointed a thick finger at Darien. "So watch out. There's been a lot of rumors over the years about the earls talking to themselves before something tragic happened." He gave them a cheerful grin. "Goodnight."

"Hang on, how many people know this story?" Darien asked.

"Now that there are no more legitimate Walpoles, it's only us Grimshaws and now you since you've seen 'im. Consider yourselves warned. Now, I'd better be off before I end up spending the night on the sofa. My missus has a thing about us going to bed at the same time." Grimshaw got to his feet.

"Thank you for the tale. We appreciate it," Juliana said. Darien could tell she didn't believe the ghost was real, and neither did he.

"The man I saw wasn't a ghost. He had a fresh black eye and used modern language, not a single thee or thou. So, unless ghosts can get bruises and learn modern phrasing, he's as alive as you and me."

Grimshaw's brows drew together before he regained his genial expression. "Think what you like, sir, but me and mine know something is going on in this hall and has been since the witch's curse. Our Liam is only the latest victim, collateral damage, so to speak. The ghost tried to warn me—and my boy survived because of it—but he'll never be the same."

"Wait, he warned you? How?" Darien blurted.

"Wrote in the dirt in my potting shed."

Darien exchanged a disbelieving look with his sister.

"And you have photographic evidence?" Juliana asked.

Grimshaw gave a snort. "Wouldn't be much of a poltergeist if 'e left evidence around, would he?"

"Of course, he didn't," Juliana murmured into her mug. Whether Grimshaw hadn't heard her, or pretended not to, Darien didn't know, but he was grateful. He didn't want to offend this man who was providing such a remarkable verbal history. He just hoped he could remember all the details correctly when he wrote it down later.

"What was the dead boy's name?" Darien asked, knowing that asking Grimshaw for proof of his story was a fool's game.

"Nicholas Thatcher. Bit ironic, really. Most people want a Nicholas coming down their chimney in December, but never in this house." With a cheery wave, he left.

They listened to his footsteps retreating and a door closing before Darien spoke up.

"The man I met said his name was Alastor, not Nicholas Thatcher."

Juliana checked her phone and sighed. "Look, I've had enough of today. It may be only nine p.m. at home, but we're running on UK time. Let's head back to the hotel. Luckily, my hire car wasn't one of the ones hit."

"I'm staying here." At her frown, Darien held up his hand. "He spoke to me before, so he might again. To be honest,

I kinda sympathize with what he's trying to do. Avoiding whoever beat him up and keeping this place intact for future generations are understandable goals. I'd rather we get him out of here quietly, without him causing any more trouble or ending up beside the Grimshaw boy in the hospital."

"That goes for you too, brother."

He gave a tired nod. "Yeah, that goes for me too. I'll be careful, don't you worry, but I'm betting he isn't dangerous. He's just a heritage warrior with too much time on his hands, hiding out from someone who beat the crap out of him. I'll see you in the morning."

"Don't forget the auction lots start arriving tomorrow."

"I remember. I'll be up and ready, I promise."

After pecking her on the cheek, he walked her out and watched until her taillights faded down the drive.

He locked the huge front door, although he didn't think it would stop the elusive Alastor from getting in or out of the building. The heritage warrior clearly knew this place like the back of his hand. Despite the Grimshaws saying they didn't know him, Darien bet Alastor was from around here; he had to be to know so much about the estate's history.

CHAPTER FIVE

The bedrooms on the first floor had modern fittings, but the second floor retained all the period features, including a lack of central heating and running water. Although Darien hadn't planned to spend tonight at the Hall, he smiled in anticipation. The excitement had everything to do with sleeping where his many times great grandparents had lived, not that the elusive Alastor might pay him a visit. He smiled to himself. Well, maybe that too.

The man's dirty mouth and his principles about protecting the estate piqued Darien's interest. Alastor's physique made Darien want to pin the cocky little bastard down and teach him a lesson, even though someone clearly already had.

What had Alastor said or done to warrant the beating? The stripes on his ass could have been an overly enthusiastic sex game by a dom who didn't know what he was doing, but not the black eye and evidence of strangulation, or at least he hoped not.

The costume could also hide a multitude of additional injuries. Enjoying a little safe, sane, and consensual punishment play was one thing, but that much abuse spoke of mental illness, possibly in both parties.

It was a puzzle he itched to solve. From the physical evidence, bondage hadn't been part of the scene, or at least Alastor hadn't struggled. His ankles and wrists had been free of marks. Although going barefoot and pantless in late October showed great dedication to his part or his masochism, perhaps both.

The puzzle intrigued him like many others had over the years. Juliana called him a magnet for waifs and strays, and she knew him well. Helping kinky youngsters
find a path in life that allowed them to express themselves safely floated his boat, but he never stayed an important fixture in their lives for long. He considered himself part teacher and part social worker for the kinky.

Others in the community wondered why he never took a boy as his own. The truth was, once he sorted out their problems, his interest waned, and he tried to pair them with a permanent partner. He knew some people thought he simply enjoyed a series of subs in his bed, but he helped kinksters of all genders who had lost their way, and he seldom became sexually involved with them. It blurred the line between help and emotion, which most vulnerable subs had trouble distinguishing between anyway. He offered time, discipline, advice, education, care, and a safety net, nothing more. As much as he wanted it, time wasn't a commodity he possessed right now.

Unless I take some vacation time.

The idea swirled as Darien climbed into the bed that had been made up to show the Hall could be used as a home as well as a business. As usual, he only wore boxers to bed, but unease itched. Yes, feeling like an intruder was stupid, but the empty corridors and rooms outside the bedroom echoed with past lives. He shivered as a draft of cold air gave him goosebumps.

No wonder the upper classes back in the days of no central heating had four-poster beds with heavy drapes to keep in the warmth. Even with added modern heating, the drapes moved in the draft from the single glazed window.

Darien lay in the darkness, twitching at every slight creak as the beams of the Elizabethan house contracted as the night cooled. *Idiot, scared of a ghost story.*

The name Alastor niggled at him. Yes, the guy might not know the name of the Elizabethan man he portrayed, but he could have chosen a period name to make his fiction more believable.

He pulled out his phone. "Cortana, who is Alastor?"

Alastor is the personification of sin passed from parent to child.

Alastor is a devil, an evil spirit, who drives people to madness or murder.

Alastor, or The Spirit of Solitude, is a poem by Percy Bysshe Shelley.

"Shelley... Wasn't he gay?" Darien murmured.

"Not as far as I know, but his mate, Lord Byron, liked lively young bodies whether they packed pussy or pricks. We had a bit of fun when he visited in 1807."

Darien's gaze shot down the bed. It depressed, although Alastor didn't appear to have moved as he lay back on one elbow near Darien's feet. His bone structure made him look as if he permanently sucked in his cheeks.

Not wanting to give the ghost fiction credence, Darien relaxed his demeanor and voice. If he reacted every time the little shit jumped out at him, it would only encourage Alastor to do it more.

Pulling himself up until he rested against the head of the bed, Darien asked, "You expect me to believe you slept with Lord Byron, a man who died in the 1820s?"

Alastor shrugged. "Him and Oliver Walpole, the tenth earl, or was he the eleventh? I forget. Long nose, weak chin, skinny when young, fat and bald when they get older; they all looked the same after a while. Byron and the Earl spit-roasted me. One in one end, the other in the other." Alastor sighed. "I didn't come that time either. Story of my life. Always the giver, never the receiver."

Darien focused on the claim that Alastor had never come with a partner. *Truth or lie?* Darien wasn't sure, and that bugged him. What he did know was that this brat was attempting to manipulate him with more sex talk.

The moonlight through the window caught Alastor's cheek. Darien could believe people had been fooled by the ghost story until Alastor spoke.

"Still keeping up with the ghost story?" he asked.

Cock-sucking plush lips quirked in a smile. "I never said I was a ghost. I've turned over a new leaf, and this century, my resolution is no lying. I'm not Nicholas Thatcher; I just look like him because of the curse. But that is me in the painting."

"So, you're what?"

Alastor pointed at Darien's phone. "Like your little box said. I'm a demon, well, only an imp to tell the truth. A bottom feeder compared to most of my kind; even sex demons have more abilities than us imps. But—" he held up a finger "—imps can get stronger and get promoted.

"The crap news for me is that if I'd been a higher demon already, I never would have been trapped by the dying curse of Agnes Thatcher. A curse that didn't need to be because Nicholas wasn't dead, at that point anyway. His plan—and it was all Nicholas's idea, the manipulative little fucker—backfired on him spectacularly. It also fucked up the lives of every man carrying a Walpole Y-chromosome who came here and every other owner of the Hall."

The youngster flopped back on the bed, boneless in his false despair. Alastor—or whatever his real name happened to be—had significant acting talent.

Is he a performing arts student? But if that's true, why is he playing to an audience of one? Darien appreciated Alastor's efforts but didn't understand them. It wasn't as if the auctioneer could legally affect the outcome of a sale. The word 'legally' hovered in his mind. How much research had Alastor done on him? Darien wasn't ashamed of his personal life, but he didn't exactly shout about it from the rooftops.

Is this all an act to get me to favor one bidder over another?

Alastor's chest rose and fell with a heartfelt sigh. "The curse was meant for the Walpoles, but it's me who's suffering for eternity. Now, thanks to all of Henry's get[1] doing their best to populate the Americas, I'm never going to be free of this place. I'll be here until the fucking sun explodes."

Darien gave three slow claps. "Great performance."

Alastor sat up, his movements fluid despite the bruises, and inclined his head. "Why, thank you, kind sir. Earls one through thirteen thought my performances were pretty damn convincing too, along with countless cousins, younger brothers, and the bastards of servants. The bastards were fun; I even regret ending some of them. The legitimate ones were mostly selfish cads, but God, they all liked to fuck." His eyebrows drew together. "Except for the ninth earl, he was a religious nut. I got him in the end, though, even though it took me twenty years."

"And how did you do that?" Darien asked, thoroughly enjoying Alastor's performance.

"He tried to exorcise me up on the roof. Throwing Holy Water around in January makes things slippery." He mimed running with his fingers, then let them fall to the quilt. "Made quite a mess. I felt sorry for the poor sods who had to scrape him up."

"So, exactly how many people have you killed?"

Alastor's lips thinned. "It would be a lot easier—and a damn sight quicker—if I could kill directly. I could have stuck a knife in every Walpole before they started breeding like rabbits. But no such luck. Death has to be either self-inflicted or at the hand of a third party." He mimed cutting his own throat. "I'm allowed the occasional accident, but the boss doesn't like those."

Now that Darien hadn't expected. "You have a boss?"

Alastor cocked his head. Darien imagined that face looking up at him, eyes watering as he forced his cock down that pale throat. He forced the thought away. Sex would certainly complicate matters, for him anyway.

"Of course, don't you?"

"Not really. My sister's the CEO, but I have autonomy as Chief Auctioneer."

"But you still have to obey rules?"

"Without some sort of framework, we'd have global anarchy. Who's your boss?"

Alastor's entire body shuddered. "Arioch. Senior vengeance demon. Scary as fuck. Flays or spit-roasts demons who disappoint. And I mean he literally spit-roasts them, not has a fun, sexy threesome."

Darien grinned at the theatrics, raising one knee as he lounged against the headboard. "Sounds like a lovely guy."

"Not really a guy, or a girl, for that matter. Arioch changes gender and appearance according to the situation. All I can say is watch out for anyone, or anything, wearing something red."

"Noted. Now, back to the deaths of my possible relatives. How many are you responsible for?"

The tip of Alastor's tongue poked out and ran across his top lip, then his mouth quirked in a dirty smile. "Not *possible* relatives, actual relatives. We couldn't be talking like this if you weren't.

"But I'm glad you've finally decided to believe me. To answer your question, I've caused enough deaths, life-changing injuries, and broken relationships that I really deserve to be punished. Held down, gagged, then pounded until I don't know which way is up. Fancy the job?"

The cocky grin faded as Darien lay relaxed and watched him with a blank expression. His bent knee meant Darien kept his straining erection to himself.

Alastor could be everything he found attractive—an attention-seeking, bratty bottom—once his issues were straightened out. Darien usually found temporary sexual partners in clubs, although he often found the people he helped there too. Mixing the two never ended well.

Right now, Alastor was a wounded puzzle in trouble, whether he knew it or not, which put him firmly in Darien's 'help' not 'fuck' category. He'd never regretted his personal moral code more. There was something about this boy, something different. Even though nothing could come of this long term, it didn't mean he couldn't provide a little guidance if Alastor stopped his one-man war on the corporate bidders.

Alastor shifted so the moonlight no longer fell on his face. The shadows transformed him into the most attractive demon, ghost, whatever, that Darien had ever met. He was damn erection-inducing as a mere human too. Whoever this guy was, Darien planned to crack his shell of lies. He paused.

Do I really want to find out that this enigmatic mystery is only an irritating rich kid getting his kicks by dishing out mischief?

Perhaps playing Alastor's ghost game, rather than getting deeply involved in his real-life issues, was the way to go. But like with any kink interaction, he felt compelled to specify the rules.

"If you promise to leave the bidders alone, I'm sure I can keep you suitably disciplined for the ten days I'm here."

Alastor scrambled off the bed, body tense. As he only stood, rather than trying to run again, Darien suppressed the urge to grab him.

"Ten days? I can't work with ten days. It's damn cruel to just—" he waved a hand at Darien "—dangle that in front of me after eighty years and then take it away. Why don't you do us both a favor and piss off to your hotel?"

The animated rant was entertaining until Alastor swore at him. Any musings about taking this to a sexual level snuffed out.

"Sit. Down."

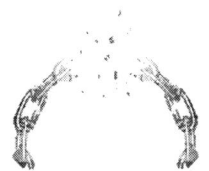

---

1. Get: Middle English for a man's descendants – from 'beget'.

CHAPTER SIX

The dominant tone went straight to Alastor's cock, and his arse hit the bed again. His breath hitched at the flash of pain in his battered backside, but he didn't lift up again. The sharp pain rather than the never-ending deep ache meant he was corporal again, and he intended to relish it for as long as it lasted.

"Well, that hurt," Darien said, matter of fact, as he leaned over and clicked on the bedside light. "What did you do to deserve the beating?"

Alastor grimaced and scratched his ear where his curly hair tickled it. It hadn't been his finest moment, but he'd been damn desperate. David Walpole had been about to leave for the war. Yes, he might have died from a Nazi rifle or in a hundred other ways, but he could also have fucked his way across Europe, leaving bastards in every town, even though his fiancée waited at home.

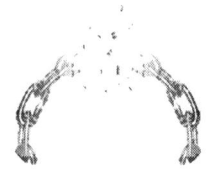

Eighty years before

The last Walpole would be leaving in a few days, and Alastor's window of opportunity to escape the curse would go with him. Tonight's dinner party was a last opportunity too good to miss. David Walpole already twitched from lack of sleep as Alastor had kept up a loud rendition of 'I'm Henery the Eighth I am[1]' all night from outside his door. When he got tired of singing, he played the same melody on his recorder, one of his few personal possessions.

The door flung open at two in the morning, revealing a disheveled, wild-haired David. Alastor relocated twenty feet away, intending to lead the poor sod a dance through the building for the next few hours.

"Shut up, just shut the hell up." As far as the staff were concerned, David shouted to thin air as he pounded through the corridors of the Hall in his nightshirt. Servants came out of their rooms, whispering about the family curse.

Given time, Alastor could probably get the staff to commit the Earl to an asylum, although it wasn't ideal. Alastor would have to remain here while David spent his life bouncing off walls in a straitjacket, but the line would end. Unfortunately, getting him committed would take more time than Alastor possessed.

After being reminded of the time by his butler the heir—who resembled a cross between a caveman and a panda—stumbled back to his bedroom.

Alastor settled down outside the door to sing again. Nine hours later, tires crunched gravel as a car pulled up outside.

Showtime. Alastor popped down to the Low Great Hall. David's fiancée and her parents, The Honorable Lady Caroline and Lord and Lady Stour, stepped into the room as their chauffeur and maid unloaded their baggage.

Alastor rubbed his hands together, anticipating this first formal visit of the future in-laws. The Earl had been driving the staff to exhaustion with his efforts to make a good impression. Everything had been scrubbed and polished to within an inch of its life. Alastor had been diligently popping in and sabotaging their efforts. He encouraged the cook to absently put salt in the puddings and the maid to overlook leaving sooty handprints on the bed linens. He also left doors open so the stable cats could bring mouse and bird corpses into the bedrooms.

These were the mild annoyances an imp should be producing, rather than causing deaths by suicide, accident, and murderous rage. Once he escaped this curse, Alastor fully intended to tell Arioch to stick the plan to 'progress his career and become a vengeance demon' where the sun didn't shine. But he'd do it politely as he was pretty fond of his skin remaining on his body. All he wanted was to go back to being a free imp, creating minor mischief and keeping people on their toes.

David Walpole, Thirteenth Earl of Tandridge, strode toward the party wearing a broad smile. To Alastor's disappointment, even with his exhaustion, the man had managed to get all his clothes on straight, and he'd even shaved and combed his hair.

Alastor popped in beside Lady Stour, mimed licking her face and squeezing her tweed-covered breast.

"Nice tits," he told David. "Can't wait to see her naked."

The Earl nearly tripped over his own feet, but as Lady Stour didn't react, David put a poor version of his previous smile back on his face.

It hadn't taken David long to work out that he was the only one who could see, hear, and touch Alastor. So far, he'd avoided being around other people when David touched him. Then, and only then, was he visible and solid to others.

David stuck out his hand. "How wonderful that you could make it, Lord Stour, Lady Stour."

The balding portly man chuckled. "Call me Gerald. After all, we're going to be family soon."

"Not soon enough," Caroline said, her expression sweet, her tone sour.

Gerald turned to his daughter. "You are not having a quick wedding; everyone will think you've been inappropriate."

Her turned-up nose scrunched. "No, Daddy, they will think no such thing. These are modern times, not the stone age. They will think my fiancé is going to war, and we wanted to get married first."

Lady Stour patted her daughter's arm. "It'll be over in a few months. He'll be back, safe and sound, you'll see."

"Like the Great War only lasted a few months? Please, mother, I'm not a child."

An awkward silence followed as mother and daughter exchanged a whole conversation with only eyebrows and eyes.

Alastor exaggerated his movements, looking from one to the other as he filled in what he thought they were saying for David's benefit in a falsetto voice.

"Mother, you're a bitch."

"Daughter, you're a greedy cunt."

"If he dies before we're married, I won't be able to hide that I've been fucking the gardener behind the potting shed for months. And I can't even do that anymore as the gardener prefers the donkey. Says it's got a tighter hole than me."

David's smile was fading by the second, so Alastor carried on.

"Try the chauffer, dear. He gobbles fannies better than the Labradors."

"Really? Better than dear old—"

Gerald looked up, taking in the vastness of the hall. "Nice little place you have here."

"Little? It's like a cathedral, a cold, drafty one. We'll be staying in London," Caroline said. Clearly, she needed more time with the Labradors.

Alastor already hated her with a passion, from her piggy nose and red lips to her carefully arranged dark hair. If David actually reproduced with this bitch, he'd see what he could do about killing off any daughters as well as the sons. Better yet, he needed to get rid of David before he had time to play hide the sausage.

The father might assume his daughter would be a virgin on her wedding night, but Alastor knew more than most what frantic fornicating beasts people were. This house was more than big enough to sneak around behind mummy and daddy's backs tonight. Caroline would need to do that if she had been playing with any of the staff.

Alastor had halted one prospective branch of the Walpoles by persuading one future bride to do that before she got married. It'd all been in vain as that Lady Tandridge's only bastard had been a daughter, and she managed a son before Alastor drove her husband mad.

Concentrating, Alastor made contact with Lady Stour's tweed jacket, right over her right tit. She frowned, brushed at the spot while Alastor wiggled his eyebrows.

"Oh, Gerald, do you think David would suck my baggy old titties while you bugger him with your embarrassing pencil prick if we creep into his bedroom tonight?"

"Right, well, I'll show you to your rooms," a red-faced David extended his arm toward the main staircase.

The thirteenth Earl wasn't any more attractive than his predecessors. He'd inherited the Walpole sharp nose, thin lips, and premature balding pattern in his dull brown hair. Fortunately, his currently muscular and fit body made up for his features. Alastor knew that if David lived to middle age, he'd follow the Walpole pattern of running to fat. Remembering him like this seemed best. His portrait already hung in the Long Gallery, so there was no real need to keep him around and every reason to end his life before he had the chance to put buns in any ovens.

As far as Alastor knew, David had only slept with him. He'd learned enough tricks to entice or annoy, most Walpoles into sleeping with him, but they'd always decided to keep the line going at some point.

Alastor popped to the bedroom allocated to the senior Stours, arranged himself on the bed, lifted his shirt, and took his cock in his hand.

Once he was free of the curse, he'd be having many, many more partners, ones who hopefully knew how to please others instead of merely using and taking.

"And this is the Blue Room. Rumor has it that James the First stayed here," David said as he opened the door, his focus on his guests.

Alastor tingled in anticipation as the older Stours stepped into the room. They took in the wooden floors, the four-poster bed where he lay, and the heavy brocade curtains.

"You can even see the—" David stopped, mid-sentence as he looked into the room for the first time. His face flushed with rage. "What the hell are you doing?"

The Stours stared, open-mouthed, at their prospective son-in-law.

Alastor gave his dick a long lazy stroke even though he couldn't feel it. "Spunking on their pillow. But have you forgotten that they can't see or hear me, Davy-boy?"

David's jaw snapped shut, his eyes round with horror as they flicked from Alastor to the Stours. Both were staring at him as if he'd grown another head.

"Steady on, old boy," Lord Stour rumbled.

Alastor smirked. "Ready for more, Walpole? I can dish it out all night, just like yesterday. I don't sleep, remember? Want me to fetch my recorder?"

The Earl's jaw worked for a second before anything came out. "I must, I must apologize. I asked for the linens to be changed in the room, and they haven't been. I'll get it seen to immediately."

Lady Stour sniffed. "Yes, it's hard getting good staff these days, but we understand."

"I'll erm, get that arranged. Dinner is at eight; feel free to explore." David gave them a weak smile and left the room, sweat beading on his forehead.

"Bit high strung, isn't he?" Gerald said as he wandered over to the window to take in the view of the long straight driveway bracketed by mature trees. Alastor remembered them being replanted nearly two hundred years ago when the first set died of old age. If praying to God that he wouldn't have to see them replaced a second time would've done any good, he'd be on his knees in a flash.

"True, but so many aristocrats are. The inbreeding gets all of you in the end," Lady Stour said.

Gerald turned, his mouth quirking up on one side. "Which is why I chose you, my naughty little alleycat."

Alastor's eyeballs nearly dropped out as Lady Stour unbuttoned her blouse to reveal a sexy red-silk corset.

"My daft little Gerry, how many times do I have to tell you, you didn't choose me. I hunted you down, just like Caroline hunted Walpole. The poor idiot didn't stand any more of a chance than you did. Shame he didn't knock her up last month, but we have another chance tonight."

Alastor had heard enough. There was no way that harridan or her slut of a daughter was getting their hands on Walpole Hall. Even though he didn't like the man, having David cheat on him pissed him off. It always happened eventually, but having it rubbed in his face by this jumped-up hedge whore was the living end. By morning, he vowed all three Stours would be hightailing it down the drive, never to look back with Caroline as unpregnant as she was now.

All afternoon he trailed David, made suggestive, derogatory remarks, playing his recorder, or singing to drown out whatever his guests said. When not winding David up directly, he whispered in the Stours' ears that David and the Hall were more trouble than they were worth.

By dinner, even the gold-digging Stours were giving David side-eyes. From their point of view, their future son-in-law and husband kept glaring at empty spaces, occasionally lunging in one direction or another while mumbling about moths they couldn't see.

Alastor had to give the man credit. It couldn't have been easy keeping your composure when you could see someone miming humping all three of your guests, dancing across the table, and trying to piss in the soup while they were eating it.

David got up from the table and went to stare out of the window of the small dining room on the first floor near the bedrooms.

Tucking his recorder under his arm, Alastor followed David, not wanting to give the man an ounce of breathing space. He had to drive David into doing something stupid enough to end his own life or at least cause an injury that would keep him here so Alastor could continue working on him.

Hoping to make David jump, he sidled up beside him. "You know I'm going to be in her room all night, don't you? Watching, touching... Licking and—"

David's hand shot out and grabbed Alastor's bicep, shaking the heavy curtain as he did so.

"Got you, you rotten little thief. I knew you were around here somewhere." Grabbing the recorder, he brandished it in the air.

Both Stour women let out squeaks of distress as Alastor twisted in David's grasp. Now that he'd been seen, he needed to pull away. Hopefully, having a person disappear into thin air would have the Stours running for the hills like spooked horses.

"I say, old boy, has he been hiding in there all this time? Guttersnipe needs a damn good thrashing!" Lord Stour announced. "Looks like he's raided some of your antique clothes too."

From the way David shook the curtain, it must have appeared like he'd pulled Alastor out from behind it.

"Why? Do you want to do it, you dirty old sod? Like boys, do you, milord?" Alastor bit out.

"Oh, I never. Please, just please take him out of my sight," Lady Stour said, her hand on her ample bosom.

"Oh, cut the crap, you old tart, you're nothing but a title chaser, just like—"

David's fist connected with Alastor's cheek. Bright white pain lanced, turning his legs to jelly, but the Earl held him up with his other hand wrapped around Alastor's bicep. For a second, Alastor thought his cheekbone had been shattered, then he heard broken pieces of wood clattering to the floor.

Anger sharper than the pain flooded him. *My recorder, my damn recorder!*

"Hit him again, Davy, hit him again." Alastor ignored Caroline's enthusiastic calls for his blood as David dragged him, stumbling, out of the room.

"It's time to deal with you, once and for all," David growled, not relenting on the bruising grip on Alastor's arm. The earl's fist fastened in Alastor's hair a moment before he released his arm. Alastor stumbled along, bent over.

Worry for his own safety tickled as instead of heading for his bedroom, David's usual choice of punishment venue, the earl dragged him down the stairs. Squeals from the female kitchen staff rang around him.

"Do you require help, milord?" the Stour's manservant called out.

"No, but attend your master and mistresses; they were quite distressed by this scoundrel."

"Don't worry about me, folks," Alastor called out. "The rich bastard is only going to beat another starving dilly boy[2] for trying to get his fair earned—"

David shook him hard as the cook gasped.

"Enough, you devil, enough," David growled as he banged his way out of the house.

"Ow, fuck, no shoes, remember?" Alastor exclaimed as the sharp gravel of the drive dug into his feet. It'd been a damn long time since he'd been on this surface while touching an heir.

The earl didn't answer as he continued dragging Alastor toward the stables. The three-sided, cobbled yard only held six horses these days, but the earl maintained them in case a guest fancied a ride.

"Grimshaw, come back later," David barked as they entered the yard.

"But sir, I've just had Prince out for a gallop; he needs unsaddling, rubbing—"

"GET OUT," David roared. Booted feet ran. A horse snorted, and horseshoes scraped on the cobbles.

"Watch it, Davey boy, don't frighten off the horsey. You might want to ride it later. Because sure as shit is brown, you won't be riding the filly up at the house tonight if I have anything to do with it," Alastor snarled.

A stable door came into Alastor's limited field of vision, and then they were in the tack room. He could feel the heir's rage through the grip in his hair. *A little longer, just a little longer.*

"What ya gonna do, bend me over a saddle and try to teach me a lesson with your tiny dick? Not that you'll get it up without me helping—"

David pushed him against the saddle on the mending frame in the center of the room. Alastor had time to recognize the whistling of a riding crop before a line of fire streaked across his backside.

He gulped, before calling out, "Is that all you got, a fucking tickle? I bet it didn't even leave a mark."

As if David was a trained spaniel obeying his master, Alastor's shirt was pulled up over his back. Fast, frantic blows rained down on his exposed skin.

"Shut up, just shut the fuck up," David snarled, the grip in Alastor's hair almost tore out the strands. It didn't matter. Nothing mattered except pushing David into doing something stupid enough to finally free him.

"Never... never gonna stop. Every day, every night, until it's just you and me. You're mine," Alastor gasped out. The blows came even harder, his backside, thighs, and back. A human would probably have passed out by now.

"You want me? That's why you're destroying my life? Well, you're fucking going to get me."

Alastor managed a tired smile as David released his hair. The clatter of the leather riding crop being dropped and hands scrabbling at clothes meant progress. Rage had taken over. The stupid bastard hadn't even realized Alastor could have vanished the second he let go of him. Now all Alastor had to do was entice an audience.

He raised his voice. "I'm sorry. Please, don't, anything but that, it was just a bet—"

"You'll be fucking sorry in a minute," David growled as he pushed into Alastor's battered backside.

Alastor squirmed, crying out loudly at the sharp sting, but what was a little pain compared to freedom?

With his blood up, the heir clearly hadn't heard the crunching gravel caused by more than one set of feet hurrying down to the stables.

Alastor upped the volume of his cries. As he'd done before, David pulled him up, wrapped a hand around his throat, squeezing hard.

"Who's the master? When I'm finished with you, you'll never—"

"TANDRIDGE!" The roar of Gerald, Lord Stour, from a few feet away was Alastor's cue to go limp. Facing Gerald, he kept his eyes open, staring at nothing.

From Stour's position, David, Thirteenth Earl of Tandridge, was fucking the body of a boy he'd just beaten to death.

David let go of him as if he'd become red hot. Alastor crumpled to the sawdust-strewn floor, but made sure one of his legs tangled with David's so he remained visible.

"It's not what it looks like. He's faking." David nudged him with his foot. Alastor let his head loll bonelessly, eyes still open.

Stour's chauffeur knelt beside Alastor, and pressed fingers to his bruised neck. He looked up at his master.

"I can't find a pulse."

David shoved the chauffeur over, then bolted out of the tack room. As the two men focused on the fleeing earl, they didn't see Alastor vanish. Shouts and the sound of clattering hooves shattered the evening air.

"After the blaggard," Lord Stour shouted. The groom, Walter Grimshaw, shoved a bridle on another horse and took off after David while the portly Lord Stour and his servant hurried back up to the house.

Time was running out. Even if the police were called, the lack of a body would be a problem. The gentry still had a lot of influence in Great Britain. The likelihood of David being convicted of murder without a body, or any physical evidence that his victim had ever existed, would be nil.

He relocated as near as he could to David's position. Scared by Alastor's pale form appearing out of the gloom, the horse reared up. The beast overbalanced, coming down on top of its shouting rider. The earl's shout of fear cut off. The gelding struggled to its feet, rolling over David in the process.

Hoping against hope, Alastor crept toward the body, expecting David to move, to groan.

Half of David's head was caved in. Blood, bone, and brains leaked onto the grass.

Alastor stared, unable to take it in for several heartbeats. Then it hit. *I'm finally free.*

Fixing his gaze on the patch of grass a hundred yards away that he'd never been able to touch, he ran, euphoria suffusing every muscle, nerve, and organ.

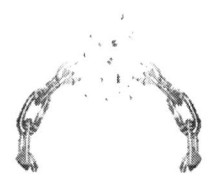

---

1. I'm Henery the Eighth I am - earworm song. https://www.youtube.com/watch?v=yxzV6dPwmwQ&ab_channel=Herman%27sHermits-Topic
2. Dilly boy: A young male prostitute, named after Picadilly Circus in London, a known cruising spot from the Victorian period onwards.

CHAPTER SEVEN

"Alastor? Did you hear me? I asked you what you did to get the beating."

The pale, battered man sitting on his bed in the middle of the night blinked as if he'd been miles away, then he shrugged.

"Irritated a guy a little too much. The thirteenth Earl. I thought I was out of here. It didn't even occur to me that there were Walpole bastards multiplying all over the world." He let out a heartfelt sigh, slumping as if the weight of the world lay on his thin shoulders. "I bet you've got a shit load of cousins."

Yes, the ghost crap was amusing, but Darien had more immediate concerns. The facial bruise seemed even worse than it'd been earlier, as if it'd just happened and was still forming.

"Have you been to an emergency room? That black eye could be hiding a fracture."

Alastor gave a wry smile and closed his eyes. "Nice try, but I'm not going anywhere."

"This place means that much to you that you're willing to risk your long-term health for it?" Darien shook his head. "Never mind. I'll look at your back, eye, and any other injuries, then we'll hunt out something for you to eat because I bet you haven't eaten in your secret hidey-hole."

A grin lit the pale face. "Not the sexiest proposition for getting naked I've had, but I'll take it if that's all you're offering." The last part of his sentence was muffled as he pulled his rough linen shirt over his head.

A second later, Alastor sat naked on the bed. He wore no underwear, and his uncut dick stood proud and flushed. Darien remembered that circumcision had never been fashionable on this side of the Atlantic except for religious reasons. He felt grateful that his own parents had bucked the trend and hadn't had their infant son cut.

Apart from the bruises on his face, neck, and one bicep, ingrained dirt showed on Alastor's neck, arms, legs, and feet. Although he didn't smell bad, it appeared that Alastor and soap were not good friends. The dirt lent weight to the 'sleeping rough' theory.

"I'm offering food, a medical check-up, and I'm adding a shower to that list. Without moving, Darien indicated Alastor's cock with a finger. "What exactly did you think I was proposing?"

Alastor's nose wrinkled at the mention of a shower. "Sex and—" he looked Darien over "—a side of pain and humiliation. Maybe pain, humiliation, and a side of sex. I haven't figured you out that far yet. All of you Walpoles like to hurt." Despite the relaxed words, Alastor held himself stiffly. *Nerves or excitement?*

"You're a masochist," Darien stated.

A frown creased Alastor's brow. "A what?"

Darien didn't believe such a worldly individual didn't know the word, but he played along. "Someone who gets turned on by being hurt and/or humiliated. That's why you push so hard; you're trying to get me to do what you want."

Alastor tilted his head. "Huh. Never thought of it like that, but yeah, I suppose so. I like it when a guy lets his inner demon out." Another smirk lit up his face. "So, now you've got me, what are you going to do with me?"

Alastor sat crossed-legged, utterly at ease being naked and aroused in front of a stranger who hadn't made a pass at him. Odd behavior. Odd man. Darien wanted to know more.

Alastor's thighs, torso, and upper arms were more muscular than Darien had guessed, but they were as pale and lacking in fat as he'd imagined. The description 'wiry' fit him perfectly. His sparse auburn body hair and around the base of his cock matched his head. No hair dye for this guy. Alastor was natural, from his reactions to his appearance. The only pretense came from the ghost fiction. *A screen to hide behind?*

"Any hard limits?"

At Alastor's questioning look, Darien added, "Anything you really don't like, sexually or otherwise?"

Those startling blue-green eyes blinked. Alastor's mouth opened.

"Not what you think I want to hear; what YOU don't like."

Alastor's gaze dropped to his grubby knees, his hair falling forward.

Pushing back the covers, Darien crawled over. He lifted Alastor's chin with a finger, then wrapped his other hand gently over the finger marks on the pale neck. He had to twist his hand to do it; the other man must have choked him from behind. Even though Alastor's face had significant bruising, the swelling was minimal, his eye moved normally, and wasn't bloodshot. No facial fractures, or at least none that required hospital treatment.

Alastor closed his eyes as if he couldn't express himself while looking at Darien. Not being able to see was a common fetish for submissives, one Darien could happily indulge. For all Alastor's bluster, he was young, nervous, and recently battered.

Even though this wasn't his sub, his business, or even his country, he wanted to find out who had hurt this youngster and make sure it didn't happen again, not to Alastor, and not to any other hapless vulnerable sub. Some people liked on-the-floor submissives, and there were plenty of those around, but it was just plain wrong of a dominant to try to break one who had this kind of spark.

"What do you want Alastor? What can I do to help you?"

Alastor blew a breath out of his nose as if no one had ever asked him something like that. Darien's heart went out to him. Like many brats, this guy hid behind bravado.

"Hey, I won't judge. I've known a lot of people like you, and I've helped most of them."

Alastor snorted. "I doubt that very much." Then he met Darien's gaze, his need oozing from him in waves.

"I don't want you to leave; I need you to stay if I'm honest. I also know you have a life to get back to, so I'll take all the memories I can get while you're here. I'll take whatever you want to dish out if you just let me stay close to you."

It was the answer of a needy, desperate, defensive submissive, but not a true masochist or someone with a humiliation fetish. Alastor wanted to be used, appreciated, not beaten. This was a vulnerable youngster searching for a caregiver to help him navigate a world he found too demanding on his own.

The bruises moved whoever had inflicted them from Darien's 'overenthusiastic and/or inexperienced dom' category to 'abusive sadist'. This submissive boy had been hurt, both physically and probably mentally. It wouldn't be the first time Darien had cleared up another wannabe dominant's mess, but with only ten days to work with, he'd better get started.

Releasing his light hold on Alastor's neck, he said, "On. Your. Belly."

Alastor complied so fast that he bounced on the bed. Darien winced at the many black and blue stripes on the pale skin. They covered his backside and upper thighs, but the ones across his back had Darien's blood boiling. They hadn't been caused by a soft flogger; those were hard impacts from a cane or crop. Blows like that could permanently damage the spine and kidneys.

"I'm going no further until you promise you won't see whoever did this to you again. In fact, give me his number; he needs to know doing this is dangerous."

The answer came too quickly. "I promise. But I haven't got his number."

"You sleep with people and don't even get their phone numbers?" This was getting worse by the second. "Did you even get his name?"

"I didn't get his number because I don't have a phone. His name was David."

Was? It clicked; the last earl had been David Walpole.

He aimed a smack at the outside of Alastor's left buttock. It was the only part of the bubble butt in front of him that wasn't bruised. Darien imagined the abuser standing on that side and whaling on the rest of him without care.

"Ow," Alastor glared at him over his shoulder. "What was that for?"

"Lying."

Alastor scowled but didn't reply as he turned to the front again.

Darien tried a new tack. "So, what did you do to the guy who beat you? Because all I see here is anger, not erotic play."

"I told him I was going to spunk on the pillows of his future in-laws."

Darien froze. Of all the things Alastor could have said, that... didn't even enter the ballpark.

"And I tried to piss in their soup. When they were eating it."

"That... that would do it. But messing around with someone else when you're getting married is a horrible thing to do."

"Yeah, he deserved it. But if I'd known I'd have to wait eighty years to be solid again, I would've waited for these bruises to heal before I popped up in front of his galloping horse."

Darien decided to ignore the fiction and get on with his first aid assessment; it'd been a busy day.

"Spread your legs."

After a pause, Alastor complied, but a hell of a lot slower than before. The state of his hole, swollen and red, provided the reason. Even if this hadn't been rape, Alastor had been battered internally as well as externally. And he'd still offered himself up for another session. Desperation, masochism, or submission? All three were possible, but after seeing the state of this boy, Darien only had care, not sex, on his agenda.

Seeing marks on consenting partners gave him a buzz, but they needed to be his marks of passion, not evidence of someone else's fury. This boy was like many of the subs he helped. He provided a place to reset, to have a timeout while giving the guidance and structure many submissives needed. He healed them, helped them understand themselves, and sent them on their way in a few days or weeks, more accepting of themselves and ready to face the world again.

Having a time limit of ten days with this needy sub wasn't ideal, but his nature meant he couldn't ignore such an unmistakable cry for help.

"Shower time," Darien announced and climbed off the bed.

Alastor dropped his forehead to the mattress but didn't close his legs. "Seriously? What is it with all the washing these days? Don't you know it strips the skin and leads to infection? A wipe down with clean linen and changing underwear every other day has always worked for me. Although I have to admit, I've had that—" he waved a hand toward the Tudor-style undershirt he'd dropped on the floor "—a hell of a lot longer than I thought I would when I put it on."

Darien rummaged in his carry-on bag and pulled out his body wash. "Hypoallergenic and pH balanced."

Wearing a scowl, Alastor heaved himself off the bed, ignored the black bottle in Darien's hand, and stomped into the ensuite bathroom. The door swung shut.

The closed door was a surprise. Alastor had been happy to show off his hole a minute ago, but he was shy about being seen in the shower?

The shower turned on, but not more than a dribble. Darien counted. He got to thirty before it slowly shut off. A grin spread across his face. *Brat.*

The door opened to reveal a scowling, still naked, Alastor. Darien strolled over, his face expressionless.

Alastor stiffened. "What? Gonna bust my arse for being too quick?"

Tension grew as Darien stood silently in front of the smaller man.

Alastor folded his arms, eyes full of bluster and challenge. "I thought we were going to get something to eat, so I hurried."

"You're remarkably talented."

Those blue-green eyes shot to his. "What?"

"Having a shower without getting wet."

Alastor's eyes stayed fixed on his. "I dried myself," he lied without a flicker of guilt.

Darien pointed at the fluffy white towels on the rail that hadn't moved an inch.

"With one of those? I'll give you one last chance. Wash." One second passed. Two. Five. Darien began to plan what he'd do if Alastor continued to be stubborn. Making the boy leave or spanking were out of the question, but—

Alastor blew a breath out of his nose, scowled, turned around. As he tried to shut the door between them, Darien's hand shot out.

"Nope. You lost your privacy privileges when you lied to me."

Alastor's brows drew together, then a bright grin lit his face. "Oh, I get it. Washing is just a..." He nodded to himself. "The Andersons got busy in the shower too."

The back of Darien's neck tickled. "You spied on them? They haven't been here for two years."

Alastor looked in his late teens, early twenties at most. How old had he been then?

Alastor's eyes rolled. "I keep telling you, but you're not listening. I'm in the painting, the one done in 1603. I've been here since this place was built. I. Can't. Leave."

"You're a ghost, but you can let down tires, open doors, and turn on faucets?" Darien pointed at the shower.

"Again, not a ghost, just a trapped imp. But yeah, I can touch things, but only objects that are original to the house are easy. Although this bathroom is new, they used an original door, so I can open it without a problem.

"Other things, like the tires and the taps—and they are taps, not faucets. This is England, not the New World— take a lot of effort and concentration when I'm on my own. And the newer they are, the harder it is; it's like they weigh a hundred times what they should and are slippery.

His brows drew together in an epic scowl. "I can't wank either. Have you any idea how damn frustrating it is to get this near—" he put his thumb and index finger a half-inch apart "—and lose concentration so you can't—"

"Turning the shower on helps with washing."

When Alastor didn't move, Darien reached in and did it for him. Holding up the bottle of body wash, he added, "Get in, get wet, apply shower gel, rinse. It's not rocket science. Even a four-hundred-year-old should be able to do that."

"It'll be pretty pointless unless you touch me. I'm not corporal without physical contact with an heir."

Darien opened and proffered the bottle, then reached out and put a single finger on Alastor's shoulder while keeping as much distance between them as possible. Keeping a straight face wasn't easy, but he refused to be manipulated into anything, including sex.

If he slept with Alastor, and that was highly unlikely given the guy's instability and the short time frame, it would be his choice, on his terms.

He'd play the game Alastor had set up—he enjoyed the challenge of a bratty sub and Alastor was the brattiest he'd ever encountered—but there was no question about which one of them would win.

Alastor frowned. "I'm going off you."

Darien gave him a bright smile. "You're breaking my heart."

"If I shrink or get the flux, consumption, or plague, I'll haunt you until the end of time."

"I thought you already were?"

Alastor stepped under the stream of warm water as if putting his head into an executioner's noose. His hair darkened as the water ran over it. Grime pooled and rushed down the plughole. Almost hairless, smooth, and lithe, Alastor's body called to Darien. He wanted to cover it with his own, to watch his dark cock sink into that pale flesh, but not tonight, probably not ever. The thought depressed him, but his libido didn't control him.

"And your back," Darien reminded and added a little pressure with his finger.

The glare Alastor shot him as he turned around had Darien suppressing a laugh. This kid really didn't like showering.

The thought made him lose his smile. Kid might be right. What adult objected to washing this much? Rather than a bratty sub, was he dealing with someone younger than he looked or with severe mental health issues? What if Alastor actually believed he was some kind of supernatural and tried to fly off the roof or something equally bizarre? *What if he's an escaped mental patient?* Darien's remaining desire fled. There was nothing he could do tonight other than stop Alastor from disappearing again. Tomorrow... tomorrow, he'd have to think again.

Alastor's hand slid down to his hardening cock. A heartfelt groan left his lips as his fist closed around his flesh.

"By God's pizzle[1], that's—"

"Ah, ah, none of that."

"Bastard," Alastor ground out.

"Nope, my parents were married. How about yours?"

"Demon, remember?" Alastor said, but he did leave his hard cock alone.

"Demons don't have families?"

"No idea. I've got no memories from before I got here."

The shower continued with Darien reminding a silent Alastor to pay attention to areas that still looked grubby.

After a few more minutes, Alastor broke his silence. "Am I done yet, milord? Because if I stay in here much longer, I'll be going down the frigging plug hole too."

Darien reached in, turned off the shower, and started to towel dry Alastor's hair. When he stopped, it stuck up like a punk's, and the rich orange color glowed. As he tried to tame the sticking-up hair, Alastor took the towel out of his hand and wiped it around his body.

"Never thought I'd have an heir as my personal fart catcher," Alastor said.

"Your what?" Darien asked, wondering if this was a new word for a top. If it was, he didn't like it. Darien stopped playing with fascinating bright hair, and the towel dropped to the floor.

"Footman, servant. You know, the guy who walks so close behind their master they catch all the farts?"

Darien opened his mouth but couldn't think of anything to say except, "You are very odd."

Alastor gave him a grin and a flamboyant bow. "Why, thank you, milord. So, now that I'm scrubbed within an inch of my life, fancy fucking me?"

"Are you hungry?" Darien asked. The longer he could keep this conversation off sex, the better.

Alastor's gaze dropped to Darien's black shorts.

"Eyes up. That wasn't an invitation to give me a blowjob. I'm tired. You must be too, and I have a busy day tomorrow—make that later today. Did you, or did you not, eat today?"

"Yeah. I nicked some food when you lot were looking for me."

Darien raised his eyebrows. The chances of Alastor making his way around the house without being seen during the search weren't great.

"Truth?"

That bright grin returned. "Would I lie to you?"

With a sigh, Darien shook his head. "I'm not even sure you know the difference between fact and fiction. But I'm not willing to argue at this point. Lie down on the bed, and I'll do your back with arnica." One look at Alastor's puzzled expression had him adding, "It's an ointment made from a plant. It'll help with the bruising."

"I don't need a poultice. The only thing that'll help with the bruises is you touching me." Alastor's hands shot up as Darien frowned. "Doesn't have to be sexual. I'm a damn good footwarmer."

Darien pulled a hand down his face. It was too late for this. "Fine. If sleeping at the end of my bed keeps you from disappearing again, who am I to argue?"

"I've gotta touch you, though. No healing unless we're touching."

"You are one weird guy."

"Yeah, but I grow on people, like smallpox." He performed another bow. "After you, milord."

Hoping that he'd hear the door open if Alastor decided to disappear again, Darien turned off the bathroom light and then the bedside light as he climbed into bed.

How the hell is this supposed to work? Alastor might like it, but he wasn't keen on having feet in his face all night, even if they were now clean.

Laying on his side, Darien pulled his feet up a little, getting into his preferred sleeping position with his top knee bent and higher than the other. Warm skin touched his lower foot, he guessed a thigh, and his upper foot nudged what he thought was Alastor's chest.

Only the sounds of the house creaking gently broke the silence as he waited for Alastor to move, to try something. Minute after minute, Alastor remained motionless. Darien drifted.

"Thanks for letting me do this, milord," he whispered through the darkness.

He'd heard a lot of terms of respect used for dominants over the years, and as it seemed appropriate given the circumstances, he let it go. Plus, he was too tired to argue.

"You're welcome," Darien mumbled and fell asleep, dreaming of touching, pleasuring, the confusing, fascinating boy at his feet.

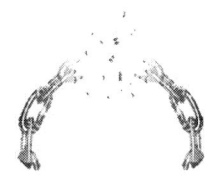

---

1. Pizzle: Early English for penis, usually used in reference to animals.

CHAPTER EIGHT

Alastor woke a few times in the night as the heir shifted in his sleep, and he lost skin contact, but it only took a slight movement to get it back. Sleep. He hadn't slept for... he didn't even want to think about it. The oblivion, the nothingness while time passed, was an unrealized fantasy he'd had for over a century. David hadn't ever let him share his bed.

The number of times that the earl before David had fallen asleep before remembering to kick Alastor out could be counted on the fingers of one hand. And it'd been longer than that since he'd eaten or drunk anything. He could ignore his grumbling belly, but the thirst... Why hadn't he drunk some of the shower water while he could?

But there might be something else he could do that he hadn't done in many decades as the heir's foot still touched his thigh.

As soon as the thought occurred, blood flooded into his cock. Trying not to move too much, he grasped his rapidly hardening cock that seemed entirely on board with this idea.

He bit back the groan of pleasure that first touch dragged from his chest. He wasn't in the ideal position. With his thighs clamped together, he couldn't easily access his balls. And there was no way to reach his ass without moving a lot and possibly waking the heir, but this, this was enough.

After licking his palm, he returned it to his cock and began to wank, using a tiny movement with two fingers around the head.

In his mind's eye, he pressed his cock into the warm mouth of the man above him. Plenty of heirs had fucked his mouth, and they always seemed to enjoy it, but he only had imagination to draw on as the receiver. Walpole heirs never intentionally provide pleasure; they used, took—

In his mind's eye, he forced his cock down Darien's throat. The big man gagged, eyes watering.

Alastor's fist sped up. *Close, so close.*

"What are you doing?"

Alastor froze at the deep, sleepy, amused voice, but as their legs still touched, for now, he began stroking his cock again.

"Scratching," he gritted out. "Don't worry, I'll be done in a minute."

"Scratching? That's what they used to call it?" Darien said, but the bastard moved his leg away. The need didn't stop, but he couldn't feel his fingers on his cock anymore. He'd never been prevented from coming like this, but as his ass still hurt from the beating the last earl had given him... *Fuck, will I be horny like this until an heir touches me again?* The thought terrified him. Reaching out, he held onto Darien's thigh, his other hand flying over his cock.

"It's always been scratching," he managed to say, even though his voice sounded strained. "This bed must have lice or something because fuuck, I need to—"

Darien pulled his leg away again, and a groan of frustration erupted from Alastor's chest, and all pretense died. "Please, just a little longer, I need—"

The warmth of Darien's skin returned. "Thank fuck, I—" Darien moved away again, and Alastor groaned, his temple resting on the wonderfully clean sheet in defeat. "I really, really hate you."

"Because I'm edging you? Although I have to say it's the easiest edging I've ever done."

"If edging means you're being a complete bastard, then yeah, you are. And if you don't let me finish, I'll pay you back a hundred-fold."

Darien stilled. "Are you threatening me, boy?"

The softly spoken question held more menace than any of the screamed insults and threats dished out by any other Walpole heir.

Alastor's choices were storming off and having a stiff, aching cock for who knew how long or backing down.

"No, no, milord, it's just I haven't done this in so very long, and without you touching me I can't—"

The heir rolled onto his back. "You can touch me."

For a moment, Alastor thought the heir was simply giving him permission to carry on pleasuring himself, but he couldn't miss this opportunity to bind the heir to himself as much as possible.

Wiggling forward, he pressed a kiss to the hairy thigh. "Thank you, milord," he said. Pushing the covers off, he got to his knees. If the heir let him suck him, he could touch himself at the same time. *Win-win.*

The heir's body was so different to his, so different to the other heirs Alastor had touched. Skinny in youth and fat by middle age, Walpole men were 'ordinary' at best. None had Darien's firm, sculpted muscles, beautiful dark skin, or delightful frizzy body hair.

Opening his eyes, he halted. The curtains let in just enough light for him to see Darien's hard cock. Long and dark with a lighter head, it nestled in a bed of clearly trimmed springy hair.

"Not what you're used to?"

"In so many, many ways," fell out of his mouth before his brain engaged.

Darien chuckled, causing his cock to lurch from side to side, then he sighed. "I'm so going to regret this, but do you still want to play?"

Alastor leaned up on his elbows, gave the cock a long lick. Hot, hard, and smelling clean with only a slight hint of musk, it made his mouth water. This wouldn't be an onerous task at all.

"I'll take that as a yes. Do you like sixty-nines?"

Alastor frowned, looked up. "A what?"

The evil smile on Darien's lips made him shiver. "Turn around and straddle me."

Heart in his mouth, not really believing this was happening, Alastor flipped around. A gasp left his throat as strong hands wrapped around his thighs and jerked him a little higher.

Lips contacted his pucker. An heir was literally kissing his asshole.

"Is this ok? Not too sore? You're still pretty puffy."

In reply, he opened his mouth and took as much of Darien's cock into his mouth as he could. Then he forgot everything apart from the sensation of Darien's tongue. Licking, then fuck... it pushed inside.

Alastor gagged as the cock in his mouth breached his throat. He pulled off, took a breath, then went back down. The tongue left his hole. Disappointment bloomed, then a finger pressed in gently as Darien guided Alastor's cockhead down into his hot, wet mouth.

This can't be happening. An heir, an actual heir, is— Something lit up inside him. He'd felt a similar spark a time or two when an heir fucked him, but Darien seemed to lock onto whatever caused the almost painfully good sensation with ease.

Alastor's mind blanked as the heir worked him, pressing on that spot inside, kneading the small area between his hole and balls with a knuckle, and sucking on his cockhead. Darien's cock had fallen out of his mouth, but he couldn't do anything but *feel.* The soreness just made it more intense. He'd thought himself fairly accomplished at pleasuring men but compared to this, he was a rank amateur.

Climax usually built slowly and had only happened when he secretly touched himself while an heir used him. This time, it punched through him like a fist through tissue paper. He cried out, spasmed, as Darien gripped his hip, kept him where he wanted.

Every muscle went limp as the last pulse faded. He collapsed onto Darien's body, not caring about the hard cock still pressing against his face.

A hand patted his thigh once and then a little harder. "Get off; you're squashing me."

"Can't," Alastor mumbled. "If I wasn't dead before, I am now. That... that was... Ugh. I've got no words."

Darien chuckled. Alastor's world lurched as he was flipped around and tucked against the heir's side. "Now, behave and go to sleep."

Snuggling in, Alastor smiled to himself. "Anything you say, milord."

He'd started to drift before it occurred that the heir hadn't gotten off and clearly didn't care. A selfless heir was a new confusing proposition, one Alastor intended to puzzle out as soon as he'd had a little rest.

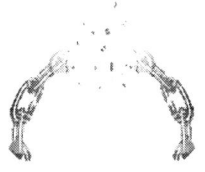

Darien's phone gave a musical tinkle, which gradually got louder. *Why can't I stay in this bubble forever?* In a few days, Darien would leave, and Alastor would return to living in limbo. No sleep, no touching, no—

A masculine dark arm sneaked out from under the cover and silenced the small black box that ruled humanity these days.

Alastor uncurled from around the arm he'd captured and stretched. His back cracked, and he grinned at the unusual sensation.

"That sounded painful." The sleepy rumble from beside him widened his smile.

"Was great, and I know just the way to demonstrate my humble gratitude." Alastor twisted around, burrowed under the covers, and kissed a hairy thigh. The hair was sparse, springy, and unlike anything he'd encountered before, much like the man whose bed he shared.

His mouth watered at the thought of wrapping his lips around Darien's shaft and returning some of the pleasure he'd experienced. He'd given hundreds of blowjobs to manipulate, to bind. Other than being able to touch himself while he did it, the thin, smelly cocks of heirs did nothing for him sexually. But the thought of licking, sucking, that clean, sweet-smelling cock had his own shaft swelling.

A hand in his hair stopped his progress.

"How's your back?"

Alastor slumped, his forehead resting against Darien's thigh. For centuries he'd hoped for an heir who actually cared, rather than the endless procession of Walpoles who were content to use him. Now he'd gotten his wish, and it wasn't as much fun as he'd thought. When they used him, belittled him, it was easy to play pranks, to drive them mad. Hurting and betraying Darien after this would be horrible, and he had so little time to do it.

A tug on his hair reminded him to answer. Instead of giving a verbal response, he pulled away. Disappointment swirled as Darien released him rather than shoving him back down to finish the blowjob.

Climbing off the bed, he turned his naked back to the heir. The bed creaked. A second later, the heavy curtains at the window were pulled back. A finger traced down his spine. He basked in the warmth from the sun streaming through the window and Darien's body heating his skin.

"These look a little better already," Darien murmured. "Thank heaven for arnica."

A hand on Alastor's shoulder turned him around. Amber eyes focused on Alastor's cheek and neck rather than looking at the person beneath. A hand came up and used his chin as a lever to tilt his face into the best viewing position.

Alastor let him look for a few moments before stepping back and dipping to grab his undershirt off the floor. Clothes newer than the age of the house simply fell to the ground when an heir stopped touching him, like the towel had last night, not that Darien had noticed.

No other options but this near rag remained to him. If he lost it, he'd be naked for eternity. It would happen one day even if he never lost it; the Elizabethan garment wouldn't last as long as he would. But he wanted to delay the inevitable for as long as possible.

The care, consideration, and pleasure Darien had shown him would be torn away within days. The memories of last night already haunted him. Having Darien hate him would be so much easier. Fortunately, he had centuries of experience in rubbing people up the wrong way.

"Does the merchandise meet with your approval, milord? And here was me thinking your slave heritage would have mellowed the Walpole genes. Guess not."

Still naked, he made for the door in stiff, angry strides.

"Stop." The dominant tone gave him a shiver, but he opened the door before looking over his shoulder.

"Or what? You'll sentence me to an eternity of being alone in this place, unable to touch, sleep, or talk to anyone? You did that the moment you decided not to stay." Alastor stepped out of the door and relocated to the bedroom next door.

"God damn it, you little shit, where did you go this time?"

The exasperation in the heir's voice mollified him a little. Next time they were alone, Darien might give Alastor what he needed—a reason to hate.

Darien's phone rang. Footsteps sounded on wooden floorboards. The heir answered the electronic burbling like a dog returning to its master.

"Yep, I'll be down in a minute. Put the coffee on." After he paused, he added, "Please put the coffee on, please, sister dearest."

With energy buzzing through his body after his fantastic night, Alastor pulled on his threadbare shirt and relocated down to the kitchen.

Darien wasn't the only person who had information about this branch of the Walpole family. Although speaking to her directly was impossible without her brother's intervention, she might let something slip.

He found a pretty, conservatively dressed woman, with sleek dark hair and paler skin than her brother, setting up the coffee machine. "How he stands it without sugar, I don't know," she murmured to herself as she put a spoonful into one of the two mugs.

Alastor moved in closer and spoke into her ear. *"When did he eat last? He has been acting odd. What sort of impression would it give to viewers if he passes out? What if he drops one of the lots coming in today? He needs a little sugar, just this once."*

Juliana hesitated; the spoon held over the sugar jar. *"Go on, you know he needs it."*

Juliana scooped up another spoonful and dumped it in the second mug.

His usual strategy to get rid of heirs was to gradually isolate them from family and friends, then tip them over the edge into madness. On several occasions, he hadn't revealed himself to the heir for months, even years, as he slowly turned people against his target by whispering in their ears.

Now, he only had a week to either find someone to kill Darien or intrigue him so much that he'd either find a way to stay or return sooner rather than later. The heir's ability to visit would depend on who bought the property. Being purchased by a hotel chain would probably be the best option. At least he'd have people to play with while he waited for this heir, or one of his male relatives, to visit.

Footsteps sounded on the flagstones outside the kitchen. Alastor relocated into the old scullery, ears alert.

"Ugh, wrong cup," Darien griped.

"No, it's the right one. I just thought you could do with some sugar this morning. Yesterday was... stressful."

The clinking probably meant Darien was getting himself another coffee.

"Since when do I have sugar in coffee?"

"It just seemed like a good idea. Any contact with our mystery man?"

Alastor changed his mind about popping in and scaring the shit out of Darien; he wanted to hear this.

"Quite a lot." The smirk in the heir's voice had anger bubbling. He was still a demon, and a human shouldn't be laughing at him even if he'd nearly made Alastor's brain turn to mush.

Juliana sighed, and Alastor imagined her shaking her head. "Only you could get it on with the invisible man."

Alastor relocated to the kitchen, leaning up against the work surface next to Juliana.

"Going to tell her you stuck your tongue in my ass?"

Darien's eyes went as round as an owl's an instant before he spluttered on his mouthful of coffee.

"How, how did you do that?"

Alastor raised his eyebrows, smirked.

"Make coffee? Seriously are you feeling alright? He didn't slip you anything, did he?" Juliana said.

Alastor mimed sprinkling something into her coffee as she frowned at her brother.

Darien scowled. "Right, ha, ha, very funny. Ganging up on me isn't fair."

"I like your sister, Darien. She's hot," Alastor said, then licked Juliana's cheek, long and slow.

Darien's gaze shot to his sister's face. Her frown deepened, and she put her coffee cup down. "Seriously, you're worrying me now. What's up?"

"You... you can't see him, feel him?"

Juliana followed her brother's gaze, looking right at the spot Alastor occupied.

"Who?" she asked.

Alastor wiggled his fingers at Darien.

"Come on, you two, this isn't a joke; we've got things to do."

"She can't see or hear me. No one can, except a direct male descendant of the first Earl of Tandridge. But I can influence her subconscious. Why do you think you got sugar this morning?" As Alastor spoke, he put a hand over Juliana's breast. "Bit small, but I can work with it."

"Leave her alone," Darien growled.

"Do you believe me yet? Because I can keep this up for hours, weeks, even years if I have to."

"That's it, no more with the ghost crap," Juliana growled. "The auction is almost in the toilet, thanks to the crap yesterday. What the hell's got into you?"

"Ok, ok, you've made your point, just... stop with the touching."

"Touching, what damn touching? What happened last night?" Juliana said, stiff with confusion.

"Question is, do I let her know I'm here, or do I carry on until she thinks you've completely lost your marbles? Do you fancy a trip back home in a straitjacket? I've done that to plenty of Walpoles. It's almost as effective as suicide to stop them producing any more brats."

Darien folded his arms, narrowing his eyes. "You don't want me to leave."

Juliana waved her hand at her brother. "Hello, earth calling Darien?"

Alastor pursed his lips. "True. So, what do I get if I show her that you're not going mad?"

"What do you want?"

Juliana threw her hands up. "For you to stop acting fucking crazy for one thing."

"To sleep with you while you're here."

"Done," Darien said, as fast as a gavel coming down.

Alastor pushed off the counter he'd been leaning against and walked around the table to the heir. Darien kept his gaze on him the whole time.

"What the hell are you looking at?" Juliana screeched. "This isn't funny anymore. We haven't got time for—"

Alastor put his hand on Darien's shoulder and gave her a grin. "Nice tits, shame about the banshee voice."

Her jaw dropped, and she seemed to lose the power of speech. Shocking people never got old, but it wasn't the most energetic reaction he'd encountered. Shrieking, crossing themselves, and often fainting were more usual. It seemed the FitzHenrys were made of sterner stuff than most Walpoles.

"Watch carefully," Alastor said and lifted his hand from Darien, knowing he'd vanished for Juliana, then put it back again. Putting on a puppy dog eyes expression, he pouted.

"Not even a gasp? I'm disappointed. I had you down as a fainter or at least a screamer." He cocked his head to one side. "Nothing to say at all?"

"W... what are you?"

Alastor wagged his finger from side to side at her. "Here was me thinking you of all people would be against putting people in boxes. What do you identify as anyway, black or white?"

"Behave," Darien ground out.

Alastor turned his grin on the heir. "Nope, not capable of that, imp remember?"

"What happened to your pants?"

"Don't you like it?" He picked at his undershirt. "This was all the rage in fashionable male underwear in the 1600s, and I kinda like the breeze. Besides, if I wore anything else, it'd fall off as soon as I stopped touching your gorgeous brother. Instant striptease without the tease."

Keeping a foot against Darien's, he leaned his elbows on the counter island between them and hoped the sight of his backside messed with the heir some more. "So, tell me, sweet Juliana, what song really pisses off your brother?"

"So, now you have proof, how the hell do we deal with Casper here?" Darien asked his sister, ignoring Alastor.

"Well, that's rude, especially after you—" A hand came down on his backside.

Slowly, he looked over his shoulder and frowned at Darien. "That is guaranteed to piss me off. What's that line in the movie about the green guy? 'You wouldn't like me when I'm angry?'"

He turned back to Juliana. "My name's Alastor, not Casper, but I can tell when I'm not wanted." Alastor removed his foot from Darien and resumed his perch next to Juliana.

The pretty woman—who looked a few years older than Darien—glanced around, then whispered, "Is he gone?"

Alastor let out a snort of amusement as he crossed his arms.

"He's leaning on the counter a foot to your right."

Juliana stumbled back and pressed a hand to her throat.

"Tell her I'm going to spy on her in the bathroom," Alastor said as he wandered over to the coffee machine where Juliana had spilled some powdered coffee.

Darien's eyes narrowed. "I'll do no such thing."

"What, what did he say?" Juliana blurted, peering at the spot where Alastor had been a moment ago.

"I can make her do things, you know, just like I made Melody Anderson and the Grimshaw boy go at it like rabbits. Why do you think she put sugar in your coffee?"

"Don't be stupid."

"Darien FitzHenry, if you don't tell me what he's saying this minute, I'll... I'll tell him what song you hate."

Alastor waggled his eyebrows and whispered in Juliana's ear, loud enough for Darien to hear.

"You want more coffee."

Juliana moved back over to the coffee machine as if programmed. "I swear, this is the weirdest job we've—" She froze, staring at the spilled coffee powder where Alastor was writing 'BOO' with his finger.

"That's it, I'm outta here, and you're coming with me." She grabbed her purse off the countertop.

Alastor froze. The heir leaving was the opposite of what he wanted.

"Well, that got his attention. If you don't want us both to leave right now, apologize to the lady." Darien nodded toward his sister, voice calm.

Apologize? Alastor had never apologized for anything, except to Arioch, and that was only because the vengeance demon scared the shit out of him.

Darien raised his eyebrows. "Well, what will it be? Politeness or being alone for another... how long has it been?"

He'd wanted to be seen for so long, but Darien's uncompromising, calm gaze had Alastor's skin prickling. Between one breath and the next, he relocated up to the roof.

What the fuck am I doing? He'll be gone in a matter of days, and here you are, trying to chase him away even faster.

Unlike the other heirs, Darien had no attachment to Walpole Hall. He could get an employee to conduct the auction or simply pull out of the contract. The man could walk out the door in a matter of minutes and never return. Yes, he'd gotten off last night, so that wouldn't be a problem again for a long time, but his throat still felt like a desert.

Sitting on the edge of the building, in front of the stone balustrade, his legs dangling into the void, Alastor gazed at the subtly changing view. Autumn was in full swing, and the trees blazed with color. The gusty breeze had flurries of leaves spiraling near the ground, but his shirt and hair remained untouched by the wind. Yet another year was dying, and here he sat, watching and apart from the cycle of life.

Since he'd first sat on this ledge, cars and lorries on tarmac had replaced carriages and wagons on mud. Houses clustered in the distance where only fields and woods had been before.

What would it look like in another century, hell, even another decade? Alastor didn't care. The living cared about things like that, and even though he wasn't the ghost most humans assumed, he felt like one. Centuries devoid of contact, of life, except for Arioch's punishments, loomed ahead.

He wished with all his heart that jumping off would do some good, or bad, according to his point of view. He knew what would happen because he'd slipped more than once. Instinct kicked in, and he relocated before he hit the ground. Even if he did actually land, being non-corporeal state, he—

The world stopped. He already knew he could be injured when in contact with an heir. Was that what the ninth Earl had been trying to do when Alastor sidestepped all those years ago? Had he been trying to take Alastor with him and save his nephew?

Would it work? Can imps die?

Alastor knew nothing about life as an imp except what Arioch had told him. His first memory had been of Arioch's office, where the demon had explained the curse, then he'd been in the first earl's bedroom.

He smiled fondly at the memory. The old man nearly had a heart attack. All he'd been able to do was point and say, "You,

you." The way he'd lumbered out the door, shouting for his servants and sons had been most satisfying.

Finding out there were already four more heirs to deal with hadn't been so entertaining. Arioch had failed to tell him that, but the demon Lord had explained that removing his memory of life before the curse was a kindness; he couldn't fret about what he didn't remember.

Arioch had lied then and probably did so all the time. Alastor did miss what he couldn't remember, but what else could you expect from a demon?

CHAPTER NINE

"What's he saying? Come on, Darien, keep me in the loop here."

Frustration bled from Juliana, but given the circumstances, Darien thought she'd taken the news that a supernatural being was stalking them rather well.

He hadn't imagined his sister fainting, she tackled problems head-on as he did, but he had expected a shriller—possibly expletive-filled—response to a ghost turning up for coffee.

"He's not saying anything; he's gone. But he's certainly racking up an impressive number of punishments."

Sinking against the counter, shoulders rounding, she pinched the bridge of her nose with her thumb and index finger. Sweat prickled on his back as he waited for her reaction.

When she looked up, his heart dropped. That wasn't worry or fright; that was downright pissed off.

"A ghost, a fucking poltergeist, and you're treating him like one of your boytoys?"

His sister constantly teased him about the seemingly continuous parade of needy submissive men who appeared in his house.

Darien couldn't suppress his slight wince, rather than giving his usual reiteration that they weren't boytoys or 'his'. As always, Juliana picked up on it. Her eyes narrowed.

"What aren't you telling me, baby brother?"

Biting the bullet, which was always the best strategy with Juliana, he spilled the beans. "He claims to be a minor demon, trapped by the curse Harry Grimshaw mentioned, not the ghost of Nicholas Thatcher."

After staring at him, open-mouthed for a few seconds, the sister he knew so well, and frankly feared a little, emerged.

"Are you fucking kidding me? A demon? You're playing kinky dominance games with a creature from Hell?"

Feeling about ten years old again, Darien muttered, "A very minor demon, an imp, he said."

With one hand on her hip, she waved the other in the air. "Oh, that's fine then. There's only a MINOR demon after your soul. We'll just carry on, shall we? Nothing to worry about."

Darien sighed. "Yes, it does sound kinda scary, but he isn't after my soul. From what he said, imps are more about mischief than Armageddon or dragging souls to Hell. He just wants to be free of the curse that keeps him here. Us turning up means he'll probably never be free as tracking down all the male descendants of Thomas Walpole is an impossible task." He looked up at his sister. "He's hurt and lost, Jules; I'd like to help him if I can."

Using the childhood nickname didn't help. Juliana threw her hands in the air, every inch tense. "Did you listen to one thing I said? He's a DEMON, which means him telling the truth is how likely? Prince of Lies, remember?"

A rattle of rain against the window made him twitch, but the dreary English fall weather was the least of his problems.

"That's Beelzebub, not Alastor." Even to his own ears, he sounded like a petulant brat making excuses. "Listen, I'll be careful. He can't do anything to anyone else. He can't even touch someone unless he's in contact with me."

"But he can touch you, little brother."

Darien inclined his head. "Yes, he can, but he's so damn desperate for human contact, I'd bet my life he wouldn't do anything to hurt me." He needed her to understand. "Just think of the history he knows. We're actually talking to a real Elizabethan man."

The tension drained out of his sister. "Always with the history. But judging by the history of the Walpole family, you are betting your life. How many of them do you think heard the lines he's spinning you before they died? If this wasn't such an important sale, I'd—" she pressed her lips together. "Just be careful, little brother."

He gave her the grin he knew always melted her heart. Alastor wasn't the only one who could manipulate people with a smile. "Trust me, boss, I've got this."

Her gaze roamed his face searching for he didn't know what. Lips pressing in a thin line, she nodded. "Ok, do what you've got to do, but if he causes any more trouble, I'll exorcise both your asses right back to Hell."

He was across the kitchen and wrapping his arms around her in the next second. She leaned into him for a moment, and he gave her a squeeze.

"You're the best sister and boss in the world, you know that, right?"

Her phone beeped with a message, and she reached into her purse to check it. "Delivery is outside."

Darien spent the morning checking the inventory of Tudor and Jacobean artifacts, including silver, ceramics, instruments, and paintings, and putting them on display in the Long Gallery.

The actual sale would take place in the Low Great Hall, as that was the largest space in the building, but the Long Gallery had far better lighting to display the auction lots.

Touching such objects usually took every ounce of focus as he checked their provenance and worked on confirming their authenticity with various scans and tests. But today, he found himself constantly staring up at the painting of Alastor or glancing around to see if he'd returned.

Juliana's heels clicking on the ancient timber floor had him focusing back on the Holbein painting of Henry VII. Something about it didn't seem right, but he couldn't put his finger on it. The FitzHenry auction house guaranteed the authenticity of everything they sold, so a mistake could result in a costly legal battle with the artwork's current owner. The guide price for this painting was £35,000.

"Go on, go see if you can find him. We've got some local dignitaries coming by for a public relations exercise in an hour; the last owners weren't exactly popular among the locals even before the attempted murder.

"I can handle them, but keeping our not-so-friendly neighborhood—whatever the hell he is—out of the way would be helpful. Besides, seeing you talk to thin air gives me the heebie-jeebies, and I don't like not knowing when I'm being watched."

"Got it," he said over his shoulder as he made his way toward the stairs.

"And don't forget to eat," she called after him. He waved a hand in the air but didn't reply.

Fifteen minutes later, after fetching his jacket from the room where he'd spent the night, he stood in the walled garden depicted in the painting. Instead of the faded blue skies and greens in the portrait, drizzle pattered down, and the leaves were golden and brown. It took a while to work out where the artist had been sitting, as the bench the main subjects had been using was long gone, but from the view of the house in the background, he was pretty sure he'd found it.

Comparing the height of the wall to where the painted Alastor had been standing, and his own height, he confirmed that 'his' Alastor had grown at least an inch. His face had also lost a little of the roundness of youth. The conclusion was simple. The person he'd spent the night with had aged since this portrait had been painted, not by more than a year or so, but he had aged. If the painting was an accurate representation.

Darien pondered the implications as he walked back up to the house. Alastor wasn't a ghost; he aged and healed. He could also be touched and injured—by a Walpole heir anyway.

His heart dropped as he saw a small procession of four cars making their way up the long straight driveway. He thought he'd have more time to locate Alastor. Three executive cars and the Grimshaws' battered red Land Rover Defender. In nine days, Darien would have no right to be here.

A faint, mournful woodwind melody rose and fell. At least Juliana had found some authentic Tudor music to set the ambiance for the guests. However, most recordings of Tudor music also contained period string instruments such as lutes, harps, or dulcimers. He paused, looking up at the hall again. The life the place had seen seemed to reach out to him. Life Alastor had seen, experienced, even if he hadn't been an actual part of it.

How would Alastor cope with being unseen, unable to interact with the world, for the foreseeable future? He'd already handled eighty years of being a ghost and had been trapped here for over four hundred years. Darien couldn't begin to imagine what that would be like. Guilt that he'd dangled a carrot of life right in front of Alastor warred with the impulse to extract every snippet of firsthand knowledge from him in their remaining time.

Something white moving up on the parapet caught his attention. He glanced up, expecting to see one of the seagulls he'd heard earlier. His heart froze as he identified pale bare legs dangling over sixty-five feet above the gravel drive.

Every drop of blood in his body froze, then he rocketed into action.

"Alastor, don't move. I'm coming," he shouted. The music stopped.

"What the hell?" Juliana blurted as he dashed past her in the Low Great Hall.

He saved his breath for running. This damn place didn't have a single straight staircase between all the floors. He negotiated corners and corridors between the flights, feet slipping a little on the age-shined wooden floors between the stone staircases. Luckily, the majority of the stairs, except for the last flight up to the roof, were shallow.

Even though he worked out, he still breathed hard by the time he burst out of the door onto the flat, grey stone roof. The urge to sink to the flagstones in relief as he saw Alastor still sitting in the same place made him swallow.

Stupid, he'd been so damn stupid. What the hell would someone do given the prospect of living in limbo for possibly centuries?

"Alastor, don't do it; we'll work something out," he said as he inched across the cold, slick dark stone.

The man turned, put one bare foot on the stone as he teetered on the edge, a wooden recorder in his hand. The instrument looked like the one Darien had put on display, but that wasn't his current priority.

"Hold on to the balustrade," he urged in as calm a tone as possible. The carved stone barrier was four feet high and set a foot and half from the edge of the building.

Alastor frowned before a smile spread across his face, lighting it from within. "Aww, Darien, are you worried about little old me?"

As Darien gaped, Alastor carefully lay the instrument down, rolled backward into a handstand, then flipped to his feet and bounced up onto the stone balustrade. It couldn't have been more than four inches wide.

Darien's throat worked for a second before he managed to speak, "Get down before you fall and break your neck; this isn't a damn joke."

"Oh, I quite agree; this isn't a joke at all," Alastor said, then performed an elegant cartwheel. The loose smock slipped up his torso, giving Darien a flash of his fit pale body and the dark marks on his ass, back, and thighs.

"Are you trying to kill yourself?"

The pale figure swiveled on the balls of his feet until he faced Darien. His back bowed, arms wheeling, until he regained his balance. Darien froze, heart in his mouth, knowing he was too far away to reach him in time if he overbalanced.

"Please get down before you give me a heart attack."

Alastor hopped down on Darien's side of the barrier. He appeared unaffected by the cold, damp stone under his feet as he drew the recorder carefully through the balustrade then faced Darien.

Bright ocean-tinted eyes peered up at him through auburn hair. "And there's the kicker. I can't kill myself. Without an heir touching me, I'm Mr. Indestructible. I can't hurt myself any more than I can wank. So, unless you fancy taking a swan dive with me, or holding on while you gut me, I'm stuck here." He waved a hand at his neck. "As you can see, giving up the squeeze too early doesn't work either."

A strong gust of wind went right through Darien, but Alastor didn't seem bothered by it. In fact, his curly red hair didn't even move.

"Mind if we talk inside? You might not feel the cold, but I do."

Alastor shrugged. "One place is as good as another, on the estate anyway. And I wouldn't mind being cold or hot. Last night was..." He shook his head, looking down at his feet.

Darien couldn't begin to imagine how it would feel to be Alastor, but he wanted to know, and right now, he was the only person in the world who could find out. The curiosity about what Alastor had witnessed during his existence—it felt wrong to call it a life—itched at his soul.

What he did know was that Alastor screamed for physical contact with every fiber of his being. As if being pulled by an invisible cord, Darien found himself walking over to the thin young man and wrapping his arms around him.

"You have no idea how good this feels." Alastor leaned into him with a sigh, burying his face against Darien's chest.

With one hand cupping the back of Alastor's neck and the other gently rubbing his back, Darien looked over Alastor's shoulder at the magnificent view of the British countryside.

It looked remarkably similar to home—damp, muddy, green, and gold. But it was the buildings on the land, how humanity had shaped this similar landscape that made the difference. Alastor had been in this place for over seventy years before the first Europeans paddled down the Missouri River. It boggled his mind.

The only previous contact he'd had, hell, anyone had ever had, with that era were the things left behind. The objects, the art, the music.

"Did you take the recorder from the exhibit?"

"Uh-huh."

"You have to give it back, you know that, right?"

Alastor didn't reply, but his entire body stiffened.

"Why did you pick that recorder? It's the plainest one out of the three. Where you worried about damaging something valuable?"

Alastor snorted. "As if money matters to me. I didn't take the others because they're reproductions. This one is real."

Darien snorted in amusement. "I assure you they're not. The provenance is quite—"

Alastor deflated in his arms, but he didn't try to move away. "Believe me, don't believe me. It doesn't matter."

"I think I need another look at those recorders. How about the other pieces?"

"The Henry VII portrait is fake, or at least the date is, although the frame is genuine."

A crow wearing a red leg ring perched briefly on the turret to their right, fixing them with a beady eye, before letting out a caw and flying off. Darien tried to imagine how much jealousy Alastor would feel for the bird's ability to fly free. He stilled. A red ring? What had Alastor said about watching out for people wearing red?

"What's up? Did you have a lot of money invested in that painting?" The muffled words came from the region of his chest. "Did I burst your bubble?" Amusement tinged his words. "Aw, has the poor little rich boy lost his shiny little—"

"Just a crow—" Darien interrupted before Alastor got into his stride, "—with a red ring on its leg."

Alastor snorted but leaned into him a little more. "You think big bad Arioch is spying on us?"

"Is it possible?"

Alastor didn't reply, so Darien took it as a yes. How weird had his life become in less than a day? He'd gone from a confirmed atheist to believing in the supernatural and cuddling with a demon. Another gust of wind battered at them, sending a few intrepid leaves up to their level. Darien spotted the crow again; its inky plumage almost hung in the air above them. It cawed, once, then again, before flying away. Darien kept his eyes on it until it disappeared into the distance.

"It's gone."

Alastor rubbed his cheek against Darien's jacket, and he tightened his hold a little. If there was one thing he'd learned being a dom it was the signals vulnerable subs gave when they craved attention and reassurance but didn't feel confident enough to verbalize their needs. A little self-esteem boosting helped in these cases.

"I liked your playing."

Alastor stiffened, tried to pull away. "I'm keeping it."

"It's not mine to give, but we might be able to work something out." Darien held on to him, amazed at himself for even considering purchasing something worth several thousand dollars for someone he'd just met.

The man in his arms gave a derisive snort that felt like a punch to the gut and trembled for a few seconds before the sound of chattering teeth disturbed the peace.

"Come on, let's go inside. You must be freezing," Darien said and let go of the back of Alastor's head. Stopping a masochistic sub from hurting themselves was something he knew back to front. With an arm around the smaller man's shoulder, he led him across the roof to the turret with the stairs.

"From what you said, being warm and eating is 'different' too, and I can guarantee they're far more pleasant."

He paused, his hand on the door to the turret room. "You can eat, right?"

The implications of the mess that would be left if he stopped touching Alastor after he'd eaten didn't bear thinking about. Did demons have digestive systems? Did they need to piss and crap?

Alastor smiled, but it didn't reach his eyes. "I can certainly swallow, even if I didn't manage it last night. But if you're wondering, no, I don't leave a mess when an heir stops touching me, or at least I haven't so far. But I also haven't eaten or drunk much."

Darien waited for him to finish the sentence with 'in the last few years, decades, or even centuries,' but it didn't come. The clear implication was that Alastor had never eaten enough to prompt a bowel or bladder movement in his entire existence.

With no idea how to handle that revelation, Darien ushered Alastor inside as his lips looked a little blue. Cursing himself for being an idiot, Darien took off his jacket, intending to wrap it around the other man, then hesitated.

"Do you need this? Or don't you feel the cold when I'm not touching you?"

Alastor put a hand on Darien's chest and took the jacket with the other hand. "Remember the bruises? I carry on feeling whatever I experienced the last time I touched an heir."

Darien blinked. "So, if I'd left just then, you would've been cold until..."

"The end of time, or when another heir turns up, whichever comes first."

The thought of anyone shivering for hours, let alone decades or centuries when he could help, had Darien resting his hand back on the nape of Alastor's neck.

A small, secretive smile twitched Alastor's lips. Prickles went up Darien's back.

"Did I do something funny?" Expecting Alastor to disappear again, Darien increased his grip on the smaller man's nape.

"Worried about something?" The amusement in Alastor's voice annoyed him, but it was probably meant to.

"Why would a guy who can't touch anything worry me?"

They stepped down into the room beside the Long Gallery. Alastor spun around, his chest pressed up against Darien's.

Mere inches away, Darien's gaze focused on the plump lip caught between Alastor's white teeth.

"But I can touch you. Last night was good, very... modern. But don't you want to know how men fucked four centuries ago? Fast, frantic, and painful for one getting fucked because real men only do the fucking. Those who let themselves be used are less than dirt. Those who got caught faced a public hanging, but only if they didn't have money. You only exposed enough skin to get the job done in case someone saw.

"Stables, cupboards, behind the garden wall in the dead of night, trying not to make a sound....

"I can give you a tour of sodomy through the centuries, but I bet you can show me more things I haven't even dreamed of, can't you, milord?"

Darien tried not to twitch as a hand pressed against his hardening cock. He could feel how cold Alastor remained even through the cloth.

"Teach me more, milord. Give me something good to remember when you abandon me."

Propelling the imp backward, Darien banged the brat against the wood-paneled wall. A gasp left Alastor's mouth. Closing his eyes, he lifted his chin, daring Darien to take what he offered.

Then and there, Darien vowed that Alastor would experience something other than fast, frantic, painful fucking in his life. Last night had been good, but it hadn't been enough by a long shot. He imagined edging this vocal boy until his begging was a genuine plea to come rather than something to end a painful experience.

"Come on. The best way to warm you up safely is a nice warm shower."

"Seriously? I had one last night," Alastor groused. "Can't I just keep the jacket?"

"Downstairs and shower, right now, or I'll ignore you for the rest of my time here."

The jacket fell to the floor as Alastor stomped down the long gallery toward the stairs that led to the bedrooms muttering, "You can try," under his breath.

Darien couldn't help grinning at his brattish behavior, but he thought Alastor was probably right. Ignoring this vibrant man, whatever he turned out to be, wouldn't be happening while he remained here. With every passing second, the need to know more, to experience more of Alastor, snowballed. But he needed to establish their dynamic sooner rather than later. Making and keeping boundaries would help anchor and relax Alastor.

He caught up. Grabbing Alastor's shoulder, he stopped him, caging him against the wall underneath the portrait of the first earl.

"Are you telling me what to do, boy?" he growled against Alastor's temple.

"Wouldn't dream of it, milord," Alastor teased, then he slumped, head falling back onto the wall. "Why does this shit always happen to me?"

"What d'you mean?"

"I really shouldn't tell you this, especially as my boss is keeping an eye on me for some unknown but damn irritating reason, but—"

Darien had had enough of distraction techniques. "Whatever it is, I'm not going to change my mind about you having a shower, and then having a decent meal."

Alastor shrugged. "Have it your own way, but unless you want to gain a reputation that'll make working in public damn difficult, you need to stop touching me. And I can't believe I just said that."

"Just spit it out so we can get to the washing."

That cheeky grin reappeared. "I'd have to have something in my mouth to spit, but as much as I'd love to oblige, a vicar is coming up the stairs."

It felt as if a bucket of freezing water had been poured over him. "What?"

"A vicar, a priest. A man of God? Not keen on demons?"

Darien's protective instincts rose. "Can he hurt you?"

Those plush lips curled up again. "Aw, you're worried about me. I knew you cared. Three, two, one, and—"

His sister's voice and that of an older man had Darien stepping back and removing his hands from Alastor.

"Ah, here he is, our Tudor and Jacobean specialist." Juliana gave him a tight smile as the group of four people around her cast polite, expectant looks his way.

"May I introduce my younger brother, Darien FitzHenry." She turned to her guests. "Darien, this is the Rt. Reverend Wildman." The stick-thin balding man looked the exact opposite of 'wild', although the lack of wrinkles pointed to a man in his late thirties rather than the older man Darien assumed went with the title.

"I can see my spend on the corner of your mouth," Alastor said from beside him. The wicked, teasing tone said the brat fully intended to make the most of this situation.

It took all Darien's focus not to look over at Alastor or check his lip as he went to greet the group.

"This is the Lady Mayoress and her husband, Mr. Bowhill," Juliana introduced. The portly pair nodded to him. "And this is Sir Stuart Brady, the member of parliament for Tandridge."

Alastor stepped out from behind the Lady Mayoress, holding her arm and grinding against her. Ignoring the 'in your face' bratty attention-seeking behavior wasn't easy. With any other sub, Darien would correct the disrespect straight away, but he couldn't in this case. Talking to thin air or grabbing Alastor to make him visible would open an uncloseable can of worms. However, as the priest's polite smile had turned into a frown, he needed to do something. Distraction first, discipline later.

Putting on a bright smile, he shook hands with each local dignitary.

"So, have any of you visited Walpole Hall before?" he asked.

"The priest has," Alastor said. "He came here as a kid. I think I pushed him into his profession by poking him. Look at him, he's still worried about being here."

"No, I haven't," the mayoress said. "I'm thankful for the opportunity, though. I've been driving past this place all my life, and I've always been intrigued about the inside. I appreciate the invitation." Her husband smiled his agreement.

"I haven't been in these parts all my life, but this is certainly very impressive," the MP added, looking at the artwork. As he focused on possibly the crudest painting in the whole collection, Darien decided art wasn't the MP's forte. Although he appeared to have nailed the bullshit part of his profession.

The priest stared up at the painting where Alastor grinned down on them. "I have. It still possesses the same dark aura."

Darien glanced at the priest, then back at Alastor, who grinned, mirroring his painted image. "Tricky not looking at me, isn't it? They'll start thinking you're odd soon, and it's a sharp, slippery slope toward a diagnosis of hallucinations. But yes, I have history with dear stick-up-his-ass Edgar."

"Oh, I don't know," the MP said, "I think any building this old has a lot of gravitas."

"This one more than most," the priest murmured.

"Do you mean the murder? Terrible business," the Mayoress's husband said.

As the four discussed the recent criminal case, Juliana caught his eye. "*Is he here?*" she mouthed.

Darien's gaze flicked to where Alastor stood behind the priest. The imp took a breath, raised his hand, let the breath out slowly, then, using the end of the recorder, poked the back of the reverend's neck.

The scrawny man's arm shot up, rubbing at the spot. The cheeky grin got wider as Alastor sidled across the polished wooden floor, waving his fingers as if he intended to touch Darien.

Having the 'ghost' appear would probably cause enough of an incident to wreck the sale or at least temporarily delay it. Trying not to make it too obvious, Darien stepped back, maintaining the few feet of distance between them.

"Wanna dance for your guests, milord? As you're already going backward, I guess you're the girl."

"Darien, I'm afraid there's some paperwork for you to fill out in the kitchen, and would you mind putting the coffee on?" Juliana said, giving him the excuse he needed.

Alastor might continue to torment the visitors, but Darien bet that the imp would rather interact with someone who could see and hear him.

He smiled at the dignitaries. "Sorry, but duty calls. Juliana will be able to answer your questions, but if not, I'm sure she can pass them on to me." After giving them a nod, he made his way down the Long Gallery, toward the staircase leading down to the next floor. With every step, his spine prickled with the need to turn and see if Alastor had followed or if he'd decided to continue tormenting the visitors.

Once he rounded the corner, out of sight, he checked over his shoulder. No Alastor. The little shit was storing up punishments faster than any sub he'd ever met, but Alastor was so different from anyone else. Darien didn't doubt that the imp craved contact, someone who could take him out of his mind and control his self-destructive impulses.

Was this how Alastor had gradually driven other heirs to madness or reckless acts that caused their deaths? The techniques would be effective on many people—especially if they couldn't abandon the family property—but he bet Alastor had never come up against an experienced dom either.

His choice was running or taking up the ultimate challenge. A smile twitched his lips. There was no contest about which route he'd take. Right now, despite Alastor's supernatural origins, Darien held all the cards. Alastor needed him, but he didn't need the imp. History would reveal if he'd break like one of his distant cousins or if Alastor would become a contented soul, at least for a while.

CHAPTER TEN

The heir leaving spoiled the fun. Alastor had been looking forward to a rematch with Edgar Wildman ever since Edgar senior had tried to exorcise him. Having an heir witness him tormenting such an upstanding, bigoted, know-it-all would have been the icing on the cake.

The reverend had been a wonderfully sensitive child, dragged along by his equally holy father to an initial meeting about the poltergeist that haunted the Hall. He'd somehow sensed Alastor even though he'd been ten. Children up to three or four could see and hear him. They lost the ability to see him by five or six, and by seven, they couldn't sense him at all.

The owner back then had three children around Edgar's age, all of whom refused to use their allocated bedrooms, thanks to Alastor.

Since moving in, Mr. and Mrs. Fisher had been unable to have any 'grown-up time' as they explained to Rev Wildman senior. Alastor called it fucking, but it'd been 'bedsport' back in the day.

Their three daughters, one by one, came galloping into their parents' room in tears throughout the night, every night. Alastor moved curtains, slammed doors, made floorboards creak, and shifted pens, coins, toys, and book pages until the girls were gibbering wrecks. They began insisting on staying within sight of their parents at all times, even though they were nine, eleven, and thirteen. Sleep deprivation was one of his favorite tactics, and it'd worked like a dream on the Fishers.

The family lasted less than a year before putting the property back on the market. He counted it a job well done as nobody had died or even ended up in a hospital.

To Alastor's joy, it appeared that Edgar had retained his childhood sensitivity as he twitched every time Alastor spoke or tried to touch him. The other visitors were oblivious, all except Juliana, who gave the thin air where Alastor had been standing the evil eye.

Yes, this was fun, but Edgar could be around for decades. Darien FitzHenry would be gone in days unless Alastor did something drastic.

He popped to where the few artifacts he could actually touch lay and sat up. The objects around him were so familiar, so safe. The pair of ugly lattice-work vases, the framed sketches of various body parts of a muscular naked male, the strongbox he'd never been able to open, and the few books and pamphlets he'd managed to steal.

The empty place where his own recorder had once sat, the one the last Earl smashed, still drew his eye. The fucker had died too fast. With a smile, he placed the new instrument on the shelf. Life would be a little easier now that he could play again.

Every word on every page of his few books was familiar, now that he could read anyway. He'd learned alongside generations of Walpole children, peering over their shoulders as they were instructed by tutors. The books he'd stolen ranged from Chaucer to a bee-keeping treatise, Latin poetry, and several quarto editions of Shakespeare's plays. The cheap pamphlets had crumbled to the extent that Alastor feared touching them, especially the one signed by the bard himself. He missed reading something new so fucking much, but not as much as he'd missed playing an instrument.

But a recorder wasn't the main thing this heir had brought him. Care. Consideration. It was as if the heir had chosen to mess with his head instead of the other way around, but he was the demon here, not FitzHenry. Letting an heir begin to think he'd gone for good before popping up again was a technique he'd used many times, but there was no time for subtlety now.

With a thought, he relocated down to the kitchen. Darien stood by the counter, watching the stream of steam from the kettle on the stove intensify.

"I'm sorry," Alastor said, trying for big-eyed contrition.

The heir didn't twitch. He just turned around, regarding Alastor with an unsettling bland expression.

"You're sorry for what?"

Alastor hadn't thought further than ingratiating himself. His mind whirled, grasping for a reason. "For scaring you up on the roof?"

Darien folded his arms. "That's one. What else?"

Alastor pursed his lips, examining his naked toes for inspiration. He looked up through his hair, an adorable expression that often warmed the heart of heirs before he screwed with their minds. "Irritating the vicar?"

"That's two. What else?"

"Pissing off your sister?"

"That's three, but you're missing a few. I'm being generous and forgetting the punishments you earned yesterday."

Alastor wracked his memory, but he couldn't think of anything else.

Darien raised a hand and started counting on his fingers. "Four, you didn't apologize to Juliana when I told you to. Five, you left the room without permission. Six, you called me a name you intended to be offensive. Seven, you stole something that doesn't belong to you. Trust, Alastor, this doesn't work without trust, respect, and being accountable for your actions."

Alastor stiffened. "Sounds damn catholic to me. What do you want? Me to confess all my sins to get absolution? You'd better be planning on staying for a few years then. Don't you get it? I'm an imp. I can't help irritating people just as you can't help being..." he waved a hand, indicating Darien's nonchalant stance.

"Being what?"

He knew the heir was baiting, irritating him like Alastor badgered others. But he had a trick to get away from Darien that the heir didn't possess.

"If you disappear again, I'll go back to the hotel tonight."

Alastor's gaze shot to Darien's face. "You wouldn't."

The kettle whistled, and Darien turned back to the stove. "I most certainly would. And I've found the perfect punishment for you. I will spend an hour off the estate for every error you make. So far, you've racked up eight hours."

The situation was slipping through his fingers like water. "You promised to sleep with me," Alastor blurted.

"I promised I would if I'm here—" Darien pointed at the floor, "—and that'll only happen if you behave yourself. But it's only one in the afternoon. There's plenty of time to rack up more hours of alone time."

Biting his lip, Alastor pondered. *Could I cope with him only being here at night, knowing he could be here all day too if I behave?*

Can I behave? He'd never tried to curb his impish nature before.

His mouth opened to voice a promise he didn't think he could keep, then shut it again.

"I'll try."

A smile spread across Darien's face. "Right answer. Trying is all I ever expect from my subs."

"What's that?"

Darien pressed his lips together. "This conversation could take some time. Are you hungry?" When Alastor didn't reply immediately, Darien's eyes narrowed.

"Can you eat? Do you need to?"

No other heir had ever asked these questions. *Is it the historian in Darien that makes him so nosey, or does he actually care?*

A hand touched his shoulder, and the chill of the floor permeated the soles of his feet.

"Truth, Alastor, always the truth with me. Lies will only get you another hour alone."

"I can eat if I'm touching an heir; it's happened every now and again."

Darien's brows drew together for a heartbeat before he returned to his previous interested expression. "Did you like it?"

"Loved it. Last time was a bit of an apple." He closed his eyes at the memory of the tart, sweet, juicy flesh in his mouth.

"That good?" Darien said, amusement clear.

Alastor huffed, embarrassed at his lapse. "Better than whatever that was last night. What did you call it? A sixty-nine?"

"That was just a fraction of what I can make you feel, but you really seemed to need it. I remember some pretty convincing begging. Question is, do you need food as well as physical touch?"

Alastor scowled at the irritating, perceptive heir. "I don't need to be touched. I've been doing—"

"That's another hour for lying."

"You are the most irritating, impossible heir I've ever—"

Darien inclined his head. "Thank you. Now, answer the question. Do you need to eat?"

"I like it, I'm constantly thirsty, but I've been doing fine without it. Imps feed on the irritation they cause; it's like..."

he paused, trying to think of a way to describe it. "It's like after I get off. Gives a warm glow, a relaxed, satisfied feeling."

"Do heirs taste better than other people?"

Alastor grinned. "Hell, yeah."

"If irritating an heir gives you a buzz, what does pleasing one do?"

Alastor blinked; he'd never thought about that before. He only ever irritated and infuriated Walpoles unless he was enticing one to do something that would later cause bone-deep guilt and self-loathing, like sleeping with him.

Darien interrupted his thoughts. "I guess we'll have to explore that one. Now, how about a croissant and a coffee? Juliana brought some pastries over from the hotel; They're keeping warm in the oven." Darien nodded toward the smaller oven in the massive stove as he moved the kettle to a metal trivet on the wooden worktop.

When Alastor didn't move, he glanced over. "Well, go on then, get them out. I'm not your servant. Heir, remember?"

Alastor held up his hands. "No touchy things without an heir, remember?"

"You held the recorder."

"I thought I explained that last night. I can touch it because it was made before the curse."

Darien snorted. "Nearly fifteen years of studying, and you can tell a Tudor fake quicker and more accurately than I can. I'd appreciate it if you checked the other lots later, but for now, come over here next to me. You can get the croissants out and put butter or jelly on yours if you like." Darien indicated a small collection of golden foil packages and a handful of plastic-covered portions of jam. "I'll pour the coffee. How do you like it?"

Alastor hesitated, never having had the stuff before, although he occasionally smelt it. The pressure of Darien's focus made him think about the sanctuary of the roof again.

This was Darien's world, a world that didn't have a place for him. But he could experience it for a while if he played this heir's game.

"Can I try it the way Juliana has it?"

Darien turned, hiding his expression, and got two mugs down from a cupboard. "Sugar and milk coming up. Well, come on, plates are there, knives in there." Darien indicated the cupboard nearest the stove and the drawer right where he'd said Alastor could stand.

He'd watched food being prepared through the ages, but he'd never dreamed he'd actually do it himself. Taking a breath, he stepped up beside Darien. Without fuss or comment, the heir put a hand on his back.

"Use the oven glove; the tray might be a bit hot."

Even though the touch on his back, the delicious, buttery smell, and the feel of the flagstones under his feet confirmed he'd become corporeal again, Alastor hesitated to reach for the modern padded black mittens hanging on the hook beside the stove. If Darien moved his hand, everything would crash to the ground, and the food would be spoiled.

The hand rubbed up and down his back. The slight soreness reminded him of the bruises that were already feeling better, thanks to Darien. Another night like last night and the physical reminders of the last earl would continue to fade. Although with each touch, each kind word, this heir was also leaving marks, just not physical ones.

"Problem?"

Swallowing, he gave Darien a grin. "No, no, problem," he said and grabbed the gloves.

"That's another hour. No lying, remember?"

Without answering, Alastor leaned down, opened the oven door, and pulled the warm black metal tray out. He probably could have used his bare hand; the oven was only warm. The rich buttery scent of the odd-looking pastries made his mouth water.

With one movement, Darien could steal all this from him. If their roles were reversed, Alastor would wait for Darien to take a bite, enjoy the taste, then, as he was about to take another bite, he'd remove his hand. He'd leave him with the taste, the memory of how it felt in his mouth, and tease him with it for hours, days, years.

But he knew the heir would never do that because Darien FitzHenry was a good man. He was nothing like the Walpoles, nothing like Alastor.

After putting the tray on the top of the stove, Alastor reached for the plates, hating that Darien had the power to give and take everything from him. Maybe he should just avoid this whole thing and—

"I'm not in the habit of being ignored by subs. Why does this make you uncomfortable?"

Lips pursed together, Alastor opened the drawer and looked at the shiny, stainless-steel cutlery. They were nothing like the cutlery that had been here when he'd arrived. Everyone back then carried their own pricker, spoon, and knife. People didn't even use single-pronged prickers anymore; they used three-prong forks.

"Alastor, you will talk to me, or I'll add more marks to your tally." Darien's calm, collected voice irritated him even more.

"I might as well keep ratcheting them up then, hadn't I? Because all this—" he waved vaguely at the stuff on the counter in front of them "—is going to end soon enough, and I'll be back to being...." He trailed off as the enormity hit him.

With a sigh, Darien pulled him into a hug. Breathing in the scent of him, Alastor let the stress leak out for a few breaths. He'd done the same up on the roof before reality stuck its stinking nose back in. He pulled away, wondering what it was about the woody scent of Darien's skin that caused the urge to be wrapped in the safety of his arms as often as possible.

Angry at himself, he turned back to the counter, jerked open the drawer, and grabbed a knife. Pain flared. Snatching his hand back, Alastor stuck his bleeding finger in his mouth.

Darien's hand wrapped around his wrist. "Let me see."

Trying to step away didn't work; Darien kept a firm grip on him.

"Look at me."

The firm words dragged Alastor's gaze to that of the heir.

"Let. Me. See. This is not a request."

Tension leached out of Alastor, and Darien pulled his finger from his mouth. Crimson drops beaded and dripped down his pale finger. Alastor watched, fascinated by the visual display of life.

"Hmm. I don't think it needs a stitch. A Band-Aid would help, though."

"It'll be fine. I don't need—"

"Band-Aids, now. Or I'll call the Grimshaws and ask. Do you really want them to see you?"

Alastor glared at him. "You're an arsehole, you know that, right?"

"And that's another mark. Now, where are the Band-Aids?"

Alastor let out a grunt of frustration. This wasn't how his interactions with heirs should go.

"If you mean plasters, they're in the First Aid box in the cupboard next to the sink."

Alastor spun, losing contact with Darien at Harry Grimshaw's deep, gravelly voice coming from behind them.

Darien glanced between Harry and Alastor. He tensed—eyes wide for a second—before the veil of control slipped over him again.

"Good morning, Mr. Grimshaw. Can I help you with anything?"

The older man snorted. "Got to give it to you, FitzHenry. You're pretty cool under pressure. He really does look like the portrait upstairs, doesn't he?"

Alastor shared a glance with the heir.

"He's still here, then? Why don't you get me a coffee, and we'll have a little chat, Mr. FitzHenry, and you too, Mr. Thatcher, if you care to reveal yourself again."

Darien's eyebrows rose in question. Alastor shrugged, then nodded. This might be the only time he'd ever get to speak with the man he'd seen grow from a mischievous little boy to late middle age.

Darien poured three cups of coffee and placed one on the other side of the table. Then he retrieved the First Aid box.

"That won't do any good," Alastor said. "As soon as you stop touching me, it'll fall off." He plucked at his threadbare smock. "It's why I still wear this."

Darien frowned. "Humor me," he said and sat down before pulling out the chair beside him.

Alastor stayed standing. This all looked a little too cozy, too domestic. Plus, if Darien got his hands on him again, he'd be unable to relocate if it got too much.

"You might as well sit down, young Nicholas. I've already seen you, and don't you think you owe me some answers about my boy?"

The knowing, accusing gaze of the closest person to family Alastor possessed had him relocating to the roof. He took a deep breath of air that would be cold if Darien was touching him. He couldn't even feel it entering his lungs. No scents, no taste, no sensations at all except his throbbing finger and the aches from the bruises. The pain was far less than his battered face, back, and ass, but it would still haunt him for all time unless he touched Darien long enough for it to heal.

"Fuck it," he mumbled under his breath and returned to the kitchen.

Darien didn't look surprised to see him. "That was a little rude, but I'll forgive you as you came back."

"I don't bite, Nicholas," Harry said, "and I probably couldn't catch you anyway. But I'd like to know what happened to

Liam. I don't buy the story Anderson told, and you were there, weren't you?"

Feeling a little like he was going to his own execution, Alastor sat down, keeping his eyes on the table. Darien's hand landed on his partially covered thigh.

"Let me look at your hand while you talk to Harry."

He put his hand on the table, took a deep breath, and looked up into Harry's grey eyes. He didn't see an ounce of sympathy.

"I'm truly sorry about Liam. I didn't, I really didn't, mean for that to happen."

Harry's lips pursed then he took a sip of his coffee. "So, you were involved?"

Looking at Darien wrapping a little bit of dark pink sticky fabric around his finger was easier than looking at the father of the innocent he'd destroyed.

Lips pressed together, Alastor nodded.

"Go on, tell him the details. The man deserves an explanation."

Another decade or two of solitude would be easier than this. Harry would be dead in twenty, perhaps thirty years. All he had to do was stay out of his way until—

"Now, or I'm going back to the airport right now." Amber eyes promised that Darien would do exactly what he so calmly threatened.

"I pushed them—not physically, I can't do that—but mentally. All three of them." Deciding he might as well try it while he could, he picked up the chunky rustic pottery mug of coffee and took a sip. He closed his eyes in bliss at the heat spreading down through his chest.

He opened his eyes as the chair opposite his creaked. Harry leaned on the table, jaw tight.

"You goaded Anderson into murdering his wife and almost killing my boy?"

Alastor wrinkled his nose. "Well, I did, and I didn't."

Harry lunged at him, but before the gnarled hand connected with the front of his shirt, Darien snapped, "Grimshaw." Harry froze. "Let him speak, Mr. Grimshaw. He came back of his own free will, and he doesn't have to be here. Right now, he's letting me touch him so you can see him. He could pull away at any time, and then you might never know what happened. He did try to warn you, right?"

Harry sat back down.

"I wanted..." Alastor swallowed. "I wanted you Grimshaws to own the Hall. I thought if they divorced, she might get the house, and then if she married Liam...." He trailed off. It was only partially a lie. "I had no idea Carl was that violent. Neither did Liam, but he really goaded Carl that day. He said he couldn't keep Melody happy in the bedroom. There was only one punch, but Liam hit his head. Anderson pushed him into the water and used the pool net to push him down." Alastor met Harry's eyes. "You and your family are the only real family I've ever had. I never would've—"

"But you did. You used Liam, and you've caused the deaths of how many others?" Harry shook his head. "No. Sorry doesn't cut it. Whether by design or accident, you're a curse on this place and every soul who sets foot in it."

"Mr. Grimshaw, I can't begin to understand the pain you're going through, but he's as much a victim as your son. He's been trapped here for over four centuries, watching life go by and unable to interact with anyone except Walpole heirs."

The chair ground on the flagstones as Harry Grimshaw stood up. He looked pointedly at Darien. "Well then, maybe someone should put him out of his misery before he causes more pain and sufferin' including his own. Thanks for the coffee." He turned to Alastor. "And don't be coming down to the cottage anymore. You're not welcome. I've had a witch put a protection spell on the place."

He walked out the door, and the pair heard the old Land Rover Defender rumble to life and drive away.

The Grimshaws were lost to him, and soon Darien would be too. An unending future of isolation with an inability to experience even the simplest pleasures in life stretched. His hidden possessions, shirt, and even the house would all eventually disintegrate. And he'd have to watch it happen, one endless day at a time.

Darien squeezed his thigh. "I won't let him hurt you."

Alastor let out a snort of mirthless amusement. "If I thought he could kill me, I'd poke him every minute of every day and night until he did it."

"Well, well, genuine guilt and regret. You'd be delicious right now if you weren't an imp."

His gaze shot to the other side of the kitchen, where Arioch stood in their full busty female form. "I think we need a little chat, don't you?"

CHAPTER ELEVEN

Alastor's gaze shot to the corner of the kitchen, and his face lost what little color it had. The imp murmured, "Oh, shite," then winked out of existence, even though Darien's hand had been on his thigh.

Somehow, Darien knew, just knew, Alastor hadn't left of his own accord. The only thing left was the ring of Band-Aid with a red drop at the center. He picked it up, if only to prove to himself that Alastor existed. Spirits didn't bleed, which meant whatever Alastor was, he was alive, at least in some way, and he needed Darien's help. In order to help him, Darien needed to find him.

He jogged outside to check the parapet. No Alastor. On the off-chance he'd returned to torment the vicar, Juliana, and the others, he went to find them.

His sister sent him a questioning look as he found the group in the library.

"Is everything alright?"

He realized just how odd he looked, having come barreling into the room. "Yes, I erm... was just—" He thanked the Lord when a phone rang, taking the focus away from him.

The reverend murmured his apologies and moved outside of the room. The others turned back to the books. Darien noted that although there were some late Jacobean volumes, not a single Elizabethan tome remained on the shelves. Given what he now knew about Alastor's ability to touch things made prior to 1600, he had a good idea that wherever Alastor had stashed the stolen recorder, there could be a small hoard of Tudor books and other artifacts.

The door opened, and the reverend returned, his expression somber. "I'm sorry, but I need to cut my tour short. I'm afraid one of my parishioners has suffered a bereavement."

"Of course, of course," the mayoress said. "May I ask whom?"

The reverend gave her a cold smile. "I'm afraid I cannot say without the family's permission. If you'll excuse me."

The Lady Mayoress reddened. "Yes, yes, of course."

Darien wished Alastor had tormented the man a little more. Reverend Wildman had enjoyed putting down the nice lady a little too much for Darien's liking.

"If you don't mind, Darien, Mr. Bowhill had a question about one of the paintings," Juliana said, trying to get the tour back on track.

Darien hoped his smile was a hell of a lot warmer than the reverend's as he led the party back out to the Long Gallery.

"Can you tell me why most of the people in the earlier paintings look so similar?" The portly husband of the mayoress asked.

It was the exact same question that had plagued Darien as a teen. Fortunately, he now had an answer. "Apart from the fact that many of these portraits depict people from the same family, many were painted in the renaissance and baroque periods. Which meant they were still highly influenced by the prevailing attitudes of Elizabeth the First. She had a stylized image and even sent out 'face patterns' to artists to ensure all her images were similar. And, of course, being much admired even after her death, the aristocracy of the time wanted to be—"

"Oh, sweet Lord, no," Juliana's pain-filled voice drew them to the towering many paned windows.

The reverend's car had stopped outside the Grimshaws' cottage.

"Oh my, those poor people," the Mayoress added.

Silence reigned for a minute before Mr. Brady spoke up. "Under the circumstances, I think it's best if we cut the tour short."

"Yes, yes, of course," Juliana said. "I'll also call the people who were meant to view later this afternoon. I don't suppose the Grimshaws will want reminders of the people who will ultimately benefit from...." She gave her three remaining guests a tight smile. "If you'll follow me, I'll show you out."

Darien remained where he was, staring out the windows as the others left. As he watched, a figure who could only be Harry Grimshaw exited the red brick house in the distance. The figure paused, facing the Hall. Darien had to resist the impulse to step back even though Harry couldn't possibly see him standing here. As far as Harry was concerned, the Hall, and Alastor in particular, had stolen his son from him.

The torment in this place needed to stop, but unlike Harry Grimshaw, Darien didn't blame Alastor. Even though he claimed to be a demon, the red-haired, confused, lonely lad had suffered more than his victims. Because, unlike them, Alastor couldn't escape his torment, even in death.

As he thought, he found himself in front of the Henry VII portrait. It still looked genuine, but maybe it hadn't been painted when Henry VII, his son, or even his granddaughter had been alive. If it dated from just after Alastor had been imprisoned here, it took a century off its estimated age. A century. A period of time that could see three or four generations, and Alastor had stood by and watched over four of them without being able to live his own life.

It was more than time that his sentence was ended. As members of the clergy had failed to exorcise Alastor, Darien decided to go back to the beginning, to the source of the curse, the vengeful spell of a witch. From what Harry had said, there were still witches for hire in this part of the world. It was an odd concept to get his head around, but then again, he'd spent the night enjoying the body of a minor demon.

Returning to his room, he climbed on the bed with his laptop and started googling. Ten minutes had him regretting his actions. The internet heaved with crap and charlatans.

A tap on the door preceded Juliana entering, her face tight and eyes glassy. "Is he here?" she asked, looking around as if she could somehow see the imp.

"No, he disappeared just after Harry left. But I don't think it was Alastor's choice. They were talking, he and Harry. Alastor admitted his part in Anderson's attack, and Harry threatened him. Something about putting him out of his misery. Did you find out if it was Liam who passed?"

Juliana nodded and perched on the side of the bed. "The police phoned, said it was probably a good idea if we delay the auction and that to keep the doors and windows locked. The officer said this place could become a target." Her lips pressed into a narrow line. "And us too because we work for Anderson. I don't think you should stay here tonight."

Darien snorted. "No way am I leaving if this place is under threat. We're responsible for the lots, and this is history, Jules, our history."

"It's a pile of brick and wood. It's not worth your life." She took a breath as if bracing herself for an argument. "You see him as a victim, but you forget that he's caused the deaths of dozens of our ancestors as well as many others. What makes you think you'll be any different from the rest of the Walpoles, Liam Grimshaw, or Melody Anderson?"

Darien shook his head. "He wouldn't hurt me; he needs me."

Juliana banged her fist down on the bed, making him twitch. "Would you listen to yourself? How many others have said exactly the same thing only to end up in early graves? He's a demon—a creature from Hell—he even admits it. Even if the historical rumors are just that, we *know* two people are dead because of him, and another's life has been destroyed. That's three families that will never be the same again. Don't make ours his fourth within two years."

Juliana's anguish and point were valid, but he still didn't agree. "I know you don't believe me, but he's as much a victim as all the others. If I can find a way to stop this, to set him free, wouldn't that be better?"

Harry's suggestion to put Alastor out of his misery came back. An heir could certainly hurt Alastor; the marks on his back and neck proved that.

There has to be another way.

Juliana regarded him with sadness. "You've made up your mind, haven't you, you stubborn bastard? Just tell me how you intend to free a demon from a curse? It's not like throwing money at a lawyer or a bail bond agent to spring someone from prison."

Her eyes narrowed, and a manicured finger jabbed in his direction. "No, don't even think about it. No deals with the Devil. You are not—"

"I thought you didn't believe in the Devil?"

She slumped then flopped back on the bed. "Shit, Darien, when did life get so damn surreal? Demons, hauntings, murders? I feel like someone slipped something into my coffee on the airplane."

"Me too, sis, me too. But I have to do something."

She turned onto her side. "Any idea what that something is?"

He turned his laptop toward her.

"The Circle of the Twilight Coven? Witches, are you for real?" She groaned. "Silly me. Why shouldn't witches be real too?"

"It's a lot," he agreed. "But I'll be safe, promise. Go back to the hotel. I'll make some calls, see what I can find out." At her scowl, he added, "And I'll keep you up to date. I promise."

"We could just go home. This isn't our problem. It's not even our country or continent." She stared at him for a few more moments. "But you've fallen for him, haven't you?"

"Not yet."

She snorted, sitting up again. "What do they say over here, complete and utter bollocks? I know you." She patted his thigh and stood up. "I also know when to pull out the big guns. Unless you stay with me at the hotel tonight, I'm calling mom."

He stared back into her determined dark eyes. "You really are a bitch, you know that, right?"

She gave him the cheeky smile he'd known in their youth. "Better a bitch with a living brother than a push-over only child. Come on, grab your stuff. You can google Sabrina at the hotel."

All the way out to the car, he kept glancing around, hoping to catch sight of Alastor. Not looking out the back window of Juliana's hire car as they drove down the mile-long straight drive almost took his last ounce of determination.

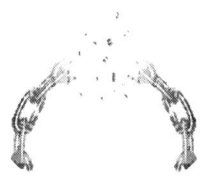

What Juliana failed to mention was that she'd arranged to have dinner with the prospective bidders who'd been due to tour the Hall that afternoon. At least the hotel was interesting, having been built in the mid-1700s as a coaching inn.

Schmoozing was the last thing he wanted to do, and the atmosphere in the bar/restaurant was subdued as it was one that Liam had apparently frequented.

He smiled, made small talk with the trio of Japanese men, and did no more than sip at a single glass of red wine for the entire meal. After dessert, the group moved to the bar area. Darien groaned inside as the little party showed no signs of winding down.

The urge to be back at the Hall in case Alastor came back from wherever he'd gone and thought himself abandoned ate at him.

If Alastor came back.

The specter of his boss, Arioch, hovered just over Darien's shoulder.

What could a demon lord do to a disappointing imp?

"I've arranged a tasting of locally made drinks," Juliana announced as the landlady brought over a tray containing five sets of shot glasses, each filled with a different vibrant colored liquid.

"Sloe gin, mead liqueur, damson vodka, gunpowder gin, and botanical gin," the wrinkled woman said. Darien eyed the beverages with trepidation, particularly the bright blue 'gunpowder gin'. He'd intended to borrow Juliana's hire car and head back to the Hall after his sister went to bed.

The landlady added, "We'll be raising a glass to a local lad who died today in the next few minutes. We hope you'll join us."

He might have been able to refuse his sister, but not drinking to Alastor's accidental victim would only create further bad feelings.

The woman returned to behind the bar and chimed the brass 'last orders' bell. The pub fell silent.

"To Liam," she announced, "may the Lord keep his soul."

Her words were echoed around the bar. Darien picked up the first shot glass full of reddish liquid and downed it, not letting it touch the sides. Gin had never been his drink of choice.

"To Harry and Lorraine," another voice called. Another drink went down. Toasts to Liam's friends and Melody Anderson followed.

The shot of blue gin remained, and Darien hoped that he wouldn't have to down it too. Juliana appeared unaffected by the alcohol, but she'd always had a far greater tolerance for it than him.

"And lastly—" a new voice, one with a midwestern twang, said, "—a drink to the curse of Walpole Hall never taking another soul."

A few murmurs of "Fat chance" and "You wouldn't get me going anywhere near that cursed place," rumbled around the bar.

Darien looked over at the voice from home. The forty-something busty woman had neat, chin-length blonde hair and wore black jeans, but it was her rollneck, blood-red sweater that took his focus.

He smiled at his dining companions as he got to his feet. "It's been lovely to meet you, but I have a little paperwork to do. I hope to see you at the sale next week."

Juliana gave him a quizzical look, but explaining he was either about to make a fool of himself with a stranger unconnected to any of this or confront a demon lord probably wouldn't lead to a quiet exit.

The woman waited at the bar, holding a glass of red wine. The blue-haired teenage boy sitting on the next stool got up and left as Darien approached.

"Darien," she greeted with a slight smile. "You've gotten yourself mixed up in a tricky situation, haven't you?"

His heart rate sped up, but he kept his stance and expression neutral. Showing fear would do him no favors with a being who fed on distress.

"Arioch, I presume?"

She chuckled. "Oh my, no, I'm not Arioch. I'm just as human as you," her eyes narrowed a little, "Well, nearly anyway." She proffered her hand, but he didn't take it.

Withdrawing it, she said, "Hmm, bright boy. My name is Shanae, and I'm a witch."

"How and why did you find me? Because you are here for me, correct?"

"I should tell you that I saw you in a crystal ball or scried for you with an enchanted crystal, but..." she smiled. "The witch council has an app that logs certain google searches."

He had to smile at the mundane answer. Life had certainly taken an odd turn since he came to England. "What gave me away?"

"Your interest in my family. I happen to be related to Nicholas Thatcher in the same way you are related to the Walpoles, but through the female line, obviously. Nicholas's mother was the daughter of my direct ancestor. After her sister and nephew were murdered by the Walpoles, Alice Flowers did the same thing as Henry Walpole. She got on a ship for the New World." She took a sip of her wine.

"We were unaware of what has been going on at Walpole Hall, and I bitterly regret that. I think that after four centuries, the Walpole family, the people who live and work at the Hall, and of course Nicholas Thatcher, have suffered enough, don't you?"

A man bumped his arm as he moved up to order a drink. Discussing centuries-old curses among recently bereaved, superstitious locals didn't seem like a bright idea, not for him and certainly not for a self-proclaimed witch. Their accents stuck out like a beacon in this place.

"Would you mind if we took this discussion somewhere a little more private? I have a room upstairs," Darien said.

A smile tickled her ruby red lips. "Aren't you worried people will talk about you ushering a woman old enough to be your mother to your room only minutes after meeting her?"

He held her gaze. "Are you worried about people thinking you pick up men young enough to be your son?"

She raised her glass, a smile hovering on her lips. "Touché."

Within minutes, they were standing in his cramped room. The black wooden floor tilted a little, and there was only space for a double bed, a wardrobe, and a chest of drawers that looked as if they'd been here since the 1940s.

Shanae looked around. "How perfectly... horrible." She turned to him with a smile.

Darien blinked at the empty bedroom; he must have dozed off after the fraud left. He remembered coming into the room with a woman and her offering a 'happiness spell' for a hundred pounds.

So much for witches.

His fuzzy head told him that trying to go back to the Hall in this state would be a mistake, even if he could find a late-night taxi in the village to take him.

Knowing Juliana would want to know what was going on, he texted her.

Woman was a wannabe witch, tried to sell me a happiness potion. Going to sleep.

A reply sounded a few seconds later.

Still can't hold your liquor, baby brother? I'm sorry that you didn't get an answer.

With exhaustion dragging at him, he managed to use the tiny bathroom, stripped to his boxers, and fell back into bed.

Sleep should have claimed him immediately. Juliana had hit the nail on the head with her comment about his capacity for alcohol. All it did was send him into a restless sleep.

Instead of blackness and the faint noises of the bar beneath him, all he saw in his mind's eye was Alastor, naked.

He'd never met anyone so filthy and needy and yet so sad, defensive, and full of bluster, snark, and life. It was an ironic combination considering Alastor hovered on the cusp between life and death, without any way apart from Darien to tip him into life.

Alastor was a supernatural being, yet Darien had the power to make his every wish come true. Those sea-green eyes begged, that full mouth pouted. Imagining that mouth around him, those eyes looking up through floppy auburn hair had his cock hardening.

His hand slid down under the waistband of his boxers and wrapped around the base of his erection. A demon, a damn demon. He shouldn't be turned on by the idea of pinning the imp down and fucking him into gasping oblivion.

Darien had done a lot of things most people would consider kinky, but this beat them all. The power of having a creature from hell begging him, pleading...

Giving in, Darien gave himself a long, twisting stroke from root to tip, squeezing his foreskin back over the sensitive head before letting it withdraw again.

Swiping his thumb over the head, he basked in the shiver it caused as precum beaded. He did it again, imagining Alastor's tongue instead of his own thumb.

Already, his balls felt tense as he continued to stroke. That soft, needy voice came back to him.

I need you, milord.

Alastor had meant the title in every way possible. Yes, he was a brat, but Darien was his lord, his master. With a few quick movements, he slipped his boxers over his legs and tossed them away. Spreading his thighs, he rolled his balls with his fingers, imagining Alastor riding him.

Slim, pale body, auburn hair falling to cover his eyes as he bounced on top of him. He'd beg, exclaim at such a fantastic dick, put his hands on Darien's chest to steady himself as he ground down, circling his hips to find just the right spot. He'd throw his head back and cry out when he found it. Darien's hand got faster. He squeezed his balls, imagining Alastor leaning back, undulating, sweat glistening on that alabaster skin as he took his pleasure.

With his heels digging into the mattress, Darien snapped his hips up, blood thrumming in his ears. Once, twice, imagining Alastor crying out as he was pinned beneath him, unable to do anything but take what Darien gave him. That small, tight white ass would be stuck in the air, his back bowed as his chest pressed into the mattress.

Please, please give it to me, milord, I need it, please.

Darien came with a stifled groan, hot cum splashing his chest. He imagined it was Alastor's as the imp cried out in pleasure as Darien filled him. His legs trembled, and he stretched them out, knowing he should go clean up before he stained the sheets. Instead, he lay there, his cum turning cold and sticky as he worried about where the boy with the devilish smile and filthy mouth was now.

CHAPTER TWELVE

"Guilt, Alastor? Genuine remorse? It's tasty but disappointing. Rather like a collapsed soufflé," Arioch said from beside him as they stood in the hospital room, looking down at Liam's still body and the disconnected machines.

Alastor hardly noticed that the vengeance demon had chosen a human female form. Whatever shape the demon chose, it intimidated him, but his focus wasn't on Arioch.

The puffy, bluish face didn't look anything like the tanned, vibrant youngster Alastor had watched grow from a babe in arms to a strapping, sexy, confident young man.

Liam wasn't the first person Alastor had seen born and die due to his antics. But Liam... Liam shouldn't have died. He should be cheerfully fucking his way through the local population until he found his life partner. Then, like every other Grimshaw, he would move his parents out of the gatehouse cottage, move in himself, and produce numerous brats for Alastor to watch and interact with until they became too old to see him.

Liam's parents stood beside the bed, crying into each other's arms. Liam didn't look asleep despite the medical team's efforts to tidy the body, that specific something, that spark, had vanished.

Alastor desperately didn't want to be here, despite it being the only place outside the Estate—apart from Arioch's office—he'd ever seen.

Being held against Darien's chest, feeling safe, appreciated, was what he wanted. He didn't deserve it and shouldn't get it. Echoes of a future that mimicked this scene and all the other permanent goodbyes he'd caused clawed at him. Imps should be about pranks, irritation, sarcasm, and dumbfounding people, not causing soul-deep heartache.

"How about we take this somewhere a little warmer?"

A thrill of fear shot through Alastor as he waited for a count of two before he found himself in Arioch's office.

In a scarlet, shimmering dress, the vengeance demon lounged in the tan, skin-covered chair, a smoking cigar in a beautifully manicured hand. As always, the walls of the small, windowless room glowed with heat. Faint screams and moans of pain and anguish provided background noise.

Dragging what pitiful courage he had up from his burning feet, Alastor stood in front of the imposing desk, looked Arioch right in the eye, and spoke.

"I'm not doing it anymore."

He braced himself, expecting a roar and instant agony. Instead, the demon's eyes narrowed as they removed the cigar from red-stained lips, a scarlet painted pinkie finger stuck up.

"Not going to do what, little imp?"

"Cause deaths. Liam didn't deserve to die."

"And the many Walpoles you've put in the ground did?" Arioch closed their eyes, drawing in a deep breath. "Ah, there it is again, guilt, remorse."

Not knowing what else to do, Alastor just stood there. There wasn't a door, and even if there was, he didn't want to experience where those noises of suffering originated.

Arioch's eyes snapped open. "Do you remember what happens to disobedient demons?"

Alastor swallowed, eyeing the pliant tan leather that hugged the vengeance demon's currently pert backside. *How much would it hurt to be skinned alive?* He bet Arioch could make it last many, many lifetimes. But at least he would have the satisfaction of knowing he would be suffering alone.

A scarlet lip lifted in disgust. "A martyr. How boring." Arioch took another puff on the cigar as Alastor awaited his fate.

He wanted to be calm, wanted to embrace his decision wholeheartedly, but the urge to take it back, to admit he was a weak, sniveling coward, itched. Every nerve felt alive, thrumming in anticipation of the coming pain while reveling in his current lack of all-consuming agony.

The cigar left scarlet lips again, and a smile replaced it. Alastor didn't think he could be any more frightened, but that smile, the evil gleam in those black eyes, proved him wrong.

"One of the rules I have to abide by is keeping a fixed ratio between specific kinds of demons and humanity. Blood and sex demons don't count because they're born, like animals, like humans." Arioch's sneer said precisely what they thought of biological procreation. "I'm not entirely sure—we don't exactly talk—but I think the angels have a similar restriction. Therefore, if you become my permanent ass hugger, I'll need another imp to replace you at Walpole Hall, and I have the perfect candidate." They clicked their fingers.

"What... where the fuck?"

Alastor wasn't sure he possessed a heart until that moment, but now he was sure as it stuttered in his chest. He didn't look, didn't want to confirm what his ears told him. Without moving a muscle, his body turned to face the now occupied chair in front of Arioch's desk.

Liam looked the same as he had the day at the pool, except he'd lost his shirt.

"I've had some freaky drug dreams, but this has got to be the weirdest," Liam said, then eyed Arioch. "Although, if this is meant to be hell, I'm in. Hi, gorgeous." He tried to lift a hand only to find black chains wrapped around both wrists and bare chest. Tilting his head, he pursed his lips. "Kinky, but

I'm game." His gaze shot to Alastor. "Although being watched by a bloke, even if he is kinda cute, is a surprise."

Ignoring the babbling Liam, Arioch focused on Alastor.

"But, you know, I think this chair still has a little life left in it, and I'm feeling mellow after making the entire weather mage college crap themselves. So, I'm going to give you a choice, imp. Either young Liam replaces you at the Hall, or you take up your role again, and I make an executive decision and send him—" the demon's gaze rose to the cave-like roof "—somewhere he probably doesn't deserve, given what he's thinking."

"Hey, this is my dream. I get to control things," Liam piped up as the two demons locked gazes.

Blood-red lips curved into a smile. "I'll throw in a free pass for you."

Alastor blinked. "You won't skin me alive and turn me into a chair?"

Arioch leaned forward. "I'm offering so much more than that. You can walk free, right now, a living, breathing, fucking, and feeling, mortal man. All you have to do is condemn Liam to your current existence, knowing that there are so many heirs that the curse will never be broken barring a worldwide apocalypse." The pert nose wrinkled. "Which might be fun, but the paperwork would be a nightmare."

Alastor couldn't process Arioch's words for a good few seconds. He swallowed as it sank in. Surely Arioch didn't mean...

"I... I could leave the estate?"

Arioch's head tilted, causing dark, perfectly curling shoulder-length hair to sway. "Of course. As long as someone is there, working on the problem, it doesn't matter who it is. I could have swapped you out anytime I chose." Arioch gave a broad smile. "I just chose not to. I must say it's been an interesting test for a prospective vengeance demon, but although you showed some early promise, your subsequent efforts have been... substandard.

"Bluntly put, you have failed your promotion review, so you can't be an imp anymore. I could just snuff you out or skin you, but—" a grin lit the cheeky face "—where would the fun be in that?"

"If you agree to him taking your place, you'll take the life he might have had if you hadn't interfered in it. You'll be able to eat, fuck, touch, and travel. You'd have the same prospects as any other human, to live, die, starve, work or pleasure yourself to death; it'd be your choice. But you'll always remember what you did to earn that life."

Scarlet lips took a long draw on the cigar, then formed an 'o' and blew out a series of smoke rings before the demon lord focused on Alastor again.

"That is damn sexy. Fancy coming over here and—"

Arioch expanded, morphing into a full demonic male form, complete with horns.

"Be quiet." The demon's roar sounded like boulders rubbing together.

Alastor had experienced the Arioch show before. It still sparked fear, although not as much as the first time he'd seen it. Liam whimpered, and the pungent odor of piss overrode the cigar smoke and sulfur for a few seconds. Alastor didn't look at him.

Freedom as an imp was something he'd dreamed about. Becoming human had never come into his wildest fantasies. One word, one word, and he could have something he'd never considered. It was like entering a competition to win a house and finding he'd won a tropical island. He didn't know what to do with it, didn't even know if he wanted it.

Demons lie. As soon as he'd thought it, Alastor couldn't push the possibility out of his head.

Arioch switched back to a female human form, and those scarlet lips curved up. "I'm not lying, not this time anyway. This is a genuine deal with a devil."

Alastor licked his suddenly dry lips, his gaze shooting to the now wide-eyed and shaking Liam before returning to Arioch.

"How long do I have to think about it?"

Arioch leaned back in the chair and crossed their shapely legs. The movement revealed one long slender thigh as the dress was slit nearly to the crotch. Another pull on the cigar.

Lips formed a silent 'o'. A tilted-up chin exposed a milk-white throat that pulsed as more smoke rings emerged. Arioch was the definition of a sexy siren, but Alastor could only think about Darien FitzHenry. As a human, he could be with him, could travel to America, and never see Walpole Hall again. He could live, really live, even get fat. *And drunk, don't forget drunk*, he reminded himself.

Arioch finished the smoke rings, then stared right at him, seeming to see into his non-existent, sordid little soul. The half-smile said the demon already knew what he'd say.

"Five..."

There were so many rules for humans, so many diseases, things you had to do, or not do. What if Darien didn't want him? How would he negotiate the world?

"Four..." The only people he knew were the Grimshaws, and they hated him. He bet he'd end up in prison with Carl Anderson or would starve to death in a gutter before a year passed.

"Three..."

He'd waste it; he knew he would. And Liam would suffer again, because of him.

"Two—"

"I'll go back. Let Liam go."

Arioch coughed, hard. A hand formed a fist and the demon thumped themself on the chest as their eyes teared. The thrill of upsetting the most powerful being he'd ever met warmed his impish heart before the implications sank in.

"What's happening? Who the hell are you people?"

Alastor turned to the bewildered human soul. "You're going to Heaven, Liam. I'm sorry it's happening so soon."

Liam blinked. "I'm dead?"

"Yes. Carl Anderson killed you. Melody, too."

Liam's eyes narrowed. "Who are you, and why did you agree to do something that sounds pretty shitty for a stranger?"

Alastor gave the soul a grin. "We're not strangers. I encouraged you, your father, grandfather—in fact, all your family for the last four centuries—to take your first steps. But I didn't do it for you. I just wanted to piss off my boss."

Liam's eyes narrowed. "Aren't you the guy in the—" was as far as Liam got before he vanished, chair, chains, piss and all.

Alastor found himself back in the Low Great Hall, standing beside an impeccably groomed, brown-skinned man in a black suit wearing a red tie.

Arioch waved a hand expansively at the room. "Get used to it because this is all you'll see until the end of time. Although I'm surprised at your less than demonic choice, I have to say I'm quite pleased. If you'd agreed, I would have promoted you, and you would've made a shitty vengeance demon." Arioch sniffed. "So much early potential spoilt by leftover morals. Shame. Maybe I'll remember to check on you in a millennium or two. Maybe I won't."

Alastor was left alone, with nothing but the slight stink of sulfur and cigar smoke and the resolve never to hurt anyone ever again.

Chapter Thirteen

Hiding from an heir felt almost as weird as being with one after all these years. Alastor needed Darien out of Walpole Hall and permanently out of his life before he got even more attached. The more contact they had, the harder it would be when Darien left. In fact, interacting with anyone ever again was probably a bad idea if he was going to keep his shiny new vow of not ever hurting anyone.

With every day that passed, with every day nearer to the auction and the day the FitzHenrys would leave, avoiding Darien became easier and infinitely more difficult.

He still couldn't resist eavesdropping on the man whenever possible. The irritating heir had already been out this morning, indulging in his new habit of walking in the open parkland while playing with his phone. Especially the parts without bushes, trees, or walls for Alastor to hide close enough to listen.

As Darien could see him, his only option was popping between locations, which took energy. Over the last few days, he hadn't dared to move around the estate or house on his own feet in case Darien spotted him.

Both FitzHenrys were busy during the day preparing for the day's visitors and the auction, but they always had breakfast together after Juliana arrived from the hotel and Darien had taken his morning walk.

Alastor popped down to the utility room off the kitchen, intent on eavesdropping on the siblings' conversation.

"I saw you coming in as I drove up. Do you still think he's here, hiding under a bush or something?" Juliana asked. Her voice sounded a little muffled. Alastor

imagined her mouth full of one of the croissants he'd seen warming on the stove earlier.

Why hadn't he tried one when he'd had the chance? Perhaps knowing that they were good would've been worse because he'd never get another. He'd never experience what Darien had done to him again either, but as much as he tried to regret that night, he couldn't. He couldn't forget it either. People thought he haunted this place, but memories of Darien would plague him centuries after the man was worm food.

A wooden chair scraped on stone. Alastor pictured Darien sitting down to enjoy this wonderfully mundane meal with his sister. Jealousy threatened to boil over yet again. It wasn't fair. He could have had this, could have left, could have… left Liam here instead.

Sliding down to the floor, he wrapped his arms around his knees and carried on torturing himself. The flips from bone-deep depression and regret to jealousy and anger were neverending.

"No, I think he's really gone. Whatever pulled him out of here frightened the hell out of him. Plus, I don't for a moment think he could resist interacting with me. Imps seem to suffer from impulse control."

"Do you think that's why they're called imps? You could do a paper on that."

Darien huffed in amusement. "I'd be laughed out of the historical society. What would I write, 'an imp told me'? I don't think so. It's such a shame, though; he could have provided a lifetime of research."

Research is all I was to him?

"Besides, he'd know as well as we do that we won't be coming back here. If he was still alive—if he was alive in the first place—he'd be irritating the hell out of us. No, I'm just touring the grounds trying to soak up all the atmosphere while I can."

Alastor rested his forehead on his knees. In two days, he'd be left with people who couldn't see or hear him. People he vowed not to play pranks on—even if he died of boredom—because that would piss off the demon lord.

If Arioch even bothers to notice.

Hatred for the vicious, well-spoken, sarcastic bastard burned Alastor up, but fuck, he would miss their attention. He shouldn't care what the higher demon thought or did, but they were the only constant person in Alastor's long existence. Even though he was stuck in this place, things changed over time.

The room beside the kitchen where he hid had been the scullery back in the day. Now it was a laundry room. The seventeenth-century kitchen staff would have been appalled at dirty laundry being kept and washed so near to where food was kept and prepared. They would have been appalled at the idea of daily washing too.

Without any real curiosity, he wondered what this space would be used for in another four centuries if it even still existed. And here he'd sit, witnessing it all like he had so far, not mattering because he couldn't tell anyone.

He'd had an heir, a genuine history fanatic, right here. And yet rather than passing on what he knew and contributing to the world, he'd irritated him and thought about nothing but himself.

I could still talk to him.

The flash of red-hot enthusiasm sputtered and died. Darien thought he was dead, or whatever passed for dead for an imp. If Darien saw him, he would never let him just talk about the past. He'd want to know what had happened the day Liam

died, how he was, maybe offer to help him eat, even touch...
No. He couldn't experience that again, knowing it would be taken away in a matter of hours.

Maybe if I really tried, I might be able to write something down after Darien's gone.

Even though moving a pen half an inch left him exhausted for hours, he had nothing but time to kill. He pictured a stack of paper, many feet high, with him adding a single word or letter each week or month. At least if he did that, he might produce something useful, something other than pain.

The uselessness of it all pressed down on him. The chances were that nobody would ever see it, even if he did somehow manage it.

"Well, let's get going," Juliana said. "We have one more tour this morning before the auction tomorrow, and then we can be out of here. I can't wait to get home."

Darien didn't answer. Alastor tensed, every fiber hoping to hear a negative, needing to know Darien didn't want to leave him.

"Yeah, I hear you, sis."

A phone pinged. "She's here," Juliana said.

"Let's get this show on the road."

Footsteps sounded on the kitchen flagstones. One set of click-clacking heels, the other footsteps were softer but just as purposeful. Sister and brother getting on with their lives. Leaving this place—and him—behind. He should just forget, should leave them alone, but every time he tried not to follow, he couldn't bring himself to do it.

Alastor relocated to the priest hole. He told himself he was only eavesdropping to find out about the bidders, so he could prod the best candidate to buy and deter the others. Listening in certainly had nothing to do with committing Darien's deep, sonorous voice to memory.

After a single night away, Darien had stayed at the hall every night, as he'd agreed. Honest, trustworthy, caring, confident, and sexy as fuck. Everything Alastor had ever dreamed about. Everything Alastor could never be, didn't deserve, and could never have.

He hid in curtains, behind doors, and followed Darien on his walks as best he could without revealing himself. He listened to Darien go about his life, talking on the phone, eating, drinking, washing, and sleeping. Each task was performed with cool precision. He didn't sound depressed or angry, but without seeing him; Alastor couldn't tell what emotions, if any, Darien experienced.

He wanted Darien to feel something, worry, grief, regret, annoyance—anything was better than being dismissed. Every second Darien stayed in the house was sweet torture as time ticked ever faster toward the moment when Darien FitzHenry left his life forever.

It's for the best. If I interact with him, it'll only be worse when he leaves.

Or maybe he'll stay.

And I'll damn well drive him mad just like everyone else I've ever spoken to.

It didn't matter that he didn't want to hurt Darien—he hadn't wanted Liam hurt either.

Sitting in the cramped, dim space above the main fireplace, Alastor continued to torment himself as he listened for Darien to greet the latest prospective bidders.

The hinges on the great front door creaked as they opened. Harry Grimshaw hadn't been back to the house since his son died a week ago, and without his constant maintenance, things were slipping.

Alastor imagined the house slowly crumbling around him. Grade I status didn't mean the house had to be maintained, just that it couldn't be changed or purposefully demolished. In another few hundred years, he could be left haunting a ruin. As much as he rejected the ghost label, 'haunting' this place was exactly what he was doing and would continue to do.

The future weighed on his shoulders like he was carrying one of the stunning heavy horses he remembered living in the warm, comfortable stables. Only cold, lifeless metal resided there now. He sighed, remembering that there weren't even any cars in the former stables now.

One set of heeled shoes tapped on the flagstones. Buying a property like Walpole Hall had always been a collaborative decision of a family or an organization with professional advisers. Curiosity spiking, he listened carefully.

"Welcome to Walpole Hall, Ms. Emerson. I'm Darien FitzHenry, head auctioneer of the FitzHenry Auction House. This is my sister, Juliana FitzHenry, the CEO."

"Darien FitzHenry," a sultry southern American voice said. "A name of importance and just a little naughty. Did you know the prefix 'Fitz' refers to a noble's illegitimate child?"

"I did, but thank you for the information, Ms. Emerson. Now shall—"

"Please, call me Shanae. It's so much friendlier, don't you think?"

"Shanae," Darien acknowledged, and his voice held no sign of irritation. "As I said, it'll be my pleasure to show you this magnificent house and answer any questions you might have about its suitability for your needs." Darien's bright, enthusiastic reply caused an ache in Alastor's non-corporeal chest.

He snorted at his own stupidity. Why would a man who could have anyone in his bed with a click of his fingers find a scrawny, loud-mouthed, beaten-up minor demon with impulse control issues the size of the moon anything but a temporary curiosity?

"I assure you, I have very specific needs that I'm hoping you'll be able to satisfy in every way," the woman continued.

Alastor gaped at her blatant flirtation right in front of Juliana. The bitch hadn't even acknowledged her. Damn rude. No woman had ever owned Hall, and he determined that this strumpet—who had fewer morals than a hedge whore—wouldn't be the first.

"I aim to please," Darien said, then launched into the spiel Alastor had heard nearly a dozen times. "This magnificent room is the Low Great Hall, built in 1599. Walpole Hall is an actual Elizabethan property constructed in what many consider England's golden age. The fireplace is one of the hall's most exciting features. The phoenix crest above the mantel belonged to the Walpole fam—"

"The passion you possess for your work is beautiful to behold. I bet you'd do almost anything legal to secure a sale."

Alastor pictured the woman eye-fucking Darien, then he stilled. *What if he beds her tonight?*

Darien's beautiful fit, muscular body moving, sweating, working to—

The flash of jealousy caused a sharp intake of breath. Alastor's delight in hurting the heirs had always been wrapped up in their privileged lifestyles and cruel or exploitative behavior. He both yearned for their attention and despised them. Even if his target felt brief surges of victory over him, Alastor always had the upper hand. Yes, they fucked him, forced their cocks in his mouth, his ass, made him beg, but as they felt ashamed of the acts, he used them as weapons. Alastor always won, eventually.

But just like a demon, Darien didn't seem ashamed of anything he did. That sixty-nine thing had been so very gloriously filthy, and Alastor would never, ever, get to do it again.

The thought of listening to Darien fuck, or sixty-nine, the confident woman turned Alastor's non-corporeal stomach. He always did his damndest to stop heirs bedding women to prevent new Walpoles from being born. But as he'd found, even on the estate, he couldn't be everywhere all the time. As much as he beguiled them and became their all-encompassing obsession, the Walpoles still managed to stick their cocks in fertile snatches.

Some heirs had delighted in knowing he watched what they did with others, but he always got them back. A grin touched his lips.

When the fifth earl had been plowing his new bride on their wedding night, Alastor had crept up behind them and touched his shoulder. The young woman looked up. Her mouth fell open in an 'o' of shock as he appeared out of thin air.

Alastor gave her his best cheeky grin. "You look like you're enjoying his cock as much as I do."

She screamed. The earl fell off the bed, mid-fuck. Oliver Walpole chased him down the corridor, stark naked, while Alastor kept just out of reach, laughing and pointing at his shriveling, swinging genitals.

His amusement at the memory of what he'd considered one of his better pranks vanished. The wife refused to stay at the Hall ever again. She returned to London, and Alastor believed his job was over. He assumed the wife would get bored and find herself a lover, and Alastor would keep Oliver occupied. But the earl spent more time in London—where Alastor couldn't reach him—than at the estate. He usually didn't even spend the night. The couple had six children. Two were boys that Alastor had eventually needed to deal with too.

It was one thing to know there were heirs out there—ones he'd never meet and couldn't possibly ever influence—and quite another to sit by and let another one be conceived almost under his nose.

Telling himself that was the reason why that woman needed to be as far from Darien as physically possible didn't stop him recognizing his own lie. The truth was that he needed the fantasy that Darien wanted him to last as long as possible.

"Shall I take this tour, Darien?" Juliana asked. "I believe you have some maintenance checks to do upstairs?"

Safe in his cramped secret space, with just enough light coming from the ragged fist-sized hole in the chimney to see, Alastor grinned. What was that modern expression, a 'high-five'? Well, he wanted to give one to Juliana.

A tinny tune sounded, one that always preceded Darien fiddling with his phone.

"Thank you, yes, I'd appreciate that, Juliana. Apologies for my rudeness, Ms. Emerson, but I have to take this."

"Don't worry about it, Darien. In the right context, I find a little rudeness makes the world go around."

"Quite. Again, apologies." Darien's footsteps receded. They sounded a little quicker, more urgent than usual. At least Darien wasn't running from him like most heirs did in the end. No one had ever been pleased to see him except when desperately horny, frustrated, or angry.

Alastor had begun to sympathize with the many Walpole heirs he'd tormented over the years. Ever since Darien FitzHenry had entered Walpole Hall, he'd been experiencing one of those three emotions most of the time—sometimes all at once—and he certainly was now.

Why had Darien been so polite to this strumpet? Could it be that he found her outspokenness attractive? Alastor froze. *Darien loved my dirty mouth.*

"So, is your brother single, and does he come with the property?" the sultry American voice Alastor was beginning to hate asked.

"Property only comes in the form of buildings and lands these days, not people, Ms. Emerson," Juliana's tone was so painfully sweet it practically exuded venom. "Although up in the Long Gallery, there's a portrait of my many times' great grandmother, who was indeed part of a property sale. If you wish to view it, come this way. If not, you know where the door is."

One set of heels clattered across the flagstones toward the staircase.

With Darien and Juliana both out of the room, Alastor relocated into the Low Great Hall. He anticipated a mortified expression on the face of a painted harlot due to Juliana's sumptuous put-down.

Rather than resembling Arioch's female form, the woman resembled a middle-aged suburban housewife, blonde-haired, wearing jeans and a pink jumper. He blinked. What were women coming to these days?

"Ah. There you are. Pleased to meet you." Blue eyes twinkled. Alastor looked around to see who she was talking to. No female, except a small child or when he'd been touching an heir, had ever seen him.

"As you no doubt overheard, my name is Shanae. I'm your many times removed cousin, and I know exactly where you've been hiding while these nice people have been worrying about you." The blonde head nodded toward the fireplace. "Unlit hearths don't often glow unless there's a spirit hiding in them."

Alastor's non-corporeal heart stopped. It was a witch's fault he was here in the first place. According to Arioch, Alastor had been relocating between one job and the next when he'd been snared by the dying curse of Nicholas Thatcher's mother.

"Now that we know you're still here, I intend to pester you until you agree to talk to me. If you don't, I'll find a way into your little hiding place, a priest hole, I presume, and destroy all the items you—"

Alastor relocated up to the roof and came face to face with Harry Grimshaw. The man grinned.

"Gotcha, ya little shite."

Alastor tried to relocate again, but nothing happened.

Harry pulled out his phone. "FitzHenry? It worked. Bring your sister up to the roof."

A gust of wind moved his shirt, his hair, and the chill of the damp autumn day wrapped around him. He couldn't see anything different, except the whole roof looked cleaner than he remembered.

"You're standing in a demon trap. And yes, it makes you visible if you haven't worked it out," a tall, skinny teenager with blue hair said in a Scottish accent. The boy leaned against the faux turret used as a store, trying to appear confident but clearly wasn't. Tension showed in his shoulders despite his nonchalantly folded arms.

"The barrier is a sphere twelve feet in diameter. If you touch it, it'll feel like electricity. A bit of a buzz at first, but it'll knock you on your ass if you push it. Traps and wards are my thing. Once a demon steps into one of my traps, they can only leave if I allow. And I'm not doing a thing unless my auntie says so. She can be—" he glanced toward the turret where the stairs were located, "—a bit fierce if you piss her off."

Going for sympathy and more information rather than bluster or anger seemed the best idea.

"What.... What do you want?" he asked as he stepped forward, hand out. His fingertips buzzed, and the sensation increased with each inch he moved. The boy's lips quirked in a smile as Alastor withdrew his hand. Maybe more force could break it, but if it was anything like the barrier that surrounded the estate, the more Alastor pushed, the harder the spell pushed back. He didn't want to end up flung on his ass on the cold stone.

As they were talking, Harry moved over to the entrance to the roof.

First Darien and then Juliana and Shanae burst through the door. Darien jogged toward him across the flagstones.

"Thank fuck for that. I thought you were gone for good, I—"

Movement behind Darien tore his focus away. Harry stepped up behind Juliana. As the older man put a hand over her mouth, Alastor shouted, "Hey, what are you—"

Darien turned, then froze as the knife Harry held against Juliana's neck glinted in the weak autumn sunlight.

"Steady there, lad. I don't want to hurt her, but I will if I need to."

"Getting back to why we're here," Shanae said brightly, "which is to break the curse and finally let Nicholas Thatcher rest in peace. So you'd best cooperate, Mr. FitzHenry. We wouldn't want to add one last Walpole heir to the tally, would we?"

CHAPTER FOURTEEN

For the first few days after Alastor disappeared, Darien feared Alastor had been imprisoned, tortured, even killed, by his demon master. Calling his name, and searching the house and grounds, proved fruitless. Two days ago, he'd caught a glimpse of fiery red hair ducking out of view.

The imp was still here, just refusing to interact. The situation seemed hopeless with the auction and the date Darien had to leave getting ever closer. If he forced the issue, let Alastor know he'd been seen, the imp might withdraw completely.

He'd tried to help subs who refused to engage before. After they realized he wasn't an asshole, some came around, some didn't, and he'd always accepted their choice. But Alastor... Alastor was different in so many ways. Apart from being human, the other subs had other options. He decided to call the imp out the next time he caught a glimpse of him, then he'd gotten a phone call from the last person he expected.

"FitzHenry? Meet me at the Red Lion pub in the village at eight tonight," Harry said and disconnected before Darien could answer.

The small, thatched pub had been on Darien's list of places to visit ever since he'd begun researching the location of Walpole Hall, but he hadn't managed to make it here yet. Made of red brick like the Hall and the Grimshaw's gatehouse cottage, it was the only other place to get a drink in the village apart from the hotel where he'd stayed that one night.

He had to duck to get in the worn, dark wood door, and the inside looked no bigger than an average home. Saggy old sofas were scattered around the small taproom. A fire flickered in the hearth, giving a warm, homely feel. The lintel above the fireplace and the walls were decorated with horse brasses that caught and reflected the firelight.

The hum of conversation stopped. Unlike the hotel, this place certainly didn't welcome non-locals. It only took a glance to find Harry Grimshaw. What Darien didn't expect was to see him sitting with Shanae and a blue-haired youth.

He walked over to the table where Shanae and the young man sat together on a burgundy leather sofa, opposite Harry, who had chosen a floral fabric armchair.

"Get yourself a pint, lad. This will take some time. Mine's a Harvey's. Best bitter in the world. The lady is drinking red wine, but—"

"They won't be drinking anything with me. This one—" he indicated Shanae with a finger without looking at her "—tried to sell me a happiness potion when I told her about Alastor. She's a money-grabbing charlatan, and if you've paid her anything, I'd—"

"Give me your hand," Shanae said, her tone mild as she held hers out.

"You've got to be kidding; I'm not—"

"You either believe I have an ability, or you do not, Mr. FitzHenry."

He met her serene blue eyes. *Witch* was the last thing that came to mind. She looked like a soccer mom, with abilities centered around her husband and teenage kids.

Stereotyping? Really?

Darien reached out, but she withdrew her hand.

"Better sit down first," she advised with a smile.

Scowling, he took a seat in the armchair next to the sofa. "Let's get this farce over with." He held out his hand.

He found himself back in the hotel room of a week ago, but things were very different this time.

Shanae gave a tight smile. "Still, you being here rather than at the Hall is fortuitous. Having this chat with Nicholas listening in would have been a little awkward." She smiled, but it didn't last long. "I don't think this was what his mother intended when she cursed the first earl. I imagine she'd be astonished at the strength of her dying spell. We have no reason to believe she was particularly strong."

Telling this witch that they weren't dealing with her long-lost relative might stop this conversation before it'd really begun, and Darien needed as much information as he could get.

"Is it possible to end the curse without the extinction of the Walpole Y chromosome? I happen to be quite fond of breathing, and I've probably got upward of a hundred relatives who feel the same way."

"Oh, I'd say upwards of several thousand, and that's a conservative estimate. Henry Walpole wasn't the only early descendant of the first earl who escaped the curse. Many Walpoles were, shall we say, very friendly before they married, and some didn't appear to consider that fidelity applied to wealthy men at all.

"However, from my brief look into the records, Nicholas has been a busy little bee in his quest to fulfill the curse."

Darien sat back on the bed, and put his feet up to claim the space without inviting her to sit. "So, how do you propose to free him?"

One carefully drawn-on eyebrow arched. "Dominance games don't impress me, young man, but it was an admirable, subtle attempt. I may be human, but I celebrated my one hundred and fifteenth birthday last week." She eyed him with pursed lips before seeming to come to a decision. "A witch may have set the curse rolling, but lasting this long and claiming that many lives? This has demon written all over it."

Something didn't ring true. "What's your angle here, Shanae?"

She stalked forward until she stood over him. He began to regret his decision to lay down. Even at no more than five feet five, she loomed over him.

Her eyes narrowed. "What aren't you telling me?"

"You first," he shot back.

"Goddess save us from men who think they know it all." She sighed, sat down beside him, and before he could pull it back, she touched his hand. In the next instant, he was back in the bedroom in the Hall with Alastor telling him his name, that he wasn't Nicholas Thatcher, about his boss being a demon named Arioch. Images flashed through his mind, Alastor's battered back, the contrast between Alastor now and the image in the painting, his bleeding finger.

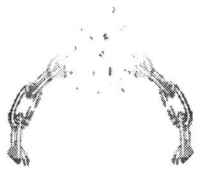

"Here, sup on this lad. It's an odd feeling, right?"

Darien screwed up his eyes and then opened them wide, trying to come to terms with what had just happened. Absently, he took the proffered pint of ale and took a swallow. The bitterness helped to clear his head a little.

"My main ability is memory manipulation," Shanae said. "Although I can also see some spells. This is my nephew, Callum."

The boy nodded but didn't speak. Although he appeared only a few years younger than as Alastor physically, a vast gulf existed between them. Alastor hadn't changed for decades, centuries. He bet this kid would grow out of his 'gothic' style in a matter of years, even months.

"The subterfuge in the hotel was necessary," Shanae continued, "as I needed to consult with my coven before determining a course of action. We couldn't risk you sharing anything with Nicholas in case his master found out. Nicholas has every reason to be scared of Arioch. There are few demons as powerful as the demon Supernatural Council delegate.

"Like all the other representatives, including myself, we remain true to our essential nature. Arioch feeds on remorse and regret, and Nicholas has helped to provide Arioch with an ongoing buffet for over four hundred years. It's time it stopped, and we need your help."

Darien blew out a breath. "I don't see what I can do. I think Arioch took him just after we found out about Liam. He's been hiding from me ever since."

"Hiding, not gone?" Shanae said, voice sharp.

Darien took another swallow of the beer that was beginning to grow on him. "I'm not sure, but I think I caught a glimpse of his hair yesterday. I didn't react, in case it made him run again, but I haven't seen anything since."

Shanae's pink lips pursed. "So, he's hiding." Aunt and nephew shared a glance.

"He physically runs? You can see and hear him?" the teenager said in a soft Scottish burr.

"He can, but he can also disappear and appear somewhere else. I could well have been mistaken. It could have been wishful thinking."

A knowing smile graced Shanae's lips. "You're falling for him, aren't you?"

Darien returned the half-empty pint glass to the table. "That's hardly relevant."

"Oh, I think it is," Shanae said. "Has he played any tricks or pranks on you? Or your sister?"

He related the sugar in the coffee incident, the deflated tires, and the way Alastor had touched Juliana that one time.

"But that was right at the start, correct?"

He nodded. The relatives exchanged another knowing glance, and Darien wondered why Shanae had brought her nephew along.

"Care to share?" Darien asked.

"Does he have a favorite place he goes when he's upset?" the teenager asked.

"Have you ever seen him with an object, something he owns?" Shanae fired at him without him answering her nephew's query.

The questions came thick and fast, but after an hour, they had the bare bones of a plan. The first step was to find out if Alastor was still in residence. The next involved making Alastor stay still long enough to talk to him.

His role would be to ensure Alastor stayed focused on him without revealing that they knew he was there. If he was still there at all.

CHAPTER FIFTEEN

Up until this point, the plan had worked perfectly, but it appeared Alastor wasn't the only one being played. Shanae claimed demons lied, that they couldn't be trusted, but that also applied to witches.

"Go stand with Nicholas, please, Darien," Shanae said. "Don't worry, the spell won't hold you. It doesn't affect humans."

Darien backed toward Alastor, hands raised. Although—as he didn't have a weapon—he didn't know why he had his hands up.

"But I'm not Nicholas Thatcher. I'm an—" Alastor blurted.

"Not helping," Darien said out of the side of his mouth.

"Doesn't matter what you are. I'm stopping this before you hurt anyone else," Harry ground out.

"Mr. Grimshaw, threatening Ms. FitzHenry is not necessary. I assure you that her brother will see it our way—just as he did in the pub—once we explain things."

"I'll see that devil bound before we get to the chatting," Harry said, eyes on Darien with his grip on Juliana still tight.

Shanae's jaw tightened. "Give us a moment to prepare. But for now, Darien, please face Nicholas. Nicholas, put your arms around Darien's waist and clasp your hands together."

"Enforced cuddles? You witches are evil incarnate," Alastor said, but he put his arms around Darien's waist and snuggled in. "Mm, I like. But I never suspected you'd pull a prank like this. Well done."

"Would you be serious? This isn't a prank. That's my sister's throat he's holding a knife to."

Alastor looked up at him, eyes narrowing as he scrutinized Darien's face, then a wry half-smile appeared. "That wasn't part of the plan, was it? You plotted to trick a professional prankster and got swindled?" Alastor huffed out a chuckle. "Oh, the irony."

"All I wanted was to know if you were still—" Darien paused. He didn't even know if Alastor was alive, even though the wiry body currently pressed against him shivered with cold. "—here," he finished lamely.

Alastor let out a heartfelt sigh. "Why, what were you planning to do? Come visit every few years so I can watch you go grey? Keep me wondering if you'll come back every time you leave? No, I think a clean break would be better, don't you?"

Darien gave him a squeeze but said nothing. There wasn't anything to say. This situation was untenable. Even if the new owners let him onto the property when he visited, his life was thousands of miles away from here.

They both knew he might try to visit regularly for a while, he would make promises, and each parting would be painful. But in the end, life would take over. The visits would get further apart until they stopped either by choice or because of Darien's mortality.

Ultimately, the man in his arms, who needed an heir's touch to experience life, would be left alone again. But was it his touch Alastor craved, or would any heir do? Despite that possibility, Alastor intrigued him more than anyone he'd ever met.

"Don't worry," Alastor whispered. "I've known Harry since he was born. He's not violent unless you're a mole or rabbit after his veg." A bright grin lit the face tilting up to look at him. "I've seen his veg. It's not worth annoying him for."

When Darien didn't react to the joke, Alastor's smile faltered. "Don't look so sad. I'm an imp, not someone you could ever introduce to your mother. If she visited, I'd probably do something to horrify you both. Let it go, let me go. Besides, I appreciate a good trick, and this is a doozy. I can't wait to see what they do next." He rubbed his cheek against Darien like a needy cat desperate to be petted. Or someone trying to draw some pain out of a black eye.

Without thought, Darien cupped the side of Alastor's head and held him against his chest, stopping the movement. Alastor relaxed a little, let out a tiny, contented sigh. The familiar satisfaction from providing what a submissive partner needed seeped into his bones.

Darien met his sister's scared dark eyes and said, "Just do what he says. Everything will be fine."

"So commanding. I almost believe you," Alastor murmured.

Darien was about to tell Alastor that he should believe him, that he'd sort this out, when the ragged, still bruised man placed a tender kiss on the exposed skin of Darien's throat.

Alastor had never displayed affection. *Is he playing me?* A gust of wind ruffled Alastor's flame-colored hair, and the man shivered.

Darien strained to hear as Alastor murmured against his skin. "Gonna miss you."

"You'll miss me, or you'll miss having an heir around to torment?" Darien couldn't keep the tinge of bitterness out of his voice.

Alastor lifted his head, breaking the skin-to-skin contact, and shrugged. "Bit of both."

Darien couldn't stop a snort of amusement. "Little shit."

Heeled shoes tapped on the flagstones as Shanae moved behind Darien.

"Well, this is a brutal punishment," Alastor said, loud enough for everyone to hear. "What are you going to do next, tickle me until I beg for mercy? Force me to eat cake until I'm overly full?"

Alastor tensed against his chest. Darien tried to let go, but the smaller man held on, his elbows squeezing tight around Darien's ribs.

"What is it? Let go. I won't have you hurt."

Alastor twitched, hissing through his teeth.

"Sorry, dear," Shanae apologized. "I know it stings, but I assure you it's quite necessary."

"What did she do?" Darien demanded.

Alastor's forehead pressed against his shoulder, breath coming in short pants, but he didn't speak.

"Shanae, tell me now, or I'll undo whatever you just put on his wrists."

"S'ok. Masochist, remember?" Alastor gave Darien another squeeze, then hissed and froze as if the movement caused more pain.

"That's it, this isn't what we agree—"

"No, no, it's not," Shanae interrupted. "And I apologize for that subterfuge. But you wouldn't have agreed, even though this is the only way to free Nicholas."

Alastor's voice wavered as he said, "Hey, FitzHenry, don't get jealous because someone else is doing the hurting. There's plenty of pain to go around."

A soft, apologetic hand landed on Darien's shoulder. "I'm sorry, but a magical bond is necessary when dealing with supernaturals. It's part of a rope from Henry VIII's flagship, the Mary Rose, soaked in Holy Water, which acts as mild acid on demons," Shanae said.

Alastor huffed in amusement. "If this is mild, I don't want to feel the strong stuff."

"I am not happy about this," Darien ground out, keeping as still as possible.

Shanae moved behind Alastor until she faced Darien over the Tudor man's shoulder.

With her expression dripping with determination and sadness, she said, "I know, Mr. FitzHenry, and it if helps, him being in pain brings me no joy either, but it is necessary. The spirit of Nicholas Thatcher has been trapped in this demonic form—probably by Arioch conducting revenge on behalf of Nicholas's mother—for over four hundred years. From what I've gleaned from family records, Agnes was not a strong witch, and she specialized in herbal potions, not curses or demon summoning. She couldn't have caused this, even if her intention was to trap her son, which I doubt very much.

"All her call for vengeance did was draw the attention of a vengeance demon who trapped her son's spirit for some unknown reason. Nicholas has been suffering as much as his victims for all this time. It's time it ended. He deserves to finally rest in peace."

The twelve-inch-long dagger Shanae proffered was dull, almost black iron with a rectangular blade. The carved dark ivory hilt had two oval swellings at the guard.

"You'll need this to release him."

Darien recognized the fourteenth-century bollock knife from examining the sale lot earlier.

Darien didn't reach for the weapon, even though he would have been itching to get his hands on it at any other time. Holding a centuries-old artifact, testing its weight, experiencing the texture, all helped him imagine what living in that time must have been like. But right now, he held a man who had lived in the era Darien loved so much. A currently living artifact, one who needed him more than anyone he'd ever met.

"Well, go on, lad," Grimshaw said. "He can't go anywhere, and it has to be a Walpole."

Darien ignored the solemn expectant faces, and Alastor's stiff body pressed against him. Instinctively, he met his sister's gaze. He might be an accomplished dominant, but Juliana had been his sounding board throughout his life. Instead of the together, calm woman whose advice always brought clarity, Juliana stood rigid, head pulled up as if keeping still would protect her from the mirror-like stainless steel at her throat. It was his turn to help her.

Keeping his voice steady, unhurried, and unpanicked, he said, "Let her go, and we can discuss it."

Harry snorted. "Discuss what? That thing you're letting slobber on you is a demon, you said so yourself. He's caused the early deaths of countless of your relatives, and I bet my lad and Mrs. Anderson aren't the first non-Walpoles whose lives he's ruined or ended. If we don't want it to continue for who knows how many generations, this needs to end now. One quick—"

"We've discussed this, Mr. Grimshaw," Shanae stated, voice hard. "That is the soul, the spirit, of Nicholas Thatcher. A boy who was abused and then murdered when he was barely an adult. He's not a demon, not yet anyway. Although I think Arioch hopes he will become a full demon in time.

"Our aim today is to release Nicholas from the control of a demon lord and let his soul continue to the afterlife as it should have done when he died in that chimney."

"Why isn't anyone listening to me? I'm not Nicholas Thatcher. I'm—"

Darien ignored Alastor's protest. It didn't matter what he was if the outcome proved to be the same. "And setting his soul free involves a bollock knife?" He nodded at the dagger Shanae still held.

Alastor tensed, but to Darien's surprise, he didn't speak or try to escape.

Shanae pressed her lips together. "I'm afraid it does. I was hoping not to scare him, but it seems that is now unavoidable.

"Mr. FitzHenry, this is the simple truth. The interference of a Demon Lord stopped his soul from being seen by a reaper, so I'm afraid he needs to die again, and that can only happen when he's corporeal. From your own admission, that only occurs when he's in contact with a Walpole heir."

"Whatever he started out as, he's a demon now. What don't you get?" Harry's voice was sharp with frustration. "Is he more important than your sister's life?"

"You won't hurt her," Darien said, hoping he sounded a hell of a lot more relaxed and confident than he felt. "You're not a murderer, Harry. Hasn't your family suffered enough? Do you really want to end your days sharing a cell with Carl Anderson?"

"Anderson wasn't a murderer either until he met that." Harry nodded toward Alastor. "If I thought Juliana here would behave, I'd do it while you hold him still. I've seen him bleed, so I know it can happen."

"As long as a Walpole is touching him, he'll be solid. So if you want to—" Darien turned at the unfamiliar male voice to see a dark-skinned man in a black suit and a red tie leaning up against the balustrade, miming an upward stabbing movement. "—go for it."

"Hey, boss," Alastor sounded cheerful, but his rigid body betrayed his fear. "How's it hanging? Got a new cover for your chair yet? I hear imp leather isn't all it's cracked up to be. Have you tried some nice soft witch hide?"

Darien didn't think he could be any more on edge. His instincts told him to protect the most vulnerable, the most in danger first. Despite the blade against his sister's throat, Alastor baiting a demon lord appeared the higher priority.

"Stop winding him up. Don't worry, we'll sort this out. I'm not going to hurt you or let—"

Alastor's head tilted. The bruises on his throat and cheek from the eleventh earl remained stark against his impossibly pale skin. "Why not? If you don't, I'll be stuck here, alone, until the end of time, unable to sleep, eat, or communicate. Or my hide will be polishing Arioch's ass forever, and knowing that fucker, they'll make sure I experience every second."

"You've got that right," the grinning demon supplied.

Alastor ignored his boss. "I've already told Arioch I won't interact with anyone again, so you might as well do it. It'd be a kindness."

For once, Alastor's eyes didn't twinkle with mischief. Instead, old eyes looked out from a scarily young face. "I've had enough, milord. I can't do this anymore. You once said you help and care for subs who don't have a permanent dom. That's me, and it'll always be me unless you help by ending this crappy excuse for a life."

A derisive snort from the demon lord took Darien's focus. The man, and that's exactly how the demon appeared, was handsome, but apart from that, he appeared remarkably ordinary. Darien even thought he was a few inches taller than Arioch.

Arioch gave him a grin that reminded Darien of Alastor and turned his attention to Callum. The young man stood near the disused turret Darien had searched back when he thought Alastor was a heritage warrior.

"Well, hello, fresh baby mage." Arioch looked over at Shanae. "What's this, work experience week? Tag along and see a human shank a demon?"

"In a way, but my nephew is already very talented in his field."

Arioch raised dark eyebrows, but Shanae kept quiet. The demon lord took a step forward. Out of the corner of his eye, Darien saw Callum tense.

Alastor turned his head so he could see. "So, boss, couldn't stay away, huh? I thought you weren't ever going to pop by again?"

Arioch shrugged, showing bright white teeth as he smiled. "What can I say? I felt your pain and thought I'd come to have a look-see. Using Holy Water on the ropes was a touch fit for a demon. It does burn so very much and for so very long, like silver to an air elemental, I'm told."

At least the pain the soaked rope caused appeared to have had a purpose. But why did Shanae want Arioch here?

"Liar," Shanae said, her tone mild. "About why you're here, anyway. The part about Holy Water is quite true. Poor Nicholas is in considerable pain, although he's trying to hide it for the sake of the three mundanes."

Darien couldn't help giving Alastor a squeeze, letting him know he was here, that he cared. There wasn't much else he could do as these powerful beings engaged in a war of words with Alastor as the prize.

"Unless it's council business—as far as I know—your only interest is feeding," Shanae said. "As this has nothing to do with the council so far, tell me, Council Member Arioch, whose justifiable revenge are you here to experience?"

"I've had enough of this," Harry growled and pressed the knife against Juliana's throat hard enough to dent the skin, but no red line appeared.

"Either take the knife, FitzHenry, or you and that demon, followed by your sister, are going over the edge. Double suicide thanks to the Walpole curse."

The outrageous threat confirmed to Darien that something was going on here that he hadn't yet grasped.

CHAPTER SIXTEEN

After seeing Liam confront Carl Anderson that day by the pool, Alastor guessed he'd just found out where the son had gotten his balls. And he knew how that had turned out.

Fear for Harry, plus regret for Liam, surrounded, suffocated, him. He had no right to be breathing when that vibrant body was in the ground, rotting, rather than enjoying life.

Liam was just the latest in a long line of lives he'd destroyed. He could almost feel their ghosts lining up to get a piece of him. Some had deserved it, but if he allowed himself to admit it, many Walpoles had been relatively decent men of their time before he'd gotten his impish claws into them. Guilt gnawed at him almost as much as the rope around his wrists. From the warmth covering his fingers, he guessed quite a lot of his blood had dripped to the damp grey flagstones.

He didn't want to cause any more pain, particularly to the Grimshaws, Juliana, and Darien, who had always been nice to him, despite knowing what he'd done. He certainly didn't want to be the reason Juliana and Darien died.

"Keep it coming; this is delicious," Arioch's deep, amused voice gave him the final push.

"You're right; it's time this ended," he said, "But I don't want anyone getting into trouble. Please don't hurt Juliana. You'd end up in prison. Think of Lorraine. She wouldn't—"

"My life ended when you killed my boy. I don't give a damn what happens to me. I'll kill you myself if someone stops these damn witches interfering," Grimshaw growled as his gaze met Alastor's.

Alastor was about to suggest knocking Darien out when the man leaned down and spoke against his ear. "The witches want Arioch in the trap."

Alastor couldn't think why the witches wanted Arioch in a demon snare, but it was a prank worthy of a far higher class of demon than himself.

When Arioch realized the ruse, the demon lord would be beyond furious. Arioch's usual reaction to annoyance was to expand to their full demonic form, and from what Callum had said, the trap wasn't that big. Getting crushed to death against a magical barrier by an expanding demon butt might be the end he deserved—hopefully, it would be quicker than being flayed—but Darien didn't.

Alastor had always known it would eventually come to a toss-up between getting promoted to a full demon or experiencing an unusual and painful death. It appeared that the coin of fate had finally stopped spinning, and it'd come up heads for Arioch. Still, it was better than it turning aimlessly for several more lonely centuries. Maybe this was a win after all.

He let out a breath, wanting nothing to distract from the last few seconds of delicious warmth and security Darien's arms provided. Even if Arioch didn't intend Darien harm, being this close to an enraged, trapped demon lord wouldn't end well for him.

It was time to grow up, and fuck, he didn't want to do that. But there was no more time.

Steeling himself, he looked up into Darien's beautiful amber eyes. One of his inky black eyelashes was a little crooked, going its own way instead of following the others.

Alastor smiled at the perfect imperfection. "Duck out," he ordered.

Black eyebrows drew together. "Are you sure?"

Alastor snorted. "Just get outta here, will you? Go save your sister. I'll dance with the big bad; it's not as if I haven't done it before."

He tried to keep his wrists as still as possible as Darien ducked down and wriggled out of his arms. He gritted his teeth as the rope bit into his skin like acid. Warmth dripped down his hands as Darien pulled away.

Darien stood up from his crouch. Eyes widening, he grabbed hold of Alastor's forearms above the wounds. "My god, you need—"

Alastor twisted away, ripping out of Darien's grasp. "What I need is for you to stop touching me," he ground out, cradling his still bound arms against his chest. Within the demon trap, Darien just being near him must have the same effect as touching, as blood continued welling sluggishly from his wrists.

Gaze on the wounds, Darien instinctively stepped forward, then seemed to realize what Alastor meant. His hands dropped to his sides.

"What can I do?" Darien asked, pain in his eyes.

Alastor closed his eyes, drawing up as much demonic strength as possible.

"Go be with your sister. Forget about me, about this place."

Darien's lips pursed, and he shook his head slowly while holding Alastor's gaze. "Playing the martyr doesn't suit you. Besides, I know you and your tricks. What are you up to? But know this, whatever happens, I'll never, ever forget—"

"You will if my aunt makes you," Callum piped up. "We can't have mundanes wandering about knowing about supernaturals." He looked at the blonde witch. "What? That's the lecture everyone keeps giving me. Don't tell the mundanes, don't talk to the mundanes, don't—"

"Callum, quiet." The blonde witch's nostrils flared like an irritated dragon. Alastor imagined steam coming out of them because Shanae looked ready to rip a strip off her nephew. Some things never changed.

"No, no, don't do that," Darien begged. "Please, don't ever—"

"How very touching, or not touching, as the case might be," Arioch said. "I'm not sure if I need popcorn or a vomit bucket. Do you think either, or both of you, might manage a tear or two if I ask really nicely?" The demon pouted, giving them puppy-dog eyes.

Alastor frowned at the being who had made his life even more miserable for four centuries. Arioch never said more than, "*It's what you're there for, but the job's not done yet,*" when Alastor announced he'd taken out another heir. Although he had occasionally received the ultimate praise of a raised eyebrow and an "*Inventive*" when the cause of death had been particularly convoluted.

"You're not funny, and you never have been," Alastor said and turned to his distant cousin.

Arioch grabbed their chest. "I'm so wounded!"

"Witch, give Arioch the knife. If the fucker wants me dead, he can do it himself. Or don't you have the balls for it? You always seem to get others to do your job for you."

"Himself? Misgendering is a crass crime that warrants capital punishment even more than being a truly appalling imp. Which you are, by the way." With a cocky smile, the sharp-suited Arioch strolled forward, reaching a hand out toward the dagger the witch still held.

The demon lord stopped and looked down at their shiny shoes. Alastor held his breath and counted, one, two—

Arioch roared, doubling in size. The suit vanished as the demon lord displayed their full-demonic form. A loud retort echoed across the parkland as a centuries-old flagstone cracked under the extra weight. Alastor dodged the desk-sized feet.

Shanae scrambled back to her nephew, pulling the now pale youngster a little further from the barrier he'd created. The trap held.

Darien joined Harry and Juliana. Harry held the puny four-inch kitchen knife toward the ten-foot-tall red-skinned, horned, and tailed demon. Arioch banged ham-sized fists on the invisible barrier and roared their fury at the witches they couldn't reach. Callum gritted his teeth, his lips moving silently, but Arioch remained contained.

The barrier might be invisible, but it might as well have been made of solid diamond for all the give it had. Arioch's height meant Alastor's head almost reached the demon's crotch as he stood between the huge demon's naked feet. At least Arioch had chosen to wear tight black leather briefs. Alastor's very brief curiosity about what a giant red cock looked like evaporated as Arioch's massive head turned down to him.

"You!" Arioch ground out, their voice like boulders grinding together.

The sound vibrated up through Alastor's bare feet, rattling his ribcage. Lifting his chin, Alastor stared into the glowing red eyes. Now the end was almost here, his fear had vanished, as long as Arioch didn't draw it out. But if an imp couldn't provoke a furious reaction, he wasn't much of an imp.

"Your breath stinks, you've got a saggy arse, and you suck donkey balls as a boss."

"If you hurt him, I'll never let you out," Callum called out, his voice wavering with effort or maybe fear.

Arioch ignored him. Twisting, the huge demon attempted to look at its behind, then lifted a claw-like hand to their face, breathed on it, then sniffed. "Really?" The voice that came out of the fanged mouth was oddly human. "I thought my ass was kinda cute, and I use breath mints and everything. Although I have to say, dating has not been going well for the last five or six centuries."

Alastor blinked. Instead of a huge male demon, a blonde, ponytailed cheerleader-type teenage white girl sat cross-legged on the roof, wearing skin-tight white jeans and a scarlet strapless top.

"So, hit me with it, Shanae. Why did you go to all this trouble to catch me?" Arioch frowned and turned to Alastor. "Were you in on this? Because plotting against a senior demon results in a world of pain if it doesn't work. Of course, it's also the quickest way to a promotion. It's how I got where I am today. Did I ever tell you how I got the better of Branigan? The poor—"

"And back to me," Alastor announced and sat down, mirroring the position of the now scowling, achingly pretty teenage girl. "Nope, I'm as clueless as you. I was trying to keep a low profile until Darien left." He nodded toward Shanae. "But that one can see me through walls. She saw me, I popped up here, and here we are, trapped until the baby witch undoes whatever he did."

"I'm a mage, not a witch," Callum mumbled, but no one replied.

The pert nose with a scattering of freckles wrinkled. "I dislike being made a fool of, especially by a human who hasn't been around as long as some of my farts. Spill it, witches, and this better be good. I'm like that—" they held up crossed fingers "—with the leader of the supernatural council." Blonde eyebrows drew together. "Actually, thinking about it, it's more like this." Arioch formed a ring with their finger and thumb, then thrust their other index finger into the ring with short sharp stabs.

Shanae wrinkled her nose as if one of the farts the demon lord mentioned was hanging around despite the chilly breeze. "Councilmember Arioch, there is no need to be crude. Callum is only seventeen. I apologize for the subterfuge, but as Nicholas does not know himself, we need you to tell us why he has been trapped here for all these years."

"He does know; he just can't remember." Arioch's head tilted. "Now, I could just tell you, but where would be the fun in that? Memories are your thing, aren't they, Shanae?"

The blond witch scowled. "You know as well as I do that I'd have to touch him to elicit a memory draw, and unless an heir is in skin-to-skin contact, I can't do that."

Arioch took on its red-skinned demonic form again, but kept to a mere seven feet tall. Reaching over, it gathered a shocked Alastor into his lap.

The demon lord's skin didn't burn, but it was definitely a few degrees higher than Alastor's corporeal body temperature. Not annoying his boss, if he had the chance to solve the mystery of his existence, seemed like a good idea.

Alastor remained quiet, passive, and waited to see what would happen. Either the past would be revealed, or Harry would be scrubbing imp blood off the roof for the rest of the day.

"I have the same effect as an heir," Arioch said and held out his other arm. "Well, come on, Councilmember Shanae, let's get all snuggly while we stroll down memory lane together." A dark red eyebrow rose. "Unless you're frightened of little old me? I promise I won't be naughty. I don't want to be stuck on this roof any longer than I have to be." Arioch pouted. "I suffer from vertigo, which makes all this terribly distressing."

Shanae's brows drew together. "I know I have a fraction of your life experience, but I'm not stupid enough to give you another bargaining—"

"I'll do it."

Alastor's gaze shot to Darien. Just for a moment, he wanted to give up responsibility to Darien's earnest, determined expression. Then he remembered what he was, what Darien was.

He scowled. "What the hell are you still doing here, FitzHenry? Think with your head, not your cock, for once. Piss off back to America with your sister." Despite the ache in his chest at Darien's disappointed expression, Alastor twisted the verbal knife again. "Did you really think you were special? You're just like every other heir. I played you, used you, and you were a lot fucking easier than most."

Hot breath scorched Alastor's ear as the demon lord whispered against his temple. "Liar, liar pants on fire. Alastor and Darien sitting in a tree, K.I.S.S.I.N.G."

Alastor gritted his teeth against the demon's taunts.

"No way are you coming in here again. I don't want you here. I never wanted you here. Besides, Shanae would still have to come into the—"

Darien's set jaw hadn't altered. "—Not if you sit up against the barrier, and we stay outside and just touch your shoulders."

"And I thought I was meant to be the devious one," Arioch said aloud, huffed out a breath, and threw their hands in the air. "Come on then, I haven't got all day to muck about here. People don't impale or eviscerate themselves, you know." Arioch's nose wrinkled. "Well, not often anyway. I do so miss seppuku[1]."

Alastor found himself on his feet, having been lifted by the demon as if he were nothing but a plaything.

And that's probably all I am to Arioch. "I don't want to," he blurted.

Arioch picked him up under his armpits and carried him toward where Darien stood with Juliana and Harry a few steps away.

Darien put his hands out, palms down, as if he could reduce Alastor's anxiety with a gesture. "I know reliving your death will be scary and painful, but if this is the only way for you to be free, you have to—"

"Please, Nicholas?" Juliana added as she clung to her brother's arm. Shanae had moved over to stand on Darien's other side. Callum remained by the fake turret as if he feared the demon would somehow be able to grab him if he got too close. At least one of the non-demons had a head on their shoulders.

"Yes, Nicholas, please," Arioch whined, batting suddenly long eyelashes.

Alastor shook his head. The humans just didn't get it. "Arioch is way too happy about this. If they're happy, it means a whole pile of crap is—"

Darien's hand shot out, grabbed his forearm above the rope wound, and pulled him forward the final step. The witch's cool hand touched his forehead.

---

1. seppuku: Japanese ritual suicide by disembowelment.

CHAPTER SEVENTEEN

Nicholas stopped playing his recorder as a deep red carriage with a pair of matched bay horses pulled up in the lane outside their cottage on this fine Sunday afternoon. His attempt to carve a similar instrument to the one his father had made him for his seventeenth birthday last year had been a dismal failure.

Nicholas simply didn't possess the feel for wood needed to follow in his da's footsteps as a woodcarver. James Thatcher always claimed to be able to see the object he wanted to produce within a piece of wood. Nicholas just saw wood.

Despite his failings, he'd still become Da's apprentice, mainly because no one else wanted him. Small and wiry, Nicholas hadn't found anything he was particularly good at, apart from annoying his mother and playing his recorder.

But father wasn't here anymore, would never be here again, thanks to a fall at the big house that loomed over the landscape a mile away. He'd been employed to add embellishments to balustrades and paneling. All Nicholas had done was move wood around the workshop and sweep up.

The money had been excellent, and despite having other projects to complete, Ma ordered her husband to take the job. She hadn't allowed Nicholas to accompany his father to install them, in case he embarrassed them with his clumsiness or stupidity. Nicholas still wondered if things would have been different if he'd been there, but both father and son obeyed Ma.

A week ago, the chairman of the build had arrived with father's body on a cart and his pay, plus another five shillings. Nicholas didn't think it much for a man's life.

As fine as the matched bay horses were, Nicholas couldn't stop staring at the crimson doublet of the fat elderly man the blue liveried groom helped down from the carriage. He had never seen such a color being worn. The Queen's sumptuary laws meant this man must either be a lord or wanted to spend time in prison.

The man didn't stop by the cottage gate like everyone else. Instead, he limped up the path toward where Nicholas sat on a stool his father had made. This gentleman clearly didn't know Ma's reputation for chasing the uninvited out with her broom.

Nicholas got up from where he'd been sitting, trying to stay out of Ma's way while being within earshot. Making her shout for him never ended well, but she found things for him to do if she saw him sitting around.

This situation could prove entertaining. Would this aristocrat receive the twig end of Ma's broom or the handle? How fast could he run with that limp that made him roll his fat body from side to side like a man taken with strong ale?

"Ma's busy. What d'you want?"

The gentleman's eyebrows rose. "And who might you be?"

Nicholas puffed his chest out and pushed his brown woolen cap back on his head. "Nicholas Thatcher. This is my cottage."

The man's carefully trimmed dark drooping mustache twitched. "Is that so? In that case, I offer you three hundred pounds for it."

Nicholas gaped. His father had been considered wealthy in the village, and he'd earned two shillings a week when he'd had work. You could buy a whole farm for three hundred pounds. Yes, the timber-framed, wattle and daub thatched cottage was sturdy and well built, with a sizeable garden for

Ma's herbs, but it only had one room, with a bed on a platform under the eaves at one end. Nicholas slept on a straw-stuffed pallet near the hearth.

His mother came out of the cottage, wiping her hands on her apron. "What brings you here, Milord Walpole?"

"You know who I am?"

Ma snorted. "Common folks aren't stupid, milord; we just have less money and opportunities. Now, as I said, what brings you to my door?"

Nicholas looked at the man with new eyes. Thomas Walpole, Earl of Tandridge, owned the newly built great house along the lane. The previous building on the site had been much smaller, and even though they'd been Catholics, his father said they'd been decent neighbors.

Five years after his birth—on the orders of Queen Elizabeth—husband and wife, a priest, and four servants, had been hung virtually on their own doorstep. Nicholas's father had been paid three shillings to make the gallows. Their crime had been holding Mass at the house.

The land had been given to Thomas Walpole, along with an earldom, for services to the crown. The old house had been raised to the ground, and they'd begun building the new Hall five years later. Construction had been going on for most of Nicholas's life, and it'd taken several lives in the process, including that of James Thatcher, master woodcarver.

"I've come to offer condolences for the loss of your husband, Mistress Thatcher." The earl touched the brim of his fashionably tall black hat.

Ma's lips pressed together. "Took you a fortnight to find out where he lived, did it? Even though you've passed the door ten score times since you arrived. Condolences don't put food on the table or clothes on our backs, Milord Walpole. And I be Agnes Flowers, not Thatcher. We never married. Now, if you'll excuse me, I have work—"

"Impudent wench," the blue-clothed, sharp-faced man who was helping the earl said. "How dare you turn your back on—"

A hand shot out, silencing the sharp-faced man in blue. "Calm yourself, Edmund. Mistress Flowers is a neighbor, not a tenant or employee. I apologize for not coming sooner, but I've been away on the Queen's business."

Ma simply stared at him, clearly not impressed by the mention of Queen Elizabeth.

Nicholas looked from one adult to the next. This was priceless. Ma appeared totally in charge, with this *lord* almost groveling for her favor.

The time when peasants needed a Lord's favor to survive had ended with the last wave of the Black Death some forty years ago. By the look of him, this Lord might have even lived through it. He certainly looked old enough. Maybe that was the reason for his politeness despite Ma being rude, but Ma was short with everyone.

"As I said to your fine son here, I wish to purchase his cottage, and by the law of the land, it is his, or it will be when he reaches twenty-one, not yours. It is the ideal location for a gatehouse for the Hall, and I'm prepared to pay handsomely for the inconvenience it—"

Ma folded her arms under her ample bosom. "Not interested, and neither is my son, even when he does get to twenty-one in three years. I was born here. My mother, her mother, and her mother were born here. Flowers women are bound to this land, and I'm not going anywhere, no matter the price. Now, unless you wish to purchase a gout remedy, be on your way, milord."

The older man's brows drew down. "The men in your family seem to have a habit of dying early if property is passed from woman to woman. Has anyone accused you of witchcraft?"

Nicholas stiffened. Being accused of witchcraft could be worse than being found to be a papist.

"People accuse me of being observant and knowing herbs, Milord Walpole, nothing more." Her gaze dropped to his feet. Nicholas looked too. One boot was significantly larger and softer than the other. "It doesn't take witchcraft to notice the swollen, painful foot of an old man used to a life of fine living. Now, do you want a poultice guaranteed to ease your pain or not?"

"I've spent the last week having the best physicians in London plastering it in foul-smelling concoctions with no effect."

Ma snorted and turned back to the cottage door. "My remedies always work if applied by the right person."

Walpole chuckled, but there was little mirth in the sound. "And pray tell me, Mistress Flowers, I take it that you are the right person?"

Ma's back straightened, and she turned back to Thomas Walpole.

"No, milord, I am not. The traditional remedy involves boiling a red-haired dog alive in oil before adding certain herbs, which is no doubt what you were given by your highly-priced physicians." Her sneer said precisely what she thought about educated men.

"However, rather than being told about it in some book, I've found a poultice made with autumn crocus works just as well without the loss of a valuable setter or hound—" she held up a finger, "—if the person applying the poultice is red-haired."

Everyone turned to look at Nicholas. He had the same bright copper hair as his father.

Touching the corpulent man's swollen leg appealed even less than fetching and carrying for Ma.

"I can't. I've got..." he paused, trying to think of something, anything, that he had to do to avoid the task. His habit of going down to the village and hanging out on the green with the other lads every Sunday afternoon had never gone down well with Ma. Father had always let him go and 'be a lad' for a while, but full-time adult responsibilities loomed in his immediate future.

"Send him with the poultice as soon as it's ready," the earl said and turned back toward the lane where the carriage waited.

"It won't be ready until late tomorrow, milord, but you haven't asked the price," Ma called out.

"My offer is apprenticing your son up at the hall instead of remaining a wastrel illiterate with no trade or prospects." He raised two fingers to the brim of his hat. "Good day to you, Mistress Flowers."

"One shilling, Milord Walpole, and you're not having my son any more than my cottage."

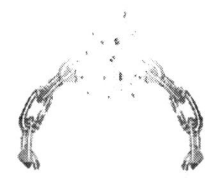

As the moon rose the next night, Nicholas found himself standing in front of his ma as she inspected him. Her nose wrinkled. "I suppose you'll do. But remember, don't dally, don't accept an apprenticeship, and make sure you collect the shilling before giving the poultice."

"Yes, Ma, I remember." He sighed, rolling his eyes as she tugged at his clothes. At least no one was here to see him treated like a child.

"Well, go on then. The moon won't be up to light your way home if you dawdle like you always do."

Nicholas found himself walking along the hard-packed dirt lane toward the big house, holding a brown, earthenware bowl the size of two spread hands. At least the now solid tallow-based poultice didn't smell as bad as some of the ones Ma made. Grease from a dead fox was one of the worst. Staying bald sounded better than rubbing that stinking mixture into your head.

Wearing his best clothes, including his pantofles[1] that he only ever wore to church, he'd set off. The past few days had been dry, and it was late summer, so he'd forgone his pattens. The wooden overshoes were ungainly but kept his pantofles clean when it was muddy.

Light streamed from the huge building up ahead. The Hall imposed itself on its surroundings rather than settling into the landscape and being part of it like his cottage. It even battled the night for supremacy. Staring up at the towering building, he couldn't even see the stars due to the light streaming from the many windows.

His cottage had two small, glassless, shuttered windows built into the thick white wattle and daube walls underneath grey thatch, but Walpole Hall was dark red brick from ground to roof.

Even from thirty feet away, he could hear male voices, loud with merriment. *Maybe this won't be so bad.* Walking up to the towering studded wooden door, he found the shiny brass bell pull and yanked it. The raucous voices coming from inside ceased.

He swallowed, thought about running, but stayed put, remembering the last switching Ma had given him. His mother might not be tall, but she wielded a hazel wand with remarkable strength.

The door creaked open. The same man from the carriage, wearing the same dark blue doublet, looked down his nose at Nicholas as if he were a fresh turd.

Nicholas lifted the bowl slightly. "Ma sent me with this. For 'is Lordship."

"The likes of you do not enter by the front door. Go around the back." The door shut in his face.

Ma was right. These people did think they were better than ordinary folk. Clenching his jaw, mind on the battering he'd get if he didn't fulfill his errand, he made his way around the huge house. Light, voices, delicious odors, and heat radiated from an open door. Nicholas peeked inside.

A stout man with forearms big enough to be a blacksmith kneaded a large batch of creamy yellow dough on one of two long tables in the center of the room. A pewter pie dish, the size of a man's chest, filled with neat slices of meat, lay next to him.

Other men were busy carrying empty plates and pots through another door. Two lit hearths stood next to each other, both the width of a dray horse. The heat almost knocked Nicholas back a step as he stood at the door, but it didn't seem to bother the eight kitchen staff.

"I've erm, got the poultice for milord's gout?" he called out.

The cook didn't look up. "Hey, Grimshaw, take—" He looked up for the first time, and a smile appeared. "Oh, you're James Thatcher's son, alright. Sorry about your father; he was a good man. Milord will be pleased you're here; his foot is beset by demons most nights."

A thin boy, younger than Nicholas, climbed out from under one of the tables and yawned.

"Come on, come on, the master's expecting him. And John, come right back. You know the Viscount is here with his guests tonight. Young Thatcher, there are leftover pies over there if you want to take one for your way home."

Nicholas considered asking what sort of pie, then decided he shouldn't look a gift pie in the mouth.

Tugging at his cap, he said, "Thank you, kind sir."

Still yawning and stumbling, the boy led Nicholas out of the sweltering kitchen and up a flight of stone steps wider than Nicholas's entire one-room cottage.

The boy didn't seem to care about his surroundings, but Nicholas gaped. Everywhere he looked were paintings and tapestries on the walls. Dark wooden chests were scattered around as if they were ten a penny. Ma had five chests, but only because Father made them for a living. The homes of his friends only had one or two.

John led him across a galleried landing, but Nicholas had to stop and stare. It felt as if he'd walked into another world, one of color, warmth, excitement, and excess in every way possible.

Beneath him, in a huge hall with a massive gray stone fireplace, men sat around a long, dark wood table, drinking out of pewter goblets and laughing rowdily as if they were in the Red Lion in the village.

The rushes on the floor and the dogs wandering around reminded Nicholas of the cramped, smoke-filled drinking hostelry, but the resemblances ended there. These men wore fine clothes. Their doublets had padded shoulders with slashed doublet sleeves that revealed fine, bright silk undershirts. Lace showed at their necks and wrist. Some even had gold braid and pearls sewn onto their clothes and boots. Despite their stiff finery, they looked comfortable, lounging, laughing, and taking drafts of wine.

Servants—all male because women only worked as ladies' maids or laundresses—stood around the perimeter, occasionally darting in to refill a goblet, offer more food, or clear finished dishes.

"See that one in black?" John nodded toward a man with a well-groomed pointed brown beard, a long face, and an aquiline nose.

"What about him?" Nicholas asked.

"That's Richard, the Earl's eldest son. The one in green is the second son, Charles. He's not too bad, not with boys anyway." Both men looked like younger, thinner, fitter versions of their father. "Don't let Richard corner you alone," John continued. "He's a mean bugger who likes to make boys cry and beg. He'll grab your balls and squeeze 'em fit to explode like ripe plums if 'e can."

Nicholas blew out a breath, uncertain what to say as they stared down on the scene of merriment.

The corner of the balustrade was crowned with a small phoenix carving he remembered emerging under his father's talented hands. Of their own volition, his fingers reached out and brushed over the carving, wondering if it had been the last thing James Thatcher touched. The bawdy laughter below him sounded derisive, callous, not merry anymore.

"Is this where it happened? Where my Da fell?" he asked.

In the back of his mind, he was already thinking of ways to torment the man laughing below while keeping him at arm's length.

"Dunno. No one tells me anything. I just scrub pots and turn spits, for now anyway. I won't be a kitchen boy forever. Come on, the master's chambers are this way. Don't worry, the countess's rooms are at the other end of the house. It's not likely that you'll bump into her, but if you do, don't look at her or her maids."

Nicholas glanced over his shoulder one more time as he trailed after John.

"They don't sleep together, the earl and his wife?"

John snorted and carried on walking. "You ain't been around gentry much, 'ave you? Marriage is for alliances and heirs. Once that's done, most married couples avoid each other like the plague. The men have their fun with the pages, stableboys, and laundresses. Plus, many keep mistresses in London."

Nicholas blinked. "They... you know, with boys?"

John shrugged. "Aristocrats are a law unto themselves. Hurts a bit, 'specially the first time, and if you don't use enough spit, but most of 'em give you tuppence[2]. Sometimes even a groat[3] or a sixpence[4]."

It sounded like a quicker way to build up money than fetching and carrying for free, but being treated like a wench?

"And the women?"

"The countess has a negro maid called Ruby. She's busy with her a lot," John said as they began ascending another broad flight of steps, but he stopped on a wide landing halfway up.

John indicated the solid door. "That's the master's room. His gentleman usher, Sir Edmund, and Robert, his page, will probably be preparing milord for bed. As milady's brother, Sir Edmund has his own bedchamber across there." He pointed at the door opposite. "Robert is meant to sleep on a pallet out here kept in there—" he waved at a chest standing neatly against a wall "—in case milord or Sir Edmund need anything, but more often than not, Richard's in with Sir Edmund. The sour old bugger likes 'is cock warmed at night, but Robert is as sour as 'is master. I don't give 'im the time of day unless I 'ave to."

John gave a jaw-creaking yawn before carrying on. "Most of the household staff sleep in the Low Great Hall, apart from the kitchen staff." He grinned. "We get to sleep in the kitchen. Warmest place in the whole of Kent, but we do 'ave to get up before the cocks crow." He paused, stifling another yawn. "Do you want me to wait, or can you find your own way out?"

"I'll work it out. Thank you," Nicholas said and watched the youngster shuffle off down the broad, shallow stone steps.

Turning to the pale, newly made door, he took a breath and knocked. "Nicholas Thatcher, here with your poultice, milord."

"Thank the Lord. Edmund, let him in."

The door opened. Nicholas came face to face with the man who had opened the door to him. He still looked as if he'd sat on a cowpat.

"You're a sir? I thought you were the footman."

A bark of laughter came from inside the room. "I told you that doublet made you look like a servant. Well, come on, man, let him in."

Edmund stood aside, looking even more sour and revolted by Nicholas than before.

"Ma says you need to be careful about your expressions. If the wind changes, you could be stuck like that." From the four-poster bed, with a rich blue canopy and curtains, Thomas Walpole, Earl of Tandridge, laughed like a little boy.

Encouraged, Nicholas carried on. "Although, thinking about it, you've looked like that every time I've seen you, so perhaps it already—" He ducked back as Edmund swiped at him.

"Careful there, sir, wouldn't want to break the pot. Ma would have both our guts for garters. Speaking of Ma, she says I have to get my shilling before you get this." He raised the pot a little.

"You think I'm frightened of a hedgewitch?" Edmund growled.

Nicholas frowned. "Ma's not a witch, but she does know how to use a switch, and I likes me arse without stripes. Now, do you want this or not?"

"Edmund, you may go."

"I can't, in all good conscience, leave you to the mercy of—"

Walpole's face lost any trace of mirth. "Begone."

Edmund bowed, stiff as a board. "As you wish, milord."

Nicholas waited until the door had closed before sitting on the bed, on the opposite side to the foot-high mound over what he assumed was the lord's gouty foot.

"Is he always that cheerful?" Nicholas asked.

Thomas Walpole shook his head, chuckling. "Have you considered apprenticing as a Fool?"

Nicholas shrugged. "I know plenty of fools, but no one who's paid to be one. What do they do?"

"They entertain, tell jokes, make fun of people, sing, dance."

"And people pay them for that?"

"They do, and handsomely too."

"Ma said I wasn't to accept any apprenticeships," Nicholas said and immediately regretted it as Thomas's expression clouded over.

"That woman is a tyrant."

"Aye, she is, but she's my only kin, except for my aunt Alice, and she's even worse." He held up the bowl, wanting to change the subject. He knew what people thought about his female-dominated family. "So, do I get her shilling?"

"After you've applied it now and again in the morning."

Not wanting to upset the wealthy man who owned more than Nicholas had ever dreamed of, he gave the man a bright smile. "Right you are, sir."

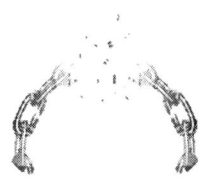

He'd started walking home and getting up before dawn to avoid his mother and make it back to the Hall in time for the Earl to wake up. After a week, the twice-daily journey and the lack of sleep began taking their toll.

Ma caught him dozing when he should have been fetching water from the well.

"Well, if you can't keep awake during the day, you might as well sleep there."

That night, after applying the poultice, he'd got the pallet out of the box John had shown him and slept on the wide steps outside the earl's room. He reapplied the poultice in the morning and went home with a smile, munching on newly baked fine bread and a wedge of fresh, creamy cheese.

The poultice didn't even smell that bad after a while, and the swelling seemed to decrease a little more every day. Milord hadn't even cursed when Nicholas rubbed the mixture into the joint of his great toe this morning.

After a long day of chopping wood at home, he was back, almost asleep, as he finished applying the poultice. The Earl's room sat above the main fireplace of the Low Great Hall, and the warmth in the room wasn't doing anything to help keep Nicholas awake.

Yawning, Nicholas folded the linen nightshirt back down Thomas's leg. It wasn't fair that by an accident of birth, this old man got to sleep on such a soft, warm bed, while hardworking folks, like himself, slept on the cold ground with a threadbare blanket worse than those the Earl's horses were given.

"Why don't you stay in here tonight? My foot's always better when you're touching it. Come on, stretch out. It's not fair that you're always rubbing my foot, and I've never touched yours."

Nicholas frowned. "You pay me for that, milord."

"I'll pay you for this too."

"How much?" Nicholas asked out of habit, although just getting to stay in the bed was enough.

"A groat."

Nicholas snapped, "Done," before the man who clearly had more money than sense changed his mind.

He'd spent the night curled up on the most comfortable, sumptuous bed he'd ever experienced, with a man so powerful, so wealthy, it addled his mind. Snuggling down, he vowed he'd never sleep on a straw pallet on a dirt floor like he did at home ever again.

A touch to his foot woke him, and the earl jerked away. He stayed still, and after a few breaths, a hand gently touched his foot again. When he didn't react, the earl eased the foot closer to his face. He heard a deep intake of breath and soft lips pressed against his bare skin.

"Hmm, so slim, so strong," the earl murmured, but he didn't do anything except gently worship the foot he'd captured. Nicholas continued to feign sleep. It seemed a small price to pay for a groat and sleeping in this bed.

He didn't go home the next day; the pot still held enough mixture for at least two treatments, and the silver coin left next to it confirmed his decision.

After spending the day hanging around the kitchen, sampling the food, he'd joined the kitchen staff in carrying food to the other household staff before taking a seat at the table for the lowest servants. No one had offered him a seat, but nobody had told him to get lost either.

It wasn't a permanent table like the Walpole family used, but a long board resting on trestles that could be cleared away. Nicholas had learned early in life that putting your elbows on the table wasn't just rude, it was downright dangerous. The board could tilt or fall, sending everything on it to the ground, much to the delight of any nearby dogs.

Most of the diners sat on three-legged stools, but the Walpole family, and the head of each domestic department, had the honor of using a chair. The chairman of Nicholas's board, who sat at the end nearest the family's table, was the head groom.

Nobody questioned his presence, but when he winced and wiggled a finger in his ear at Sir Edmund's woeful attempts at singing while playing the lute, several men nearby stifled grins. He felt seen, wanted, and included for once in his life, and he didn't want it to end.

One of the hounds snuffling amongst the rushes for dropped food gave him an idea. He nudged the man next to him, one of the stable lads. Lifting his wooden ale cup to his lips to cover what he was doing and provide a louder noise, he let out a long, reedy howl.

Sir Edmund fell silent, as did everyone else in the hall. Clothing rustled as they all turned to where Nicholas sat. He stood up, pretending not to notice that he was the center of attention.

Wagging his finger at the dog, he said, "Bad dog, Sir Edmund is singing, not howling. Stop joining in."

Snorts and then outright laughter ran through the Hall from the low tables to the high one. Nicholas turned and feigned surprise at everyone looking at him. Only Sir Edmund didn't look amused. Even the countess, Edmund's sister, bit her lips as if trying not to laugh.

He pulled his cap from his head as he addressed the top table. "Forgive me, my lords, my lady, but he—" he waved to indicate the dog, "—seems to be under the impression that there was a contest, and he fancied his chances. I'll take him out." Surrounded by laughter and not bothering to hide his own grin, he grabbed the broad leather collar of the hapless hound and dragged it out to the kitchen. He gave the beast a piece of piecrust and a pat before returning to the hall.

"Well, go on, Edmund, play something. Just don't sing in case the rest of the dogs think they can beat you too," the earl managed to get out between chuckles.

With a scowl that threatened dire retribution, Edmund took up his lute again.

The groom beside Nicholas elbowed him. "Bet you won't do it again."

"How much?" Nicholas immediately returned.

"A farthing, but only if he doesn't play for the rest of the week."

Nicholas shook his head. "Not worth it. I could get whipped or dismissed."

The stableboy nudged the man next to him. A furious whispered conversation ran up and down the table, with men dipping into their pockets.

In the time it took Sir Edmund to launch into a second melody, an older man Nicholas knew to be a senior groom wandered down from his position higher up the board table.

"If you stop him caterwauling for a week, this is yours." A weather-beaten hand opened to reveal six farthings.

"Done," he said and reached for the pile of coins. The man closed his hand.

"When he's been quiet in here for a week, you'll get it. But if you tell anyone you've been paid, the deal's off. Got it."

Nicholas gave him a grin. "Got it. Now go away and let the master work."

With a snort of amusement, the man returned to his seat.

Nicholas waited a handful of notes before he got to his feet. Cocking his head this way and that, he wandered around the hall, looking under tables, even getting on his knees to check under the carved chests placed against the paneled walls.

As he'd hoped, out of the corner of his eye, he saw the diners elbowing each other, whispering, as they wondered what he was doing. Gradually, he worked his way toward the top table. The volume of conversation in the hall dropped, and even the servers stopped in their tracks.

Ignoring the seven family members at the table, Nicholas dropped to his hands and knees and peered under their table, while making kissing noises.

"Well, I never," the countess exclaimed as Nicholas began crawling along the floor, but he made sure he'd started at the end furthest from where she sat. Being accused of trying to see a lady's ankles would not end well.

Sir Edmund stopped playing. "Get out of there, you brazen varlet[5]," he called out.

Nicholas got to his feet. "Shhh, you'll scare it," he said in a loud whisper.

Sir Edmund frowned. "By God's teeth, what are you on about now? Are your brains addled?"

Nicholas gave him his best wide-eyed innocent expression. "The cat, sire. Didn't you hear it screeching? I thought someone must have trodden on the poor thing's tail, but it seems to have gone quiet now."

The silence lasted several heartbeats. Nicholas began to think he'd made a huge mistake.

"A cat with a squashed tail," the earl exclaimed and burst out laughing. He smacked his eldest son, seated next to him, on the shoulder. "That is what he sounds like, am I right?"

With the earl giving his support, the rest of the family and the household joined in the laughter. Even Edmund was forced to give a tight smile.

Nicholas bowed and backed away, then returned to his seat. As he passed between the tables, people praised him, patted his back. He might not have a crown, but at that moment, he felt like a king.

Face aching from smiling so much, he settled back onto his stool. John immediately came over to fill his cup with ale, the strong stuff, not the standard weak brew.

The food, the life, and merriment at Walpole Hall beat Ma's cottage a thousand times. She'd warned him not to accept an apprenticeship, but that was only because she wanted him to be her lackey for the rest of his days.

Yes, the cottage would technically be his in a few years, but he had no illusion that things would change. Agnes Flowers knew her own mind and didn't bow to pressure, even refusing to marry the man she took to her bed. She didn't even seem ashamed of herself or have the least grain of regret for making a laughingstock of Nicholas and his poor dead father.

But these people were laughing with him, not at him. It felt damn good. This place, these people, were his future, not that dirt-floored, cramped, single-room cottage down the lane with its grouchy, demanding, unappreciative owner. All he had to do was wrangle a permanent position here, preferably one that didn't involve backbreaking work in all weathers.

He headed up to milord's chambers when the old man retired despite not being summoned. Sir Edmund left the room with a sniff as Thomas bid him enter after he knocked on the door. Yes, he might have made an enemy, but Edmund hadn't liked him since he set eyes on him. That wasn't likely to change whatever Nicholas did.

He'd finished helping the earl get ready for bed, folding his sumptuous clothes carefully and helping him wipe off the grime of the day with a clean linen square. After applying the poultice, Nicholas blew out the beeswax candle in the brass wall sconces, took off his leather jerkin, breeches, and hose, and climbed into the big bed, feet almost on the Earl's pillow.

He lay tense, sure the earl would punish him for his presumption both in the Hall and in his bed. Instead, the earl pulled Nicholas's foot to him again, kissed it, and stroked his leg. His fingers moved higher and higher, pushing up Nicholas's linen undershirt, brushing his fingers over the sensitive skin at the back of his knee. The bed creaked as the earl shifted so he could reach Nicholas's backside.

He froze. This was what John had been talking about. A vision of Ma coming at him with her favorite switch made up his mind. *How bad could it be?*

"Do you know what a fool does?"

He did, but the earl seemed to enjoy educating him. "Makes stupid mistakes, sire?"

The earl chuckled. "No, young Nicholas, a fool does not make mistakes. He uses his wit and skills to distract his master from tedium and duty through jokes, music, parody, and any other means he can, as you did this evening."

"I hope I didn't offend Sir Edmund too much."

"Oh, don't worry about that old windbag. It's me you need to concentrate on pleasing. Would you like to be my Fool, Nicholas? I'll pay you well, you'd live here, travel with me, and fools are exempt from sumptuary laws[6]. You could wear whatever I wear."

A vision of Ma coming at him with her favorite switch made up his mind.

"Yes, milord, I'd like that very much."

Thomas patted his leg. "Good." It was odd having such a momentous conversation lying only partially clothed in a man's bed, but he didn't suppose being a professional fool was a normal occupation.

"Do you know how to please a man, in private, Nicholas? Because pleasing your master—in all ways—is part of a Fool's role."

He didn't think what the earl said was true, but did it make a difference? Was refusing worth going back to Ma? It didn't take long to decide. How much worse could it be than rubbing poultice into the man's diseased foot?

"No, no, sir. I've never done anything with a man—or a woman to tell the truth. Ma doesn't let me out much."

The earl hummed to himself. "Sensible woman. I wouldn't let you out much either if you were mine. Do we have a deal? Will you be mine for ten pounds a year?"

It wasn't a bad offer, ten pounds was more than farm laborers earned, more than John and the stable lads earned, but he'd never get personally rich on it.

The earl must have sensed his hesitancy. "If you keep quiet, keep yourself just for me, and do what you're told, I'll give you sixpence every time we know each other."

"Will..." He swallowed. The thought of this corpulent man heaving on top of him, taking his pleasure in his body, turned his stomach. "Will you want to know me like a man knows a woman?"

"No, my sweet boy, I'm a student of the human form, an artist without a medium, if you will. I would enjoy touching you, learning your tender, untouched body."

"I can do that," he whispered, hoping to hell and back that he could.

The earl's hand reached higher. His bollocks were gently rolled while the earl exclaimed how beautiful they were. He touched, even talked, to Nicholas's cock and hole with the utmost reverence, calling them pure, unsullied.

It was the oddest thing he'd ever experienced, and it didn't turn him on at all, but sixpence was sixpence.

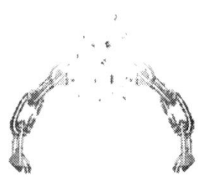

Well-rested, well-fed, and well paid, Nicholas whistled to himself as he approached his mother's cottage, which looked so much poorer now.

Ma straightened from where she'd been digging in the garden. The sneer on her face drained the joy out of him like a hole in a bucket.

"Enjoying yourself, boy? Have you forgotten who and what you are? Do you need a reminder?"

Ma's reminders were universally painful. Between one heartbeat and the next, he'd had enough.

"Well, Ma, you've just given me a reminder of what a scold you are. You ought to be careful, lest they use the branks[7] on you."

She started toward him, arm raised. "Why you—"

Nicholas ducked back out of reach and carried on running.

"Don't think I'll be making any more poultices for that Lord of yours," she called out after him.

Nicholas pulled up, hung his head. The job of Fool to Milord Walpole involved making him happy and distracting him from pain. A job that would be far harder, perhaps almost impossible, without the poultices. No poultice would mean no reason, no excuse, to be in milord's private chamber. Hopefully, last night had given him a reason, but he could hardly admit that he spent his nights in the Earl's chambers because the lord liked playing with his balls.

Putting on the sad expression that had always worked on his father, he headed back to the cottage gate.

"Sorry, Ma. I guess my head got turned a little. Milord Walpole offered me an apprenticeship as his Fool. Ten pounds a year, he said."

"And I bet you snapped the offer out of his hand like a starving dog rather than talking to me when I *told* you not to accept an apprenticeship."

She looked him up and down, huffing in derision. "A fool? I guess it's all you could hope for. The Lord knows you're useless for anything else."

He hung his head, tried for contrite. "I'll give you some of my pay to—"

"Some?" She snorted as if he'd told the funniest joke she'd ever heard. She held out her hand. "Coins," she demanded. "It's not like you need any when you're living up there. I'll let you keep two pounds a year if you work the garden one full day a week, but I'll be keeping that too if I need to pay someone to do your work here."

He fished in his pocket, regretting that he'd put everything he'd been given in one purse. She looked inside, snorted, and slipped it in her apron. The vain hope that she'd let him keep a penny or two died.

"Now, does Milord Walpole's Fool want his switching in the house or out here so everyone can hear him howl?"

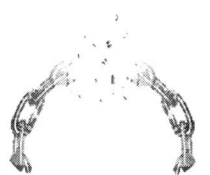

1. Pantofles: Slip-on leather shoes with cork soles
2. Tuppence: Coin worth two pence.
3. Groat: Siver coin worth four pence.
4. SIxpence: Silver coin worth six pence. Twelve pennies made a shilling. Twenty shillings made a sovereign – worth a pound.
5. Varlet: A dishonest or unprincipled man.
6. Sumptuary Laws: Laws regarding apparel–color and cloth/fur/embellishment types–intended to reinforce and maintain social hierarchy.

7. Branks or Scold's bridle: An iron framework that enclosed the head with a bridle bit that pressed down on the tongue and stopped the wearer from speaking.

CHAPTER EIGHTEEN

The walk back to the Hall was a great deal less comfortable than the walk home had been, but he'd secured another basin of the greasy poultice. He'd also grabbed the only possession that meant anything to him, his recorder. He tucked it down the front of his shirt to leave his hands free for the basin. From now on, he'd leave nothing of value at the cottage for his mother to destroy or sell. Besides, Fools were meant to entertain, and he knew he could do a much better job than Edmund. He might not be able to play the lute or an aristocratic virginal[1], but he played well and had a fair voice. He certainly didn't miss notes or destroy melodies with awful timing as Edmund did.

The Hall loomed ahead, and the sun sank behind it. The sound of a cantering horse coming from behind him caused him to step aside. Rain the night before had left puddles, and he didn't want his clothes muddied.

The horse slowed. "Nicholas, is it?"

He looked up to see Richard, Viscount Challock, heir to the Earldom, atop a fine chestnut stallion. The man was in the prime of life, in his late twenties, and resembled the portrait of his father painted a score years ago.

The twenty-eight-year-old heir to the earldom styled himself as a modern man and sported a narrow lace collar laying flat against his wine-red doublet, unlike the large stiff ruff that usually cradled his father's thick neck. The expensive, carefully disarrayed clothes drew his eye. So did Richard's fetching pointed dark beard, long mustaches, and slim, powerful body.

Nicholas wore one of his two undershirts, with his brown sleeveless jerkin, worn breeches, and hose. There was no hiding their status difference, yet the heir to the entire Walpole estate had stopped to talk to him, just as his father did.

"Yes, sir. Nicholas Thatcher. I'm going back to the Hall to help your father with his leg." He raised the bowl, and Richard wrinkled his nose.

"Are you hurt? You seem a little awkward."

"Aye, sir. I am a little sore."

"Did Uncle Edmund beat you for your prank last night? I haven't laughed so much for ages."

"No, sir, this is…something else." Being beaten by his mother when he was a grown man wasn't something he wanted to throw out there. He was meant to be a Fool, not an idiot.

"Want a ride?"

Nicholas opened and shut his mouth. Refusing would be rude, but riding with his poor bruised arse would be damn uncomfortable. Then he remembered what John the kitchen boy had said about Richard.

Shading his eyes with his hand against the bright afternoon sunshine, he squinted up at the man who was so far above him in every way.

"You mean on the horse, right?"

Richard's mustache twitched as he smiled. "Most definitely. I promise to behave myself, for now, anyway."

The flirtation was clear as the sky on this late summer day. Perhaps this was an opportunity to replace some of the money Ma had taken.

Nicholas touched the brim of his cap. "Much obliged by the offer, but sitting a horse right now would be mighty painful."

Dark brows drew together. "My father didn't beat you, did he?"

Nicholas grinned. "No, sir. T'was none of the fine folk at the Hall, and your father has been nothing but kind and generous. He's even offered me a job as a Fool." He dropped the smile for a mournful expression. "T'was my mother. She beat me for staying out without sending her notice. But your father asked me to stay. Says his foot is better if I sleep at the end of 'is bed. He looked so pained I couldn't refuse. She took the wages 'e gave me too, didn't leave me a farthing."

The viscount frowned. "That's all you do, sleep at the end of the bed?"

Having the interest of two lords had to be more lucrative than one. Besides, how much longer would Thomas be the Earl rather than Richard? This could be his best opportunity to establish a long-term relationship with the heir.

Nicholas wrinkled his nose. "What else would I do? He's a fat old man, not like a handsome fit fellow like yourself, milord. No disrespect intended."

"None taken." Richard smiled at the compliment and shifted back on his saddle. "Come on, you can lay across the front of me, save your poor rump."

"Like a sack of grain?" Nicholas shook his head. "Everyone would laugh and not in the good way they did last night. No, sir. I think I can manage astride, although I'm no horseman."

'No horseman' was a gross exaggeration. He'd never sat a horse and had only ridden in a wagon as a child when helping with the harvest.

The viscount pulled his foot out of the stirrup and held out his hand for the bowl.

Nicholas swallowed. If the basin of poultice got broken, he'd have to go back for another, and it took several days to make. Mother would be even angrier, and the earl might—

"Don't worry, boy, it'll be safe. Father hasn't been nearly as bad-tempered since you started the treatments. So, it's in all our best interests that they continue."

Praying the viscount was telling the truth, he handed up his precious burden. Richard passed it to his other hand before reaching down again for Nicholas's hand.

With a little hop and a jump, Nicholas found himself sitting in front of a viscount on a horse worth more than his father had earned in a year.

"Try not to drop it." The viscount gave him the bowl back and urged the horse into a walk.

The horse swayed from side to side more than he expected. He clutched the bowl to his chest with one hand while grabbing the horse's mane with the other. The recorder poked at his ribs, but he couldn't spare a hand to readjust the instrument.

"Squeeze your thighs, lift up a little. Take the pressure off your poor buttocks," Richard whispered against his ear.

Nicholas tried to do as asked, but Richard urged the horse into a trot. He drew in a sharp breath as the bouncing sent pain radiating up his spine and the mouthpiece of the recorder jabbed into his left nipple.

"Does it hurt, little Reynard?"

Being likened to a fox wasn't new, and Richard appeared to be enjoying his pain, just like John had said. *But would he pay for it?*

"Aye, milord, but a penny will lessen the sting."

Richard chuckled. "If a penny lessens the sting, let's see what you'll take for a shilling."

Richard snaked a hand around his waist as they rode, pulling Nicholas back against him.

"What do you have hidden in here?"

"My recorder, sir. I thought I might give Sir Edmund a little more competition than a howling hound."

Breath warmed his ear. "I'd like to hear you make sweet noises too, but not on a recorder."

Through his breeches, the viscount's cock—hard and eager, pressed against his lower back. The father might not be capable of using his tool these days, but the son certainly had no such deficiencies.

"Do you have an instrument in your breeches too, sir?"

The viscount chuckled. "Oh, you are a feisty one. Keep teasing, and our duet might be louder than you intended."

The horse clattered into the brick yard, and a groom ran up to take the reins. This was the last time Nicholas could back out of this situation without losing face.

"Don't worry, Hugh. Nicholas and I will see to Morello."

"Yes, sir," the wiry middle-aged groom said and turned away without glancing at Nicholas. He'd been the man who collected the money last night, but it appeared Hugh didn't want to rock any boats with his future employer.

Hugh's clothes were better than Nicholas's, but the man looked tired, worn, despite being far younger than the earl. Hugh probably worked from before dawn until after dusk for years just to feed and clothe himself while his employer ate and drank himself into his grave.

Nicholas didn't want to spend his life working like a dog for the scraps others left. He wanted to be the one leaving the scraps, and for that, he needed more money than honest, risk-free living could ever get him. Those who didn't stand up for themselves—who didn't take risks—stayed poor, like the groom, like Nicholas's father.

Richard didn't appear to want a Fool or to admire Nicholas as if he were a piece of art. The chances of gaining long-term employment with Richard were low.

The Walpole heir wanted something far more carnal and quick. Getting as much money as possible, so he could travel and seek his fortune when the earl died, perhaps in London itself, sounded like a dream come true.

Despite his resolution, apprehension crept along every nerve and tightened every muscle. So it might hurt—would probably hurt—according to John. But he hurt already, and his current pain had lost him money. From now on, Nicholas resolved that if he had to be in pain, it would damn well be profitable.

Richard slipped off the horse and led it into a loose box with Nicholas still in the saddle. The stable floor was strewn with sweet new straw. It smelled clean, wholesome, and much better than most peasant homes Nicholas had entered.

Richard reached up, grabbed Nicholas's waist, and lifted him down as if he were a maiden or a child. The nearness of his larger, muscular body had Nicholas trying to step away when his feet touched the straw. Richard held onto his arm.

"Don't be shy. Let me see the damage; it might need a salve."

Nicholas's gaze shot to the half-open stable door. Anyone could come past. He'd accepted this would happen, but with an audience?

Richard reached over, grabbed the upper half of the door, and pulled it shut. Light still peeked through the cracks in the door, illuminating the gloom and the viscount loosening the tie of his britches.

"If getting buggered is good enough for the King of Scotland, it's good enough for the likes of you. Put the bowl down. Wouldn't want it broken, would we?"

Nicholas's jaw dropped. "You buggered the Scottish king?" Saying the words felt so very bad, but it also gave him a thrill, similar to the one he'd gotten from his prank at Edmund's expense.

Richard snorted. "He loves it. Show him an upstanding prick, and he's drooling like a dog at a haunch of beef."

Nicholas dragged his gaze up from Richard's groin. He wasn't quite salivating, but going where a king had been? Oh, yes, that appealed.

"Do you want that sixpence or not?" Richard's voice now held an edge of annoyance.

Biting his lip, he looked up through the hair the viscount admired so much. "A crown[2]? Silver, not gold, of course." It was an audacious request, so he quickly added, "It's my first time, sir. I can't get it back."

"Turn around, drop your breeches, and brace yourself against the wall," the viscount said, voice rough with desire.

Nicholas put the basin against the wall, then turned back to the viscount. "Crown first."

Richard's brows drew together. "You sure you haven't done this before?"

"If I had, I'd only be asking a sixpence."

The viscount chuckled. "You're too clever for your own good, but if I think you lied, the beating your mother gave you will feel like a tickle in comparison."

He reached into a pouch hanging on his belt and withdrew a bright shining silver crown.

Nicholas reached for it, but Richard snatched it back before offering it again. This time, he let Nicholas take it.

"I intend to get my money's worth." He spun his finger in a circle.

Swallowing, praying it wouldn't hurt too much, Nicholas turned around, took a breath, pulled the recorder from his shirt. Then he undid the tie on his breeches, let them drop, and braced his elbows against the brick wall of the stall, one fist tight around the coin, the other wrapped around the recorder his father had made him. One breath, two. He hated having his bare skin exposed, imagining some foul miasma[3] invading his body through his skin.

If John can do this, so can I.

He jerked as a finger stroked across his bare flesh.

"Oh my, she really got you," Richard's voice was low. "Red, white, and a touch of blue, most artistic."

The horse stamped a foot and shook itself as if reminding them that it still wore its tack. The noise almost covered the viscount hawking and spitting into his hand.

Body heat warmed Nicholas's flesh. He screwed his eyes shut, clenching his fist around the shiny coin. He'd never had this much money in his—

Huge and blunt, the viscount's member pressed against his hole. A hand grasped his hip, hard enough to bruise.

"If you cry out, I keep the crown," the viscount murmured, then shoved forward.

He went up on his toes, trying to tuck his backside in and away from the ripping pain. A strong arm slipped around his hip, grabbed his balls.

"You squeal, and I'll rip them off, got it?"

Nicholas put the side of his fist in his mouth and nodded. The viscount thrust, again and again, working his way inside until his hips pressed flat against Nicholas's rump.

Harsh, panting breath warmed his ear. "By God's bollocks, you feel good."

"G...glad to be of service," Nicholas choked out, then he cried out as the Viscount sped up. Buttoning his lips, he told himself he could do this, would do this.

Richard squeezed his balls hard, and Nicholas instinctively pulled back, impaling himself on Richard's cock even harder. The man seized against him, shuddering as he took his release. After a final pull on Nicholas's still soft member, Richard stepped back, his spent member sliding, slick and wet, from Nicholas's battered body.

Nicholas stayed in the same position, wondering if it was blood or seed dripping down his bare thigh. A slap on his buttock brought him back to himself.

"Better cover up, boy. If you stay with your arse sticking out like that, Morello will want a go too."

The speed with which Nicholas snatched at his breeches and pulled them up, while trying to keep hold of the coin, made the viscount laugh. "If you want a shilling, come find me in a few days when you're healed, and you can warm my cock again."

The viscount opened the stable door. Nicholas blinked at the bright light as Richard walked out, leaving Nicholas holding up his breeches with one hand and his forearm on the wall for support.

Hugh walked in and simply began unsaddling the horse as if Nicholas wasn't even there. He felt like a ghost, unseen, forgotten, and dismissed by the living, yet last night, he'd been the center of attention.

Then he reminded himself that he'd had the Earl and his heir's entire focus for a little while. Not many could claim that. That and the money would have to be enough.

When the groom left, Nicholas refastened his breeches properly, tucked the crown into his shoe, the recorder into his shirt, picked up the bowl of poultice, and made his way up to the Hall. Every step reminded him of the pain in his back passage and the coin in his shoe. Where there was one crown, he vowed there would be many more. These arrogant Walpoles owed him for his father and his pain.

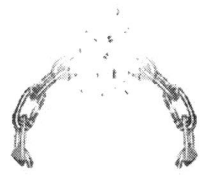

---

1. Virginal: An early keyboard instrument.

2. Silver crown worth sixty pence or five shillings.
3. Disease was assumed to be carried by the air, so uncovering and exposing your body to air or water was thought risky.

CHAPTER NINETEEN

Stopped by the heat when he stepped through the kitchen's open door, Nicholas didn't think he could love this place any more than he did already. Heat, hurrying bodies, shouted instructions, platters of salted fish, baked eel, cheeses, pasties, and eggs for the lower tables. The biggest baked salmon that Nicholas had ever seen was carried past by two kitchen workers, no doubt destined for the top table.

"Out, out, you're in the way," the head cook grumbled. Nicholas retreated outside to wait for dinner.

Leaning up against the sun-warmed brick, Nicholas watched small birds hop about, looking for scraps among the flagstones in the fading evening light. A light breeze brought the scent of herbs from the large kitchen garden as well as the muffled sounds of the kitchen workers preparing dinner. He couldn't imagine going back home and joining his mother in their typical silent evening bowl of barley pottage and coarse dark rye bread.

His immediate plan was to increase his purse by stopping Sir Edmund from playing for a week without getting into trouble. His pranks had gone down well last night, but he didn't want to make any more of an enemy out the man than he had already. Spreading the target of his pranks might work, but that could easily go wrong too. Right now, only one person in the household wished him gone. If that number increased, his position might become unstable.

As if his thoughts had summoned the man, Sir Edmund's reedy, off-key voice drifted down from one of the upper windows as he attempted to accompany himself on the lute. He's sounded like a tomcat calling for a wife, and the diners would likely be subjected to his efforts again tonight. Yes, Edmund came from noble blood, but he couldn't sing or play for shit.

He pulled his recorder from his shirt, lifted the warm wood to his lips, and started on the melody Sir Edmund was currently disemboweling with every string plucked. After the opening refrain, the lute and voice fell silent. Nicholas's music spiraled up into the autumn evening. Even the hubbub in the kitchen faded as he played.

Several windows above him opened. Sir Edmund leaned out. "Stop making that infernal racket."

"Who's playing?" the earl called out from the next window.

"Nicholas Thatcher, milord. Sorry if I disturbed you."

"You're playing tonight at dinner."

"But, I always—" Edmund protested, but the earl's window clanged shut.

Nicholas played a jaunty little trill, then ducked as an apple flew down from above. It landed too near the poultice basin for his liking, so he snatched up the bowl and headed inside.

"I thought I told you to get out?" the cook groused. "I can't have wastrels clogging up my kitchen. Take a seat in the Hall."

"I'm meant to be playing during dinner, so I won't be—"

The cook growled, snatched up a hunk of spiced wheat bread, a quarter wheel of mild cheese, and a wooden cup of ale. "You can eat there." He gestured at a spot near the door to the scullery.

Nicholas was finishing the last of the bread, when Sir Edmund's muffled voice rose above the general hubbub as he announced the presence of the Earl and Countess. In his mind's eye, Nicholas imagined the married couple making their way—slowly, because of milord's gouty foot—to their seats on the raised platform under the galleried landing. He wondered how long it would be before he also took the role of Master of Ceremonies from Sir Edmund.

It would be at least an hour or two before the earl wanted to retire. Rather than carrying the foul-smelling poultice into dinner, he decided to take it upstairs while everyone was beginning their meal.

As always, he stopped on the landing above the Low Great Hall and trailed his fingers over the phoenix carved into the newel post. Would James Thatcher accept what his son was doing to better himself? He didn't think so, but his father had always been obedient and content with his lot in life. Hard, backbreaking labor for little reward and a nagging, domineering wife that had led to nothing but an early grave. Pressing his foot down on the wooden planks, he felt the coin's outline. No, that life wouldn't be his. Walpole Hall would just be a staging post to something bigger and better.

Queen Elizabeth only had female Fools, but the Queen was old and childless. Rumor was that James of Scotland would become King of England, and Richard's comment about his Royal Highness's preference for men gave Nicholas hope. A fool's role was to entertain, and what better place to be entertaining than a bedchamber?

Although he couldn't see them, the earl and the countess would be side by side at the center of the top table. The rest of the family would be seated according to status. All would be wearing their wealth to enforce their position. By luck of birth, Nicholas would never sit at that table, but he could get damn close as a fool.

"Please, master, please stop—" the distressed, accented, female voice drew Nicholas from his contemplation.

"Come on, you haven't lifted your skirts for me in six weeks, and your mistress won't be back for at least an hour. They won't miss us," a male voice murmured. "Be a good girl. If you don't make a fuss, I'll give you some pretty lace. Come to my chamber, we—"

"Sir, I have my courses. I cannot—"

The wheedling tone vanished. "I don't care. You have two holes for a reason."

The girl gasped. "Please, Master, I beg you, not when I have my—"

Whistling a cheerful tune, Nicholas strode forward. The second eldest Walpole son, Charles, had caged a small, dark-skinned woman in an embroidered pale green dress against a wall. His fingers fumbled with the ties at the front of her gown.

Both looked at him. Ruby's wide eyes and trembling chin pleaded wordlessly for help. Charles's promised pain. Nicholas put on a deferential, polite expression and lied through his teeth.

"Ah, there you are, milord. Your father is asking your whereabouts."

The dark-haired man with the same long nose as his father and brothers gritted his teeth. "Get lost, boy."

Nicholas schooled his face into polite inquiry. "Shall I tell him that when I return to his side, sir? I was just going to deliver this to your father's chamber before heading back down to play at his request."

The young man pulled away from his victim with a growl and turned to Nicholas.

"Just because father favors you, it doesn't mean we all want you here," he spat at Nicholas, catching him with his shoulder as he shoved his way past.

Ruby stood, head bowed, with a hand over her lower belly. The countess dressed her up like a doll, like an accessory, which, Nicholas supposed, she was. After all, she'd been bought and paid for like Richard's stallion. The family would sell Morello's offspring, but this girl wasn't livestock; she had feelings that the damn Walpoles didn't appear to possess at all.

His hand hovered over her arm. The poor girl didn't look any older than him. "Can I do anything?"

Her head shot up, eyes blazing. "You can leave well alone. You think a boy who howls like a dog and offers himself to be used as a woman is better than me? He was about to offer me a—"

"I do not—" he glanced around to ensure they couldn't be overheard, then hissed, "—get used like a woman."

She put a hand on her hip. "Your mouth denies but your body speaks the truth. I know, it's happened to me plenty of times. Buyers pay more for virgins, but that doesn't stop traders using both girls and boys." Her lips pursed. "If you want to help, you can assist me in convincing Henry that I carry his child."

"Are you with child?"

"Not yet, but I'm working on it. It might even become the truth if I can incite the others to take up sodomy."

"Others?" Nicholas asked.

She snorted. "Hoping to find more who will give you pennies for your tender behind? Who was it?"

"Richard."

Her nose wrinkled. "No wonder you're walking funny. He's a brute. Charles is almost as bad, and Edward always follows his brothers, but he hasn't got their confidence yet. Henry's the best of them. Sir Edmund's cock is so skinny I can hardly feel it."

Nicholas gaped at her audacity, then had to laugh. The countess might dress Ruby up like a doll, but it appeared she had a mind and a will of her own. Nicholas hadn't had much to do with the youngest Walpole, but the servants only said good things about the boy who shared Nicholas's birth year.

"You're a woman after my own heart, Ruby. Perhaps if we work together, we can run these aristocrats ragged."

She tilted her head, assessing him. "You can start by using my name, Yaingo, when we're in private."

Blowing out a breath, Nicholas tried to get his head around what she'd lost. Home, family, even her name. And she was still trying to get one over on her owners. He had to admire her for that.

"Where were you going? Do you want me to walk with you?"

"I'll not lift my skirts for you, Fool."

"I wouldn't ask, Yaingo," he replied truthfully.

"Because I'm a slave?"

"Because you don't have a significant purse," he said and offered his arm.

After leaving the poultice in the earl's room, he saw her safely back to the countess's rooms which lay at the opposite end of the building to her husband's.

Despite the ache in his abused behind, he trotted back to the staircase. Keeping the Earl and his family waiting wouldn't get him any coin.

As the earl bit into a chunk of salmon speared on his eating knife, he spotted Nicholas coming into the Hall.

"There you are. I thought you'd gotten lost."

Nicholas bowed. "Apologies, milord. I encountered Milady's maid as I was taking your poultice in your room. She felt she might swoon, so I escorted her back to Milady's chambers."

Henry's head came up, concern in his eyes. Maybe Yaingo had gotten further in her plan to ensnare the youngest Walpole than she'd thought.

"You didn't tarry with her, did you?" The earl ground out.

"Why would I do that when I could be playing for you?" He raised the dark, wooden pipe and gave the man a smile.

The earl's suspicious frown smoothed. He nodded, then took a swallow of wine from a silver goblet bearing the family phoenix crest.

The countess, with her carefully powdered wig and ruff, glared at him, as did Charles, who had just taken his seat next to his younger brother, Edward. The twenty-two-year-old listened as the second in line to the earldom whispered in his ear.

The countess had popped out a baby every two years for a decade, but the last had been a stillborn girl. Kitchen gossip said she'd banned the earl from her bed ever since.

The two middle sons could have been twins as they displayed equally sour expressions. Henry, who sat at the end of the table, picked at his food, looking as if he'd rather be checking on Yaingo. Fish wasn't Nicholas's favorite either, but he bet the salmon on Henry's plate tasted much better than the eel on the lower tables.

After the last few nights of moans and groans at Sir Edmund's efforts, Nicholas had an idea of the musical taste of the residents, or at least of those seated at the lower tables. He started with a lively tune he'd heard played in the village pub that never failed to get feet tapping.

Edmund shot his brother-in-law a questioning look, but the Earl smiled, waving his finger in time with the melody. Edmund scowled and motioned to a server to refill his goblet. If Nicholas hadn't been playing, he would have grinned at the man's discomfort. Tormenting the sour, stuck-up man gave him just as big a thrill as the night before, but now he had additional motivation.

Paying Edmund and his nephews back for the pain they inflicted on others would be his pleasure. The line he walked was a thin one, but the post of Fool gave him a license to tease that nobody else possessed.

Henry had barely waited for the main course to be removed before rising from the table. Nicholas turned to melodies Edmund and his sister preferred to give Henry and Yaingo a chance to be together. His efforts kept Edmund and the countess in their seats after the last course had been removed.

One by one, the remaining three Walpole sons left to seek further distractions or their beds.

Sir Edmund escorted his sister from the hall an hour after the meal. The earl stayed in his chair, staring into the fire as if the flames held the answers to everything as he nursed his rich wine. Nicholas continued playing even though his ass ached and his eyelids drooped.

The dozen or so members of the household who slept in the hall hid yawns as the kitchen staff cleared, wiped down, and then stacked the trestle tables. Two of the youngest were already curled up on pallets next to the hearth, sharing the warmth with the half dozen dogs.

In contrast, Nicholas Thatcher—the illiterate wastrel—would hopefully sleep in the most sumptuous bed in the county while someone who had the monarch's ear cuddled his feet. The beating from his mother would hopefully be enough of an excuse to stop the earl trying to touch his sore hole or balls tonight. Thomas enjoyed his 'purity,' and Nicholas certainly wasn't that anymore.

Starting the same slow tempo sleep-inducing piece for the third time, he wondered if he could sleep while standing and playing. It certainly felt as if he were playing in his sleep.

"Come on, boy, I'm ready for my poultice," the earl ground out as he used the table to heave himself to his feet.

Nicholas blinked, realizing that the recorder's mouthpiece had dropped from his lips. "Come on, come on, under my arm. Can't you see I'm in pain?" The stink of sack[1] on his breath merely reinforced their social distance. No praise, thanks, or even an acknowledgment of his service were offered for the three or more hours Nicholas had played for him.

His "Yes, milord" might not have been as deferential as it could have been. But the extent of his caring had melted almost as much as the candle stubs in the chandelier hanging high above him.

Holding the recorder in one hand, Nicholas slipped under the earl's shoulder. The man's weight nearly bore him to the ground, but somehow, Nicholas managed to keep going. It took an age to get to the bedchamber, with the red-faced earl huffing, puffing, and swearing with almost every step.

He bit his tongue on the urge to tell his employer that this would become a lot easier and less painful if he spent less time eating and drinking. Maybe in time, as a favored Fool, he could poke gentle fun at the earl, but not yet.

Once through the door of the earl's private chamber, he led the earl to the bed, then replaced the almost burned stub of the fine beeswax candles in the wall scones at the head of the bed.

Blinking and smothering jaw-cracking yawns that barely let him breathe between, Nicholas removed the earl's rich clothing. Yes, it would be tricky to undo all the ties and pins on your own, but the earl's lack of flexibility and his level of drunkenness meant he simply couldn't have gotten ready for bed on his own.

Making sure that as little skin was exposed to the air at any one time, he wiped the fat body with a clean damp linen square while helping the earl into his calf-length, long-sleeved nightshirt. Once the dirt and sweat had been removed, he ducked under the earl's shoulder again and helped him into the garderobe where his fine, closed stool lay.

Like everything else in life, where you pissed or left your night soil depended on your social status. Nicholas either pissed outside or into a fire. Night soil was a vital fertilizer that went directly into the garden or into a chamber pot in poor weather.

Once the earl was done, Nicholas heaved him off the padded seat, wiped him with soft lambswool on a stick, then assisted the sweating, complaining man into his grand, canopied bed.

"Boy, you are an angel on earth," Thomas moaned, thoroughly out of breath by the effort. Without replying, Alastor put the used chamber pot outside the door and set the clean one in position.

"Hurry up, my foot is killing me."

Without speaking, Nicholas retrieved the poultice basin from where he'd left it by the chest at the end of the bed.

Kneeling on the wooden floor beside the tall bed, exhaustion, the pain from the beating, the fucking, the way he'd been used and dismissed weighed heavier than the earl.

It wasn't fair. The preachers claimed that 'the meek shall inherit the earth' well, they could shove it up their vestments. Religion and 'Good Queen Bess' only worked to keep the likes of Nicholas in his place while the rich lived in luxury. But as he liked his neck its current length, he'd stay quiet and try to work the system to his advantage.

He didn't even experience much disgust as he carefully unwrapped the bandage on the swollen foot. Thomas hissed through gritted teeth as Nicholas carefully wiped off the salve from this morning. Yes, the foot remained discolored, but even in the flickering candlelight, it looked better than when Nicholas started doing this two weeks ago. And yet, apart from the hard-earned crown in his shoe, he had nothing to show for his work except a sore backside, bruises, and being more tired than he could ever remember.

Scooping up a dollop of the thick, yellowish, sour-smelling, greasy salve, he smoothed it over the earl's foot. Even his feet were fat. He could hardly tell where the ankle turned into his calf.

How much good living does it take to have fat feet?

"Nicholas, whatever is the matter? You haven't said a word all evening. And take off your outerwear; you don't want to get the poultice on them."

With a wince, he pushed to his feet and took off everything but his undershirt. It took no more than a minute to remove the belt that held up his breeches and take off the battered leather jerkin that had belonged to his father. As he knelt and tucked everything under the bed, he said, "It's not your problem, milord."

"It is if I have to look at your sour face."

Nicholas looked up. The Earl sat propped up in his opulent bed, his mouth puckered like an anus.

The only pain Thomas Walpole had was from overindulgence. Nicholas bet the man had never been beaten for anything in his life, just like his four sons. They lived charmed lives, did what they wanted, to whom they wanted, whenever they wanted, and all because they had money and the luck to be born into a particular family. Nicholas was probably in as much pain as this fat old man, yet he had fewer prospects because of an accident of birth. Maybe it was time the earl heard a little about the lives of others less fortunate than himself.

"Ma beat me for spending too much time here and for accepting the apprenticeship. She took my entire purse, even the vails[2] you gave me."

"I'll replace it if you do something for me." The earl licked his lips, his hungry, lustful expression mirroring that of his sons.

Nicholas was merely another entertainment for what seemed like the whole family, but he could use them too. He might have a sore arsehole, but he also had a crown in his shoe that he hoped wouldn't be lonely for long.

"Do you want me to play again?" he asked, even though he'd bet the coin in his shoe that the earl wasn't after music.

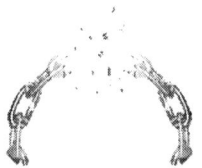

---

1. Sack: Fortified wine from Spain, that evolved into sherry.
2. Vails: Tip, gratuity.

CHAPTER TWENTY

The earl swallowed, then said in a hoarse whisper, "Have you been up to the long gallery?"

Nicholas frowned. "You want me to play up there? Now?"

"No. I was wondering if you'd noticed something missing from my grandfather's armor."

"I haven't been up there, sir, sorry. But I'm sure it looks perfectly—"

"Look in the chest." Thomas nodded at the trunk pushed up against the end of the bed. "Right at the bottom wrapped in the red chemise."

He lifted the garment out. The lump in the cloth was metallic, about seven inches long and half as thick as Nicholas's fist. He glanced up at the earl.

"Well, go on, open it."

Blowing out a breath, he unfolded the cloth. The revealed dull silver metal threatened like a headsman's ax.

"It's a codpiece." The earl's voice broke his stupor. "They were fashionable in the early part of the century. My grandfather served with the old king and had the armor made for the Field of the Cloth of Gold tournament in France in 1520, although he never wore it."

Nicholas looked down at the eighty-five-year-old hollow metal cock. Thomas's grandfather had either been a very well-endowed man, or he'd been trying to convince everyone around him of that fact.

"The armor or this?" he raised the codpiece.

Mirth bubbled up as he imagined Thomas's father turning up with a bigger armored codpiece than the legendary Henry VIII and having to surreptitiously remove it. Henry VIII had ordered people beheaded for far lesser offenses.

"Both. He fell from his horse while practicing for the tournament and died a month later."

"Oh. Sorry. Erm... What do you want me to do with it?" Nicholas asked, although he had an idea that it would involve pain for him.

Thomas drew himself up, lifting his chin as if that could disguise his fat neck. "You may never speak of this."

Nicholas straightened, looked the earl in the eye, and lied through his teeth. "Sire, I'm a poor fatherless wretch, and you have taken me in. You have my loyalty, always."

Thomas pursed his lips, nodded to himself, then lowered his gaze to his gnarled hands. "I wish to occasionally experience the freedom of being a woman within my chambers."

Nicholas forced his mouth to shut. This day couldn't get any stranger. "You want me to... with this?" He gestured with the codpiece.

"Yes. I can no longer manage alone."

Nicholas nearly dropped the codpiece at the thought of the corpulent old man buggering himself with it. But this had to be worth more than what he'd charged Richard.

"For an angel[1], I'll strap you first, you wicked harlot."

The earl's eyes lit up, and he clutched the green embroidered bedcover to his chin. "Oh sir, please don't."

This felt stranger than when Ma once used the wrong mushrooms in their pottage. But the power this man offered, even though it was only pretend, intoxicated.

"If you turn over quick, I'll use my hand, not the strap."

Thomas heaved himself over. It was the fastest Nicholas had ever seen the man move. Pushing down the covers, the Earl pulled up his nightshirt to reveal a broad saggy white backside reminiscent of a pony's rump. Nicholas grimaced. A quick glance confirmed that if Thomas had inherited his grandfather's genitals, his grandfather had grossly exaggerated the dimensions of his manhood when he'd commissioned the armor. The thought of getting any nearer to that turned his belly, but he'd manage for an angel.

He brought his hand down in a stinging slap, causing the flesh to ripple. The earl jerked, muffled a cry of pain in his pillow, but he didn't say "stop." Nicholas did it again and again, enjoying it a little more each time. He could feel the heat coming off the reddened skin from two inches away as the Earl of Tandridge sobbed and begged for mercy *from him*. The boy everyone labeled a worthless wastrel.

Grabbing the codpiece, he thrust it into the basin containing the tallow-based poultice, then pulled one of the cherry-red cheeks to the side.

"I'll teach you a lesson, my girl," he cried and shoved the cold metal against the Earl's wrinkled hole.

"God's teeth, be careful!"

Nicholas ignored him, drowning in his act. "Strumpets don't deserve careful," he said and pushed the codpiece in.

The earl cried out, and all thoughts of his own discomfort vanished as power coursed through him. He dealt the red, wobbling flesh another stinging slap.

"Sire? Are you well?" Nicholas froze at the call through the door.

"I'm fine," the earl choked out as he pushed himself to his elbows and turned toward the door. "Don't come in."

"Thomas? Is that boy in there with you?" Nicholas met the Earl's wide eyes at the sound of the countess's voice. "Sir Edmund says you dismiss him every night in favor of that boy you stared at all night. I'll not tolerate being made a fool of in my own home again."

The earl heaved himself upright, scrabbling behind himself to yank the codpiece from his flesh. "Move the stool; there's a chamber under it," he hissed.

Heart thumping, Nicholas grabbed his recorder, and the coin from his shoe, then scrambled to obey as the earl clambered off the bed like a great bald bear.

The wooden, padded stool in the privy was as heavy as it looked. The damn thing must have bricks in the bottom to provide ballast as Thomas strained to relieve himself.

"Pull it that way," the earl hissed, then called out, "No one's here, my dear. I'll be there in a moment, just using the privy."

With a heave, Nicholas shifted the heavy box, but he didn't see a hatch.

"There, there." The earl jabbed the codpiece he still held at one plank. "If she finds you, she'll petition the Queen like she threatened last time, and both our necks will stretch."

Nicholas scrabbled at the tiny crack between the floorboards but couldn't get any purchase.

"Use this." The earl shoved the codpiece at him. The part meant to fit against the rest of the armor was flat. Not caring that he held the end that had been inside the panicking man behind him, he pried the section of planking up. It revealed a two-foot square hole. Nicholas couldn't see anything below, nothing but a vague sense of a tight space.

"Hurry, get in there." The earl shoved at his shoulder. Heart in his mouth, Nicholas picked up the recorder—and the crown he'd suffered so much to get—sat down, and slipped into the hole.

He fell a little over the length of his body, but only got a glimpse of the brick walls around him before the light vanished as the earl replaced the hatch. Scraping came from above, and Nicholas imagined the earl pushing the stool back into place.

Footsteps and multiple furious muffled voices. Nicholas crouched, heart thumping, ears straining. Heat radiated from the far end of the narrow space. As his eyes adjusted to the darkness, a dim light source came from the opposite end of the eight feet long, four feet wide secret compartment. Trying to orientate himself, he worked out he was somewhere above the central fireplace in the Low Great Hall. The dim light revealed a wooden shelf behind him, holding a foot-long metal-bound wooden strongbox, and a pair of gaudy pale blue-green glazed vases with an odd, open lattice pattern. A two-foot-tall painting of a beautiful naked man rested against the wall beneath the shelf.

Remembering what he held, he grimaced and put the codpiece on the strongbox. Keeping all Thomas's favorite illicit items together seemed appropriate, but how had it all gotten in here? There was no way Thomas could have carried them in himself; he'd barely fit through the hatch, let alone climb back out. Besides, what was the point of hiding things in here? At least some people would know this chamber existed, the carpenter who had created the hatch and the shelf for one.

His heart went cold. With trembling fingers, he felt along the underside of the shelf for the brackets. The shape of a hooked beak on a smooth head with spread wings to take the weight was unmistakable. His father had made this shelf, and knowing him, he would have insisted on installing it himself.

How accidental had that fall been? Hiding no longer seemed like a healthy idea. The earl could wait until no one was around and kill him as he'd killed his father. The more people who knew he was here, the better. Even if the countess made an accusation, he'd have a better chance if he got to put his case to the authorities.

After laying the recorder and the coin on the floor at his feet to keep both hands free, he pushed on the hatch. It didn't budge. The earl must have gotten the closed stool back in place; maybe someone was even on it.

Whoever was in the room above, they were about to get a surprise. He banged on the wood with the side of his fist and called out, "Hey, let me out."

A man coughed loudly, and a boot stomped on the floor directly above him. He froze. Had his father faced this situation? What had he done?

His father's reputation had been one of honesty and truthfulness, and he'd still died to keep a secret he wouldn't have told anyway. This hidey-hole might have been why his Da hadn't let him come to the hall. Nicholas had always been a little loose-tongued and impetuous. Da had been protecting him from these people, from himself.

Nicholas might have his father's hair, but that was all he'd inherited, and he'd be damned if he'd die to protect the secrets of these people. He'd make them pay, one way or another.

He banged on the hatch again. "Hey, I'm trapped under the privy; let me out."

He waited, heart in his mouth, as sweat broke out on his back. The temperature in the secret chimney room and the playing had already dried his mouth, and a headache pinched right behind his eyes.

Milord Walpole had messed with the wrong Thatcher this time.

Moving over to where light flickered through a fist-sized gap in the chimney wall. Squinting against the heat, he called through the gap. "Oi, you in the hall, wake up. I'm stuck in the chimney."

"Did you hear that?" John said.

He drooped in relief, and an idea occurred to him. The Earl had backed down to Agnes Flowers once, and he might do again. "John, it's me, Nicholas. Go tell my mother I'm stuck."

"Really? It's the middle of the night. Just wait until the fire dies and come down."

Threatening to reveal the earl's secrets to the servants would be a swift way to an early grave, but hopefully, his mother would be able to help. Ma could be real persuasive when she put her mind to it.

"Can't. She's expecting me back, and you don't want a woman like my mother aggrieved with you."

Straining his ears, he caught some hasty, muffled conversation.

"Alright, alright, I'm on my way," John called back. "But you owe me a shilling."

"Done, now get going."

Footsteps and hurried conversation—three maybe four people—came from above him.

Something heavy scraped on the floorboards. A grin of relief stretched his lips as he went to stand under the hatch. He might even be able to turn this to his advantage. Yes, his mother was a harridan, but he had no doubt she'd come to defend him, and then beat his behind again.

The hatch lifted up. Nicholas squinted at the three figures looming over the narrow access. The three eldest Walpole heirs.

"Keep quiet if you know what's good for you," Charles, the second eldest, snarled. The contempt in his voice had anger flaring in Nicholas's gut. He'd done nothing to deserve this treatment, and respectable honesty hadn't helped his Da.

"The people in the Hall know I'm here, and I've already got one fetching my Ma. Unless you want me shouting about him—" he poked a finger in Richard's direction, "fucking boys and paying them to keep his perversion quiet, and you getting the black maid in the family way, I'd be digging in your purses damn quick."

None of the men looked remotely worried. In fact, the youngest, Edward, sneered. "You think to threaten us, you foul, lying cur? Our father has the ear of the Queen. He wanted this land, and he got it, all but the piece you own, which he'll get in the end. Why do you think he's even bothering with a—"

Jaw clenching, he snatched the codpiece from the strongbox. "What does it say about your sainted father if he pays a cur like me a sovereign to spank his bare behind, call him a wicked wench, and shove this up his shithole?" He held the cock-shaped metal aloft, and the candlelight reflected off it.

"Why you lying—" Edward growled. Pulling his bollock knife from the back of his belt, he crouched as if intending to climb down into the space.

"No, son, don't." The earl's voice reeked with defeat. "He only did what I ordered him to do. He's innocent, but the devil has corrupted me. If you want to punish someone, punish me."

"He's no innocent," Richard said. "He rubbed himself against me when I was giving him a ride home and then said he'd be a woman for me for a crown. He's the devil, luring men to the sin of sodomy."

The earl's stricken face appeared above him. "I trusted you."

"Don't worry. He won't be spreading his lies for long," Edward snarled and jumped down into the space.

Nicholas held his hands up. "I've got no issue with you Edward. I just want to—"

Edward's fist shot out, hit Nicholas's chin. Stumbling back, he fell, head banging against the wall. Everything swirled. Nicholas blinked, tried to work out what was going on as he felt himself pulled and pushed, hands grabbing for his wrists and feet.

He must have fallen asleep, as the next thing he knew, was brick against the side of his face and some cloth stuck in his mouth. His head ached something fierce, worse than when he fell out a tree as a boy. When he tried to reach for the cloth, his arms remained behind his back, and his ankles were also bound together.

The light coming through the fist-sized gap in the chimney wall was less than before, so he guessed it was nearing morning. All seemed quiet below.

Would it be that quiet if Ma had come? His mother was many things, but quiet wasn't one of them. Maybe they'd been calling out for him while he'd been senseless.

He shouted through the gag, and drummed his heels on the brick floor, then stopped, listening for a reaction. He could hear people moving about below, probably getting ready for the day. Sweeping, preparing breakfast, getting ready to stoke the fire.

It was already hot, and he didn't want to be here when the fireplace was fully lit. Getting nearer to the gap would probably help him be heard.

Despite his head throbbing, he wiggled like a caterpillar, bumping, inch by torturous inch, nearer to the chimney wall, sweating because of the heat.

Finally, he sat up against the chimney wall. Squinting against the pain he knew was coming, he drew in a breath, screamed for all he was worth, while thumping his bare heels and the back of his head on the brick. The pain just added to his fury, and he let it out, put everything into making noise.

Lack of air forced him to take a breath, and the spike of pain in his head caused him to freeze.

"Did you hear that?" A male voice asked from below.

Nicholas tried to call out again, but the amount of noise he made was pitiful, so he banged his heels on the floor again.

"Hear that? He's still up there." John's voice sounded tense, concerned. At least someone cared about him.

"I'd be quiet if I were you, Grimshaw," Richard Walpole said. "If you hadn't gone to his mother last night, a lot of this trouble wouldn't have happened. Stoke the fire up. Give him a bit more incentive to come out."

"But sir, if—"

"Do you want my attention again, boy?"

"No, no, sir. I'll erm, get the wood."

"You bastards, you fucking bastards," Nicholas screamed through the gag, but the light got brighter, and the temperature rose.

He had to stop trying to shout as his head buzzed too much to move. Taking shallow breaths, trying to keep from increasing his headache, Nicholas imagined all the ways he was going to get his own back on the Walpoles.

He'd take all this stuff, which was clearly valuable, and start a new life. One day he'd come back, buy this house, and throw the fuckers out on their arses.

He dozed or maybe passed out again. Grinning demons and images of hellfire danced before him. A scarlet, horned, forked-tailed version of himself used a trident to shove a screaming Richard down into a roiling magma lake. Richard screamed, twisted as his body blackened, one hand reaching out for salvation that would never come. Nicholas laughed at the funniest thing he'd ever seen. In the next heartbeat, he was the one in the lake with a grinning Thomas looking down at him.

"You brought this on yourself, all you had to do was be honest, but no, you thought you were better than us. Well, you're not, and you never will be. Dirty, stinking peasant." The trident reached toward him.

Hoarse screaming woke him. He pried his crusty dry eyes open and realized the cries had come from his own throat. Sweat soaked his body. The side facing the chimney burned worse than when he'd gotten so sunburned as a small boy that his back blistered.

He'd been dizzy, confused, and sleepy that day, but nothing like this. Ma had dunked buckets of water over his head, saying he'd gotten sunstroke, that he could've gone to sleep and not woken up.

He had to get away from the heat; otherwise, he might not live long enough for Ma to tell him he was stupid or strap his backside ever again.

He tested his bonds again. They'd used the woven silk ties from the curtains on the four-poster bed around his ankles, and another likely held his wrists. Even if he had the strength of ten men, he probably couldn't break them.

I've got to cut them. He looked around for something sharp. The only thing that had a vague edge within reach was the codpiece.

It seemed to take hours to maneuver himself around enough to pick up the foul thing and then position it so the edge of the plate rubbed against the tie holding his wrists behind his back. All his concentration went into the tiny back and forth movement. The far wall almost glowed with heat, and sweat dripped from every pore. His eyes burned with salt, but he'd long since given up opening them except for an occasional blink to check if the fire had lessened.

Gritting his teeth, he released the slick metal codpiece and wiped his sweaty palm on the back of his shirt. He'd try again in a minute. A little rest, that's all he needed.

At least he was flexible enough to do this. The fat bastard that had caused all this would just lay here like a landed fish, unable to do a damn thing. Dying like that would be too easy for the earl. Nicholas wanted him to hurt, to be frightened, to cry and wail. He wanted to poke Charles's eyes out so he could never letch over another woman. He wanted to cut off Richard's cock, stuff it in the bastard's own ass and see how he liked it.

The light from the chimney rose and fell, but it never died down. Time must be passing, but Nicholas had no idea how much. His hands cramped, then went numb. He was tired, so damn tired. But he couldn't, wouldn't, give up.

Two minutes more sawing, another rest. A little more. Fuck, his head hurt. He kept his eyes shut as much as possible, and couldn't remember how long it'd been since he'd been able to swallow; any attempt felt like swallowing knives. He'd even stopped sweating.

He lay still again, utterly exhausted and every fiber of his body crying out for moisture. He'd kill, hell, he'd kill every person in the fucking hall for a swallow of ale.

Nobody is coming. *I'm going to die here.* He rolled the thought around in his mind.

Forgotten, unwanted. Nobody will even remember me in a few years except Ma.

He dozed again, dreams fevered with people asking "Nicholas who? Never heard of him."

"Well, that's it then, the whole family's gone."

"James was a good man, but I was never sure about that wife of his."

It took several dizzying heartbeats to work out that the voices weren't in his head.

"Well, she's dead now too, and good riddance to the lot of them. Did you hear her curse our whole damn family?"

The other voice snorted. "Why d'you think Charles pushed her back into the flames? Who knows what an angry witch could do? She could have brought the Black Death down on the whole damn village."

It took a few more torturous, slow heartbeats to comprehend what they'd said. Ma was dead, just like Da. Fury exploded. What gave them the right?

Nicholas had Edward's bollock knife in his hand, and he plunged it into one Walpole male after another. Blood spurted, fear, begging, he wanted, needed—

Slow clapping came from above him. A red-skinned man, no more than a hand high and wearing odd black clothing, sat on the shelf next to the strongbox.

"Such wonderful hate."

"Who—What are you?" Nicholas said, then stopped as he realized he was no longer restrained.

"The skin and size don't give it away?" the man asked. "Well, as you—and your entire family to tell the truth— have been having a very bad day, I'll spell it out. I'm a vengeance demon, and you are about to meet a reaper who will carry your soul to its final destination. Which, given your less than pious existence, will be—" he gestured downwards.

"I'm dead?"

The demon held out their hand, wobbled it from side to side. "Technically, no, not yet, but you won't wake up again." He rubbed his hands together. "So, what'll it be?"

"I don't understand."

The devil huffed and looked at an odd, jeweled band encircling his wrist. His dark jacket and breeches were made from a cloth unlike any Nicholas had ever seen. Close-fitting, they lacked a single embellishment.

"Ok, I'll make this quick. I've got places to go, souls to torture, you know the sort of thing. Both you and your mother put out strong calls for vengeance with your last conscious thoughts. That's like a beacon to my kind, so I popped by.

"Your choice is, I leave and arrange for something unfortunate to happen to one Walpole for both you and your mother, or—"

Nicholas's mind whirled. He was sure Thomas had started this because he wanted their land, but Richard was an utter callous bastard. He could have helped with the plan—he was the heir after all. But Charles had killed Ma. They all deserved pain and anguish far greater than he had suffered. None should benefit from—

"Nice seething, but hardly productive right now. As I was saying, I can let a hard-working reaper collect your grubby little soul, although I doubt ultimate paradise will be your destination given your—" he paused and grinned, showing sharp, elongated eye teeth, "—tricky nature."

"Or?" Nicholas prompted.

The devil's dark eyebrows drew together. "Again with the interrupting? You really are an irritating little turd."

"Says the pizzle-sized demon," Nicholas spat back.

A deep rolling chuckle came from the tiny devil. "I knew I liked you. Or I recruit you as a probationary vengeance demon, and you can personally make sure no heir will ever know true happiness."

"Done." Nicholas stuck out his hand.

The demon gave him a toothy white smile. "Sorry, kid, but you still have to die."

Nicholas found himself back in his body on the ground, unbearably hot, pulse thumping oh so slowly in his ears.

A fever dream, nothing but a fever dream.

He vaguely acknowledged that his hands were no longer behind his back, but he didn't have the energy to move them. Instead, he tried slip back into the dream where the Walpoles would pay.

His heart beat so loud he could feel it.

Ba-dum.

Ba... dum.

Ba

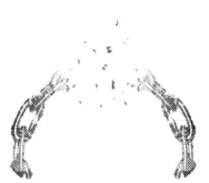

---

1. Angel: Gold coin worth 10 shillings.

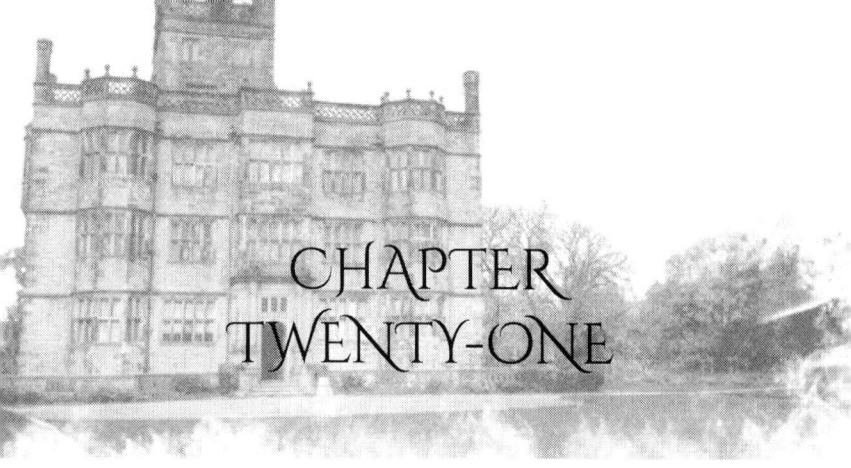

CHAPTER TWENTY-ONE

Shanae touched the boy's milk-white forehead, and Alastor collapsed in Darien's arms. Dread seized his chest. It couldn't end like this.

"What did you do to him?" Shielding Alastor from a further touch, he eased the scarily limp body to the ground. He'd seen subs pass out before, but they usually got woozy, slurred, and stumbled first; they didn't just 'stop'.

Pressing two fingers under the point of the pale jaw, he willed there to be a pulse, even though he wasn't sure if Alastor even had a heartbeat under normal circumstances.

"Eliciting memories, but I've never done it to a spirit or a—"

He tuned her out, putting every ounce of concentration into his fingertips trying to sense life. Still nothing. Alastor was too alive, too vibrant to just—. A slight flutter that might have been wishful thinking tickled his fingertips. Holding his own breath, as if he could force Alastor to breathe if he didn't, he pressed a little harder, trying to confirm the—

Alastor lurched in his arms. His chest rose, and a groan tore from his throat before he relaxed again, but his body was no longer boneless.

"Oh, thank God," Juliana gasped.

Arioch snorted. "God's got nothing to do with anything that little fucker does."

Cradling Alastor in his arms, Darien stroked the boy's face as a cool breeze ruffled his hair. He should take him inside before the scantily clad boy became chilled. If he could, he'd pop straight to a warm bed with Alastor, pamper him, care for him like no one had ever bothered to do before.

Auburn eyebrows drew together. Sea-green eyes fluttered open and tugged Darien's soul into their bottomless depths.

"Hey, welcome back," he said. Unsure what Alastor had just experienced, he gave a gentle, hopefully reassuring smile. "You're safe. Just take your time to process—"

Alastor screwed his eyes, opened them wide, and focused on Darien's face. Then he rolled over, body spasming as he heaved, but nothing came up. Darien rubbed his back until the taut body stopped surging.

He gathered the trembling young man back into his arms as if holding him could dispel the internal terrors and ward off the external threats. Alastor's were closed tight against something only he could see.

"It's ok, you're here with me. Whatever you saw, it's over; you're with me." As Darien carried on babbling reassurance, he realized how useless it was in their present company. How could he protect Alastor from a demon or his past?

Useless or not, Alastor's fingers clutched at his suit jacket despite his earlier declaration that he wanted Darien to go. Mouths could lie, but bodies seldom did. Alastor wanted him here, at least for now.

"Do you remember anything more? Who you are? Who cursed you?" Shanae asked, her voice loud and intrusive from over his shoulder.

Alastor took a few deep breaths, and little by little, the trembling grew less and vanished. Darien could almost see this fascinating man packing away whatever had scared him, whatever he'd seen.

Alastor opened his eyes, and Darien swore he was looking at history itself in those sea-green depths.

"Yeah," he croaked, swallowed, and tried again. "Yeah, I remember."

"So, you remember being Nicholas Thatcher?" Shanae pressed.

Alastor shuddered and shook his head. "I don't want to think about it."

"Start with something small, something pleasant," Shanae encouraged. "A favorite gift, or a meal? A game you enjoyed as a child?"

Silence stretched as Alastor turned his head, seemingly fascinated with the view. Perhaps he was trying to reconcile the differences between his memories and his current reality.

"Give him some time, it must be—"

"My Da gave me a recorder he made for my birthday."

"Was it like the one in the sale?" Darien asked.

Lips pressed together, lost in the past, he nodded. "Until just now, I had no idea where it'd come from, but I kept it until the last earl smashed it." His lips pressed together.

"And you killed him for it. Fair exchange, don't you think? The life of a promising young man for an old wooden instrument?" Arioch said.

Alastor's jaw clenched as he glared at the demon. "I never claimed to be a saint. I just wanted to travel, sleep in a bed, and have more than one set of clothes."

"Not doing very well then, are you?" Arioch said. "I can see where you were born from here."

"Arioch," Shanae ground out a warning, but still kept several feet from the painted lines on the stone roof.

"I remember the second earl fucking me for a coin, which hurt more than Ma's beatings. The first earl offered me an apprenticeship as a Fool if I buggered him with the codpiece from his grandfather's suit of armor."

Nothing in this world or the next could have prepared Darien for that last sentence. He stared at Alastor, mind as blank as new-fallen snow.

"Did you?" Callum asked.

Shanae turned on her nephew. "Callum, this is not for your ears."

"What d'you want me to do, take them off?" the lanky, blue-haired youngster grumbled.

"Fucker squealed like suckling pig."

Darien looked down. Alastor's grin lit up the world around him.

If the devil really did trade in souls, at that moment, Darien knew he'd hand his over to keep Alastor.

"I also remember being in that damn hole, shouting and crying, while everyone in the hall pretended I wasn't there," he said, eyes haunted.

"Well, that escalated quickly. So much for little happy memories," Arioch mused.

A hole opened up in Darien's chest as Alastor pulled away, but all he did was swivel around, so he sat almost in Darien's lap, with his back pressed against his chest.

With a slight huff, Alastor took Darien's wrist and pulled his arm around him. "Better," he announced, then tilted his head and pressed a kiss against Darien's chin.

Shanae's hand landed on his shoulder. "So, as you seem to be ok with the tough stuff, was the first earl the one who cursed you?"

Did Alastor kiss me because he wanted to, or to piss off the witch?

Darien shrugged her hand off, hating that he doubted the man in his arms.

"Does it matter?" he ground out. "He's long dead. Let's stick to helping the living." He squeezed Alastor, just in case he didn't realize who he meant.

"Only the living matter, hmm?" Arioch said, examining their nails for a moment before looking up. The demon now resembled a Hollywood blonde bombshell in a sequined scarlet dress that clung to every curve as they stood within the demon trap, one hip cocked.

"In that case, you'd better step away from that boy you find so fascinating, unless you're into necrophilia, which—" Arioch held up a finger "—isn't as uncommon as you might think, but that's a tale for another day.

"Unfortunately for you, dear Nicholas is still as dead as the day he died from heatstroke and dehydration, which was Tuesday, 17th of September 1602, in case you were wondering what you should put on his gravestone."

Darien tightened his arms around the tense, wiry body. "I can feel his pulse; he's as alive as I am."

Darien wanted to wipe the condescending false smile off the demon's face. The femme fatale disguise didn't fool him. If anything, Arioch looked more dangerous in this form than in the horned and forked-tailed version.

"So did Agnes's curse do all this?" Shanae asked.

Alastor stiffened in his arms.

"You seem so intent on apportioning blame, Shanae. We're not in a council meeting now. No one is on trial. Not me, and not Alastor. Whatever happened was a legal act of vengeance, claimed, proved, and executed."

"I'm just trying to get to the details. If we know who caused Nicholas to be trapped here, the easier to free him."

"Get on with it, Arioch," Darien added. "He's in shock, cold, and getting colder."

The demon pouted. "Aw, poor boy. I forgot he's revoltingly human while touching an heir. If you don't want him to feel cold, you might want to move away from—"

"Not happening," Darien and Alastor said at the same time, and grinned at each other like schoolboys, although Alastor's smile dropped away quickly.

Something wasn't right here. The banter seemed to be diverting everyone from something neither Arioch nor Alastor wanted them to know.

Arioch rolled their eyes. "Please, stop. You're vomit-worthy. So, as you rudely insist, I'll carry on with this sad tale. Unless you want to?" The demon raised perfectly sculpted blonde eyebrows at Alastor.

Alastor shrank back against Darien's chest. "I don't want to think about any of it."

"After the codpiece squeal, which his wife heard, the earl shoved Nicholas down into the priest hole, for want of a better description. Although as a staunch protestant monarchist, I doubt Thomas Walpole ever thought a catholic priest would be seen dead there." Arioch grinned. "See what I did there? Seen dead there? Because—"

Even young Callum joined in with the "Get on with it."

Arioch sighed. "Everyone's a critic these days. Video really has killed the art of good storytelling. Well, if you must have just the plain facts, after creating a scene outside the hall, your mother was escorted back to her cottage. She even banged on the side of the earl's carriage as it went past. Such a wonderfully spirited woman."

Alastor scowled. "She made my Da's life a misery, beat me with a stick, and stole every penny I got."

"And yet when you were in trouble, you called for your mommy like a babe still on the tit." Arioch cocked a carefully shaped eyebrow at Shanae. "Nothing to say in defense of your illustrious relative?"

"In Agnes's defense, Nicholas couldn't have been an easy child, and corporal punishment for children was accepted, even promoted at the time."

"So, getting beaten was my fault?" Alastor said, and tried to get up.

Darien held him in place. "Settle down," he murmured. "Rest for a bit. You've had—"

"She tried to force him into a mold he didn't fit," Arioch said, "whereas I have always fully appreciated his—"

Alastor pulled out of Darien's arms and climbed to his feet with a hiss of pain.

Holding his forearms out, he examined his bound wrists, then presented them to Shanae. "See what you did?"

Red and raw, blood drips were still making their way sluggishly down his skin. They looked far worse than Darien imagined from Alastor's reaction when the ropes were tied. The boy must have a high pain threshold or—*Was he not reacting to protect my feelings?*

The prospect sent alarm bells ringing. A sub, particularly a masochist, who hid their pain was a dominant's nightmare. And he should not be thinking about that. Alastor wasn't his. Hell, he didn't even know if the man he'd held in his arms was technically alive.

Darien got to his feet. "Let me see," he said, but Alastor ignored him as he confronted the witch.

"This is not the way to encourage me back to the bosom of my loving family. A family who ignored me for over four fucking centuries. And my name is Alastor, and I'm an imp. I was only Nicholas for eighteen years; I'm not that boy anymore." Alastor's body almost vibrated with the lie.

"I don't even know if what I remembered was real. You're a witch, and they're a Demon Lord. You could have just—"

Arioch sighed, hung their head, and all the color drained downward, leaving a slim white man wearing white jeans and a white shirt with a red 'coke' logo. The demon's raunchy, sarcastic attitude drained along with the siren character.

"Shanae is the memory specialist, not me. What he clearly doesn't want to acknowledge is that his death was largely his own fault. He shouted about what he'd done to the earl, so they tied him up and gagged him. They left him there and nailed the hatch closed. It was a brutal, drawn-out, lonely, cruel end. The story passed down to Harry was pretty accurate. He kicked and thumped, screamed, cried, and tried to free himself for days before he succumbed to dehydration."

"And you watched every second, didn't you?" Darien said, feeling sick as he imagined what Nicholas had gone through.

Shanae's eyes narrowed. "Whose revenge was it?"

Arioch rolled their eyes. "Things don't have to be so linear. Agnes's dying call for revenge was on my to-do list, but several of the Walpoles weren't exactly fans of his either. His loose lips could have doomed the whole family. All that rage and revenge centered on one person with an added witch twist? I couldn't help myself." Arioch shrugged. "By the time I got there, Nicholas was out of time, not that I have a habit of saving the kin of witches. Your kind has been a thorn in my side for as long as I can remember.

"When the earl came back a week later, Alastor was sitting on the bed, grinning at him like nothing had happened."

Alastor clicked his fingers. "I remember pretending to read the play script he brought back from London. I knew who he was, and about the curse, but that's all. All I said was 'Good evening, milord.' He ran out, crying and begging God for forgiveness. I followed him around all day and most of the night, asking what ailed him, and if I could help, until a month later—" He made his fingers run, jump and fall. "Right here." He walked over, patted the stone balustrade, and stared out at the view. "If he'd been born now, his preferences wouldn't have mattered. None of it would have happened." Bowing his head, he remained silent. A gust of wind ruffled his hair and undershirt. "Thomas never entered that bedroom again."

"Probably didn't like the idea of sleeping near your body," Arioch mused. "I bet you stank after a while. Although, if you were baked to a crisp, there might not have been much of a smell."

Darien felt a little sick as he looked over to where the chimney from the Low Great Hall reached toward the sky.

Alastor shook his head. "I've been in that priest hole thousands of times. There's no body in there. Just a strongbox, a painting of a fit, naked guy with a disappointing tiny cock, a pair of really ugly turquoise lattice vases with goldfish on them, that damn codpiece, and the books and the instruments I put in there."

Arioch rolled their eyes. "You were there, trust me. You just couldn't see yourself. Although, making someone sit with their own corpse as it rots might be just the thing to—"

The brief description of the vases short-circuited Darien's mind. A decade ago, a similar vase, dated to 1740, had been sold for over $65 million. He didn't want to even speculate how much an earlier matched pair would be worth. They could be Kangxi, Shunzhi, or even from the reign of the founding emperor of the Qing dynasty, Nurhaci. His mouth almost watered at the thought of finding such a piece. "Can you describe the vases?"

The gaze of five humans, one demon, and whatever Alastor was, bored into him.

"What? They could be worth a fortune."

Arioch smiled. "Avarice, how... predictably human."

"A fortune that belongs to the owner of the Hall," Juliana stated, "if the pieces even exist." She paused, her eyes widening as she stared at Alastor. "I can still see him, and he's not touching Darien."

Slow clapping came from Arioch.

CHAPTER TWENTY-TWO

"At last," Arioch said. "I thought I'd be here for another decade while you humans worked it out."

Humans? Alastor looked down. His feet were outside the dark red pentagram inscribed on the roof. A pentagram he hadn't been able to see earlier.

He met Arioch's gaze, and the vengeance demon smirked. "Ta da, not a demon anymore. How's that for a magic trick?"

Concentrating, he tried to relocate down to the kitchen, but nothing happened. He looked up at Darien, who looked as shocked as he felt.

"I'm alive? I can eat, touch, heal?" He'd never dreamed this could happen. The most he'd dreamed of was being released from the curse and moving on as a free imp. Elation soared, and he ran forward.

Darien caught him in his arms, squeezing him tight. "We'll get you a passport. I can't wait to take you home." Darien paused, leaned back. Amber eyes bored into Alastor. "You do want to come home with me, right?"

Alastor blinked. "You really want..." he trailed off, unable to complete the sentence in case he was wrong.

"I want to show you the world if you'll have me," Darien said and gently brushed his lips to Alastor's. Warm, soft, considerate. This man, this Walpole heir, was everything he could ever— His mind stuttered.

His legs nearly went out from under him as the devastating truth and his new-found memories combined. Pushing away from the heir, he stumbled over to the balustrade. The stone felt cold under his palms as he leaned on it. It felt so damn wrong.

"Alastor? What's wrong?" Darien asked. A warm hand landed on his back, and he twitched away from it as if burned. He didn't want to say it, didn't want to break the wavering, fragile soap bubble of Darien's happiness.

Staring out over the autumn parkland, he finally had some idea of how the eight Walpole men—his victims—had felt before they jumped to their deaths.

"Mm, delicious. Definitely worth waiting for," Arioch slurred as if they'd had a shot of morphine.

Alastor dry heaved, belly spasming. A silver glob of saliva fell from his lips, disappearing as it fell. He imaged the ground rushing up to it before it hit, disintegrated. The Walpoles hadn't disintegrated. They'd been twisted lumps of flesh, eyes staring, limbs bent in impossible— he heaved again.

"What are you talking about?" Darien's sharp question was ignored as the demon began chuckling.

"Well, are you going to tell lover boy, or shall I?"

Alastor shook his head, denying the truth. If he didn't voice it, maybe it wouldn't be true. It couldn't be true.

"Darien is still alive, but the curse is broken." The quiet, sorrowful, hauntingly young male voice said. "It means Nicholas being trapped here for all this time had nothing to do with ending the Walpole line."

Alastor didn't move, tried not to breathe, wished he was as invisible to everyone as he had been an hour ago.

"Give the boy a prize," Arioch said. "Quite a delicious ruse, don't you think?"

A hand, firm, confident, reassuring, landed between his shoulder blades. "This is Arioch's fault, not yours. They manipulated you, lied—"

"Arioch is a demon," Alastor interrupted, voice flat. Darien needed to understand, and he patently didn't. Because if he did, he wouldn't be touching him, wouldn't want to be within a mile of him.

Turning around, he leaned his butt up against the balustrade, achingly aware of the drop behind him. The misplaced concern, the care in Darien's eyes was almost too much. Facing it was so much harder than leaning backward and simply stopping in a matter of heartbeats.

He still couldn't prevent himself from reaching up to cup Darien's jaw, but he dropped his hand before actually touching him.

Four hundred years ago, he'd been a mouthy, manipulative brat, only interested in his own pocket. It was time to grow up, to take responsibility as an adult. He blew out a breath and met Darien's gaze.

"Yes, Arioch's a demon; they can't help it. But I agreed to Arioch helping me dodge a reaper so I could get my revenge on the Walpoles, but I meant the ones I knew, not... every damn one of you. I drove your relatives to their deaths, caused many others pain, and cost them their lives, including Liam."

"So, what are you going to do? Kill yourself because you were duped?"

Alastor blinked at Darien's blunt question.

The man who had come to mean everything to him indicted Arioch with a finger. "That would make Arioch's day. Hell, it'll probably make their century."

The demon grinned, held up their palm, and wiggled their fingers in reply.

"You can't change the past. At least, I don't think you can?" Darien's gaze found Shanae.

Alastor's breath stilled in his chest. So much had changed today. Facts had become fiction, and fiction had become fact, so why couldn't things be changed in the past? All those lives saved, all that pain vanished.

"You could bring my boy back?" Hope ached in Harry's voice.

Shanae held Darien's gaze, didn't look at Harry. "Even if it was possible, which it isn't, how far back would you go? Two years to save Liam and Melody? Who might have been born, or not born, if they were both still here? Eighty, to save the last Earl, which could mean several new generations of Walpoles? Back to when Nicholas died? What might the world look like now? Henry Walpole might not have gone to America, you might not—"

Darien held up his palms. "Ok, ok, I get it. It's not a good idea. We deal with what we have. Which means we complete the auction tomorrow and then get the hell out of here."

Arioch's eyes went wide. "Did I say he could leave?" He wobbled a hand from side to side. "Curse, spell, demonic revenge, it's all so confusing and interchangeable, isn't it?"

"Why you—" Harry growled and started toward the demon who still stood within the confines of the trap.

Arioch expanded, clothes vanishing, skin turning red as their full demonic form emerged again. In a voice like distant thunder, the demon ground out. "Wanna dance, little man?"

Shanae's voice rang out. "Councilmember Arioch, if you want to be released any time in the next decade, you will refrain from threatening anyone."

The demon shrank back down in the blink of an eye, returning to his male college student form. "Formality, how quaint. Well, if we're being all prim and proper, may I inquire, Councilmember Shanae, how you intend to explain your unsanctioned imprisonment of a fellow delegate to our esteemed colleagues? I'll let you in on a little secret." He looked from side to side as if someone might be listening in. "I have a bit of a thing going with the leader of the council. He loves my horns, all three of them."

Shanae tucked her chin in, looking at the demon as if peering over a pair of glasses like a classic schoolteacher.

"Avery is an incubus. He has a 'thing' going on with every sexual member of the council, their guards, and possibly the caretakers, not that I've ever seen whoever keeps the council chambers tidy."

Arioch's head tilted, a smirk playing on his currently masculine lips. "Do you wish to test Avery's affection for me? Besides, even if he doesn't miss me immediately, he'll come looking if I don't appear at the next council meeting."

The threat didn't seem to faze the witch. "Which is in three and a half weeks. I hear it gets mighty cold up here at night, and there's a storm due over the weekend. How much do you enjoy being cold, wet, and bored?"

Arioch blew their cheeks out and folded to sit cross-legged on the stone. "I don't think I can squeeze much more angst out of this anyway. What do you want to know?"

"You said you made him an imp, but that doesn't explain why he couldn't leave the estate."

I've examined the boundaries of the estate, there are no wards to stop anyone entering or leaving," Callum said.

"There has to be. I bounce off the damn thing."

"Bounce off, or get pulled back?" Callum asked.

"Quiet, I'm thinking," Shanae said. It seemed that his modern female ancestors weren't any more tolerant of their young male relatives than his Ma had been.

Callum's sigh and eye roll probably mirrored what he'd done as Nicholas Thatcher many times, but at least Callum didn't seem to be facing a beating. Or he wouldn't until aunt and nephew were in private.

"If you really wanted the Walpole line extinguished, you would have let him hunt them wherever they went. Was it Agnes' curse that held him here?" Shanae asked Arioch.

"Does it matter?" Darien said, but both demon and witch ignored him.

The conversation was about him, but neither party seemed keen to involve him. Like Ma and Thomas Walpole, they both thought his opinions, his emotions, didn't matter.

The only one here who didn't appear to see him as a problem to fix was Darien.

The man was like a magnet; his warmth, his compassion, drew Alastor like nothing ever had. He inched sideways, and as if he couldn't help it either, Darien's arm curled around his waist. Basking for a little longer couldn't hurt, right?

"At first, yes," Arioch said.

Shanae's eyes lit up. "I knew it! She wasn't strong enough to do this, nor was Nicholas. It was you, wasn't it?"

"You know, I so enjoy proving people wrong. It almost ranks with justifiable revenge as far as I'm concerned. But to answer your question, no, it wasn't me, not directly. I just used one stone to kill a remarkable number of birds." Arioch stretched out, leaning back on his elbows and crossing his ankles as if the damp, cold stone roof was a featherbed.

"Nicolas and Agnes both swore revenge on the Walpoles, but they weren't focused on a never-ending blood feud. I do so love those; they can provide almost endless reciprocal calls for revenge.

"But I digress again. Dear roleplaying, codpiece-loving Thomas was so upset about Nicholas betraying his trust and playing with his eldest son too that he cursed him never to rest until he had true feelings for a Walpole. I was just—" a predatory smile quirked his lips, "—a little economical with the truth when I explained the curse to my shiny new imp.

"I did need another vengeance demon, and now I still do, thanks to this—" he wrinkled his nose and waved a hand toward Alastor and Darien "—quite nauseating emotion. So, simply put, young Nicholas brought this on himself by having such a wonderful deceitful, jealous, greedy, and impish nature. Now, release me."

After a nod from Shanae, the thin, blue-haired teen stepped toward the nearest dark line painted on the flagstones.

Not thinking seemed a damn good idea. If he thought about it, his remorse would just be feeding Arioch that little bit more. The fucker had already bled him dry for centuries.

He couldn't see any more of what the young witch did as he refused to move an inch. Pulled against Darien's chest, Alastor let the warmth, the love, seep into his being. A kiss pressed against his temple.

"That was you then. It isn't you now. You've broken the curse yourself by caring for me. See, I told you it's going to be ok. I'm sure Shanae can sort out the paperwork, and as soon as she has, we'll be on a plane home."

"As long as dear Nicholas is happy being transported in a coffin in the hold, I'm sure you'll have a fantastic honeymoon. Personally, I prefer partners who are actually capable of breathing," Arioch said.

Darien gave him a squeeze. "Are you claiming he's a vampire now? Give it rest. You've lost; deal with it."

Arioch chuckled. "A vampire? What quaint ideas you humans have. For your information, sunlight doesn't bother blood demons, nor does garlic or crucifixes. No, dear Nicholas is not a vampire; he's not even dead in any sense of the word, not yet anyway. He's simply four hundred years old.

"Walpole's curse might be broken, but his mother's dying spell tethered his soul to this place until he gets a decent, Christian burial beside his father. Who, for your information, was buried in an unmarked grave in a cemetery that became a housing estate in the 1930s. I believe they reinterred all the remains... somewhere. But I digress. It's a wonderfully annoying habit I'm trying not to break." They sat up, crossed their legs, and leaned their elbows on their knees.

"What it comes down to is, if dear Nicholas puts one foot over the estate boundary—as it was in 1602—he'll revert to his real age.

"I know some people have a thing about geriatrics, but I doubt even a kinky soul like you will find a four-century-old corpse sexy." He tilted his head. "Although, you might be able to sell him as a museum exhibit." The demon swept his hands in twin arcs, looking into the distance. "I can see the tourists shuffling past his glass case, wondering how he died."

"Give it a rest, will you? Haven't you tortured him enough?" Darien ground out.

Alastor remained still and quiet within Darien's embrace, even though the chill of the stone under his feet and the autumn breeze seeped into his bones. A matter of hours ago, he would have appreciated being able to feel the low temperature. Now, he didn't know what to think. He remembered the winters of his youth, how people sometimes froze to death and weren't found until spring.

"All I did was put a stasis spell on his body before he died so the reapers didn't find him. He's been popping about the estate via astral projection, except for when an heir touches him. Then, and only then, is he released from stasis, temporarily of course."

Arioch poked a finger in Darien's direction. "You're the only one who has ever noticed that he looks older now than in the painting. I should have known you'd be as much trouble as Yaingo. Now there was an imp candidate if ever I saw one. It's such a shame those pesky reapers got to her before I did.

"Anyhoo—" the demon rubbed their hands together, "—I have lives to ruin. There never is any rest for the wicked. I'll be back for the very emotional goodbye. I wonder what dear Nicholas will decide to do if the new owners of Walpole Hall don't want a permanent, penniless, unwanted squatter on their land?"

The demon grinned, then vanished.

CHAPTER TWENTY-THREE

Alastor pulled away from him and looked out over the parkland that must have been so familiar to him. Surely being alive, being able to touch and experience life was a positive outcome? Alastor's body language screamed the opposite. Perhaps he was merely processing his change in fortune and his own part in it. After four centuries, it had to be a hell of a shock.

Darien wrapped his arms around the shivering body from behind. Alastor leaned his elbows on the balustrade, revealing his raw, bleeding, and still bound wrists as they poked out of the loose sleeves of his undershirt.

"Come on, let's get you downstairs, warm you up, find you some clothes, and see to those wrists."

A gust of wind carried stinging drops of icy rain. Alastor didn't move, didn't speak, just carried on staring out at the view.

"Come on, you'll catch your death out here." Darien winced as he realized what he'd said. "Look, we'll work something out. At least you're alive now; you can eat, drink, and—"

"Get arrested for trespass and die as the police haul me over the boundary? I bet the coppers will shit themselves." A small smile tickled his lips for a few seconds, then it died, and he hung his head.

"I suppose it's fitting that my last prank will be such a doozy. Because after that…" His shoulders heaved as he took a gulp of the cold, damp air. "I'll be a real ghost trapped here for all eternity without even a Walpole heir to see or touch me. Yeah, that will be so much better than being an imp. Thanks for that."

He glanced at Darien before turning back to the view. "You and Shanae, you think you've saved me, like on one of those superhero films Anderson made. But I enjoyed it most of the time. Well, the irritating and pranking people bit anyway.

"I did it back when I was Nicholas too. Anything to make the important people smile and hand over some coins. After I—" He huffed in amusement. "I don't even know what to call it anymore. Became an apprentice demon, I suppose.

"I couldn't even get that right. Arioch said I had to break the curse to be promoted to vengeance demon, but I never wanted that. I had my heart set on being a free imp, roaming the world, losing keys, unplugging phones, flattening tires, spilling drinks, taking the last cigarette or condom, or leaving windows open so vermin can get in. All the little irritations that piss people off but don't kill them.

"I told myself that I was Arioch's personal Fool, that my pranks had to be deadly because my master was a demon, but the joke's on me. I'm well and truly fucked, thanks to the inability to keep my mouth shut and all your epic help, folks."

Alastor lifted his head to the view as if it held the answers he sought. Darien had never felt more impotent. All his life, people had looked to him for answers, for help, both in his professional and private life, but he had nothing to offer for this.

The other people on the roof didn't appear to know what to do or say either. That their plan had succeeded, had freed Walpole Hall from the curse, no longer seemed such a bright, pure ambition. Alastor had been happy, at least at times. Now, he had what?

Callum squinted at the gray sky and shoved his hands into his pockets. Alastor must be verging on hypothermic if Callum was cold when fully dressed, including a thigh-length black wool coat.

The former imp wasn't the only one who could do with a hot, sweet drink and a warm blanket. The big answers were beyond Darien for now, but he could solve the immediate, practical issues.

He nodded at the witches and his sister. "Let's go get warmed up. After you, ladies."

Harry Grimshaw held the knife loosely at his side as if he'd forgotten it was there. "Come on, Harry, give me the knife so I can get those ropes off Alastor."

Harry looked down at the knife as if seeing it for the first time.

"No, not until we have first aid available, that's a magical wound," Shanae said, then looked over at Callum. "Have you got that sterile water?"

The lad produced a clear plastic bottle from his pocket.

Alastor ignored everyone but the man he'd known all his life. "Would you have killed me?"

The two held each other's gazes as Darien willed Harry to deny it.

"Aye, lad, I would've, but only as a last resort. The curse had to be stopped, one way or another."

Alastor pressed his lips together, nodded, and turned back to the view. The linen shirt looked old and threadbare as it hung on his body. It appeared to have been made for a bigger man, and it probably had been. Few people of Nicholas Thatcher's age and social station would have had any new clothes. Historians should be examining it. No peasant garments remained from Alastor's time, except leather shoes and a fragment of a knitted sock found on the Mary Rose. His auctioneer brain immediately started calculating a reserve price, but he shoved the thought away.

"Alastor, come on, let's go get warm, see to those wounds, and get you something better to wear." He pictured Arioch's eyebrows lifting and a smirk appearing on the dark red lips as if the demon knew how much he itched to preserve the precious artifact before Alastor could damage it.

Cupping Alastor's hair rather than his shoulder was simply establishing physical contact. It had nothing to do with protecting the priceless Elizabethan garment. In Darien's imagination, Arioch laughed at his self-delusion.

Alastor turned at the touch but stared at Darien as if he had no idea who he was for a moment. Moving out of Darien's reach, shoulders rounded and arms held protectively against his breastbone, Alastor followed the others.

He looked so alone, so downtrodden. With a couple of quick steps, Darien caught up, pushed down his instincts, and put his hand on Alastor's shoulder to provide the physical reassurance many subs craved. The instant shrug and twist away felt like a punch to the gut.

"You don't need to touch me all the time now. I'm not going anywhere. Not now, not ever. And if you think I'm letting anyone pour something a witch gave you over me, you're crazy."

Alastor's bare feet were as silent on the stone steps as they had been when he'd been a ghost. No, not a ghost, an astral projection. Darien had heard of the phenomenon but assumed it was pseudoscience at best, crackpot wishful thinking, or simply a scam at worst. He'd had the same opinion of magic, not to mention demons and curses.

He'd come here hoping to learn a little more about Tudor life, his own heritage, but this was so much more than he'd ever imagined in his wildest—

"Leave him be for a bit. He needs time to process," Harry rumbled from behind him. Darien could have said the same for all the people on the roof, including himself.

"Would you have hurt Juliana?" he asked Harry.

"No, lad, I wouldn't have hurt your sister. It was an idea Shanae came up with to get you to cooperate. The demon was linked to young Nicholas, so we used his pain from the ropes to draw it here. We didn't think you'd allow that."

"You're damn right I wouldn't have done. He's as much a victim in all this as anyone," Darien said and moved in front of Harry, not wanting to be separated from Alastor.

"No, he's not. He chose to do the things he did, and he did most of them with a smile. We'll have to see if being free from Arioch changes his ways. Personally, I doubt it."

As he went down the flight of spiral stairs, Darien brushed his fingers along the wall that his so many times great grandfather had probably touched. And the man a few feet ahead had actually known him, not as a name on a screen or as a figure in a painting, but as a person.

A man everyone in the world could now see and touch. He'd been Alastor's everything, the focus of his entire existence. The fascinating man had needed him like nobody else ever had. Now, Darien was just like everyone else who crossed the estate boundary.

Every sub he'd ever been involved with moved on sooner or later. He'd always taken joy in helping them gain the confidence to go out into the world, proud of who they were. So why did he feel so hollow when he looked at Alastor and tried to imagine being away from him? The last few days had been horrible, even though he'd got a thrill from knowing that the curse had been partially broken because Alastor cared about him.

Many of the subs he'd helped developed temporary crushes on him over the years, even though he didn't encourage them or sleep with them. He pushed away the damning knowledge that he'd already broken his personal code with Alastor.

Could a mere crush break a centuries-old curse? Or did Alastor feel more for him than that? His chest warmed at the thought, then realized that the Tudor man's affection, possibly love for him, just made everything much more painful. Alastor couldn't leave this place, and in less than two days, Juliana would hand the title deed to someone else, and they'd leave.

"Harry? Where are you?" a frantic female voice came from below.

He jogged down the last few steps and moved out of the way as Harry's wife ran down the Long Gallery to him.

With a poker clutched in her fist, Lorraine wrapped her arms around her husband. "I thought, I thought—" she choked out.

Harry kissed her temple, murmuring, "Now then, none of that."

Lorraine sniffed, stepped back, and delivered a cracking slap to her husband's face.

The witches who stood a little farther into the Long Gallery mirrored Darien's surprised expression.

A lone snort of amusement broke the silence. "Go, Lorraine."

Shanae glared at the smirking Alastor, mouthed 'behave'.

Still holding his abused cheek, Harry asked, "What was that for? I was just—"

Lorraine raised the poker. Harry stepped back. "Just what, Henry John Grimshaw? Trying to ensure your wife has two funerals to arrange in the same month?"

"I wasn't doing any—"

"Liar," she spat, almost vibrating with stress, her cheeks red with anger. "I could see whatever that was up on the roof. Which is why I—" She brandished the brass-handled poker.

Darien had to give the woman points. Intending to attack a ten feet tall demon with a poker took guts.

"Callum, I thought I told you—" Shanae started.

"Don't look at me," Callum said, "I put up the wards you asked for."

Lorraine waved a hand at Shanae. "Don't go getting your knickers in a knot. I couldn't see it until I drove up to the cottage. Seems only those on the estate could see it."

"You know, you were such a sweet, shy thing when you first came to the cottage," Alastor mused as he leaned up against the paneling, arms held awkwardly against his chest.

The wounds on his still bound arms, and the long lines of his pale, naked calves and knees, dotted with occasional bruises, proved how much he needed someone to look after him.

Lorraine walked over to Alastor, a frown drawing her blonde eyebrows together. She peered at Alastor. "I know you."

He returned her bold stare with raised eyebrows. "True. I used to play with your son when he was small, but he stopped seeing or hearing me when he turned four. But I promise I spied on Liam in the shower far more than you."

For the second time in two minutes, Lorraine's hand contacted a male face.

Alastor staggered and crashed into the easel holding the portrait of Henry VII. Alastor, painting, and easel hit the floorboards. Darien's heart stopped at the sound of cracking wood.

Darien and Juliana both rushed over. Alastor looked up at them from the wreckage of the painting.

"Huh. Guess not being able to pop around will take time to get used to."

Juliana swallowed, looking at Darien. "The insurance claim could sink us."

"For this lump of firewood?" Alastor poked the broken frame.

Darien turned to his sister. "Alastor thinks it's a reproduction, or at least it wasn't painted before his..." He paused.

"Death? Former life? Pre-demon period?" Alastor nodded to himself, his dark red corkscrew curls bobbing with the movement. "Yeah, that'll do. I can have a pre-demon, demon, and post-demon period. Makes me sound classic, rather than being an animated corpse."

Lorraine took a step back. "You're a what?"

Alastor rolled to his feet, ignoring the destroyed picture frame. To Darien's relief, the actual canvas, although bent, didn't look to be damaged beyond repair. The portrait might not be pre-1602, but it could still be Jacobean and valuable.

Alastor walked forward. Lorraine backed away. "Former ghost, failed demon, a zombie in the literal sense, and you just hit—"

Lorraine looked more likely to use the poker she still held with every word Alastor spoke. The picture could be taken to a specialist conservator to be repaired. Alastor couldn't. Hell, he couldn't even get an x-ray if it was needed.

Darien got up from his crouch. Brattish behavior was never acceptable, but this was odd, possibly suicidal. "Hey, stop it. Yes, hitting you was out of order, but so was what you—"

Alastor turned on him, every inch tense. "Finally noticed me, have you? After all, I'm not as important as a fucking painting, am I? All I've got is this." He plucked at his shirt. "Four and a quarter centuries, and nothing has fucking changed. Those with money control those with nothing, and I've had enough of it."

Alastor took off down the Long Gallery, bare feet slapping on the dark floorboards.

Juliana made shooing motions. "Go, go, I'll put the coffee on."

Darien chased after him. In the state Alastor was in, he didn't know what he'd do. At least he hadn't headed back up to the roof.

The main door in the Low Great Hall hung open. He sprinted toward it, picturing Alastor running for the estate boundary. He had no desire to see if Arioch had told the truth for once.

A damp linen-wearing figure sat slumped, forearms resting on drawn-up knees, on the bottom of the steps leading up to the entrance.

Not trying to hide his presence, Darien headed down the steps and sat next to Alastor, close enough to touch if the young man wanted but with enough distance not to put any pressure on him.

The chill from the stone seeped through his pants within heartbeats. He sat, not talking, as the fine drizzle turned to heavier rain.

Eventually, Alastor said, "It's raining."

"Yep."

"The gravel's damn sharp."

"That's why I'm wearing shoes."

"I haven't got any shoes."

"I'll get you some."

Alastor nodded slowly, kept staring out at the darkening view. "Being cold isn't as interesting as I remember." He held out his arms, displaying the rope around his raw, bloody wrists. "These suck too." With a deep sigh, Alastor leaned his head on Darien's shoulder.

Bone-deep satisfaction warmed Darien from the inside.

"What the fuck am I going to do? Everything works on paperwork these days. There weren't even birth or death certificates when I was alive before, just parish registers. I'm alive, but I can't prove it to anyone. Who the hell would believe me?"

"I would." Darien got to his feet, bent, and gathered Alastor to his chest before standing up again. "Let's get you sorted out. We'll deal with everything else later, don't worry."

Alastor rested his forehead against the side of Darien's face. "You're a terrible liar."

"True," Darien stated as he carried Alastor inside and used his back to shut the door, and the world, out. "It's because I get very little practice. And I'm not lying now."

Darien headed toward the kitchen, hoping that at least some of the guests had left. Alastor didn't need anyone else he could torment to distract himself from his new situation.

"You can put me down, you know. My legs do work," Alastor said, but he didn't wriggle.

"I know. But I want to keep hold of you. You're damn fast, even if you have lost your disappearing mojo."

"You really think I'm fast?"

The hope in the question almost made Darien stumble. Everything had been torn from Alastor, and he needed to know he was worth something in this new existence he'd been thrown into.

"I know so," he said as he shouldered his way into the modern kitchen that probably took up less than half the space of the one that had been here in Nicholas Thatcher's day. It was still one of the biggest non-commercial kitchens he'd ever been in.

Harry sat opposite the witches around the huge solid oak kitchen table. Juliana played with the coffee machine, and Lorraine swirled steaming water in a metal teapot. It appeared neither trusted the other to make their favorite hot beverage.

Shanae's chair scrapped on the flagstones as she shot to her feet.

"Here, put him here. What happened?"

Darien lowered Alastor carefully onto the vacated chair. "He's cold, wet, and tired, and I need the first aid box for—" Darien stopped talking as those gathered stepped into action. Callum stood and draped the cream blanket that had been on the table around Alastor. Shanae reached down and produced the First Aid box she'd had on the floor beside her.

"Coffee?" Juliana asked.

"He'll have hot, sweet tea," Lorraine said firmly as she turned and set a red mug on the table in front of Alastor. "He's English, not American."

"Thanks," Alastor said. Lifting the mug to his lips, he blew on it and took a sip.

And he's doing it all without me needing to touch him. The stab of jealousy hurt more than it should.

Alastor's attention was on Lorraine. "Sorry I was rude. Not being an imp is going to take a bit of getting used to."

A smirk made her plain features appealing. If Liam had been anything like his mother, Darien could see the appeal, and the devastating regret Alastor felt over his part in the youngster's death.

"Don't worry about it. I think I got my revenge with the slap." Her lips pressed together. "Which was wrong because violence is never the answer, no matter the provocation. I should know that more than most. I apologize."

Alastor shrugged. "Times change. People lived by 'spare the rod and spoil the child' in my day. Beating your children showed you cared." He gave a wry snort. "My mother cared a hell of a lot."

"Mothers know their children, but we don't always get things right. Liam was quite capable of getting himself in trouble, and he did have an eye for a pretty girl. Maybe if I'd been harder or lighter..." She sighed, pursed her lips.

"Maybes don't change anything, but they only hurt if you let them. The past can't be changed, but it can only shape the future only if you let it." Darien had used the line many times but it had never sounded so trite or inadequate as it did now.

"Out of all the people I knew back then, I'm glad John Grimshaw ended up on my land." A smile ghosted across Alastor's lips. "He was a mouthy little shit who slept under one of the kitchen tables, right about—" he paused looking around to orientate himself "—there." He pointed to a spot near where Juliana stood, then looked back into his mug. "He was my friend, and I think I could have been friends with Liam too." He met the eyes of each of the Grimshaws. His lips pressed together as his eyes became glassy. "I really am so very sorry."

"Being sorry doesn't bring my boy back," Lorraine said.

"No, no, it doesn't," Alastor said. "But he's not in a bad place. Arioch offered me freedom if Liam took my place here. I told him to shove it where the sun doesn't shine." A brief smile twitched his lips. "Liam liked that."

"So my boy's in Heaven?" Harry choked out.

Alastor met the gaze of Liam's parents. "Yes."

Darien glanced at Shanae, who gave a slight shrug. He itched to ask more but questioning Alastor's statement in front of the Grimshaws would be cruel. Although after all the weirdness he'd seen here, perhaps Heaven and Hell existed after all.

Wiping her eyes, Lorraine said, "I need to get something from the car."

"I'll help," Harry rumbled and the Grimshaws made their way out.

Darien hadn't expected anyone to suggest that Alastor live with the Grimshaws, to almost literally step into the shoes of the boy whose death he helped to cause, but the seed of a relationship had been planted.

The door opened again, bringing a blast of cold, damp air. Lorraine leaned in, put a full black bin bag just inside.

"I was going to take these clothes to the charity shop. Seems they could be better used here until he gets his own stuff." Not waiting for an answer, she closed the door again.

They listened as Harry's Land Rover rumbled to life, and the sound of the engine faded as the couple made their way home.

"Is everyone ok with coffee?" Juliana asked. "I don't suppose any tea I make will be worth drinking."

Alastor took another sip of his tea that had to be almost cold by now.

"Put your arms out, and we'll get those ropes off," Shanae ordered.

Alastor kept his two-handed grip on his mug as if someone would try to take it from him. Darien leaped at the opportunity to regain the upper hand from the witches who seemed to have taken over. They'd already isolated and surrounded

Alastor with Callum on one side and Shanae hovering behind him.

"Don't worry, I'll see to him."

"Haven't you done that already, Mr. FitzHenry?" Shanae asked, one eyebrow raised.

Darien leaned back on the counter, folding his arms. "That question is inappropriate in this company," he nodded at Callum, "Although I have to wonder what my personal life has to do with you when you openly admit sleeping with an incubus."

Shanae waved her hand dismissively. "All witches do that. It extends our lifespans."

"Not all witches," Callum grumbled.

"Your mother said no, and that's the end of it. I also happened to agree with her."

"Callum do this, Callum do that," the boy mumbled under his breath.

"This incubus, Avery?" Alastor said, "You haven't got his number, have you?"

Darien was struck dumb for a moment before a chuckle burst from him.

"Callum, if you wouldn't mind?" Darien asked, raising his eyebrows.

The blue-haired teen glanced at Shanae, who narrowed her eyes, then nodded. "Go pick out something for Nicholas to wear, dear."

Darien sat in the vacated wooden chair next to Alastor and motioned to the First Aid box. "You do that one; I'll do this. Jules, can you order a pizza or something? It's been a damn long time since Alastor ate anything."

CHAPTER TWENTY-FOUR

Pizza with everything was every bit as good as Alastor imagined, including the olives Darien carefully removed from his slices. Even his wrists felt more comfortable now that they'd been washed and smothered in a salve from a squeezable metal tube and wrapped in bandages.

Dressed in a pair of gray sweatpants and a matching plain stretchy long-sleeved top, he felt out of place, out of his time, but at least his belly was full. He couldn't remember ever being this satiated, this comfortable.

And he was still torn over the disgruntled pizza delivery driver. The prank hadn't gone according to plan at all.

He'd been wearing his new, old clothes for twenty minutes when the brass front doorbell clanged. It wasn't the original one, but it wasn't much different.

Darien got to his feet, but Alastor was quicker. "Can I? I've never answered the door before."

Darien stared at him as if assessing his ability to perform such a mundane task, then he nodded. "Go on then."

Alastor shot him a grin and hightailed it to the main door in the Low Great Hall. Taking a breath, he drew himself up and channeled Sir Edmund as he opened the door.

The red and blue hat made the young female delivery driver look more like a professional Fool than Alastor ever had. She proffered two huge flat boxes. When Alastor didn't immediately take them, she said, "You did order pizza, right?"

Alastor stuck his nose in the air. "The likes of you do not enter by the front door. Go around the back." He expected the same reaction that he'd had all those years ago; shame, anger, and embarrassment.

His mirth died as the girl sneered and dropped the boxes on the doorstep. "Have or don't have it. It's paid for, so I don't give a shit. And if you put in a complaint, I'll tell my boss you tried to grope me." As she drove off, she gave him the finger.

Alastor bent to pick up the thankfully undamaged boxes. In every way he could think of, things had changed, and he didn't fit anymore.

When he'd been Nicholas, everything had been about accumulating money and power. When he'd been an imp, it'd been about ridding the world of Walpole heirs to gain his freedom. Now, the future was such an unknown that his mind shied away from it. Basking in the moment, having a full belly, soft clothes, and being warm seemed so much easier.

"You can stay here all night if you wish, but Alastor is almost asleep in his chair, and so am I. We're going to bed," Darien said. The no-nonsense tone brought Alastor back to the conversation.

Shanae leveled Darien with a look worthy of the strictest headteacher. "Nicholas has been pushed around and exploited enough in his life; he doesn't need to add you to the tally. He can go to bed. You are coming back to the hotel with me."

Alastor's heart dropped. He didn't want to be alone again, but there was no room for compromise in Shanae's voice.

Darien didn't twitch at her demand.

Alastor found that if he squinted a bit, and imagined Shanae with different clothes and darker hair, she was the spitting image of his mother.

"No." Darien didn't even try to offer a reason. Under that narrow-eyed glare, Nicholas Thatcher would have been babbling excuses. Alastor the imp would have simply popped to another room. Now—mainly because he couldn't escape them—he simply sat and watched the show. Although if they didn't hurry up and make up their minds, he would take a leaf out of John Grimshaw's book and climb under the table to take a nap.

Shanae leaned forward. "While I was bandaging his wrist, I took a proper look at his memories. You pulled him away too quickly for me to see anything up on the roof."

"Just because he gave you permission once, it does not give you the right to poke around in his—"

"I'm sorry, but I needed to know. My ancestors failed him. Agnes Flowers all but pushed him into the arms of the Walpoles, who then abused him from almost the moment they met. I won't do the same."

Neither of them looked at him. Alastor nudged the pizza box with a finger. It moved, proving that the spell hadn't somehow resurrected itself. Being ignored when you were insubstantial was one thing, but this was just plain rudeness.

"I don't have to explain myself to someone who caused his current injuries and attempted to get me to stab him to death," Darien said as if he were discussing pizza toppings.

Shanae's lips thinned. "That was to save lives, not personal gratification. Did you think I wouldn't investigate your past? I've met dominants before. The head of the Supernatural Council has a wonderful Mediterranean island dedicated to feeding himself and other sex demons. He has a club for your sort there, so I know what your type does, especially to the young and vulnerable."

Alastor couldn't help it. Her sour expression was like a red flag to a bull. Leaning an elbow on the table—the height of bad manners in Nicholas's time—he rested his chin on his fist and gave her every ounce of his attention.

"So, what goes on in a club like that? As someone who is incredibly young, inexperienced, and oh so very vulnerable, I think I need details. Lots of very explicit details."

Shanae's eyebrows drew together, but Darien's lips twitched.

"Do not try to play me, young man. Those clubs cater to those who enjoy inflicting pain and humiliation."

"And I thought you were a woman of the world," Darien drawled. "I don't know about this demon club you mentioned, but human kink clubs cater to anyone with sexual desires outside what is commonly considered normal. Yes, that includes sadists, but the masochists they play with aren't forced to attend. Every club I frequent has staff watching for coercion. I perform that role myself at my local club."

Darien policing people who went too far fitted his personality. Alastor couldn't wait to see him throwing a bully, someone like Richard Walpole, out on his arse. His enthusiasm died as he realized that would never happen.

"Sadism and masochism are only part of the kink community," Darien continued. "Many kinksters don't indulge in either."

"What about you?" Shanae asked Darien, but Alastor ignored her.

"What else do they do then?" he asked with genuine interest. As far as he'd seen and experienced, sex was quick and functional unless the man had to persuade the woman to give in. In those cases, smiles, lies, kissing, and soft touches preceded the same quick act of planting their seed inside.

"Roleplay, which can involve human professions, ageplay, or animal roles, exhibitionism, voyeurism, humiliation, bondage without sadism, fetishes involving objects, body parts, clothing—"

Shanae held up a hand. "Stop, that's quite enough. Neither Nicholas nor I need to know about—"

"Speak for yourself, Witchy; I want to know what the big guy is into." He wriggled in his seat, noticing the pain in his ass had almost gone entirely. "Come on, Darien, throw a guy a bone. Speaking of which—"

"Boy, we are not alone, and you are offending our guest."

Alastor frowned. "Boy? I'm no—"

"Does your kink involve a term beginning with D?" Shanae interrupted.

"I take the penny finally dropped?" Darien asked, eyebrows raised. "Although I prefer the term caregiver for myself."

"What are you two on about?" Alastor looked from one to the other.

Shanae got to her feet and locked eyes with Darien. "You don't want me as your enemy, Mr. FitzHenry. If you've lied about your... predilections, I will find you wherever you hide. If you are genuine... you might be exactly what he needs, for now anyway."

She turned to Alastor, fished in her bag, and pulled out a simple mobile phone. She held up it. "Press this button, then one, then the phone symbol. It'll connect straight to me. Call me. Anytime. Understand?"

Disappointed, he held out his hand for it. He'd been hoping for something far less mundane.

"Or you could pinch your left earlobe and say, 'family is everything' and I'll be here in a heartbeat."

"Really?"

She held her stoic expression for a heartbeat before her face lit up with a grin. "No, not really. You're not the only one of the family who likes pranks, Nicholas. If you need me, phone me, ok? I'll see you in the morning."

To his utter surprise, she rounded the table and enfolded him in a hug. The first genuinely platonic embrace he'd ever experienced.

She rubbed his back and talked against his cheek. "I meant what I said. I'm here for you, whatever you need. I'll work on the spell that Arioch claimed exists. Just don't try testing it in case it's real.

"Be good, and if you can't be good, be careful. I don't want to lose you now I've found you. There is magic in you, Nicholas, which is probably why you caught Arioch's attention. Demons and witches have been scoring points off each other for as long as we've existed."

She raised her voice so Darien could hear. "And if he ever oversteps the mark, just click your heels together and say 'Skidaddle skiddoodle, your dick is now a noodle.'"

Alastor snorted and pulled back. "Now I know you're a relative. That was truly awful."

Her lips twitched. "If you don't believe me, try it sometime. The spell lasts a day, but you have to be touching the person you want to affect. But tonight, I want you to sleep, nothing more.

"Oh, and I'll have Callum set up some wards against those with ill-intentions entering the estate. Sleep tight, boys."

CHAPTER TWENTY-FIVE

Darien kept two steps behind Alastor the entire way up to the only furnished bedroom in the building. So much had changed in the last day that Darien found it hard to process. He had no idea what was going on in Alastor's head.

What he did know was that Alastor being alone tonight wouldn't be a good idea. The guy was fickle, impulsive, and way too unpredictable. Jumping off the roof, burning the place down, or simply heading for the boundary were all possibilities. Whether Alastor needed a sounding board, silent sympathetic companionship, or another distraction, Darien vowed to provide it.

Usually, auctions got his blood racing, but he wished this one would never happen. When the final hammer came down, his interaction with Alastor would become a hell of a lot more complicated. He couldn't change that, but he could give this fascinating, needy, vulnerable man everything he could while trying to solve the issue.

He wasn't sure when he'd decided to stay permanently, but he couldn't contemplate walking away. Worries about getting a work visa, or even permanent residency, swirled in his mind. As far as he knew, things like that had to be applied for back in the US, and leaving Alastor alone caused a hollow sensation in his belly.

Boxing up his own emotions, he concentrated on his sub's needs because that was what a good dom did. Once they were both in the bedroom, Darien leaned against the door, assessing Alastor's mood.

Alastor stood near the bed they'd briefly shared and raked his fingers through his hair. The urge to step forward, to stop the physical manifestation of stress, bubbled. Control the body, control the mind, his mentor had told him, and the strategy had always worked with distressed subs before. But Alastor was unique, among subs, among the whole of humanity as far as he knew.

As soon as he levered himself away from the door, Alastor fixed him with a hard look, halting him in his tracks.

"You should go back to the hotel with your sister and the witches. The auction is tomorrow, and you've probably got lots to do."

"I know, but you—"

Expression fierce, he poked a finger in Darien's direction. "I don't need your pity, and I'm not a child who needs looking after, not by Shanae and not by you. Hell, I've seen more of life than you could ever hope to.

"We don't know each other, and we won't see each other again after tomorrow. You'll be carrying on with your career, your life and family and—" his next words rushed out, "—and I don't want to know how good it could be if it's only going to be one more fucking night."

Alastor flopped back on the bed, forearm over his eyes. "Just go before I make an even bigger fool of myself than I have already."

To his knowledge, Darien had never encountered a sex demon like the ones Shanae mentioned, but if he had, he bet Alastor would outshine any incubus. Attitude and neediness. Dark red hair curling against the white bedding, hard cock outlined in the soft sweatpants. Everything felt designed to hit his every desire. Two inches of pale skin were revealed as the borrowed gray sweatshirt rode up. That stripe of exposed flesh begged to be worshipped, and the man it belonged to protected.

Darien strolled forward, the creaking floorboard telegraphing his movement. Alastor held his breath as Darien took his time, gaze roaming over him. Yes, Alastor wasn't a virgin, but Darien bet that he'd only experienced fast, furious, hidden, or angry sex before the other night, never a sensual experience for mutual pleasure.

Being together wouldn't be easy, but he vowed it would happen. Tonight, he intended to give Alastor something to hold on to if things took time to sort out.

Moving slowly, so Alastor had the opportunity to object if he wished, Darien put one knee on the bed and then the other. Then he shuffled up until he straddled the narrow hips.

Alastor moved his arm, opened an eye. His Adam's apple bobbed as he swallowed. "What are you doing?"

"What I've wanted to do since that first night." Darien ground his ass gently against Alastor's cock.

Alastor's pale throat vibrated as he let out a groan. Tilting his hips, he pressed his hardness against Darien.

"And I thought I was meant to be the demon," Alastor murmured, thoroughly distracted. But the former imp wasn't the only one finding it hard to concentrate.

Darien's cock, already hard and desperate, pressed against his zipper, but even though they both clearly wanted this physically, he wouldn't go further without verbal consent.

"I don't pity you, Alastor," he said and ground against him a little harder. "I want to watch you writhe and moan. Remember the day we met when you told me you wanted to know what noises I make when I spill?"

Leaning forward, he caged Alastor's head between his forearms. The world faded but for those few inches of distance between them. "Well, I want the same. Can you do that for me?"

"Ugh, using my own lines against me is pure evil." Alastor groaned, his hips thrusting gently as if he couldn't help the movement. "Impulse control has never been my strong point."

A smile tickled Darien's lips. "I've got enough control for both of us. If you don't think this is a good idea, we can simply share the bed like we did the first night."

A pink tongue poked out and wetted plump lips. Darien's cock lurched, but he resisted the urge to palm himself.

"Tell me the truth about something first."

"Go on."

Alastor's eyes bored into him. "Do you want me for me, or do you just want to tick 'fuck a Tudor man' off your bucket list?"

Darien smothered his laugh by leaning down and taking Alastor's lips.

Alastor pushed a hand against Darien's chest. Darien pulled back. Had he gotten it wrong? Did Alastor not want this?

"I'm not a girl. You don't need to kiss me."

Darien failed to hold back his grin, but it vanished as Alastor began to struggle.

"Hey, hey, calm down. I know you're not a girl." He ground his hips down, pressing his cloth-covered balls against Alastor's still hard cock. "I just happen to like kissing. If you don't, we can—"

Alastor turned a delightful shade of red. "I've never, erm—"

To save him further embarrassment, Darien leaned down—slow enough that Alastor could stop him if he wished—and touched their lips together. At first, Alastor stayed passive. Then, as Darien began exploring his lips, he hesitantly reciprocated. When Alastor's hand grasped his hair, controlling the kiss a little, Darien groaned in appreciation.

Darien gathered Alastor to him, lowering one leg so he could grind their lengths together. Alastor groaned into his mouth, his sweet, pizza breath invaded and intoxicated.

Needing air and a break before he simply took what he wanted, Darien pulled back but left their foreheads touching and their breath mingling.

"So—" He swallowed as his voice sounded hoarse and breathless and tried again. "—So, do you approve of guys kissing now?"

Alastor squinted and pursed lips swollen by Darien's kisses. "Might need another trial, just to make sure."

With a smile, Darien obliged. Alastor moved against him, hands stroking, exploring, grabbing his ass, testing the muscle of his arms and shoulders.

If all Alastor wanted was to kiss and grope, that's what he'd do, even if his cock felt ready to explode just from rubbing against Alastor. But he needed to know now, so he could make quick use of the ensuite before his little head overwhelmed his resolve.

"What do you want, Alastor? We can keep doing this all night, we can get some sleep, or we can go further. You're calling the shots here, little imp."

Sea-green eyes looked up at him, and a smirk curved puffy lips. "You still think I'm an imp?"

He couldn't stop his answering grin at finding the perfect pet name. "Hell, yeah. And I'm damn thankful it's me you're teasing tonight."

Alastor circled his hips, increasing then decreasing the pressure on Darien's cock. Darien gritted his teeth. "You're asking for it, imp."

"Well, you'd better give it to me then, hadn't you?" Alastor's self-satisfied smirk tore down every remaining barrier Darien had put up to keep his heart safe. In that moment, Darien knew he'd tear down the world to protect his imp, including Alastor's self-sabotaging tendencies.

Darien skated his hands under the gray sweatshirt, found taut, smooth skin. Unable to help himself, he slid down, knees hitting the floor. He needed to see, to taste, to bring pleasure.

Licking, nipping, and sucking, he marveled at the speed Alastor's alabaster-like skin reddened at his touch. Obeying Darien's insistent pushing, Alastor pulled the sweatshirt off, revealing the beautiful pale skin that was fast becoming Darien's obsession.

Tugging at Alastor's sweatpants, he found that the modern concept of underwear still hadn't reached the Tudor man.

Slim and curved, the reddened cockhead glistened with precum. He ran his nose along it, taking in the musky, mouth-watering scent. Like before, he wanted Alastor to explode in his mouth, to writhe, gasp, beg, and forget everything but him.

Alastor tugged on his shoulder. "Get up here. I need more practice at this kissing thing, and get this shirt off."

Darien didn't object to prolonging this as long as possible. Teasing each other for hours on end seemed just about perfect. After pulling off his shirt, he crawled up Alastor's body, eager to taste those lips again.

Alastor smirked. "My turn."

Darien found himself on his back, looking up at the former self-proclaimed demon.

It started with a kiss. For a beginner, Darien had to admit Alastor was a damn fast learner as he nibbled, licked, and placed open-mouthed kisses along his jaw and then down his neck. Darien lifted his chin to give more access to the sensitive skin, but Alastor didn't stop there.

He slid downward, paying attention to each nipple, each line of muscle on his belly until he got to his navel. Darien shuddered as Alastor stuck his tongue into the dip. Darien's hips twitched. The sensitive spot had always felt as if it had a direct connection to his cock.

Alastor smiled against him as if he'd somehow won a point in a competition. The little shit mouthed down his happy trail and then back up three times before Darien broke and pushed on his head.

Alastor might not have any experience with twenty-first-century underwear, but he didn't hesitate to pull down the waistband of Darien's boxer shorts with his teeth. The cloth pulled his cockhead up, then released it to slap back against his belly.

"Well, well, all happy to see me," Alastor murmured. Looking up at Darien, he bit his lip, gave a lopsided smirk. "How much do you want my mouth around you, milord?"

Before Darien could process, Alastor didn't waste any time and pulled off Darien's pants and shorts, then engulfed his cock with his hot, wet, mouth.

His tongue swirled, outlining the veins and the base of the head; Darien gave up counting the techniques Alastor used as the sensations overpowered him. Kissing might not be something Alastor had experienced, but hell, he knew how to suck a cock.

Darien's hips bucked, pushing himself further into that tight, wet heat. The tingle in his balls grew as Alastor expertly sucked and pumped the shaft. This wasn't how he'd wanted it, wasn't how—

"Stop, not so fast, I—"

Alastor sped up, dragging a groan out of Darien. Gritting his teeth, he grabbed a handful of Alastor's curls.

"I said, stop. I'm right there, and I don't want—"

Alastor increased the suction, so Darien pulled him off. His cock popped out of the imp's mouth with a dirty slurp.

"You don't want to spend? I think you might be lying because if you didn't, I wouldn't be able to—"

Even though Darien had his hair in a firm grip, it didn't stop Alastor reaching for him and pumping his cock for all he was worth, while tugging on his balls with the other hand.

Already on edge, the final erotic shot of half pain, half pleasure sent him over the edge. Darien's climax ripped from him, cum shooting from his slit, hitting Alastor's cheek, his eye, and Darien's belly in four sharp pulses.

Darien blinked as he came down from the nerve-jangling high, only to see Alastor wiping cum off his cheek. He sucked his cum-covered finger with a mischievous twinkle in his eye.

Alastor sucking him off hadn't been Darien's intention at all. Someone here had been played, and it wasn't the former imp.

"Come on, it's your turn," Darien said, wanting to make Alastor's eyes roll back in his head as much as he'd just experienced.

The smile dropped from Alastor's face, and he sat up, elbows on his knees as he gave Darien nothing but his back. A back that still bore the fading marks of the last Walpole heir. "I'm good, just really tired."

Darien had never been turned down in such a situation, and it confused the hell out of him. Alastor had clearly wanted what they'd done, had enjoyed it, or had he?

Alastor had been acting, playing, Walpole heirs for centuries. Alastor had called him milord. Darien's mind stuttered. Was that because Alastor couldn't remember his name? After all, he was only the latest Walpole to take Alastor to his bed.

Was this an attempt to secure his sympathy, to bind another heir to him, or had Alastor simply been going through the motions because his body was the only currency he had?

Was it even true that the curse had been broken because Alastor loved him? Demons lied, and there had been two of them up on that roof.

Or had he refused Darien's touch because he wasn't turned on anymore and didn't want him to know? *Fuck, is he even gay?*

The thought that Alastor hadn't enjoyed what they'd done, had assumed he had to have sex with him out of obligation or as *payment,* drained away any remaining pleasure from the orgasm.

But maybe this was for the best. After all, once the auction concluded, their fledgling relationship could depend exclusively on the assistance of Liam Grimshaw's parents.

The former imp's best bet for a secure future would be creating a bond with whoever bought this place.

Perhaps the blowjob had been a 'thanks for the memories' act. Darien felt a little sick at the thought, even though he'd had plenty of 'goodbye' sex in his life. This seemed so different, so wrong. But he'd never left a sub without talking through a situation, especially a sexual one. It was part of the dom code, his code.

Reaching out, he placed his palm gently on Alastor's shoulder. "Look, we need to—"

Alastor twitched his shoulder away and choked out, "What you need to do is stop touching me."

"You're upset," Darien said firmly. "I can't leave you like this."

"Wanna see if Shanae's noodle dick spell works?"

Having this conversation naked in bed would complicate matters. Darien reached for his boxers, then pulled on a pair of sweatpants and a t-shirt.

He paused at the door. "I'll be back soon, and we'll talk, but please, stay in here. I'm too tired for another round of midnight hide and seek."

Chest hollow, he headed downstairs, intending to bring back some tea or decaf coffee so they could discuss things like sensible adults. Alastor needed help, and he intended to provide it, even if the Tudor man didn't want him long term.

Chapter Twenty-Six

By leaving, Darien confirmed he was just like every other arrogant, selfish Walpole heir. All that 'I care' shit had been to get in Alastor's pants, and now that he'd taken his pleasure, he'd pissed off.

Alastor sighed, flopped back on the wrecked bed, and stared at the ceiling. If this had happened a decade ago, hell, even yesterday, Alastor could have chosen to follow the heir, tease him some more, or simply disappear back to the priest hole.

Four hundred years in this place, and it still felt like he didn't fit. There was one place he did belong. After pulling on his familiar Tudor undershirt, he left Sir Edmund's old room.

The layout of the Hall had been altered over the years to accommodate the changing needs of the residents. The master suite of the first earl hadn't lasted long after his death as his son also refused to sleep in there.

Sir Edmund's old room became the main bedroom. The first earl's bedchamber got divided into two and had served as guest bedrooms, a children's nursery suite, and hobby rooms, but nobody wanted to use the part where Milord Walpole's privy had been for long.

The space had been a storage closet for linens and cleaning equipment for the last century. Alastor slipped in, squinting at the automatic harsh electric light.

He hadn't viewed the space from this angle for several centuries, so it took a little thinking to work out that a short round vacuum cleaner sat exactly where Thomas Walpole's closed stool had been all those years ago.

Usually, he just thought about the priest hole below and found himself there. It'd been his space, his sanctuary, and the pull of the familiar among all these crazy changes drew him like a magnet.

Dragging the red cleaner out of the way, he began tugging at the hideous green 1930s linoleum.

"Alastor?"

Instinct kicked in. He pictured the space beneath him, willing himself to be there. His attempt to relocate failed like every other time he'd tried since the scene up on the roof.

Would Darien move on if he stayed hidden? He dismissed the ludicrous idea. Darien was a persistent bastard and would track him down like a damn hound if the light and the partially open door hadn't already given him away.

He sat back on his ass, ignoring the slight pain from the last earl's beating. "In here."

The door creaked open. Without saying anything, Darien came in and sat down beside him, at ease in his sweatpants and t-shirt.

"Well, I have to say that Sardines[1] beats Hide and Seek."

Alastor ignored the lame joke, but he yearned to lean against the big, solid man and take the comfort he offered, but it'd only make tomorrow more difficult. Even though he wore his old undershirt, the bandages on his wrists proved how much—and how little—things had changed. Despite being corporal again, he remained doomed to haunt this place forever.

"You must be cold in just that."

Alastor wrapped his arms around himself, ignoring the sting in his wrists. "You're not having it. It's mine."

Darien pursed his lips, nodded slowly. "It is. But it could be worth over forty thousand pounds to one of the bidders tomorrow afternoon. Selling it to a collector or a museum could provide you with a nest egg."

"Is it enough to buy this place?" Alastor asked, even though he knew the answer.

"Sadly, no, but it could give you a little independence."

Alastor snorted at the ridiculous statement. "And where am I going to keep or spend all this money? It's not as if I can stroll into a bank or shop or get one of those little plastic cards. People don't keep all their money in strong boxes like the one down there anymore." He nodded at the area of the floor he'd cleared.

"Is that where you..." Darien trailed off.

"Died? Yeah, that's where I am, was, whatever." He couldn't take his eyes off the spot, couldn't stop the emotion welling up. "Wish I was still there."

Darien pulled him against his side, and though it would probably damn him, Alastor didn't resist.

"Do you want to look? I hate to say it, but with the sale tomorrow, it might be the last—"

"Yes." The word shot out of his mouth.

Darien huffed in amusement. "Don't want to think about it for a while?"

"Just move your ass, FitzHenry. If this old shirt is worth forty thousand, the stuff down there has to be worth a hell of a lot more."

Darien halted as his fingers had been about to pry up the linoleum. "Alastor, everything in the house belongs to the estate, even objects Carl Anderson doesn't know about. If they are valuable, they'll be sold individually, along with the auction pieces in the Long Gallery, before the estate is sold."

The irony that the objects he'd sat beside for so long would get to leave when he couldn't, caused a huff of amusement. The prank was worthy of a top-class imp. He didn't care about most of the things—he'd already committed them to memory a thousand times—but his heart clenched at the thought of losing the most recent object.

"You're even going to take the recorder, aren't you?"

"I don't have a choice about that—it belongs to the seller—but I'll buy you another."

Alastor pictured one of the ugly, soulless plastic instruments the last resident children had used. Between one second and the next, the last thing he wanted to do was see the priest hole and the things he'd thought of as his for so long.

Pulling away, he got to his feet. "Knock yourself out with the cataloging. I'm going to get some sleep."

"One question first."

Alastor sighed like a bolshie teenager and dropped his hand from the door handle, but he didn't turn around. Of course, Darien wanted the last word. This must have been how the heirs had felt, unable to escape their tormentor.

"What?" he ground out.

"Why didn't you want me to reciprocate in the bedroom?"

All the tension drained away, leaving only depression in its wake. "Because I wanted you to be angry, to hate me, so I could hate you back. It's what I did to all your relatives because it made what I had to do to them easier, and it'll make it easier when you leave. So stop being so fucking nice."

Throwing himself out the door, running, finding somewhere to hide until Darien left forever went through his mind, but his body refused to complete the actions.

The floor creaked as Darien got up. A hand on his arm slowly turned him around.

"Let go, let me take the stress, just for a while," Darien murmured and pulled him into a gentle hug as if he were made of glass.

One second. Two. A hand rubbed his back, promising so much. Lying.

Alastor broke. Tears welled up and poured down his face, turning Darien's pale blue shirt dark.

"It's ok, just be. I've got you. No past, no future, just now." Darien continued whispering nonsense in his deep calm voice as he swayed them from side to side and drew circles on Alastor's back. Alastor hung onto the sound, the feeling of being surrounded, like a drowning man holding a life vest.

When he ran out of words, Darien hummed a slow tune as they slow danced above Alastor's grave in the middle of the night.

"Idiot," Alastor said against Darien's shoulder as he recognized the tune as 'Don't Worry, Be Happy,' but he didn't stop the slow, shuffling circle. No past, no present, just now, seemed a wonderful idea, and Darien had given it to him.

Without thinking, Alastor kissed Darien's neck, not caring if the salty taste was from his tears or the sweat of the man who held him with such consideration and compassion. A man who, despite Alastor being a brat and pushing him away so many times, was still here.

A slight squeeze told him that Darien didn't mind the attention. For the first time ever, Alastor let go and did what he wanted, rather than focusing on his partner's emotions. He left open-mouthed, sloppy kisses across the stubble on Darien's chin, then down his neck. Leaning back, he shoved at Darien's t-shirt, needing access to that perfect skin. Skin that was different from every other Walpole, just like the man inside it.

"My little imp," Darien said against his hair, "let's go back to bed and forget some more."

Alastor's cock lurched, the spike of lust blanking his mind of any thoughts except getting down and dirty.

Grabbing Darien's hand, he reached for the door handle, opened it, and began towing Darien through it.

---

1. Sardines: Game similar to hide and seek but seekers hide with the first hider when they find them. The last person to join the group becomes the new hider.

CHAPTER TWENTY-SEVEN

Having someone else's pleasure in his hands wasn't new for Darien, but it had never been more important than this moment. It felt as if every sexual encounter before this had been preparing Darien for this moment.

He wanted to find all the secret places on Alastor's body that made him gasp and twitch, not only the ones common to everyone. The majority of guys got an electric pulse to their cock if you hit their prostate just right, but most had a special place that made them purr or gasp when they were played with—feet, fingers, the back of the knees, armpits, belly button, throat—everyone was different.

As soon as they entered the bedroom, Alastor reached for the hem of his undershirt. Darien put a hand on his shoulder.

"I want to make you feel better than you've ever done before, so you need to tell me if there's something you want or something you don't like, ok?"

Alastor bobbed his head, and his hands reached for his shirt again.

"I need words, little imp. None of this works without communication."

His frown was adorable as his curly auburn hair fell over one eye. "Is this part of the kink thing you and Shanae were going on about?"

"Intimacy without consent is just abuse," Darien said, a little frustrated that his own rules had disrupted the spontaneity.

"In that case, Milord FitzHenry," he pulled off his shirt and performed a florid bow, erect cock bobbing, "you have my solemn, everlasting vow that I will—"

Darien shoved his chest, causing Alastor to fall back on the mattress. He crawled up the bed, straddling Alastor's thighs as he had earlier, but he wouldn't let the imp take control this time. He wanted him feeling, not thinking or plotting mischief.

"Well, this is a little sudden, I—"

Darien leaned down and took his lips in a searing kiss. When he pulled back, Alastor's pupils were wide, lips spit-slicked, and his chest rose and fell as if he'd been running. Satisfaction warmed Darien's chest. For once, Alastor wasn't cracking jokes, being bratty, or trying to manipulate him.

"Do you want to play a game?" Darien asked. Without waiting for a reply, he lifted Alastor's arms—avoiding his damaged wrists—above his head. "Can you keep them there while I feast on you, little imp?"

Alastor's nose wrinkled. "Well, I'm willing to give it a —"

The attempt to distract earned him a bite on the neck. Alastor gasped, hips rocking up. *So he likes being bitten.* Darien grinned against the pale skin. With each utterance, each movement, Alastor gave Darien a little more ammunition in the fight to distract him.

Inch by inch, Darien raked his fingernails up Alastor's chest, admiring the red trails he left behind. When he got to his nipples, Alastor arched, chasing the sensation.

Taking a pink bud in his mouth, he sucked and licked, but it took a nip and a pinch to make Alastor gasp. Moving over to his armpit caused Alastor to bring his arm down.

"Ah-ah," Darien reminded.

"I don't like it," Alastor blurted.

Darien moved back up, letting Alastor see his smile. "Right answer. I'm proud of you for telling me."

Alastor opened and then shut his mouth. Pressing his lips together, he turned his head away, eyes glassy.

Has no one ever praised this boy? He couldn't believe that he'd somehow been granted the privilege, the honor, of rectifying that travesty.

"You are the most remarkable man I've ever met, and not just because you've seen so much." He placed a gentle kiss on Alastor's chin, then pushed himself down a few inches.

"I've never met anyone so resilient," he added and bit at Alastor's nipple, making him gasp and twitch.

When he got to his belly button, he tongued it with a dirty slurp. "You are funny, talented, and so fucking sexy that you blow my mind."

Heat radiated from the now rosy skin beneath him. "You're just saying that because you want to suck my cock."

If this was the only way he'd get Alastor to voice what he wanted, he'd take it. Sliding down, he stopped to admire the slim, reddened cock that bobbed, begging for attention, from a bed of wild red hair. He usually liked his subs shaved or sculpted, but this primitive, natural sight had his balls buzzing. A bead of precum appeared at the slit.

"You don't have to if—"

"Oh, I want to, my imp; I'm just admiring. You really have the most perfect cock I've ever seen."

Alastor snorted. "Yeah, right. Like I don't know a line when I hear one."

"I seem to remember you saying, 'Believe me, don't believe me, it doesn't make a difference.' That applies here too."

Darien sat up, then grabbed the lube from his bag on the floor beside the bed. "Do you know what this is?"

Alastor frowned and leaned up on his elbows, legs spread. He looked magnificent, hair mussed, the pink marks of Darien's attention stark on his skin, and his cock hard and flushed against his belly. "Some kind of healing gel like you used on my wrists? They're fine. I don't need—"

As Alastor spoke, Darien squeezed a little of the clear, flavorless gel onto his fingers, then fisted Alastor's beautiful cock.

"Ah, by God's balls, that's good. Did the witches—" Whatever Alastor had been about to say turned into a gasp as Darien played him. Fast then slow, full fist, then two fingers, Darien used every edging trick he knew until Alastor's glistening body bucked, his thighs, belly, and arms twitching as he fought to stay in the position Darien had ordered.

He wondered if Alastor had any idea that he was controlling the speed and tightness of Darien's fist. His other hand stayed on Alastor's balls, enjoying the weight, testing, assessing, how near his victim was to exploding.

Darien slowed his ministrations when Alastor's breaths came in pants and his belly tightened. When his breathing evened a little, Darien used his entire palm, making sure he twisted and rubbed his thumb over the exposed slit to bring his boy back to boiling point.

Alastor tensed, his balls tightening as they got ready to spill. This time, rather than slowing down, he gave Alastor's sack a sharp tug and squeezed the base of his shaft, effectively stopping his climax.

"Are you sure you're—" Alastor swallowed "—not a vengeance demon? Because this is fucking torture."

A few rapid pumps had Alastor's hips thrusting in time, so Darien let go again. "Well, if you don't like it, I can always stop."

Alastor's eyes blazed. "If you don't finish what you started, I'm gonna jump off the fucking roof so I can haunt your ass forever."

Darien brushed damp curls away from Alastor's forehead, lips twitching.

"You want my ass, little imp?"

Plush lips parted in utter shock, and a damp Adam's Apple bobbed. "I've, I've never—"

Darien decided the man beneath him might just be the most beguiling thing he'd ever had the privilege to meet, but now was not the time to teach him about topping.

Darien bent over, took the cute, flushed cock into his mouth until it pushed against the entrance to his throat, then swallowed. The deep grunt of pleasure and the heaving, damp thigh under his hand was all the pleasure Darien needed.

He bobbed—making obscene wet sounds—until he ran out of oxygen and pulled off to breathe. A silver strand connected his lips to the rosy cockhead. Bending again to his task, he sucked and bobbed, jerking the part not in his mouth with his fingers.

Alastor thrust up, almost pushing himself into Darien's throat again.

He pulled off. "Ah, ah, my turn, not yours."

"Ugh, I've changed my mind. I'm going to haunt your evil ass whatever you do."

Darien raised his eyebrows. "Really? Then I have no reason not to do this." Holding Alastor's gaze, he licked two fingers, then pushed them, one by one, into his hole. "I want to feel you come from the inside too."

Alastor's eyes went round. Darien held his gaze, pumping his cock gently as he probed his slick, wet heat.

Apart from feeling the bumpy rounded surface of his gland, Darien knew he'd hit the spot as Alastor lurched up, hands grabbing mindlessly for Darien.

"Settle down, boy," Darien growled.

Bandaged wrists shot back up. Time to reward his obedience. Darien wrapped his lips back around the rock-hard cock and sucked while tapping Alastor's prostate.

Alastor wailed into the night as he shot down Darien's throat, clenching on his fingers. Darien worked him, taking pulse after pulse until the former imp collapsed, boneless, satiated, and hopefully with his mind blown.

Slowly, carefully, he released Alastor's spent cock, and withdrew his fingers from his body. Taking his eyes off the limp, spread-eagled, fucked-out man in his bed proved impossible. He wanted nothing more than to lie down beside him, but tomorrow was auction day, and he had to fit in at least forty-eight hours of work before reaching for his gavel. It seemed an impossible task, but for Alastor, he'd manage somehow.

Leaning over, he pressed a kiss to the damp forehead. Alastor opened heavy eyes.

"That was—" he blew out a breath, and a tired smile lifted his lips "—Sorry 'bout being mean before. It's difficult to trust, y'know?" He lifted a hand, cupped Darien's cheek. Those sea-green eyes drew him like a siren. "I didn't think demons could love, but—"

Darien bent, brushed his lips with a tender kiss. "I'm here to look after you, little imp. Trust me to do it. Get some sleep. I'm going to grab a shower."

Alastor frowned and started to sit up. Darien used a hand on his chest to encourage him to lay back down. "You can't shower because of your wrists. For once in your life, do what you're told and go to sleep. I've got you, don't worry."

For a second, he thought Alastor would object, then his eyes closed, and he murmured, "Kay."

When Darien came out of the bathroom minutes later, Alastor lay curled up on his side, sound asleep. The bruises and marks from the last earl, and their lovemaking were still stark on his pale skin, as were the bandages around his wrists. He took a moment to watch him sleep so innocently, then gently pulled the cover up over his shoulder and smoothed it down.

Alastor made a happy little sound and rubbed his cheek against the pillow. Darien's heart melted and then hardened. Simply being in a bed, being warm and comfortable, brought the Tudor man so much joy.

Yes, Alastor had done horrible, probably unforgivable things by many people's standards, but nobody had ever given him a chance. A destitute, grieving peasant boy had been exploited first by the Walpoles and then by a demon.

It would end now. Alastor needed choices, and Darien vowed to somehow give them to him. But he couldn't do it alone.

Grabbing a clean set of clothes, he picked up Alastor's Tudor undershirt and left the room, phone in hand.

CHAPTER TWENTY-EIGHT

So damn comfortable. Alastor drifted, dozed, stretched, and luxuriated in warmth, softness, and safety. But something itched like a mental bedbug bite. Pulling the fluffy pillow over his head, he fooled himself that he was still asleep for another few moments. Shoes tramped across the wooden floorboard of the Long Gallery above him.

With a sigh, he flung the pillow off of his face and cracked open his eyes. Bright sunlight stabbed through the two-inch-wide gap in the heavy green drapes. He smiled. It had to be at least mid-morning.

Wanting to thank the man who had given him this decadence, he felt behind him, expecting to touch a warm, male body. His hand brushed across the cool sheet and then the edge of the mattress. His heart missed a beat.

He'd never been alone in a proper bed in his entire existence.

Yesterday crashed back into his consciousness; Arioch, his identity, the sex, the pizza. The... fuck. *Did I tell him I loved him?* Wracking his mind, he couldn't remember Darien getting back into bed after he left to have a shower.

Darien's open case sat on top of the chest of drawers. Being corporeal again meant he could do something he hadn't been able to since he'd been Nicholas; snoop in an heir's possessions. He didn't think he'd find an armored cod-piece in Darien's case, but he might find some clues about the man.

The blue passport grabbed his attention. He opened it, and a folded sheet of paper fell out. After glancing at the passport, including the many entry stamps, he opened the sheet of paper.

It was a return flight booking. Darien's flight back to America took off from London Heathrow airport tomorrow. He stared at the numbers, mind numb for a moment. He needed to find Darien, to ask him if he intended to leave right after the sale.

Dread made his stomach drop; Darien had been damn interested every time he'd mentioned the things in the priest hole. He ran across the broad landing that separated Sir Edmund's room from the cleaning closet.

The light came on as he opened the door, but he didn't need the artificial light to see the gaping hole in the floor. As if he'd been pulled by another damn spell, he stepped forward and looked down. Nothing remained except the shelf his father had built.

I've been played like a fucking fiddle.

His belly rebelled. He ran for the ensuite in Sir Edmund's room and threw up in the toilet. His heaving body only reinforced that he was alive, really alive, and it meant nothing. It felt like someone had presented him with the ultimate shiny prize only to discover it was a frozen turd covered in gold paint.

He could rage, make Darien's auction a complete farce, but the Hall would be sold whatever he did. The likelihood that the new owner would let him stay if he made a scene was zero to nil. To survive, to live in the new world, he'd have to swallow the humiliation and carry on like he'd done so many times before. It was the only way to beat Arioch and show another damn Walpole that they couldn't hurt him.

Alastor had possessed a purpose before Darien strolled into his world with his designer suits, beautiful dark skin, and knowing smile. Now, he had nothing but a life he didn't know how to live. But he would. Because if he gave up, Arioch and the damn Walpoles would win. Besides, being a real ghost didn't sound like any sort of option.

He looked himself in the eye in the mirror above the vanity unit. The face looking back at him was far more like his father than he'd ever imagined. The man had worked hard, had loved and accepted his unusual wife, and been patient with his inept wastrel son.

I want him to be proud of me.

Seeing his collarbones sticking out reminded him of his nakedness. He knew exposing his skin to the air wouldn't make him sick, but even after all this time, it still made him uncomfortable. Time for this Fool to give the performance of his life, and for that, he needed clothes.

The spot where he'd thrown the coarse linen undershirt last night revealed nothing. His heart lurched. Darien couldn't have stolen that too, could he? He ducked to look under the bed, tossed his borrowed clothes aside, then rifled through Darien's expensive suits hanging in the wardrobe.

Second by second, as his search revealed no sign of his shirt or the phone Shanae had given him, anger at himself for being so fucking gullible heated his blood a little more. The stuff in the priest hole was one thing, but the shirt had been his since Da died. It was only a bit of worn cheap cloth, but it was the only tangible connection with his father.

After every Walpole heir throughout history had proved to be arrogant and exploitative, he'd still fallen for pretty words and an even prettier face. He'd wanted what Darien's crocodile smile promised so much that he'd lost all sense. Arioch was right about him not being fit to be a demon.

He couldn't even fuck-up the FitzHenrys' precious auction in revenge. He needed the new owners to take him on as a live-in employee or permanent guest, but what, by god's teeth, could he offer the new owners? Knowing his epic luck, the new owner would be a straight man with no sense of humor.

Pulling on a dead man's clothes, he left the room and headed up to the Long Gallery.

The hum of conversation got louder as he reached the top of the stairs. Usually, he had hours, weeks, sometimes decades, to plot his next move. Now, he only had seconds. Everything was coming too fast, too frantic, but he was determined to work the situation to his advantage. If he could also manipulate the situation to make Darien regret his actions, he'd grab the opportunity with both hands.

Standing at the top of the stairs that led into the Long Gallery, Harry Grimshaw tugged at his starched white shirt collar. He looked out of place and awkward in a dark gray suit rather than his familiar corduroy pants. Dressing a handyman up as a security guard didn't make him one.

Liam Grimshaw's old clothes didn't stop Alastor from being an imp either but alienating Harry could really bite him in the ass if the new owner didn't like him.

He gave the older man a smile. "Have you seen Darien?"

Harry turned away and called out, "Ms. FitzHenry?"

"Ah, here he is," Juliana said brightly. She stood with perhaps a dozen smartly dressed people clustered around a row of stands that hadn't been there yesterday.

Plastering on a smile, Alastor strode forward, wondering which of these people would hold his life from now on.

Juliana held her hand out toward him. "May I introduce Nicholas Thatcher? He's the direct descendant of the famous Walpole Fool depicted in this portrait." She waved at Charles Walpole's painting. "He also happens to be the world's premier authority on Walpole Hall. No one knows more about the history of this magnificent estate than him, although his particular specialty is Elizabethan and Jacobean entertainment." She gave him a wide smile. "What he doesn't know about Fools isn't worth knowing."

Everyone in the group looked at him expectantly, thanks to Juliana's glowing introduction.

Having the Grimshaws, witches, and Juliana see him yesterday had been damn stressful, but he'd been able to kid himself that it was due to Darien's influence as an heir. But Darien was nowhere to be seen. It brought home how vulnerable he'd become. A slip, a fall, an infection or illness, even a piece of food going down the wrong way, and he'd be as dead as his parents and all the Walpole heirs he'd finished off.

"So, what do you know about these late editions to the catalog?" A thin man in a three-piece 1920s-style brown suit asked.

Alastor glanced in the direction he indicated. Everything he remembered from the priest hole sat on stands and tables in front of the tall windows. The erotic nude sketches sat next to his pinned-out and framed undershirt. But the pair of hideous green vases held pride of place.

"They all date to before the first Earl's death in 1602," he managed.

"And you know that how?" A woman scoffed. "You don't look old enough to have finished a first degree, let alone become an expert."

Age, background, clothing, or appearance, they always found some reason to put him down. But like the delivery driver last night, he refused to roll over and play dead this time.

"All these items were found in a recently discovered priest hole. The iron nails holding the hatch shut were individually hand forged." He gave the bigoted woman a sickly-sweet smile. "Of course, that doesn't prove anything except someone used genuine Tudor nails to seal the chamber. Although, you'd have to wonder why someone would do that when cheaper, machine-made nails were available from the early 1600s.

"In addition, the most recent item," he indicated one of the pamphlets, "is dated 1602 and signed by several of The

Lord Chamberlain's Men, the group who owned and ran the original Globe theatre, including Shakespeare and Burbage. One of them, William Kempe, died in 1603. Nothing found in the priest hole dates after 1602."

The expressions of his audience had begun to soften, so he pointed to his undershirt. "This shirt belonged to the carpenter who constructed the priest hole, James Thatcher. The Walpoles killed him to silence him on September 5th, 1602. The shirt was passed to his son, Nicholas Thatcher, the man in the painting. It's been in my family ever since."

"And you're selling it now? Why?" the thin man asked, brows pinched in suspicion.

Alastor gave him a winning smile that tore his heart out. "I'm willing to sell for the right price. As for why, that's my business."

The woman pushed a glossy photo of the twin vases at him. Darien had indeed had a busy few hours.

"FitzHenrys's claim these are Ming, but they're in the later style of Qianlong."

Alastor shrugged, not having a clue about the names she'd mentioned. "They are certainly pre-1602, but apart from that, I'd make up your own mind if I were you."

The woman snorted. "Very true. I like your attitude, Mr. Thatcher; it's very refreshing."

The group moved on, and Alastor looked a little more closely at the information on the photo.

'Pair of reticulated Wanli Emperor vases. Dated 1575-1600. Guide Price £20,000,000.'

He read it once, then again. The numbers were unbelievable. He couldn't even work out a word for a number with that many noughts. And the FitzHenrys would get a percentage of everything sold today.

A hand landed on his arm. He looked up to see Juliana's sympathetic smile. Beneath her make-up, she looked tired. Darien must have left him fucked out in bed and immediately called his sister to help catalog the priest hole treasure. The pair must have laughed themselves silly at his naivety while calculating their commission.

"Why don't you go and grab something to eat? These last-minute items have created quite a stir. We've pushed the auction back a couple of hours so new bidders can assess them."

"Where is he?" he blurted, then hated himself a little more. The man who had literally rocked his world wasn't his concern anymore.

"There's no show without the auctioneer." Her smile appeared concerned, but he'd been lied to too many times to believe it. "He'll be here, I promise."

"You think I care?" He scoffed.

Her sympathetic expression said she saw right through him, even though he was corporeal. He pictured the priest hole as it had been, but he remained exactly where he was.

"So, do you just study Tudor Fools, or do you emulate them?" A large Asian man in a black suit asked.

"What?" he blurted, unsure about the rapid conversation change.

"I'm Bo Ayers, from The Foresters Group. We're hoping to buy this place to turn it into an authentic Tudor experience and theme park."

A theme park would be better than a private buyer. They'd need staff, hopefully live-in staff. Alastor shook his hand, managed a smile. "Pleased to meet you. May I offer my services as a consultant?"

The man blinked, and Alastor hastily backtracked. "I'd be happy to work here for little more than room and board. This place," he cast a glance around himself, "is my life. I'd do anything to stay here."

"Anything?" the man's lips quirked in a smile he clearly thought seductive.

Alastor knew that look and hated it. He still returned the guy's smile. He'd serviced enough men he didn't desire to get what he wanted over the years. One more wouldn't make a difference. At least that was what he told himself, but his balls were trying to climb back inside him at the thought of this man touching him.

"Nicholas? Why don't you take this and go down to the gallery to provide a little mood music?"

He couldn't resist the recorder Juliana proffered, even though it wasn't the one he'd taken before. This one was finer quality, but post-dated his death. "Sure."

Ayers touched his arm. "So, you play? What else do you do to be an authentic Fool? I heard Fools were the ultimate confidants for their masters and would do anything to entertain and distract them."

Alastor cocked his hip and grinned as his skin crawled. "Want a private demonstration?"

A slim dark hand closed around the recorder. "I'll put it back on display if you're not going to play it." Juliana's frown told Alastor exactly what she thought of his flirting.

What did she expect, loyalty to a man who had stolen from him, then abandoned him a few hours before walking out of his life forever?

He tugged his forelock and began bowing and backing away. "Yes, your Ladyship, anything you say."

Ayers looked thoroughly amused, but Alastor felt hollow. He didn't want to sleep with the man any more than he'd wanted to sleep with most of the heirs.

Even though everyone could see and touch him now, he felt more alone than ever. Darien had appeared to care, and the fact that he didn't, had merely been playing him as Alastor had played so many of his relatives, sucked to high heaven.

He bet Arioch was watching and loving every second of his torment. Revenge was a bitch, and Arioch had always been the biggest bitch on the planet, whether they chose to pack a prick or a pussy.

To distract himself—and show how little this affected him—he folded into a backward roll. Juliana gasped in horror that he might have damaged the valuable auction lot.

She hustled forward and hissed, "Be careful."

"Worried about your auction lot?" he sneered.

"No, you idiot. If you break a leg or your damn fool head, how the hell are you going to get treated?"

"I'm surprised you aren't egging me on, Ms. FitzHenry of FitzHenry auctions. It'll be easier to sell this place without a sitting tenant. And if you see that brother of yours before I do, tell him he can stick his apology where the sun doesn't shine."

He turned and walked away, gratified by her shocked expression.

"Nicholas?" she called out. When he didn't turn around, she tried, "Alastor?"

He kept going. He didn't have to impress the FitzHenrys anymore; he only had to beguile the new owner of Walpole Hall.

As he strolled past Harry Grimshaw, the man said, "I would tell you to behave, but I don't think you're capable of it."

Alastor carried on past without speaking. Ghost, imp, irritant. Four hundred years hadn't changed a damn thing. Nobody had ever wanted him around for long. Walking across the gallery above the Low Great Hall, he looked down on Lorraine Grimshaw and two other women he didn't know setting out folding chairs for the bidders. They faced the area underneath Alastor where the Walpoles had dined on a raised platform while looking out over their employees. The lesser beings who made their luxurious lives possible.

A pair of big men stood by the main door, with another by the entrance to the kitchen. By their dark uniforms, they were security operatives hired to stop any pilfering or fights between rival bidders if such a thing ever happened at these events. Any prospect of reclaiming his shirt died. Getting arrested and hauled across the estate boundary would literally be the end.

To be truthful, if suicide wouldn't make him a ghost or put a smug grin on Arioch's face, he'd consider it. This modern world was so different from what he knew. As an imp, the differences that came up as the decades and centuries rolled past hadn't really mattered. He hadn't needed to understand how to dress, behave, buy, and prepare food, operate appliances, vehicles, or communication devices.

Now, he needed to negotiate this new digital, electronic world, and he didn't have a clue where to begin. Grief washed over him again. He'd felt so safe with Darien for those few hours last night, even if it had all been an illusion, even if Darien hadn't been there for some of it. He wanted—needed—someone to help him through this, someone who cared rather than exploited or felt an obligation.

Someone who might need him in return.

His jaw clenched against his stupid naivety that such a person—if they even existed—could walk into the life of an evil shit like himself.

As always, the worn, barely recognizable phoenix his father had carved on the newel post drew his fingers. He wished he could go back in time, could try a little harder to be what his father had wanted. Maybe if he'd applied himself more, he would've become a better woodcarver, and his father would have asked him to come along to the hall. If he'd been here, maybe his father wouldn't have fallen that day or any other day. Maybe Nicholas Thatcher would have lived out his life four hundred years ago.

With pointless maybes piling up like dung on a midden, he lifted the recorder to his lips. The melodies he'd performed for Thomas Walpole the night everything had gone so horribly wrong flowed out.

People arrived, collected shiny catalogs, and went to view what felt like his bones up in the Long Gallery. Gradually, the seats below him filled. Alastor continued to repeat 'Greensleeves,' mind blank because he didn't want to consider the future or his past errors.

The patient crowd began to shift, the murmurs increasing as the prospective bidders checked their phones and watches. Alastor carried on playing, not knowing what else to do. If it hadn't been for the occasional glance up at him, he would've assumed he was again invisible to these wealthy people.

Juliana hurried across the length of the Low Great Hall, phone clamped to her ear, as she headed toward the kitchen. She beckoned to Lorraine, who followed her out of the hall. Harry came down the stairs and walked over to the two guards. After a brief conversation, the men headed back toward the stairs, leaving Harry standing next to the main front door as if daring anyone to leave.

Lorraine appeared from the kitchen with trays of white wine and what looked like orange juice, but it didn't seem to mollify the bidders. But at least their focus was taken as the guards began bringing the lots down. Alastor imagined the space under the gallery gradually filling up. But when the last item, as far as he could remember, was in place, the mutterings in the crowd got louder.

Where the hell was Darien, and what was the heir doing apart from avoiding him? If Darien didn't turn up soon, Juliana would have to conduct the auction herself. He couldn't help thinking that had the plan all along. Darien talked the talk, but it seemed he had a yellow streak a mile wide.

The betrayal burned like acid, and he hated himself for falling for the prank. It didn't stop him from wishing with all his heart that what he'd imagined had actually been true; that something had finally gone his way.

Ma had always claimed he was stupid, and it seemed she'd been right all along. She'd tried to beat some sense into him, but had still died because of his greed and stupidity.

Ayers looked up at him. Smiled. How he kept playing he didn't know, but he did, if only to bug the demon who must still be fucking with him. Nobody else could be so damn cruel.

Darien strode through the door from the kitchen, straightening his tie. Alastor stopped playing, recorder still at his lips.

Darien smiled up at him, winked as if nothing was wrong, and disappeared from view as he moved under the gallery.

As if his feet had a mind of their own, Alastor headed for the stairs. It wouldn't do any good—would probably make it hurt even more—but he needed to see the man who had played and betrayed him for every minute they had left.

"Welcome, ladies and gentlemen. I apologize for the late starting of this unique auction of fifteenth, sixteenth, and seventeenth-century artifacts," Darien's deep voice rang out. He sounded so self-assured. The sophisticated American had every right to be smug.

Whatever he was now, Alastor had been an imp for four hundred years, and he appreciated a fellow trickster's ability. This was first class work. It was just a shame they were on opposite sides, but with his epic luck, he shouldn't have expected anything else.

"Please raise your paddles to bid, but be aware that we are also taking phone and internet bids." Alastor's heart fell. The new owner of the Hall might not even be here?

How the hell am I meant to influence someone I can't see or talk to?

"Lot 1. A late Elizabethan decorated silver wine taster dish, one inch high and three inches wide, dated to circa 1570-80. The bowl is decorated with an Elizabethan lady and gentleman, a unique, attractive piece from a private collection. I have five thousand pounds online. Fifty-five hundred anyone?"

Alastor nearly dropped the recorder. He remembered the small drinking bowl on one of the stands, but surely, he must have gotten it wrong. No one would pay that much for such a small thing, would they? This had to be another prank, and Alastor needed to see the bidders' reaction. Would Darien's ruse fall flat on its face, or would he play the knowledgeable crowd with the same expertise he'd used on Alastor?

He took the steps two at a time, reached the bottom, and slid, barefoot, into the Low Great Hall. The heir commanded the room, utterly at ease with all the attention. He stood in front of a waist-high table, a laptop open on either side of him.

Beside him, Lorraine held up the small piece of silver Alastor remembered from upstairs.

Darien banged the gavel down. "Sold for seven thousand, six hundred pounds to an internet bidder." Eyes down, he made a note on a sheet of paper then looked up. His smile froze as he looked over Alastor's shoulder.

Darien swallowed, put a professional smile back on his face. "Ah, it seems we have another volunteer to present the lots. Come up here, Alastor."

All eyes turned to him.

CHAPTER TWENTY-NINE

The night before

"Are you completely crazy?" Juliana screeched down the phone. Darien winced, glanced toward the half-open closet door.

"Keep it down, Sis, he's sleeping. And yeah, I know this sounds loco, but if you could see what I'm looking at…" he tailed off.

Resisting the impulse to touch the artifacts he'd so carefully lifted from the priest hole wasn't easy. His first look into the hole, illuminated by his phone torch, made him feel like Howard Carter discovering Tutankhamun's tomb.

Carter's companion, Lord Carnarvon, had asked, "Can you see anything?" Carter had replied, "Yes, wonderful things."

The artifacts might be several thousand years newer than those found in the boy pharaoh's tomb, but they were every bit as wonderful to Darien.

Dust covered everything except an Alastor-shaped space on the floor. He had no doubt that what the imp and Arioch claimed was true. From the dust pattern until recently, a body had lain here, and nothing in here had been touched for a significant length of time. Before climbing down, he'd taken a great many photographs.

"And you're sure they're genuine?" Juliana asked.

He snorted and ran a hand over his hair. "I don't think any single person is qualified to authenticate a lost Michelangelo drawing of David, maybe the most expensive pair of ceramics ever found, and the only non-legal document example of Shakespeare's signature, but I'm sure they're genuinely that old. This chamber was sealed with sixteenth-century nails, and Alastor said it's been undisturbed since he died."

The deep groan on the line made him smile. "We can hardly use 'a former ghost slash demon said so' as provenance, can we?"

"We can't admit they exist at all until I get my name on that deed."

Silence dragged. "Darien," she sighed. "I know you want to help him, I do too. But even if it works—and there's a list of 'if's' as wide as the Atlantic—you know how this'll be seen by the auction community.

"It'll finish FitzHenry Auctions and our careers, even if there's no legal challenge. No one in the auction or antique business will ever trust us again."

He could hear the big fat 'no' loud and clear. His ridiculous idea had been to secure ownership of the Hall, so that he legally owned the items in front of him. He'd then sell them to pay for the building. It could, theoretically, work as long as it happened within the same banking day.

The items sang a siren song that was hard to resist, almost as much as Alastor. If he was correct about their value, these few small pieces could buy the Hall outright, and they'd be plenty left for renovation.

But as his sister said, the practicalities were ludicrous. He'd still kidded himself that he could make a mad dash to Wormwood Scrubs, secure an emergency visit, and persuade Carl Anderson that having an American owner who promised a business use for the Hall would be better than relying on the vagaries of an auction. Plus, he'd also somehow catalog the priest hole items, gather international interest in these one-of-a-kind items, get back to the sale at two, and have the money in his bank account to pay Anderson before the end of the day.

"Brother, I love you, but it's not logistically possible. We'd need a miracle to get all of that done in," she paused, and he imagined her checking the time, "thirteen hours? Even cataloging the items properly would take longer than that, not to mention getting independent verification of their authenticity."

Darien held in a growl of frustration. As always, Juliana's practical nature had shot him down, although the authentication wouldn't be a problem. Any history expert would hightail it here to see if his claims were real, but she was right about his plan to buy the Hall.

"We'd need a miracle or.... Get over here, sis; I have another idea."

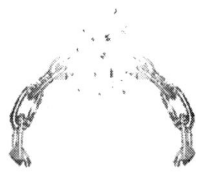

A heavy-eyed Juliana had gone back to the hotel to get changed for the sale after taking the images they needed for the extra sales pages and the website. The hired security team would be here to secure the building in an hour. Experts from the Museum of London, the Victoria and Albert Museum, and the British Museum were on their way to authenticate the finds and perhaps bid on them. The ordinary bidders would arrive from eleven a.m. He still wasn't sure if the final lot of the day would be the building. If he had his way, the new owner of Walpole Hall would be decided before he picked up his gavel.

Darien poured himself a much-needed coffee as he waited for the help Shanae had promised. Slipping into the room where Alastor still slept and taking his phone to call Shanae had seemed like a betrayal. But getting Alastor's hopes up and then dashing them would be damn cruel.

Initially, he'd hoped the witch would somehow be able to magic up the funds to buy the Hall or buy it herself. But it appeared even witches couldn't lay their hands on millions at such short notice, but she said she knew someone who might.

She'd also said that she wouldn't be attending the auction as she didn't want her nephew and the intended 'help' to interact. That she'd happily let Callum annoy a demon lord ramped up his anxiety about this mysterious helper, but he didn't have a choice.

The clock on his phone seemed to have sped up since Alastor fell asleep, but now it inched along, with every second longer than the last. *What would they do if he couldn't pull this off?*

Yes, Alastor might persuade the new owner to let him stay—he'd certainly had a lot of practice at beguiling people—but what if they refused? The Grimshaws were their only hope, but he couldn't picture Lorraine and Harry playing house with Alastor in the near future.

He opened up a google search for RVs. Maybe parking one on the Grimshaws' land would be a possibility. Despite the glowing sales pages, every vehicle looked like a miserable excuse for a home compared to where he sat. He couldn't picture the vibrant Alastor sitting in such a vehicle, alone and cold, until he died of boredom or irritated Harry into killing him.

Darien nearly spat his coffee out as a couple appeared opposite the kitchen table. One was a stick-thin, blue-skinned figure with pale flowing hair, wearing what looked like a Tudor undershirt. Despite that unnerving sight, the man holding its wrist drew Darien's attention like a magnet.

The blond man personified masculine perfection in every way. Tall, but not intimidating, muscular, fit, but not muscle-bound. His expensive tailored suit showed off thighs and an ass Darien could worship for decades.

Darien was a natural top, but if the blue-eyed man waved a finger, he knew he'd be on his knees offering his ass, his mouth, in a heartbeat. He'd never gotten hard so fast in his life.

"Thank you, air elemental. I'll call when I need you again." Even his voice, which reminded Darien of smooth, dark chocolate, caused his cock to lurch. The blue figure vanished, but Darien hardly noticed.

"You're an incubus," Darien blurted the only explanation that made sense.

The man smiled. If anything, it made him even more attractive.

"I'm Avery, Leader of the Supernatural Council. Shanae said you had a little—" the demon's gaze dipped to the front of Darien's straining pants, and his lips quirked again. "—or not so little problem that I might be able to assist you with."

Not letting Callum meet this man made perfect sense.

Darien swallowed, trying to pull himself together. Were all sex demons this overwhelming or was Avery in charge because he was special? Whatever the case, Avery was a demon, and in Darien's minimal experience, demons didn't do anything for free.

"What do you want in return?"

"Straight down to business, I like that."

Avery pulled out a chair and sat down, every movement fluid and purposeful. Darien bet he fucked like that too, playing his partner with effortless ease, turning them into a pool of mindless lust without the slightest—

He gritted his teeth, trying to push down the desire clouding his thoughts. He needed to think with his head, not his balls.

He stood up, needing a distraction to get back on track. "Can I get you a drink? Something to eat?"

Avery's lips twitched as his gaze slipped to Darien's bulge again. "I guess Shanae didn't tell you too much about my kind, but we'll get to payment and food later. First, I'd like a tour, starting with this imp that's got two members of my council squawking at each other like broody hens."

"You're not going to fuck him, are you?" Darien blurted. "He's had a really tough few days, and he's sleeping, so I—"

Avery's head tilted. "Hasn't stopped you playing with him in the last few hours, though, has it?"

Darien's face heated. "That's none of your business."

A chuckle rose from Avery's chest as he stood up. "Human morality. It still surprises me how crippling it can be, but at least they don't hang sodomites anymore. But they did when this boy of yours was born, didn't they?" He indicated the kitchen door. "This way, I presume? I'd like to see what I'm being asked to invest in."

Despite what he'd said about seeing Alastor first, the suave demon strolled around the property, looking into every room and peering at the displayed lots in the Long Gallery. And all the time, Darien couldn't pull his focus away from the demon's body. His ass, lips, and even his hands, promised more pleasure than Darien's mind could imagine.

"Mind on the job, Mr. FitzHenry," Avery murmured. "This is business, not pleasure."

"Sorry, you're erm..."

"A demon designed to be overwhelmingly attractive? Yes, I am, but that's not all. I'm also a businessman and a collector of beautiful things, including property." The incubus indicated the portrait, his tone no longer relaxed. "That's him? Shanae's great, times eight or so, uncle? What was his birth name?"

Alastor's painted smile pulled Darien in even more each time he saw it. He couldn't help stepping forward as if getting closer to the painting could somehow protect Alastor from the demon beside him.

"Yes, that's him, Nicholas Thatcher. The world, and Arioch, screwed with him for centuries. I want to change that."

Avery's devastating focus flicked back to Darien. Somehow, they'd ended up only inches apart.

"Thatcher, not Chaumier?" Avery asked, tense for the first time. "Could he be French?" The demon shook his head. "This would be so like Arioch."

Darien blinked. "He doesn't have a French accent, but Shanae said her family had been here for generations before Nicholas was born; she didn't mention his father's history so—"

Avery brushed a finger across Darien's cheek. "Your desire is so very bright," he murmured. "But it's not all for me, is it, boy? Even when I'm right here, you're thinking about him. Do you have a savior complex, Darien FitzHenry? Is it simply about sex or something more? Have you given him a token, something he keeps with him?"

Darien foggily focused on the last question. "No, nothing; I should though, he—"

"Will you give him to me if I promise to give him the world you never can? Say yes, and you can have me, any way you desire, right here, right now. Do you want to hold me down, fuck me, bite my perfect, round ass? Do you want my lips wrapped around your hot, hard cock? My tongue in your hole? Feel how much you turn me on?" Avery took Darien's hand and pulled it toward his pants.

Avery's touch and dirty words went straight to Darien's cock. Nobody was here yet. He could rip down Avery's pants, feast on that peach of an ass, make him moan, beg and—

"Ah, ah, not until you give the little imp to me."

Darien glanced up at the painting again. Alastor's smile appeared false, strained.

Gasping, he pulled away from the blond, stumbling back a few steps as his knees felt as if they were made of rubber. "Stay, stay away from me, demon," he managed to get out. "Alastor's not mine to buy and sell."

Between heartbeats, his intense lust dropped from 'about to come on the spot' to a high simmer. The touch, it had to be the physical contact that caused the lust-fueled brain fog.

"Not just sex then, which is a shame but not insurmountable. But he is a sub and you are a dom," Avery confirmed as if they'd hadn't just been about to get down and dirty. "But that encompasses so much. Tell me about you, about him. What sort of dom are you?"

The quick change of subject had Darien blinking, trying to re-focus, but he still replied to the demon's overly personal question.

"I'm a caregiver and a disciplinarian, rather than a sadist. Alastor's a brat, but—"

Avery snorted. "The best ones always are, but please, continue."

"He has submissive tendencies. Although I doubt he's ever had a chance to fully explore his sexuality, he has used it to manipulate people over the—"

"Enough." The word was softly spoken, but Darien's mouth still snapped shut as if he'd been slapped.

Avery turned and strolled over to some of the easels and tables to examine the artifacts. "Let's get back to business. You say he can't leave this estate?"

"We haven't tested it, but that's what Arioch said," Darien answered, frustration growing. It was clear Avery's interest wasn't only in Walpole Hall, and Darien began to think he'd made a huge mistake. Had he handed Alastor over to be another demon's plaything?

"You know, many supernaturals live incredibly long lives, and all this," he waved a hand at everything around him, "is all very nostalgic. It would be wonderful to have this place restored to what it was like back in the day."

He brushed long, fine fingers along the recorder that was again safe on its stand. Darien's cock lurched at the thought of those fingers playing his body like a musical instrument. He palmed his cock but couldn't stop the groan of frustration slipping from his throat.

Avery smiled but didn't stop examining the auction lots. The bastard knew how he was affecting Darien. Arioch might get his jollies by torturing people's consciences, but this demon fucked with their desire. Both demons used people like him and Alastor without a thought.

"You have something to say, something to... ask? You know what they say, 'ask, and you will receive.' What would you like me to give you, Darien?"

Darien pushed down his lust and stared the incubus down.

The demon inclined his head. "Impressive. Now, I need to see him."

"He's sleeping."

That devastating smile appeared again. "I said, I need to see him, perhaps a brief touch, not wake him."

"Why?"

Avery pursed his lips. "Because he might be related to the man who was my life; he certainly looks like him."

"He can't leave here. You can't—"

Avery stepped forward, put a hand on Darien's shoulder. "Calm yourself, guard dog. He needs you, and I wouldn't change that. Come, let me see him."

Darien found himself leading a demon to where Alastor slept, even though every fiber of his being screamed that it was wrong.

"In here?" Avery indicated the bedroom door.

Darien's head nodded without his conscious choice. The demon slipped into the room. Darien remained silent despite every instinct screaming at him to tell Alastor to run.

He followed the demon inside. Alastor lay on his side, with only his head and the top of his shoulder exposed. For several long minutes, Avery stared down at the sleeping man. Then, oh so gently, he reached out a finger and brushed it once across Alastor's cheek. The boy's nose wrinkled; his hips tilted as he rubbed his face against the pillow before settling again.

Avery's lips pursed, then he strode out of the bedroom without a backward glance. Darien followed him back down to the kitchen, where the demon turned to confront Darien.

"There is something there, but he is not.... what my Frederick was. Which is a tragedy for my kind, but maybe not a bad thing for him. However, there is enough resemblance to make seeing your Alastor—" His lips pursed, gaze lost for a moment before his lips curved into a wry smile. "—remarkably painful." Blue eyes focused back on Darien. "Tell me, does the world seem brighter when he smiles?"

Darien huffed in amusement as Avery had nailed it. "It does, even though he deserves a damn good spanking most of the time. He has to be the biggest brat in history."

They shared a smile, and for the first time, Darien felt a connection other than lust with this extraordinary man.

"To make sure that smile stays in the world for as long as possible, I'll buy this place, but only if you agree to several non-negotiable conditions. One, neither you nor Alastor can ever reveal the existence of supernaturals to ordinary humans. Two, with Alastor's help and my money, you will return this building to what it was like in the 1600s so that—"

"We need the signature of the current owner, Carl Anderson, on the paperwork before the auction starts, otherwise we have to go through with the sale, and the price might be—"

"Where is this Anderson?"

Darien shifted his feet. This was where the whole thing could go up in smoke. "Her Majesty's Prison, Wormwood Scrubs, in London. He killed his—"

Avery waved a hand in dismissal. "As long as it wasn't a supernatural, I don't care."

"Fair enough, but we only have a matter of hours, and it took me ten days to get an emergency visitation order to—"

"A prison, you say?" A devilish smile curved Avery's lips. "I haven't visited a prison in almost a century. If I remember rightly, I went into a food coma for almost three days afterward. Draw up your sale document, FitzHenry, and we'll—"

"What about the visitation order? They won't let us in if we turn up on the doorstep. There are procedures, passes, and—"

"When was the last time someone told you 'no' when you were really trying to get them to do something for you, Darien?"

His face heated, remembering Alastor turning him down a few hours ago.

Avery laughed, eyes crinkling with mirth. "Oh, I have got to hear about that. But for your information, the last time a human I really tried to influence told me 'no' was 1540, and he was… extraordinary." A cloud passed across the demon's face. Darien didn't have to hear the name again to realize the man he spoke about must have been Alastor's double.

Avery gave him that devastating smile again, and everything seemed right in the world. "I don't think a bunch of bored British civil servants will break that streak, do you?"

When Darien didn't answer, Avery made a shooing motion. "Well, go on, go get ready for a prison visit. I'll have an air elemental pick us up. Speaking of which, it's probably not a good idea to eat anything. Travel by air elemental can be a little unsettling the first few times."

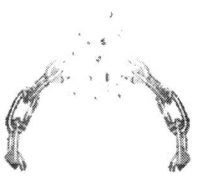

'Unsettling' didn't cover the sensation Darien could only describe as being turned inside out while on one of those whirling rides on maximum acceleration.

He'd spent the previous few hours frantically cataloging the pieces from the priest hole. Despite telling Avery that the visitor center didn't open until eleven a.m., the demon insisted they leave soon after dawn.

The air elemental left them outside the now-familiar gothic entrance of the prison, with Darien clutching his laptop case and churning belly.

"There'll be a pass for you at the door at eleven. I'll see you in there," the demon said, completely unaffected by their travel method.

"Where are you going? You just can't—"

"Oh, I can. And I do believe breakfast is about to be served."

"They might have started cooking it, but I don't think they serve food before—"

A wicked smile that went straight to Darien's cock appeared on those perfect lips. "I'm not talking about food for the inmates. This place is full of sex-starved desperate men. It's an all-you-can-eat buffet for an incubus. Have fun."

Darien watched the demon stroll up to the security booth. After a brief exchange of words, he walked right into the prison while fixing a visitor pass to his jacket.

Shaking his head at what his life had become, Darien jogged across the road and went into a seedy café. Setting up his laptop, he began putting together his auction notes on the bidders he knew hoped to attend. Knowing the preferences and background of potential bidders was almost as important as in-depth knowledge of the lots. A good auctioneer could always squeeze a little more out of a room, and Darien worked at being the best at whatever he attempted.

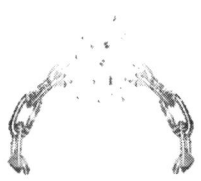

A tap on the window next to him had Darien looking up. He'd almost been asleep in his third coffee.

Avery's scowl as Darien came out of the café didn't bode well. "Come on, time to go."

"But I haven't seen Anderson yet, we—"

"And you're not going to. He just had a heart attack. He's not dead, but it's not looking good. There's already a reaper standing by. Actually, he didn't look good before that, but his cellmate wasn't bad."

Darien scrunched and then opened his eyes wide, trying to take the information in. "What was he doing to make him—"

Avery grinned. Darien shook his head, held up a hand. "No, I don't want to know. What now?"

"Looks like we do this the old-fashioned way after all. I was going to come to the auction anyway; I haven't been to one in years. Plus, I'm still curious about this boy of yours. He—"

"You're not having him," Darien blurted.

A perfect eyebrow rose. "Possessive much? I thought you and Shanae were all about giving him choices?" He looked Darien up and down. "Although I don't think you'll be much competition in your current state. You look dead on your feet."

Darien's feet did feel as if they were encased in concrete, but he wouldn't give this suave demon the satisfaction of knowing he'd been close to dozing off. It pissed him off that the incubus—who could have sucked or fucked dozens of men in the last couple of hours—still looked as perfect as when they'd met.

"Yes, well, us mere humans don't have the advantages of demons. Now can we call your little blue friend and get back to the Hall? I want to check on Alastor."

"You have a phone, don't you?"

He'd phoned Juliana half an hour ago, and Alastor hadn't come out of the bedroom yet.

"I do, but I don't want to wake him up if he's still sleeping."

Avery slung an arm over his shoulder and began leading him down the street. "Tell me the truth, what would you be doing right now if you were at the Hall?"

"If he's not awake, I'd be helping to set up the auction room and the lots. It's considered bad practice for the auctioneer to talk to bidders on auction day in case of bias.

"Actually, I'd probably have him doing that too. You know what they say, idle hands do work for the devil, and Alastor is—" he paused, wondering if he'd just offended another powerful supernatural.

"Alastor is what?" Avery prompted.

"Prone to creating his own entertainment, which usually involves irritating someone."

"So, you'd be doing manual work anyone could do?"

He paused, turning to the demon. "Yes, and? People do stuff like that; we can't all click our fingers and magic things."

"In that case—" Avery held up his arm, and a black cab pulled up. "—we'll take the scenic route. I get so tired of never experiencing the journey."

They climbed into the cab, and although the driver objected to the distance at first, a few smiles from Avery and they were on their way.

"So, tell me more about what you want to do with the Hall. How would Alastor and I fit into your plan?" Darien asked.

Avery tore his gaze away from the many people on the street near the shopping mall they were passing. Darien supposed that the busy cosmopolitan street was akin to a food court to the demon.

The demon frowned. "Darien, you're dead on your feet. Take a nap."

"Nap? I haven't got time to—"

The demon's eyes glowed, and he felt a hand touch his. "Sleep."

The command resonated deep inside. His eyes closed.

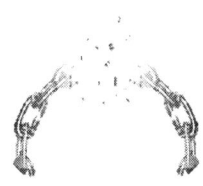

"Hey, mate. Wakey wakey time."

Darien blinked and looked around himself in confusion. The black cab was sitting outside Walpole Hall, and he was alone in the back seat.

"What happened to the other guy? Did he go inside already?"

"He got out soon after you dropped off. He paid me first, though. Good tipper."

He'd thought falling asleep so quickly was unusual even though he'd been tired, but the cabbie's words proved Avery had done something. What cab driver would say he'd already gotten a tip when there was no one to say otherwise?

"Oh, ok, thanks." He got out, stretched his back, and winced at the number of cracks and pops coming from his spine and neck.

There were at least thirty cars parked on the wide gravel drive in front of the main door. He went from dozy to wide awake in a matter of seconds and grabbed for his phone to check the time.

14:45. Fuck, the auction should have started half an hour ago. The main door led into the Hall where the bidders would already be waiting. Without saying anything more to the cabbie, he jogged around the side of the building, glad that all the bidders were hopefully inside and wouldn't see his less than professional entrance.

He banged through the kitchen door to find Juliana waiting with a fresh shirt and tie.

"Don't ask. Some guy called and said you'd want these. He also said we were going on with the sale," she said. "Laptops are set up and ready, notes are on the desk, but the natives are getting restless. As the place still belongs to Anderson, we're starting with the unconnected lots, then the pieces from the Hall, with the estate as the last lot."

She batted his hands away as he attempted to fasten the dark blue silk tie around his neck. "Hold still," she growled.

"Is Alastor up? How is he?"

"I told you not to ask," she said and almost propelled him toward the door that led to the hall.

The recorder music drew his eyes up as soon as he entered the hall full of restless bidders. He did his best to reassure Alastor with a smile and wink. There was no time for anything else. But if looks could kill, Darien would be pushing up daisies.

The position of the podium meant he couldn't see Alastor, so he gave a quick apology and an even quicker introduction to the sale and got the first lot underway.

Seconds after concluding the first lot, Alastor slid into the hall as if he were on a skateboard. His bare feet, messy hair, haze of new stubble, and sweats looked out of place among this sophisticated, wealthy, academic crowd. Everyone turned to look. Most of the bidders frowned, some lips lifted in disgust. Several glanced toward the security guard by the door as if he should leap forward and throw out the only person who wasn't trespassing.

Darien hoped he appeared more relaxed and professional than he felt. Avery slid into a seat near the back of the Hall, just behind where Alastor stood glaring at him. The incubus eyed Alastor with interest.

A tall, elegant, fine-featured man approached the security guy from the kitchen. The security guard's expression blanked, and he headed toward the kitchen, not looking around him. The man in the dark, three-piece suit took up his position, met Darien's gaze, and raised a thin eyebrow.

Even with the large room full of people, for several heartbeats, they seemed utterly alone. A shiver of fear went up Darien's spine. The man wasn't beautiful enough to be an incubus, but after meeting several supernaturals, Darien had no doubt that this was another one. It felt like he was a punchbag, swinging after being hit, only to be jabbed again.

And Alastor was walking right into a situation he knew nothing about, just like with Arioch. Guilt weighed in his belly. The tall man met Darien's gaze and his lips twitched. Darien knew, he just knew, that this man—this demon—could feel, perhaps taste his anxiety.

Darien swallowed, trying to get his mind moving. Shanae's scheme had worked up on the roof, and he had no choice about trusting her again even if she wasn't here. But having Alastor closer to either demon than he was to him had every nerve jangling.

Thinking fast, he called Alastor up to help present the lots. Despite a scowl that promised painful retribution, Alastor stalked down the aisle left between the chairs, getting further away from Avery and his minion with every step.

CHAPTER THIRTY

"Hold up your shirt. I want to get it sold before shit hits the fan," Darien said out of the side of his mouth. Then he smiled at the packed room, utterly confident that Alastor would obey like a damn slave.

"Now, ladies and gentlemen, one of the late editions to the auction. A genuine late Elizabethan undershirt. A unique piece. Who'll start me at thirty thousand pounds?" Darien's voice rang out.

Alastor gaped as a ripple of paddles rose in the air before he'd even presented his framed shirt. The bidding went up quickly, as five, no, six people vied for his only possession.

They didn't want him. No one wanted him, particularly Darien, who'd walked out without saying a word and intended to leave the country with a fat commission. History, and this auction, were all that had ever interested FitzHenry, and he'd played Alastor like a professional.

"You want me to present the lots? Well, present this, you arsehole." He pulled off Liam's old sweatshirt, grabbed the frame holding his carefully pinned-out shirt, and punched the glass.

The crack echoed along with several gasps from the crowd. Not caring about cutting himself, he tried to rip the shirt out of the frame.

Darien's hand closed around his wrist. Pain flared, but FitzHenry didn't care about Alastor's physical wounds any more than he cared about inflicted mental torture.

"What are you doing," Darien hissed. "This is neither the time nor the place. If you didn't want me to sell it, you just had to—"

"The auction is over. You bid, but didn't win. Go home." Calm, almost bored, the man in the black suit addressed the bidders with his back to the podium.

Chairs scraped. As one, the bidders gathered their things and headed to the main door.

Alastor blinked. The man was now by the open front door, whispering to the bidders as they left. No human could move that fast. Within a minute, the echoing, double height hall was empty, except for the dark-haired demon—he couldn't be anything else—and a stunningly beautiful man who sat in the back row of seats, one leg crossed over the other as if he had all the time in the world.

"Is the internet still working?" The blond asked.

"What?" Darien said, his hand still on Alastor's bandaged wrist. It stung, but Alastor didn't pull away. Drawing the attention of either of these demons seemed like a very bad idea.

"The internet, Mr. FitzHenry. Is it still working?"

Darien glanced at his laptop. "No, no, it's not."

The blond raised his paddle. "I bid twenty-two million for the estate and all its contents." The beautiful man looked around himself. "Any other bids?" he asked the empty room.

Between one heartbeat and the next, the dark-haired man stood in front of the podium. Darien and Alastor both jerked back, and Darien's grip on his wrist tightened.

"I think the appropriate thing to say is 'Going once, going twice, sold to the smug demon at the back,' or has the cat got your tongue?" The guy's lips curved in an arctic smile. As Alastor watched, a pair of white fangs dented his thin lower lip.

Darien's mouth hung open, then he swallowed and asked, "What, what are you?"

"Vampire," fell from Alastor's lips.

"Have you met any of my kind?" The man's head tilted to the side as he examined Alastor. "No, I don't think you have. You're worried, but not scared. If you'd met any of my—"

"Silas," the blond man said as he strolled up the aisle. "Don't torment them. I didn't bring you here for lunch."

"Why not? I keep telling you I'm not my father. Fabian would have rounded everyone up and taken them back to Scotland as a takeout.

"I won't hurt him. I just want to see if he tastes as unique as his background. Besides, he's already bleeding." Silas nodded toward Alastor's hand.

Bright red beads welled from a small cut on his index finger.

Darien pulled him back by his sore wrist. "No. You're not having him. I didn't say anything about Alastor being part of the deal, Avery."

Avery smiled. Alastor's cock stood up and begged like a dog at the thought of those plush lips around it. He wanted, needed—

Blue eyes met his. "Now, now imp, mind on the subject. But if you let Silas suck your finger, he'll stop it bleeding for you, although—" A line appeared between perfect eyebrows as Avery's gaze ran over his naked torso, taking in the bandages on his wrists that had been hidden by bedclothes last night. "Turn around."

The command was softly spoken, and Alastor began to obey. He found himself pulled against Darien's chest.

"Leave him alone. You might be demons but—"

Silas's eyes reddened. "Step away from him."

Darien gasped, stumbled back as if shoved.

"Did I ask for your assistance?" Avery asked the vampire, brows drawn together. "I may not possess your level of compulsion abilities, but I'm not entirely without talent."

The redness vanished from the vampire's eyes, and he bowed his head. "Apologies, Council Leader."

With a curt nod for his subordinate, Avery turned back to Alastor and smiled. It was like the sun coming out. Despite the whimper of distress from behind him, all Alastor wanted to do was please this glorious man and perhaps be granted the honor of touching him.

"Would you show me you back?"

Without hesitation, Alastor spun.

"Push your pants down."

The words sounded like honey, and despite being uncomfortable about exposing his skin in such an open space, Alastor pushed his sweatpants down, then looked over his shoulder.

Avery and Silas both stared at his butt, hunger on their faces. As if it had a mind of its own, Alastor's fist closed around his cock, stroked.

"Alastor, please, don't." The choked voice tugged him to the edge of the lust cloud fogging his mind. Darien's brows were pulled down, his lips twisted as if in pain. "He's an incubus. He just wants—"

A spike of anger dispersed his lust like a thrown pebble disturbed the surface of a millpond. "What does he just want, Darien? Sex? At least he's honest about it. He's not pretending he's concerned to trick me into giving up—"

"Darien." The dark eyes dulled at Avery's command. "Tell me the truth. Did you make those marks on him without his consent?"

Alastor looked over his shoulder. Both the demons were focused on Darien. The incubus looked disappointed, but the vampire licked his lips as if he was about to receive a treat.

Yes, Darien had been a shit, but Alastor didn't want to be responsible for another death.

"No, no, he didn't do it," Alastor blurted, "It was—"

Avery glanced at Alastor, and his eyes pulsed with an orange glow. "Quiet."

Alastor's lips sealed as thoroughly as if someone had put a hand over his mouth.

"Some of them." Darien sounded drugged.

Keeping his soft smile in place, the incubus strolled forward, brushed a tanned thumb over Darien's dark cheek, then he leaned in and kissed the lips that had brought Alastor so much pleasure.

"Show me which ones you made, using your tongue." Alastor barely registered Avery's command before Darien was in front of him, kissing and licking down his naked chest.

The American fell to his knees to get better access to Alastor's belly. Alastor concentrated as if he could force Darien to take his cock in his mouth by sheer force of will.

A hand stroked over his ass, and he tore his gaze away from the sun-kissed hand resting on Darien's tightly curled hair. Lips met his, and he groaned at the wave of lust that threatened to collapse his knees.

"And you told me off for wanting to have a nibble?"

Alastor's mind didn't make sense of what the vampire said before Avery pulled away, a mischievous smile on the lips that had been devouring him a second ago.

Desire dropped away so fast it left Alastor's head spinning.

"Telling truth from lies is easier when lust lowers the barriers," Avery said. "FitzHenry didn't beat him, and I don't think he'd ever go further than a probably well-deserved spanking."

Darien gaped at the demon but then seemed to shake off the lust haze. He hauled Alastor's sweatpants up as he got to his feet.

"That... that was assault," Darien said, his voice uneven.

A blond eyebrow quirked. "You think so? Seemed like you were doing all the touching to me. However, it doesn't feel right that Alastor should remain in pain. The wounds on his wrists are part magical. They'll heal eventually, but it'll take weeks and will scar unless they get a little help." He raised his voice. "I require an air elemental."

A blue, stick-thin being appeared behind Avery. As he was the only one to twitch in surprise, he guessed Darien had already been introduced to the odd creature. But by his less than enthusiastic expression, he had no wish to see it again.

"You called, oh master?" The blue being's tone reeked of sarcasm.

"Do the air elementals wish to renegotiate their agreement with the supernatural council?" Avery asked, his tone mild.

The air elemental stiffened and bowed deeply. "No, Council Leader. I apologize for my attitude. I have a few family issues that I shouldn't have let interfere with my work."

"Anything I can do to help?" Avery asked.

"Unfortunately not, sir, but I appreciate you asking. Now, what can I do for you?"

"Could you fetch a pup to do a little healing?" He nodded toward Alastor. "It's awkward conducting a business negotiation when one party has trouble sitting down."

"Any pup in particular?"

"One of Henry Lloyd's pack should suffice, but pick one with a brain?"

The air elemental snorted in amusement. "That cuts out at least half," it said, then vanished.

"Do you mind?" Alastor turned to the vampire, who indicated Alastor's hand with a finger. "Seems a shame to waste it."

"It's alright; he won't take any more than is necessary to close the wound," Avery said.

Darien huffed. "As if he's going to trust you after you made me—"

Avery quirked an eyebrow. "Made you what? Molest him or prove you didn't abuse him?"

Darien drew himself up, looming over the shorter blond man. "Look, you were meant to secure the hall, not—"

"Council Member Shanae asked me to help her relative, and that's what I'm doing."

Fed up with other people making decisions about him, without bothering to ask him first, Alastor turned to the vampire and held out his hand. Blood had flowed down his wrist, staining the bandage. "Knock yourself out."

Darien grabbed his shoulder, pulling him back a step. "He's a demon, don't trust—"

Alastor twisted away. "Don't push it, FitzHenry. I was a demon as well less than a day ago. As for trusting a demon, so far, neither of these two have broken their word. I can't say the same for you."

Darien looked like he'd been punched in the gut. Avery slung an arm over Darien's shoulder and led him away, murmuring to him. The demon's hand slid down Darien's back to his ass. The man who had promised Alastor so much didn't resist the touch.

"Don't worry. Avery won't hurt him, although he might take another sip of lust. That's how sex demons feed. On the other hand, I feed on blood, and I can tell a lot about a person from just a taste. Do you want to know what you are?" Dark eyes met his in a question.

"Be my guest."

A cool hand closed over his forearm, and then wetness enclosed his cut finger. The demon held Alastor's gaze as his tongue swirled over his finger. Avery might be a sex demon, but Silas was damn erotic too. He wondered how much it would take to make the vampire lose control, wondered if it would be the last thing he'd ever see.

After a single long lick down his hand to clear up the main blood trail, the vampire licked his lips with a thoughtful expression.

"Well?" Alastor asked.

"You're... interesting. Old with a tang of youth. There's also something I can't quite... A little more would help. A finger really isn't enough. May I?" he asked, indicating his own neck.

"Not going to drain me, are you?"

Silas snorted. "And end up in my own prison? Sorry to bust your ego, but you're not worth that."

"Is he?" Alastor nodded toward where Avery stood talking to Darien near the fireplace.

The amusement dropped from the vampire's expression. "I don't feed on incubi."

Alastor's interest piqued. "Why? Can't demons feed on each other?"

"If they are different species, yes."

"So why not incubi?"

Silas's brows drew together. "You're a nosy little shit. Are you sure you're not a fae?"

"Is that what the blue thing is?"

"No, that's an air elemental; you're not one of them either. Question is... what are you?"

Alastor pointed to his neck. "Knock yourself out."

Before he could even gasp, pain lanced in his neck, and arms held him like steel bands. Every worry and anxiety drained away, leaving only bone-deep relaxation and simmering lust. Alastor pulled the demon closer rather than trying to push him away.

One mouthful, two.

A growl broke the silence, and Silas lifted his head.

Alastor's hand found the back of the demon's head. "No, not yet," Alastor pleaded; it felt so damn good.

"Sorry, kid, but shifters don't like my kind anyway. There's no need to antagonize one." After a last swipe of his tongue, Silas steadied him and turned to the new arrival.

The vampire's booming laugh echoed around the Low Great Hall.

A small, curly-haired guy who looked in his mid to late teens stood next to the air elemental, showing his teeth as he growled at Silas. A patch of white showed on the side of his otherwise chestnut brown hair.

"A poodle? You brought a poodle?" Silas laughed.

"I'm a barbet, not a poodle," the boy ground out, then added, "not that there's anything wrong with being a poodle, even a mismarked miniature one. And my name's Idris, not that anyone was polite enough to ask."

Avery approached, a line between his brows. "I know I said a pup, but I didn't mean an actual puppy. We need someone capable of healing."

Idris, who wore blue jeans and a faded black, heavy metal band t-shirt, puffed out his chest. "I'm plenty old enough." He waved a hand at Alastor. "I'm at least as old as him."

"I doubt it," Avery said. "He's four hundred and thirty, give or take a few years."

The boy's eyes widened, and he sniffed loudly. "Doesn't smell like a vampire."

"And how many vampires have you met before me, pup? I don't expect your alpha lets many of my kind near his packhouse."

"Not the point," the boy grumbled, looking precisely like a disgruntled, sulking dog.

"Well, you're right about something," Silas said. "He's human, mostly. But there's a touch of smoky old magic and demon spice there too. I reckon you got to him just in time, Council Leader. A few more decades under Arioch's influence, and you'd have another fully-fledged vengeance demon on your hands."

The strange company, incubus, vampire, air elemental, teenage canine shifter, and the bemused human, all stared at him, waiting for his reaction.

"So... I really am an imp?"

Silas shrugged. "If there is such a thing, and I've never heard of one, I guess you're it."

For some reason, that made Darien frown. Alastor couldn't help smiling at his discomfort.

"Definitely an imp," Avery said wryly.

Idris rubbed his hands together. "Ok, who's my patient?"

The air elemental rolled its eyes. "Take a guess, Einstein."

"The name's Idris, not Einstein," he mumbled under his breath as his gaze flicked between Darien and Alastor. The shifter bit his lip and frowned, so Alastor held up his arm, displaying the bandage on his wrist.

With almost comical determination, the youngster strode up to him and reached for his forearm.

Alastor held it away from him. "What does this healing involve?"

Idris nodded toward Avery. "He's got a magic cock, vamps control people with their voices, and us canine shifters have healing tongues." As if to demonstrate, Idris poked out his tongue, which looked more like a dog's tongue than a human one.

Avery shrugged. "He's not wrong. Let him do it, so we can get on with things."

Having his wrist licked by a boy who looked younger than Liam felt all kinds of wrong, but it didn't hurt. When Idris turned to the other one, Alastor couldn't help staring at the pink, newly healed skin when only raw oozing wounds had been minutes before.

Idris wrinkled his nose. "I wish people wouldn't use antiseptic. It tastes awful."

When he finished Alastor's other wrist, he asked, "Anything else?"

Avery said, "Yes," at the same time Alastor and Darien both said, "No."

"I am not having a kid licking my.... other injuries," Alastor ground out, face getting hotter with every heartbeat.

Avery sighed. "He's a canine shifter. They go naked most of the time. Seeing your ass is not going to embarrass him."

"The man said no," Darien said from beside him. Even after everything the auctioneer had witnessed over the last few days, he still clung to his 'I'm in charge' attitude. Alastor didn't know whether to kiss him or clip him round the ear for being so damn stupid.

"I'll just erm... look around while you decide. I've never seen anything quite like this before," Idris murmured as they continued to argue.

"Want me to compel him?" Silas asked.

"No," Avery, Darien, and Alastor said together.

Silas shrugged. "Fair enough. So, as you don't need me anymore, council leader, I've got evening rounds at the prison. If I don't do it, Grikx won't send anyone else. All he does is sit in his office, staring at the records."

Avery frowned at Alastor. "You're adamant about him not dealing with the bruising?"

"Yep. It doesn't really bother me anyway."

Avery sighed. "Fine. I guess we're done here." He turned to the air elemental. "Who knows you borrowed Idris?"

Blue shoulders shrugged. "No one as far as I know. I asked, he agreed, so here we are. The rest of the pack were out working the fields. He was the only one in the packhouse for some reason."

Avery frowned and focused on Idris, who was doing an abysmal job of being inconspicuous as he looked at the lots.

"Why were you grounded, Idris?" Avery asked.

"Huh? I wasn't grounded. I was just doing a homework assignment."

Alastor had done enough lying in his time to recognize a rank amateur, but as the boy had healed his wrists, he didn't want to repay the kid by calling him out.

"Truth?" Avery asked.

The curly hair bobbed as Idris nodded frantically. It was almost as if he thought the more he nodded, the more he would be believed.

Avery's lips pursed. "Ok. I'll give you a pass this time, but only because you helped. You can take him home now."

The air elemental reached out to touch Idris's shoulder, then pulled its fingers away as if burned. "Silver, he's got silver."

Idris's eyes went round then he tried to bolt from the room. One moment Silas was propped up against the podium, the next, he was carrying a squirming Idris back toward them, one arm wrapped around the boy's belly as if he weighed nothing. In his other hand, he held the sold silver wine tasting dish.

"Keep it away," the air elemental hissed as it backed away.

Darien stepped forward and took the piece from the vampire.

"I think a few days with me might teach him about property rights." Silas sounded cheerful at the prospect.

"In the prison?" Idris squeaked and started squirming.

"Is that really necessary?" Alastor stood up. "The kid didn't ask to come here, and—"

"Yes, yes, I know that," Avery groused. "Put him on his feet." The incubus stared at the youngster, who lifted his chin and stared the far older and more powerful supernatural in the eyes.

Alastor remembered doing the same thing many times with his mother. It'd always resulted in a beating whether he was guilty or not. Although to be fair to Ma, she'd usually caught him bang to rights, just as they'd caught Idris.

"He can stay here with me," Alastor blurted. "Who's better to keep an eye on a thief than a thief?"

Avery sighed, pinched the bridge of his nose. "And have the most powerful canine shifter on the planet, not to mention a member of my council, going nuts because his son is either missing or in prison because I borrowed him without asking?"

"Would he know?" Alastor said, then hastily added, "That you took him, not that Idris was missing."

"He'd probably thank you," Idris said mournfully.

Silas checked his watch. "Tick tock, Avery. There might be unsanctioned snacking if I don't supervise the prison staff."

"Tell him you got Idris a job," Alastor blurted. "He can help with whatever you want to do with this place." Alastor paused, heart dropping. "You... you do want to do something with the Hall, with me, right?"

Avery smiled, and everything seemed fine in the world. "Yes, I want you to do something with this place. I promised Shanae, and I quite like having the witches owe me a favor." He smiled, and for the first time, Alastor felt a little afraid of the beautiful demon. "But we can discuss that later. Now, let's get Idris home. I think it's best for everyone if your father thinks you've just fallen asleep somewhere rather than having been transported across the country and then caught stealing by the leader of the supernatural council, don't you?"

Idris mimed locking his lips and throwing away the key. "My lips are sealed. You have my word."

"Where do you go when you're trying to avoid your father?" Avery asked.

Idris wrinkled his nose. Alastor wondered if he'd ever been that obvious when lying to his mother, but he had to admire the kid's balls for trying.

"Never mind," Avery said, "Silas, wipe him, and have the air elemental take him home."

"As you wish, Council Leader." No sooner had Silas stopped speaking, than he, Idris, and the elemental vanished.

CHAPTER THIRTY-ONE

One moment he'd been standing in the Low Great Hall, facing four supernaturals, the next, Darien sat at the kitchen table, with Alastor beside him and Avery opposite. By the darkness outside the window, at least several hours had passed.

"Drink your coffee," Avery indicated the steaming red mug in front of Darien as if nothing had happened. Darien ignored him as he tried to work out what he'd missed.

Alastor wore a soft cream button-up shirt and black jeans. He looked down. Instead of the suit he remembered, he wore his blue jeans and his favorite long-sleeved black ribbed t-shirt.

Had Avery simply purchased some new clothes for Alastor or had he helped him out of his old sweats and into them? Alastor had already flashed his backside at the incubus, but did things go further? With Alastor, *with me?*

He felt violated, but jealousy over Alastor stung, fired his blood. He pushed it down; he had no right to the emotion. Alastor wasn't his, but fuck, the thought of that smooth bastard touching him, whispering lies, feeding on him, burned.

"What happened?" he ground out.

Blond eyebrows drew together. "None of your business."

"I've lost at least two hours. Taking people's memories, their free will, is not acceptable."

Alastor now appeared modern and so in the world, compared to the ragged, bruised Tudor peasant only he'd been able to see, to interact with. *Not mine anymore.*

His mind stalled, revolted by the selfish, visceral urge to have that situation back. He'd always helped subs move on in their lives. He'd never held someone back or denied them their freedom. And yet, with Alastor, he craved turning the clock back.

A tap on the door caused Alastor to call out, "Come in."

When had the power in this house shifted from the incubus to Alastor? What the hell had gone on that he couldn't remember? Why had his memory been blocked?

Lorraine Grimshaw came in, wearing the same black skirt and white blouse as earlier. To Darien's amazement, she bobbed a curtsey to Alastor. "Ground floor is all done, Milord. Will there be anything else?"

"Er, Lorraine?" Avery tugged at his own shirt collar.

The blonde woman's face reddened, and she pulled the collar of her blouse a little closer to her neck. It still didn't hide the red hickey.

Darien couldn't stop staring at the incorrectly fastened buttons on her white blouse.

"Thank you for your help today," Alastor said with a relaxed smile.

Alastor didn't require him to interact anymore, but it didn't soothe the itch that perhaps he needed Alastor.

Lorraine bobbed a curtsey, murmured her thanks, and headed out the door into the night. Before it finished shutting, Harry Grimshaw popped his head in.

"Right then, that's me done too. Everything's locked up." He tugged at the peak of his tweed flat cap.

Had he entered the twilight zone? What was with the 'milord's' and curtsies? Neither of the Grimshaws had behaved like this before.

Harry still wore the dark suit from earlier, but the zipper on his pants had definitely been done up before, unlike now. The older man's underwear showed white against his charcoal pants.

"Well, you didn't remember to lock your—" Darien started.

Harry stood a little straighter. "I beg your pardon, but I locked everything, sir, as I do every night."

Alastor's lips twitched, but instead of making fun of the man as he would have done before, he said, "No, that's quite alright, Harry. You may go."

Harry gave Darien a hard stare before saying, "Right you are, Milord. Goodnight."

The door closed behind Harry. Darien was left looking between Alastor and Avery.

The demon glanced at Alastor, then regarded Darien with a sour expression. "Everyone needs to eat, Mr. FitzHenry." Avery bent and placed a black briefcase on the table.

The thunk of the twin locks opening shook Darien out of his stupor. "But Harry?" he asked.

A line of distaste marred that perfect forehead. "Shame on you for assuming older people don't experience desire. With my assistance, Mr. and Mrs. Grimshaw enjoyed quite a busy afternoon." The devilish smile promised all kinds of sin.

"Did they consent?"

"What?" Avery said as he shuffled through paperwork Darien couldn't see behind the upright lid of the case.

"It's not a difficult question, Avery. Even though you are a demon and the head of that council of yours, explicit consent is always required before every sexual act."

The beautiful blond man tilted his head, examining Darien as if he were an alien. "Everything is so very black and white for you, isn't it? I think I envy you, but life isn't that simple. Sometimes you have to do questionable things for the greater good.

"For example, do you think the Grimshaws talking about what happened here yesterday would be good for them or for Alastor? Ranting about real demons and witches roaming Kent?"

"You took their memories," Darien ground out, even as he wondered if he could trust his own recollections.

"Silas adjusted them, Juliana's too." Avery dismissed the issue with a wave of his hand.

Guilt jabbed at the mention of his sister. He hadn't even thought about her since the auction. "Where is she?"

"At the hotel, packing, I presume," the demon said as if it was a pointless, unnecessary question. "You have a flight home tomorrow morning, remember?"

Darien pulled out his phone, kept his gaze on Avery.

"If you say anything untoward, I'll have to send Silas to see her again, but he'll be unsupervised this time." The demon's eyes promised that an unsupervised vampire wouldn't end well for Juliana.

Darien still hit dial.

Juliana picked up on the second ring. "Hey, brother. Are you nearly finished there? I thought we could stay in an airport hotel tonight, so we don't have to panic about morning traffic."

Not looking away from the demon, he said, "Don't worry about me. I'll make my own way. I might even stay for a while."

Alastor's jaw tightened at the last sentence, but he didn't comment.

Juliana snorted. "I thought as much. Who would've thought the new owner and that heritage warrior knew each other? Pretending to be a ghost is the oddest auction tactic I've ever seen, but I guess it worked. Besides, I know he caught your eye. Knock yourself out. You've earned a break, and we haven't got another auction until mid-November. See you at home." The line clicked off.

He placed the phone carefully back on the table. At least he knew the spin on events that Juliana had been forced to remember. The grain of truth would make the lies easier to swallow.

"See, everything is fine," Avery said. "It was for their own good, and Alastor whole-heartedly agreed."

Darien concentrated on keeping his body language bland and non-threatening as he turned to Alastor. He'd deal with Alastor's upset over his less than enthusiastic declaration about staying, but he couldn't let this violation go. If he accepted it, he'd be setting a precedent that he was ok with having their memories altered.

"You agreed to a demon messing with my sister's head, or did he make you think you did?"

Alastor scowled. Because Avery still watched them, Darien resisted the urge to smooth out the line between the imp's brows with his lips.

"I could have had him change your memories too," Alastor said as if he'd done him a favor.

Darien snorted. "He did. I don't remember the last two hours or my trip back from London. Do you really believe a demon's word that he didn't alter anything else? He could have made you forget too."

"I made you sleep on the way back because you needed it, and after you got changed you've been sitting here doing nothing so you didn't get in the way of what needed to be done."

"How do I know that?"

Avery sighed, glanced at Alastor. "This is a pointless, circular argument, and the reason I suggested wiping him too. The story about you having a phobia about traveling would have worked. Now, let's get on with this as this place is starting to bore me."

Avery began dropping documents from the briefcase onto the unpolished table. "Birth certificate, passport, driver's license, contract of employment, bank account details... everything's here. Welcome to the new you."

As Alastor didn't move, Darien reached for the nearest document, a burgundy UK/EU passport. He scanned to the main details page on the first right-hand page.

Forename: NICHOLAS ALASTOR JACQUES

Surname: THE VISCOUNT CHALLOCK

Nationality: BRITISH CITIZEN

The left-hand page, reserved for official observations, contained:

THE HOLDER IS NICHOLAS ALASTOR JAQUES CHAUMIER, THE VISCOUNT CHALLOCK.

"Viscount Challock? Jacque Chaumier?" Darien asked.
"Chaumier is French for Thatcher," Avery said. "Jacque Chaumier changed his name to James Thatcher when he came over from France to escape religious persecution." A sad, distant smile curved his lips before the charming façade reappeared. He closed the case and snapped the latches closed. "It appears that Alastor is the grandnephew of my dear Frederick. We added the minor title of the Walpole family because—" he delivered one of his devastating smiles, "—why not? besides, many humans are impressed by such things."
Darien blinked, his mind boggling at the array of documents. "How did you do all this in a couple of hours?" he asked as he pulled one of the many documents closer. The contract named Nicholas Chaumier as Managing Director of Walpole Hall Ltd.
"Most supernaturals have lifespans that far exceed humans, but we can't, unfortunately, ignore your modern bureaucracy. We've become efficient at creating new human identities, although this is an impressive rush job by the fae council

representative." Plush lips pressed together. "I now owe him a favor, and believe me, fae never forget a damn thing. Unfortunately for me, they are also non-sexual."

Avery's chair scraped as he stood up. "Hopefully, this place will earn me far more favors in return, including a great many from you. That is, if you can make it authentic enough to convince people who also remember the late Elizabethan period first-hand."

"Not a problem, although I take it you'd like to keep modern bathrooms rather than reinstating pissing in the fireplaces?" Alastor said, tone bright, but his fist tightened on his lap. The Elizabethan man wasn't nearly as confident as he wanted to appear.

"Few, if any, demons need toilets, but they'll be needed for the shifters, witches, and—" He tilted his head. "You know, I have no idea what elementals or fae do in that regard. I should look into that, know thy enemy and all that."

He refocused on Alastor. "Anyway, remember, as far as the Grimshaws and Juliana are concerned, nothing happened on the roof yesterday. They don't remember the witches, Arioch, or that Alastor is anything but a minor British aristocrat with a passion for history.

"I bought the Hall at the auction to turn it into an authentic Tudor experience and installed Alastor as my representative. Which is all perfectly true. He just happens to look like his distant relative in the painting." He pressed his lips together. "And option two remains open. Are you sure a year isn't too long a test?"

Alastor's shoulders hunched, and he spoke more to his hands in his lap than the demon. "I'll let you know if it is."

"Option two is?" Darien asked, but it seemed he was as much a ghost now as Alastor had been as both men ignored him.

"What about him?" Avery nodded at Darien. "I can still send him home with his sister. Rounding up some more suitable assistants will not be a problem."

Alastor looked up. Darien almost held his breath as sea-green eyes met his. He had no doubt that his memories lay in the former imp's hands.

Without a trace of a smile, Alastor kept his focus on Darien and said, "I'll let you know about that too."

"As you wish." The suave incubus stood then strode out into the night without saying another word to Darien. He'd never felt so dismissed in his life.

The auction was finished. Alastor's future was secure. He should be happy that he could leave yet another sub in a better position, both mentally and financially. So why did he feel so damn empty at the thought of walking away?

He wasn't foolish enough to believe he'd keep his memories if he left here. That damn vampire probably lurked outside, waiting to send him on his way, oblivious like Juliana and the Grimshaws.

Darien stared as if he could commit Alastor's features to memory by sheer force of will. The sharp line of his too-thin face, the errant red curl falling into the sea-green eyes. Eyes that had lost the merry spark that captured Darien from the moment they'd met.

Heart heavy with grief, he reached out, brushed his thumb down Alastor's pale cheek then cupped his chin. "I don't want to forget you."

Alastor's eyes closed, and he leaned into Darien's hand. A crystal teardrop sparkled on his eyelash before it trailed down his cheek.

Without thought, Darien gathered Alastor onto his lap. Holding his head against his shoulder, Darien breathed in his woodsmoke scent and placed a gentle kiss on his hair.

"Don't worry, little imp, things will turn out fine. You have a magnificent future ahead of you. This place will be full of people every day, and it'll always be your choice who and how you want to interact with them. You deserve that more than anyone I've ever met."

"It's too big, too much." Darien strained to hear Alastor's words. "It's easy to pretend when he's here. But, I... I don't know how the modern world works; hell, I hardly knew how things worked in 1600. Even back then, the furthest I ever went was the village."

Alastor shifted, tilting his face up. He swallowed, pain creasing his forehead, but his brave little imp managed to say what bothered him.

"Option two was making me a shiny new twenty-first-century man who had lost his memory. He said that might totally break the curse. I might be able to travel, do anything I wanted."

"Why didn't you take him up on it?" Darien asked although he couldn't imagine Alastor without his history.

Alastor's brow wrinkled in frustration. "You don't get it, neither did Avery and Silas. Losing my memory will be like killing everyone I've ever met." He tapped his temple. "They're all here. My mother, father, all the Walpoles, Yaingo, even John Grimshaw. Nobody in the world remembers them except me. If I forget, they'll be gone." He made a starburst with one hand. "Some might still be in a painting, a name on a family tree, or some other record, but it won't be *them*, understand?"

"You could write their stories down." Darien paused as he realized the enormity of the task. "But that would take several lifetimes."

An impish smile curled Alastor's lips. "Well, we'll have longer than most people. Sleeping with sex demons prolongs human lives."

Darien groaned and let his head fall back, equally appalled at being violated and pissed off that he'd missed having sex with a demon designed to provide the ultimate sexual high. "I knew it. I just knew it. Do you remember it?"

"Nothing at all. He woke me a few minutes before he woke you, said thanks for the snack, and told me his plan for this place. Said it was up to me what happened to you. Did I do the right thing?"

"Yes, you did the right thing, little imp," Darien murmured, but he knew that wasn't what Alastor wanted to know.

The unspoken question, 'Do you want me enough to stay?' hung between them.

He'd always imagined finding the right boy one day, integrating that special someone into his life, hopes, and dreams. Someone who would fit in with him, not the other way around.

That could happen if Alastor lost his memory. He pushed the thought away, disgusted at himself for even considering violating the principle of consent that had ruled every sexual interaction. He knew the guilt would cripple him.

If I remember asking for it.

The prospect of a memory wiped for them both itched at his conscience. He could ask Avery to arrange a normal meeting between them, and they could go forward like any other couple.

But what if one or both didn't feel this pull between them without their shared history? They could walk right past each other and never interact. The plan also relied on a fickle demon doing something neither he nor Alastor would remember. Shanae probably wouldn't object as long as her relative was safe.

Erasing history for his own selfish reasons went against everything he held dear. It would be like bulldozing this place and destroying everything in it.

The house creaked and groaned as it settled. It felt alive, as if it was trying to tell the stories of all the people who had lived and died here. But the only person who could do that sat cuddled on his lap.

His own life would be swallowed by the man he held if he agreed to stay. If he didn't, he knew Silas would pay him a visit. He wouldn't remember Alastor as anything other than a passing acquaintance, at least consciously. He couldn't believe he wouldn't experience some sense of loss, of something missing left behind.

Would he spend his life looking for Alastor, going through club after club, looking for the 'right' sub when he'd already walked away from him?

Am I too damn selfish and prideful to admit I can't put Alastor's needs before anything else, permanently? It wasn't a pretty thought. But could he base the rest of his life on knowing someone for just ten days?

This could be like any other vacation romance, fantastic in a different environment but then everything dissolves once real life comes back to bite you in the ass.

But some people manage to live their dreams.
Is this mine? Is he?

Alastor's soft words broke into his tumbling thoughts. "I'm going to need help, a lot of help. I need someone to rely on, someone to be with, talk to, someone who understands my nature and the modern world and helps me with both. I'm a little shit, and I'll probably stay that way. I can't help it. Being with me will never be easy."

Darien placed an absent kiss on the dark red curls. "The word you're looking for is brat, and I happen to—"

"Silas told Avery he could find someone for me, that he'd have plenty of volunteers," Alastor blurted. Darien's arms closed around Alastor a little tighter at the thought of some demon or shifter taking his place.

"But I don't want someone who thinks I'm a burden they're paid to keep an eye on or is coerced to be here. I won't be a preferred prison sentence for some supernatural."

"I'll stay." The words were out of Darien's mouth before he could think about them, but they felt right in every fiber of his being.

Alastor tilted back, eyes examining his for signs of truth, so he said it again. "I'll stay. Avery asked if a year is enough of a test. I think it's more than enough time for us to drive each other completely bat-shit crazy if it's going to happen."

He gave a lopsided smile at the hope radiating from Alastor. "I accept who you are, little imp, but you must accept who I am too. I don't tolerate disobedience, and I expect you to obey because I will never ask you to do something unnecessary, pointless, or that you won't ultimately enjoy."

"I can do that," Alastor blurted way too quickly.

The little imp had no idea what he'd agreed to, but if he couldn't take everything Darien was, this wouldn't work long term. If they didn't truly complement each other, there would only be heartache, bitterness, and ultimate failure ahead.

"In that case, let's take it upstairs. We can start with a shower."

"Again? Seriously, you have to get over this constant washing thing; it's bad for the skin."

"Fifteen minutes," Darien said calmly, although his belly knotted with anticipation. "Fifteen minutes of punishment for not doing what you're told, brat."

Alastor shot off his lap and began backing away from him. "Hell, no. I'm not letting you or anyone else beat me ever again."

Taking a breath, Darien pushed down the flare of anger. "If you think I would beat you, you don't know me, and perhaps you never will. I am not, nor have I ever been, a violent man. But I have, and intend to do so in the future, spanked a misbehaving sub. But only with their agreement. Some are even naughty on purpose because they enjoy it so much."

Alastor licked his lips, his face flushing. "You want to spank me? Like over your knee with your hand for fifteen minutes?"

"Not this time. This time, I'm not going to touch you at all."

Keeping a straight face while the wheels turned in Alastor's head took all his dom abilities.

"You're not going to make me eat something horrible or piss on me, are you? Because that's not—"

"Thirty minutes."

"You're going to make me stand in a corner or sit on a naughty step, aren't you?"

"No. Forty-five," Darien announced, loving the stark confusion on Alastor's face. "And I'll be adding another fifteen minutes for every minute you don't get your butt in the shower upstairs." It occurred to him that Alastor's problem might not only be with washing; exposing his skin in general might be an issue. "Actually, you might as well strip now."

Alastor's pretty sea-green eyes went round. "Here?" he squeaked, looking around himself. "In the kitchen?"

Darien leaned back, folding his arms. "There's no one within a mile of you except me. You need to learn to trust my decisions if this is ever going to work."

"Being naked is my punishment?"

"One hour. No, I want you naked because I like looking at you."

A slow smile spread across Alastor's sinful lips. Mesmerized, Darien froze. Avery might be a sex demon, but he'd never seen anything as hot as Alastor's wicked expression.

"Is that so, milord?"

The honorific went straight to Darien's cock, but he couldn't let the brat get the upper hand this quickly. This first play session would be a test for them both.

"Shirt off. I won't ask again." As soon as he said it, he wondered what the hell he'd do if Alastor refused.

With that wicked grin still in place, Alastor carefully began unbuttoning the cream shirt Avery must have supplied. Darien made a note to do some online shopping as soon as possible.

His sub wouldn't be wearing something purchased by another man, even if that man was a richer than sin demon.

The buttons might have been undone slowly, but as soon as Alastor reached the last one, he tore the shirt off, shoved his jeans down, and sprinted for the door as if having his skin exposed for a second longer than necessary would be fatal.

Chapter Thirty-Two

Having cool air brushing his skin as he ran across the echoing Low Great Hall only increased the butterflies in Alastor's belly. He knew intellectually that no one remained in the hall, but exposing himself in a large open space still felt all kinds of wrong. It also sent a thrill up his spine.

The heat in Darien's eyes had been damn real. He could almost feel the man's touch, his tongue at his hole again. No one had ever wanted him for him before. Even Shanae had helped because of a familial sense of obligation, and Avery wanted the witch to owe him.

Darien wanted him enough to give up his entire life. Excitement bubbled at having snared his chosen prey, just as Avery claimed he could.

Twenty minutes later, Alastor cursed the incubus with everything he had. Sitting in the shower tray, naked as the day he'd been born, Alastor gritted his teeth, his body and mind burning with the need to come.

Avery said he saw lust like a glow around a person, but right now, Alastor bet he shone like one of the WW2 searchlights. Wearing only his black boxers, Darien squatted in front of him, playing jets of warm water over Alastor's rigid cock. Just as he thought it would finally happen, Darien moved the stream to the inside of Alastor's thigh. He'd lost count of the number of times it'd happened—once had been too much.

This was worse than being unable to touch himself for all those years. Darien played him with maddening frustration, a small smile on his lips. The stream played over his cock, stroking it until his balls fizzed and his hips flexed, then it moved to his thighs, nipples, armpits, anywhere but where he craved it. As soon as the urge to come receded a fraction, Darien moved it back to his cock, making him jerk, twitch, and moan all over again.

He blinked the water dripping from his hair out of his eyes and again considered using the spell Shanae had taught him on Darien. But knowing FitzHenry, he'd probably carry on torturing him until it wore off. Instead, he gripped the toweling belt of the bathrobe wrapped around the shower fitment a little tighter and tried to calm himself before the water hit his cock again. He both wanted it fast and feared that Darien would leave him hanging.

Every swearword, every attempt to let go and touch himself, resulted in additional torture time. The water hit his cock again. He jerked at the jab of painful pleasure. At first, it'd been embarrassing, uncomfortable both physically and mentally. He'd squirmed, swore, and twisted away as the jets hit his cock. Then Darien began talking, and bit by bit, he'd gotten hard and wished for higher water pressure.

"So damn beautiful," Darien murmured, gaze fixed on Alastor's straining, red erection as the water played over it.

No other thought existed except not irritating Darien so he'd finally let him come. Harry and Lorraine, Silas, Avery, even Arioch could walk through the bathroom right now, and he wouldn't try to cover up.

Nearly, so damn close, just hold it there a little longer, shake it, right on—

Darien changed the target of his weapon to Alastor's chest. He bit back a curse.

"Ready to say the magic words yet, little imp?"

He'd already tried 'sorry,' but all Darien had said was, "Try again; I already know that."

Begging he understood, but it'd never been begging for pleasure, only for pain to end, but this was pretty damn near the worst torture he'd experienced.

The harsh electric light dimmed, and he looked up. Darien stood over him, his boxer shorts bulging with his straining, untouched erection. Alastor's cock lurched, slapped against his belly, his mouth watering. He wanted it any way he could get it.

"Say the magic words, and this could be my mouth." The hard needles of water moved down again, and Alastor's cock twitched as if reaching for the sensation it needed. *One second, two, more, just a little more and—*

The stream returned to his inner thigh, causing a deep groan to rip from his chest. He'd had enough. Darien would clearly drag this out to the whole hour, by which time, Alastor was sure his cock would explode and not in a good way.

Closing his legs, he drew them up, protecting his cock.

"Spread your knees, little imp."

"You lied; you're a sadist," he choked out.

Water hit him full in the face, and he gasped, getting a mouthful of water. Twisting his head, he screwed up his eyes, tried to breathe the moisture-laden air. He coughed, failed, and spread his legs again.

In the next heartbeat, the water switched back to his cock, going from his painfully tight, drawn-up balls, up the shaft, before concentrating on the head. He twitched, jerked, as needles of water battered his slit.

"Please, I can't—"

Darien's voice sounded equally thick as he said, "Are you ever going to moan when I tell you to shower again?"

He looked up. Darien's eyes were hooded, his expression raw, almost as desperate as himself. *I did that.*

Without thought, a tired smile curved his lips, and he said, "Every fucking time."

Darien growled. His hand shot to the faucet and turned it off. A big dark hand wrapped around Alastor's pale bicep, and he found himself on wobbly feet.

Bracing Alastor with his hip, Darien grabbed the shower gel. A squelch sounded a heartbeat before a blue plastic bottle landed near his feet. Rough hands swirled over his ass, pushed into his crack then Darien pressed up against him.

"Say yes, god, say yes," Darien gasped against his neck as his hardness thrust blindly against his crack.

Not trusting his voice, Alastor braced his forearm against the tiles and stuck his ass out. He expected pain, expected to serve as he'd always done, but Darien wrapped a fist around his cock and jerked him until Alastor's hips thrust in time.

"Say yes, damn it," Darien's growl was as rough as Alastor felt.

He swallowed and forced his mind and lips to form a few rough words. "Yeah, yeah, do it, please do—"

The pain of Darien pushing into him only made him soar higher. His climax punched out of him, and his world closed down to sensation.

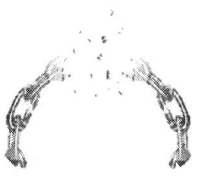

Light irritated his eyelids, but this time Alastor didn't luxuriate, didn't bask in the softness and warmth of the bed. His hand shot behind him and contacted a warm body.

Darien grunted with the force of the near punch. "Warn a guy, will you?"

Alastor flipped over and took in the sleepy face that held not an ounce of regret or disgust at being in bed with him.

"You're still here," he confirmed.

A soft smile grew on Darien's lips. "I am. And I will be until you kick me out."

"Even after last night?"

A hand snaked over Alastor's hip and squeezed his butt. "Especially after last night. If you'd given up immediately, I would've been disappointed. I like a challenge, and I can see you challenging me for the rest of our days."

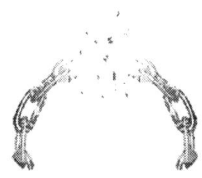

Want to see what Avery got up to during those missing hours? Click or snap the QR code to find out today!

The series continues with Domino and Jude, a silent siren with a death wish, and a leopard shifter bounty hunter trying to turn him in for cash. Click or snap the QR code to find out how Arioch sticks their nose in again.

Want to see where the DeMMonica universe began? Click or snap the QR code to check out INCUBUS SEDUCTION to start the adventure.

Afterword

Thank you for reading **IMPrisoned.** Reviews are crucial for helping readers just like you discover new books to enjoy. If you want to share your love for Alastor and Darien, please leave a review.

recommending my work to others is also a tremendous help. Don't hesitate to give IMPrisoned a shout-out in your favorite book rec group to spread the word.

Next in Series

It started with an ordinary bounty job. Sparks fly, but will Jude's heart soften enough not to hand the intriguing silent siren over to an uncertain fate?
If you love enemies to lovers, opposites attract, angst-ridden dark paranormal romance with a scattering of familiar characters, read Pied Piper today.

About Emma

Emma was destined to be a little quirky after being born as an unexpected twin in Hungry Bottom (Yes, it's a real place).

Known as the Queen of Angst because she loves putting damaged, often sweet and funny characters through hell before letting them have a HFN or HEA ending. Visit her website for a complete list of her books.

Emma blames her rebellious muse (who looks like Chris from the Paint Series) for the erotic aspects tickling the angst and the humor climbing into bed with the erotic.

When not writing or reading in leafy Sussex, England, (with the help of Loki the Rottie) she herds Birman cats and sons; both groups argue that there are too many of the other sort.

See you in the next book – Emma XX

Printed in Great Britain
by Amazon